DUPLICITY

OF

POWER

WILD HERITANCE, BOOK 1

S. LYNN HELTON

ISBN (Paperback): 978-1-7326763-0-5
ISBN (eBook): 978-1-7326763-1-2

Scripturio Books
www.ScripturioBooks.com
25.07.04

DEDICATION

To my family: my wonderful husband, kids, mom, and the best in-laws a person could have. And especially to my dad. I think you would have been pleased, Dad.

ACKNOWLEDGMENTS

Thank you to my beta readers: Elaine, Mark, and Vickie. You helped so much to improve the story with your great insights and suggestions!

CHAPTER 1

The night held a hint of something beyond the sense of the changing seasons. Namid felt the difference. She shifted in her chair, trying to rub out the itchy, twitchy sensation running across her back, and surveyed the tavern room to see who was watching her, certain that someone was.

But no one was.

Whenever someone opened the door and slipped in or out, a chill breath of air from the darkness outside drifted in. The chill trailed virulent promises across her skin and disturbed certain abilities of hers, abilities that most people called magic, but others—herself included—called Power.

This final night of the autumn fest, the rest of the city of Rhadanthus reveled, oblivious to any dark intimations. No matter that Rhadanthus—once a prosperous trading center a century or so in the past—now belonged less to farmers and traders and more to the dregs and outcasts of Paronia, middlemost of the Six Realms of the Monarch.

Any excuse for a party.

But in the rundown West Ring Tavern, the patrons showed little sign of autumn revelry. In the single, smoky room, Namid witnessed many of the same disreputable people engaged in the same arguments, with the same, almost always violent results.

However, as she watched the other patrons from her customary seat, back to the wall in a darkened corner, Namid realized a tension had been building for several days. She wondered how soon something would crack beneath it. It loomed over everyone now, potent enough to affect even those who knew nothing of the Power, like the others in the tavern. Their arguments had grown louder and their drinking more desperate than usual.

Namid set her mug of Karinthe on the table when she realized that she, too, had been drinking more than usual. She glanced at her two cohorts, seated elsewhere in the room so they could watch areas that she could not. A wise precaution here, if one had friends, or at least associates, that one trusted.

One of her cohorts looked grim, a common expression for her. The other gave Namid a crooked smile. Relax, his smile seemed to advise, in spite of the tension, the strangeness in the air, no one here, or in all Rhadanthus for that matter, will annoy you, a leader of the Shadowers, or your people. His smile sent that message, although they all knew it was not entirely true. But close enough.

Namid had just refused the server's offer of another drink when the door crashed open, hurling a blast of frigid air across protesting patrons. But the complaints petered out when the cause of the disturbance stumbled in. A big man, Gwelasius was, and his unkempt brown hair hung in his eyes. Denizens of this ring of the city knew him for his strength, his disregard for anyone's life but his own, and his love of drink. Few dared to cross him. Fewer lived to tell the tale.

Gwelasius swayed in the doorway, looking uncertain about what came next, and Namid saw movement in the gloom outside. In the silence, a soft voice spoke from behind Gwelasius, telling him to move aside. He ignored it.

The demand came again, and again he ignored it.

With the other patrons, Namid watched the little drama at the door. She caught expressions of anticipation on some of the others' faces as a second man pushed his way past Gwelasius and into the room. Namid got a brief impression of fine clothing and a young-looking face before Gwelasius attacked the stranger.

The two men slammed against the wall, shaking down dust, and the stranger slid to the floor. But a moment later he stood, one hand on the hilt of his long dagger.

He said something, which Namid missed because his weapon seized her attention. She felt that particular tingle that told her there was something special about that dagger, some Power about it. The moment passed as the stranger drew his knife and lunged for Gwelasius. But the feeling persisted, and Namid watched the fight with greater interest.

In avoiding the stranger's attack, Gwelasius tripped over his own feet. He fell to the floor and seemed dazed. The stranger stepped back to allow him to recover, and onlookers shouted for him to finish the downed man. One of Namid's Shadowers attracted her attention and asked to intervene, using the hand signals the Shadowers used to confer without speaking aloud. Namid waved him back from the fight. Better to wait until they finished.

While the taunting distracted the stranger, Gwelasius staggered back to his feet. Without warning, he grabbed the younger man from behind, pinned his arms, and lifted him off his feet. The dagger fell to the floor as the stranger struggled to escape Gwelasius' crushing grip.

A flash of lantern-light reflected from the dagger drew Namid's attention from the stranger's plight. She half rose to her feet to get a better look at the weapon. One of her Shadowers, seeing her interest, snatched it and brought it over to her. When Namid touched it, the curious, familiar warmth of Power seeped out from the dagger and washed over her hand. But the Power had an odd feel to it, a sense of turbulence she had not felt in Power before. Perhaps the stranger might have something interesting to say. She stepped out from behind her table.

"Gwel. It'd be just as well to let the young pup go," she said, loud enough to carry over the noise of the fight.

The stranger shot her an annoyed look, she assumed because of her choice of words. Now that Namid saw him better, she guessed he had more years than her own score plus. He was nobility, judging by his fine clothes and arrogant bearing. She felt the attention of the other patrons as they realized what she was trying to do. She tended to avoid involvement with the frequent fights that occurred in town, so this was something new.

Gwelasius relaxed his grip enough to allow his opponent to breathe. "Aw," he said. "Namid's taken a likin' to him, has she?"

Namid gave Gwelasius a cold look and tapped the dagger on her palm. She noted that, while not designed for throwing, it had a nice balance, despite its length and the sense that the hilt was oversized somehow, maybe better suited for a longer blade. Gwelasius paled, knowing her reputation with small, edged weapons.

"Just let him go," Namid said, adding the smallest, subtle touch of Power to her voice. Gwelasius had no choice but to obey.

The young noble looked ready to start the fight again. Namid caught his attention as one of her Shadowers stepped up behind him.

"Leave off," Namid advised.

The noble glanced back at the fierce-looking woman who stood at his shoulder, able to enforce Namid's advice. He nodded. They watched Gwelasius stagger out the door, cursing Namid all the while. Namid felt certain Gwelasius would cause trouble later, if he could. She smiled to herself, unbothered by the possibility.

After she signaled to her Shadower to return to her drink, Namid invited the stranger to sit with her and studied her guest. When standing, he had topped her by almost half a head. He wore his light brown hair shorter than the fashion in Rhadanthus and he sported a thin mustache. His skin was shades lighter than Namid's, and somewhat flushed, perhaps from the fight. His fine clothes of green silk marked him as wealthy, and a newcomer to Rhadanthus. They also screamed for someone to rob him. In this city of thieves and assassins, harlots and renegade mages, probably someone would.

"I thank you, my lady," he said with a frown, biting off his words.

Namid gave him a hard look. She had not been called 'lady' for a long time and the word brought back memories that she had worked hard to bury. She had, however, been called many other things in Rhadanthus.

"I'm Namid," she said. "Not 'lady'. Certainly not *your* lady. If you're in Rhadanthus looking for amusement, you'd better try one of the other, better parts of the city. All you're likely to find in this ring is a messy, probably painful death in a dark alley."

He looked startled, and perhaps alarmed. Then he drew himself up. "I'm not looking for anything," he said. "And you shall return my dagger—"

"Of course," Namid interrupted as she slid the dagger across the table to him. "I have some knowledge of edged weapons, and that one strikes me as a bit unusual."

He gave her a sharp look, his green eyes narrowed. "Oh? It's just a dagger, if a bit long."

"Is it?" Namid said, to give him something to think about. Perhaps even to warn him that others might take an interest in the Powerful weapon. She wondered then why she was bothering. The best course of action in Rhadanthus, she had learned years ago, was to mind one's own business. Maybe that tension in the air had gotten to her.

He ignored her remark. "I am Enric Rapha—"

Namid set her mug down with a bang, startling him into silence. After the people nearest them turned back to their drinks, she leaned across the table.

"Quietly!" she said, her voice just louder than a whisper. "The Earl is well hated here." She cocked her head at the corner near the bar.

The man seated there, one of her Shadowers, had lost his tongue to Earl Raphahan. The illustrious Earl had also gifted him with his scarred, disfigured face.

Enric nodded. "I know. In fact," he said, "that's really why I'm here. To get away from the Earl's influence."

Convenient, Namid thought. And maybe even partly true. But she wondered about his real purpose in coming to Rhadanthus, and to this disreputable ring of the city in particular. Nobles did not frequent this part of the city so far from the center ring, with its finer houses and the temples dedicated to each of several gods worshiped by the many peoples of Rhadanthus.

"If you're going to stay here any length of time and expect to stay alive," she said, "you'll want to curb that tendency to issue noble mandates. Or someone else will do it for you."

"I'm perfectly capable of taking care of myself!" he said as he stood up. Then he stalked out the door.

Namid considered chasing him down to find out more about that dagger, but somehow felt that they were not yet through with each other. She had learned to trust this sort of feeling. She sipped her Karinthe and let her thoughts run where they willed. Then a shadow fell across her table.

She looked up into the smiling face of Aahmes, a former Shadower and a man who seemed to delight in provoking her. Unfortunately, they were well acquainted with each other.

To their shared annoyance, they found themselves mistaken for relatives by most people seeing them for the first time. She and Aahmes did look like they could be related, with their similar lean builds, red-brown skin, and black hair. Their eyes differed, his were a gray-brown while hers were light brown. Aahmes wore his hair shoulder-length, swinging free most of the time, while Namid's hair fell below her waist when loose. A fringe of bangs covered her forehead and she wore the rest of her hair in a single long braid down her back most of the time. Their faces were much the same shape, his somewhat thinner, making his nose rather prominent. This sometimes reminded Namid of a bird of prey. Or maybe that was just his attitude.

Aahmes stood over half a head taller than she did and was clean-shaven. Namid had never seen him with a beard or mustache. He was a native of Rhadanthus, while she was not. Her childhood home of many years ago was much different.... She buried the memories, as she always did when they threatened. They were best left behind.

"Mind if I join you?" he said. Without waiting for her answer, he pulled a chair around the table and set it at an angle to hers, so his back would also be to a wall. He dropped down onto the chair, then tilted back to lean against the wall, all in one fluid motion.

"In fact, I do mind," she said, "but don't let that stop you."

"You planning on carrying on Dar's tradition? Taking in poor, helpless strays and training them up to Shadowers?" He brushed his hair back from his face with one hand and tilted his head to give her a sidelong look. "I have to tell you that one looks pretty hopeless." He gestured in the direction Enric had taken.

Namid shrugged. Aahmes had long seemed to resent Dar's aid to her when she first came to Rhadanthus, and more recently that Dar had named her one of his Seconds in the leadership of the Shadowers, as the select group of thieves in the city called themselves.

"You should've let Gwel take care of the noble," Aahmes said while he toyed with one of the many knives he carried openly. "Even with your help, he won't last long. Or maybe even because of your help."

Namid shrugged again. "Why should what happens to him matter to me? Or you? We both know it's everyone for themselves here."

"Of course," he said. "So why *did* you help him? Hoping he'll be grateful and show you a good time? He won't live so long." He leaned toward her and gave her an intent look. "But if you're looking for some fun…."

She stared at him. Was he—?

Then he placed the knife he had been fingering on the table, hilt toward her.

Namid laughed, leaned back in her chair, and waved the dagger that she had just lifted from him.

"Are you sure you're ready?" she said, challenge in her voice.

Although she chose not to display the arsenal she carried, from their shared days in the Shadowers, Aahmes knew how well she could handle herself. He glared at her a moment, then his expression eased into nonchalance. For several years, they had both skirted the question of who was better with a blade. Namid almost hoped he would take her up on her challenge.

"Another time," he said. "I'd better be going." He snatched back his daggers and sauntered out the door.

Namid watched him leave, idly noting his confident swagger, and considered what he had said. She had no intention of letting him know why the young noble interested her. But what was this Enric, one of Earl Raphahan's brood, doing with a dagger of Power, anyway? She had felt no sense of Power about Enric, but that might not mean anything. She had a sudden feeling that Aahmes planned something concerning the noble, so she signaled her Shadowers to do as they wished with the rest of the night, then dropped a generous number of korz—the copper coins of the Six Realms—on the table and followed Aahmes.

Outside the tavern, widely spaced lanterns along the street attempted to light the night with their feeble candlelight. Namid saw better in dim light than everyone she knew, so the murk did not worry her. None of the moons were visible. A dense haze hung in the air. Namid feared she had lost Aahmes, then she noticed motion at a corner to her right and spotted him slipping around the edge of the building, his gray clothes blending well into the murk. She stole after him, paused at the corner, and peered around it. She saw the edge of his cloak as he disappeared into an alley. She followed.

They skulked in this manner through many of the streets and alleys of Rhadanthus, and ended up near Shadow Keep, Namid's residence and the Shadowers' base. That entire area was deserted at that time of night, except for those who preferred to conduct their business after sundown.

Aahmes glided into a shadowed doorway, and as Namid did likewise, she was forced to admit to some admiration for the man. He had to be one of the slickest sneak-thieves she had ever seen. With her skills and Power, she should have found it much easier to follow him than it had been. She watched his hiding place for close to a candle-mark before another figure appeared on the street, coming from her right. As the figure approached, she saw that it was Gwelasius. She shrank back in the shadows as he passed her.

Aahmes stepped out of his doorway to meet Gwelasius, the mist swirling around them both, and they talked in quiet voices for a brief time. Namid saw Gwelasius hold up a pouch that looked full and Aahmes' laugh carried to her. Then he said something that caused Gwelasius to back away, shaking his head, hands raised in front of him. Aahmes lunged at him and Gwelasius scurried away, toward Namid's hiding spot. He jabbered something.

"Then we'll go back and get it!" Aahmes said. He shoved Gwelasius in front of him, snatching the pouch in the process. He hooked it on his belt. After they passed her, Namid stepped out and followed.

The two men hurried back through the streets, with more noise than Aahmes had made alone. Their noise masked any that Namid made in her effort to keep up.

Before long, they all came to a narrow back street in an area of broken, crumbling buildings. The two men turned down the street, while Namid remained in the shadows near the entrance. At the base of one wall, not far down the street, lay a dark lump.

When they reached the lump, Aahmes shoved Gwelasius aside and knelt, searching. A moment later he stood, the gleam of a dagger in his hand.

"Lucky for you it was still here," he said to Gwelasius. "Come on. We'll divide the rest somewhere else."

They started toward Namid, and she scrambled back into the closest crevice. As Aahmes passed her hiding place, deep in conversation with Gwelasius, Namid saw the opportunity and lifted the pouch off him. She hoped he would not notice until he had gotten far away. She tucked her prize into her overtunic.

After the two men disappeared into the night, Namid edged closer to the lump on the ground. Maybe Aahmes and Gwelasius had overlooked something. If so, the city's latest casualty would not need it. And the Shadowers might.

She rolled the body over and hissed in surprise. It was Enric. She shook her head at herself. She should have guessed it. She wet a finger and held it under his nose. The faintest breath cooled her finger. She put two fingers to her lips and whistled a summons.

While she waited, Namid searched the noble. On the back of his head she found the wound from his attacker. Gwelasius must have been drunker than she had thought, for him to have failed to kill the young noble with that blow. Gwelasius' victims rarely survived to miss what he had taken from them. Or maybe Aahmes had forbidden it. He was a thief, after all, not a murderer.

Enric's dagger was gone, and any money he might have carried, which Namid realized she probably had now. She collected his rings and ornate cloak pin, with a thought that they would be safer with her. She grinned to herself at this. Maybe she would give them back if he recovered. And then again, maybe not.

She heard a low whistle from nearby and straightened up

as one of her Shadowers appeared out of the thickening mist. It was Thes, the older man who had long served as one of Dar's Seconds and had stepped back to let Namid fill that spot. Thes now helped her as a kind of Second of her own.

"What took you so long?" Namid said.

Thes grinned, the expression almost lost in his gray tangle of beard. "Had t' finish m' job!" He displayed Enric's dagger and placed it in Namid's hand. "Found Aahmes with it. And Gwel. Figured it'd look a mite better with you."

Namid noticed a deep slice across the back of Thes' left hand. "Your fingers are getting slow, Thes. Looks like he caught you lifting it."

Thes grinned even wider. "Naw, not really. Just had a wee bit o' difference o' opinion with the lad. Aahmes ran after I counted his ribs for him." He held up his own dagger with a flourish.

Then he chuckled at the astonished look she gave him. "Aye, I got a lucky slice on him," he said as he tucked away his dagger. "I woulda chased him down, but I heard you call."

"And Gwel?"

Thes shook his head. "The lad had just sent him off t' do somethin' or other. Now that I think o' it, Aahmes did seem a mite put out about somethin'...."

Namid nodded, but only gave Thes a grin. She indicated Enric. "Would you get him back home to the Keep and have Elnathan tend to him?"

Thes gave her a dubious look, but hoisted Enric up and draped one of the noble's arms over his own shoulder to better drag him along. "You sure you want to bring one o' his type back to the Keep?"

Namid gave him a puzzled look. "He needs some Healing and no one else is about. Is there a problem?"

"Naw. Just don't want him to be settin' City Warders on us. And what if his people come lookin' for him?"

Namid considered this. "If he recovers, we'll just make sure that he won't be able to find his way back to us when we let him go. I'll check around and head off any of his people if they do come looking for him. But I have a feeling that he's here on his own."

Thes gave her a questioning look, but then shrugged. "You're the boss m' girl. You stayin' out all night?"

"I think so. Why?"

"Some o' the others were wonderin'. And Dar, o' course. They hadn't seen you leave. And there's somethin' funny in the night t'night."

Namid shook her head in mock irritation. "It's just a heavy mist, Thes." She clapped him on the shoulder. "You all try too hard to watch out for me. You know I'll be fine. Tell everyone I'll probably be the whole night. I feel a need to be out." And yes, she added to herself, there is something funny in the night and I'm going to try to find out what.

Thes gave her a dubious look but nodded. He shuffled off with his burden and passed from sight after a few steps.

CHAPTER 2

Namid returned to the Keep at dawn, tired, yet still restless. She had not discovered the reason for her disquiet, nor had she been able to escape it.

Her unexpected guest slept in one of the Shadowers' rooms, under the influence of one of Elnathan's nauseating potions, she suspected. No one reported any mishaps during the night, just the normal scrapes and cuts. She emptied out her collection for the night and gave it to Thes to parcel out as needed. The Shadowers were not at all poverty-stricken, but they always needed to supply gifts in certain quarters. It never hurt to cover their tracks, even before they might need covering.

She headed to the second floor of the Keep, to check in with Dar, a habit she had started when she became one of his Seconds. The stocky leader of the Shadowers was not in the small room he liked to call his office. But when Namid turned to go, she spotted him further down the hall.

He paced toward her, head down and lost in thought. The widely spaced lanterns in the hall showed Namid the fatigue in his stance. His thinning auburn hair and light, freckled skin looked lackluster in the dim light.

But when he looked up and smiled at the sight of her, the impression of dullness and fatigue fell away from him.

"Ah, you're back. Have a good night?" He stopped next her. "I hear you've brought us an unusual haul."

Namid shrugged. "The night was fair, anyway." She stifled a yawn. "Hope it's all right I had Thes bring the noble. Gwel got to him and he might not have lasted the night afterwards."

Dar pondered this a moment and nodded. "No harm that I can see. Just get him out of here as soon as you can, with as little knowledge of us as possible."

"Of course."

Dar peered at her. "Now, take yourself off and catch some sleep," he said. "And leave your old leader to his dull tasks. I'm heading out for a few candle-marks, need to speak with someone, but should be back before you wake."

Namid grinned. "Never old," she said over her shoulder as she started toward her room to follow his advice. On the way to her room, she left word to be informed when Enric awakened.

Namid was one of the privileged few who had a private room within their rundown, but comfortable-enough building. The room might not have a window, but it was hers alone. Nice to be one of the leaders.

She opened her door, then remembered her candle had burned down. She grabbed one of the lanterns from the hall and felt a whisper of a breeze as she did so. She spun to see who was there but saw no one. And none of the flames in any of the other lanterns in the hall were flickering.

The night's strangeness must be affecting her more than she had thought. She turned back to her room, brought her lantern in with her and closed the door behind her.

She dropped her gray cloak on her narrow bed and set her lantern on a shelf above the bed. She hid Enric's cloak pin and rings and, after some thought, the dagger too. Her curiosity could wait until after she had rested. She did, however, take the time to examine the contents of his pouch. The coins and small gems she poured into her hands amounted to a fortune! Enough to live at least half a year in Rhadanthus, in considerable comfort. That fit with Enric's story of who he was. The Earl Raphahan was said to be generous with his children, at least regarding material goods. Namid poured everything back into the pouch and placed it with the rest of Enric's things. Then she prepared for rest by shedding her small arsenal.

The two daggers in her boots she left there and just removed the boots. The small dagger in a sheath on the back of her belt came off with the belt. She unlaced the leather armguard on her left forearm to better examine the stiletto hidden within it. The knife was new to her, and she was not yet certain of it. Her matching right armguard she seldom removed. She had no wish for a certain small tattoo hidden beneath it to become common knowledge. Also, the stiletto tucked within this band had a rare poison on it.

As she set her armguard on a small table by her bed, she noticed the full sleeves of her shirt looked more a dingy brown than the light gray they were supposed to be. She frowned. The color might be better to blend in, but it was an irritant just the same. Still, she had learned to live with such things, rather minor compared with much of what one found in the city.

Perhaps she should see about dyeing the shirt the same darker gray as the rest of her attire… overtunic, undertunic, trousers, and boots. That shade of gray faded well into the dimness of the city streets at night.

Namid shook her head at her wandering thoughts and stepped through a series of relaxing exercises that she had learned as a novice in the temple of Ilenii, she who was known as the secret god. The exercises did not help. When she finished, Namid felt as restless as before.

She paced next to her bed and played with the finger-long dagger in its sheath that hung from a silver chain around her neck. This was a memento from the night that she became a Shadower. She shrugged at herself and tried to put aside the strange feelings.

Namid glanced in her mirror, a luxury item in Rhadanthus. She looked worn and worried, matching how she felt. She looked away and started unbraiding her hair.

A sound behind her caught her attention. She started to turn, then froze when she felt a cold, sharp point in her side.

"You have something that belongs to me," whispered an all-too-familiar voice.

"What could that possibly be, Aahmes?" She tried to sound as innocent as possible. Somehow, she could not resist baiting him, even when her life might be at risk.

The knife pressed harder and she felt a small bead of warmth run down her side. She turned her head enough to see him in the mirror.

He looked somewhat wan. From loss of blood, she assumed. The front of his tunic and the shirt beneath were torn, the dark stain there damp-looking. Through the tears, Namid saw a gleam of white cloth wrapped around his midriff. Maybe she would be lucky enough to have him drop right there, without any help from her.

"What you took from me last night," he said. "What's mine."

Namid shrugged. "If you can't hang on to your own treasures—" She broke off as the knife pressed even harder.

"I'll have to get it," she said.

The knife eased up. "All right. Wait… I don't want your poison in me. Take off that other armguard."

Without warning, Namid twisted away from him, and kicked him in his wound.

He gasped and fell away but held on to his dagger.

A twist of her wrist and her stiletto dropped into her hand from its wrist-sheath.

Namid leapt toward him, but he eluded her. His knife missed her face by a finger-width.

Aahmes caught a foot on a loose floorboard and he crashed to the floor. The dagger spun out of his hand.

Namid lunged for him, her stiletto reaching for his

throat, but he rolled, catching her off guard.

He scrambled for his knife, but she was ahead of him and kicked it out of range. He swayed off-balance, and she slammed him back against the wall, gathering a fistful of his tunic.

Her blade caressed his neck without breaking the skin. Yet.

"Now my turn for demands," Namid said. "Tell me how you got into the Keep without anyone knowing." She knew that someone would have told her, if they had known he was there.

Aahmes gave her a weak grin and shook his head. "You haven't learned all the Keep's secrets, have you?"

Namid twirled her blade in front of Aahmes' eyes to give him a good look at the bluish ichor-like liquid on the tip and edges.

"How much do you know about this?" she said.

He started to sweat. "There's supposed to be no cure," he said.

She nodded. "And would you like to hear how a person dies if this is in the wound?"

Without warning, her door crashed open. Thes and several other Shadowers charged into the room.

"Are you all right?" Thes said. "The apprentices said they heard sounds o' fightin'...."

Namid turned, leaving Aahmes slumped against the wall. "I'm fine. I just found a rat in my room."

Thes looked at Aahmes and his eyes widened as he recognized him. Aahmes made no move, just leaned there, one hand pressed to his wound.

"How'd he get in here?" one of the others said.

"That's what I'd like to know," Namid said. She gave Thes an intent look. "Any ideas?"

Thes glared at Aahmes. "I'll take a look int' it. You wanted t' know when his lordship woke up? Well, he's awake, and fightin' mad. Seems some o' his stuff's missin'." Thes grinned at Namid, and she heard a soft chuckle from

Aahmes.

Namid nodded. "I'll come. Have someone get him something to eat—"

"It's already on the way."

"Good." Namid pulled on her boots, grabbed her other armguard and laced it back on as she started out of the room. "Have him watched closely." She indicated Aahmes.

She paused in the doorway. "On second thought, bring him too. I want to keep my eye on him. But search him first."

Two of the Shadowers searched Aahmes. After they relieved him of several knives, they reported he carried no other weapons. They dropped his weapons on her small table and hauled Aahmes upright. He groaned as he straightened, still clutching the wound he had taken from Thes' blade the previous night.

"How deep did you cut, anyway?" Namid asked Thes.

"Not deep enough, I'd say," one of the men muttered.

Aahmes glared at him. "The cut was nothing," he snarled at Namid, "until you kicked me."

"Don't be such a baby," Thes told him and chuckled. "No doubt you'll live."

Aahmes gave him a nasty look, but kept his mouth shut.

"Bring him," Namid said, and headed toward Enric's room. Thes and all but two of the other Shadowers headed the other direction, to discover Aahmes' means of entry, Namid hoped.

Aahmes and his two guards caught up as she approached the noble's room. A crash from within brought her up short, just as the door burst open and one of the younger Shadowers scurried out, followed by a glass bowl, which shattered on the floor.

"A royal tantrum," Aahmes said from behind Namid, and she had to laugh.

"I want my possessions now, girl!" Enric yelled as he appeared in the doorway. He still wore his fine clothes, now wrinkled and minus the cloak. And the bandage wrapped around his head had fallen over one eye. When his attention fell on Namid's group, the young Shadower disappeared down the hall with a grimace for Namid that showed her opinion of the noble. Namid smiled back at her.

"You!" Enric pointed at Namid. "I insist my property be returned immediately!" He ruined his imperious demeanor by trying to shove the bandage back off his eye.

"Is this the way to talk to someone who saved your life?" Namid said, walking toward him.

He backed up, like he was afraid to touch her. She waited for Aahmes and his guards to follow her into the room and closed the door. She faced Enric and leaned back against the door.

"Perhaps we'd better start out with a bit of honesty." Namid heard Aahmes snort and ignored him. "Your property is safe," she said, "for the moment. Now, if you'll just share a little about the real reason you're here in Rhadanthus," and what that Powerful dagger has to do with it, she added to herself, "we should be able to come to some arrangement."

"I told you earlier."

"You told me a story I conveniently set up for you." Namid turned away. "But perhaps you'd be more willing to talk with one of my people. Do you remember the man I pointed out to you? I'm sure he'd be glad to be introduced to you." She glanced over her shoulder at Enric, pleased to see his worried expression. Then he pulled himself together.

"I'm not amused by your threats, nor am I intimidated by them. Return my possessions!"

"It's good to know that threats don't bother you." Namid opened the door and called for Fellin, the man disfigured from Earl Raphahan's attentions. Fellin arrived less than a quarter candle-mark later. She ushered him into the room and secured the door again.

"Fellin, I'd like you to meet someone. This is Enric—"

"It's not anything important!" Enric broke in.

"But if you're so unwilling to talk about it," Namid said,

"it must be at least interesting. Maybe even profitable."

"I doubt it would be of any interest to you."

"As I was saying—"

"All right. I'll tell you about it."

Namid smiled and thanked Fellin for coming. He asked by hand-talk what was going on, and she replied the same way that she was just getting some information. He grinned, signaled her good luck and left.

She turned back to Enric and saw Aahmes trying to hide a smile. Somehow, she had forgotten that he also knew this silent language of the Shadowers. Feeling a sudden kinship, she impetuously winked at him. He gave her a startled look, then a cautious smile.

"We're listening," Namid told Enric.

"As I said," he began, "it's truly nothing to interest you. I'm pursuing a quest and came here to find a guide."

After a breath-of-time of dead silence, Aahmes began laughing. "Pursuing a quest!" he managed to gasp and laughed even harder.

Namid tried to ignore him. "What kind of quest? Don't tell me there's some fair, helpless maiden needing rescue from a vicious monster…."

At this, Aahmes laughed so hard that he had to lean against the wall to remain upright. His two guards grinned.

"Do you always break the dishes of your host?" Namid said, changing the subject.

Enric stared at her and blushed. "I apologize for my behavior, earlier. I offer to replace the damaged dish." He gave her a meaningful look. "Of course, in order to do so, I will need my belongings."

"Tell me more about this quest of yours," Namid said.

By then, Aahmes had quieted, and stood watching them.

Enric sighed and sat on the edge of the bed. "My quest is to find the blade of Akavos. The only clue that I possess so far is a name. I believe it might be a city in this area, or possibly further to the west, in the realm of Yiruny. And that's why I need a guide."

"Akavos," Namid repeated. The word meant nothing to her. She glanced at the others, but her Shadowers shook their heads, and Aahmes shrugged.

"The blade of Akavos?" she asked Enric. "Who or what is Akavos?"

"Akavos is a magical sword," he said. "But at this time, it exists only as a hilt."

The mention of magic reminded Namid of the young noble's dagger. "Why do you want a magical sword? You've already got that dagger."

Out of the corner of her eye, Namid saw Aahmes look up sharply. She wondered at the startled look on his face and decided he must not have known the dagger had Power.

"Well?" Namid prompted, when Enric just looked at her with his mouth hanging open.

"Maybe this dagger has something to do with Akavos…" Aahmes said.

Enric gave him an anxious look, but still said nothing. An idea came to Namid.

"That dagger is Akavos!" she said.

Enric nodded, a trapped look on his face.

"But it's already got a blade," Aahmes pointed out.

"The hilt can be made to hold a common blade," Enric said. "But for no more than several weeks, maybe as long as a season, at a time. Its rightful blade is hidden. But, when the hilt and blade are joined, the sword is supposed to be so magical as to rival the most powerful mages in all the Monarch's realms!"

"Nice fairy tale," one of Aahmes' guards muttered.

"This guide you're looking for…" Aahmes said. "Are you paying well?"

"Of course," Enric said.

"Planning to leave us so soon?" Namid asked Aahmes. "But you've only just arrived. And such an entertainment I had planned…."

Aahmes' guards gave him speculative looks. He glared at everyone in the room.

In the momentary silence, Namid heard running footsteps in the hall. Thes burst into the room, out of breath, with fear in his eyes.

"You'd better come!" he gasped.

A shiver of premonition slithered down Namid's spine. She felt the tension of the past days had been leading to this. Without hesitation, she followed Thes through the building, marginally aware that the others followed her in turn.

Thes led the small procession to the roof, from which they could look out over much of Rhadanthus. Namid focused on the dark green-gray fog that boiled to the south. A slight breeze from that direction carried shrieks of fear and agony that turned the warm morning cold.

"Belaraketh preserve us," Aahmes muttered.

"Sy'shythys," Namid said, noticing the tremor of fear in her voice as if it belonged to someone else. She felt odd and detached.

Sy'shythys, or the Death Vapor, was said to be a magical fog that killed swiftly and corroded everything, even metal and stone. The highest caste of the priesthood of the evil god Sesaisyd—called the Dark Prince by many in the Six Realms—had created and used it. Old tales told of Sesaisyd's destruction centuries ago. His worship was supposed to have ended with him. Namid had first heard about Sy'shythys during her studies in the Power.

She had never expected to see it.

"It can't be," Thes said in a hushed voice. "There's nobody left—"

"Well, someone somewhere doesn't know that!" Namid broke in. "Tell everyone, if they don't already know, and send them out of here! Head north. We'll meet outside the city." She did not wait to see Thes follow her orders. She turned to Aahmes' guards. "You two, get out of here!"

"But what about—"

"Go! Save your skins. He's not important now!"

They fled.

Namid looked at Aahmes and Enric. "You're both free

to live. If you can."

She darted back inside and charged down the stairs from the roof level. She was surprised to hear their footsteps behind her. She also heard others running in the building. The Shadowers escaping, she hoped.

"I said you could go," she shouted over her shoulder.

"My weapons," Aahmes said. "I'm not going out there unarmed!"

Enric nodded. Namid noticed he had already brought his cloak with him. He must have taken it along when they headed to the roof.

Namid laughed. "Then follow me."

"How fast do you think it's approaching?" Enric said as they crowded into Namid's room.

She shrugged, snatched his things out of hiding and threw them on her bed. She stepped over to a certain spot near her mirror. The wood there had once been a rich, polished red-brown. Now it was a nondescript gray. She pried out a specific knot to open a hole just large enough for two fingers.

"What're you doing?" Aahmes demanded as he retrieved his weapons. "We've got to get out of here!"

Namid ignored him and instead felt within the hole with one finger. She fought against the beginnings of panic and forced herself to move slowly. In addition to what she wanted, traps also lurked for the careless within that small hole. After interminable breaths-of-time, her finger touched the solid lever. She pushed it to the side. A panel near her knees popped out and moved aside.

She grabbed the long bundle inside, which held a family heirloom: an ornate, golden-hilted sword, and its sheath and belt. She had long ago wrapped the hilt in strips of leather to hide the decorations, but the sheath and belt, both of tooled leather, would draw attention on their own. She could not leave the sword behind, no matter the delay. In passing, she also grabbed the belt she had taken off earlier.

"Is that everything?" Enric said.

At her nod, he grabbed her arm. "Then come on!"

He pulled her out the door, and they ran down the hall. Namid was surprised to find Aahmes at her other side. She shrugged off Enric's hand, so she could buckle on both of her belts, but kept the pace he had set, even as her sword threatened to trip her. As they approached the outer door, Aahmes tossed her cloak around her shoulders, and they dashed into the street.

People fleeing for their lives filled the street, hitting and shoving each other as they all tried to escape. Namid felt Sy'shythys drawing ever closer, and moving faster, too.

"Link hands!" Aahmes shouted.

Namid ended up between the two men as they fought their way through the crowded street. The panic-stricken mob yanked them this way and that. Several times they were almost separated.

The din hammered at their ears. Namid shuddered as the panic she had tried to push aside crept up on her. She thanked the gods that she was not trying to plow through the mob on her own.

At the first cross street, Aahmes came to a halt. "Look!"

He pointed down the street to a pair of horses hitched to an empty wagon.

"Go!" Namid shouted.

They struggled against the throng to reach their one hope of escaping Rhadanthus in time. They could not see Sy'shythys but Namid felt the oppressive nearness of its Power. Just around the next corner, it seemed.

The horses acted as frantic as everyone else and resisted their efforts to calm them. Namid glanced down the street toward the south and saw a man come staggering from that direction. A dark miasma clung to him, writhed around him almost as if alive, and he shrieked without pause. He bumped into a woman and some of the darkness flowed over to her. She screamed.

"Don't let them touch you," Namid told her two companions. "It spreads that way, too."

Finally, they calmed the horses enough for Aahmes and Enric to each grab a horse's reins while Namid cut the horses free of the wagon. Enric had a struggle to mount the fussing horse. Aahmes mounted his with no trouble and reached down for Namid. He clasped arms with her and hauled her up behind him. She grabbed him around the waist to keep from falling right back off.

"Which way?" Enric cried, his fear evident both in his eyes and his voice. His horse screamed. Namid grabbed its reins as Aahmes headed toward an alley that looked less crowded. Between the two of them, Enric and Namid, they managed to control his horse. How Aahmes managed the horse he and Namid rode, she never knew.

Their flight through Rhadanthus was a nightmare of screams of the terrified and dying, hundreds of clutching hands determined to pull them from their mounts, and confused people running all directions, many headed back toward the danger. They threaded their way through the twisted, terror-filled streets, with Sy'shythys dogging their heels. Both men struggled to guide the horses, which had long since caught the sense of panic and horror.

As they crossed one wider street, Namid looked down it and dread enveloped her. A tendril of Sy'shythys flowed parallel to them, like it was trying to outflank them!

She looked the other way at the next street. It was there too. She could not shake the weird feeling that Sy'shythys hunted the three of them. If it came between them and the edge of town....

"Faster!" Namid screamed at Aahmes, hoping he heard.

The air filled with a shrieking roar that stabbed into her head. She fought it, refusing to give in to its numbing spell. As she caught a whiff of the sickly sweet killing fog, she prayed to Ilenii to deliver them from this horror.

Aahmes found the one straight street that led to the North Gate and urged his horse to a gallop. Namid dropped the reins to Enric's horse and heard him just behind them.

They plowed ahead, overrunning all in their path.

Everything narrowed down to a race for the gate through a passage of death.

Just as they sighted the gate, a thin finger of the deadly fog reached out for them.

And they saw that the gate was closed and barred.

Namid shouted a warning.

A figure enveloped by the green-gray fog staggered toward them, toward the gate. The head titled up toward Namid. Through the miasma, and beyond the melting flesh, Namid recognized the leader of the Shadowers.

"Dar?!" Namid cried.

Aahmes turned, also spotting him.

"No," Aahmes said, just loud enough that Namid heard him.

Dar gave them a single nod and half fell against the bar on the gate, shoving it aside. With one hand, he grabbed the edge of the gate and leaned his whole weight back to pull it open. He used his free hand to tell them—by the Shadowers' hand-talk—*Don't trust anyone else!*

The fog thickened around him and he toppled to the ground.

They plunged through the open gate.

The malignant fog closed off the passage behind them and silence fell.

CHAPTER 3

For the next couple of candle-marks, the three sat atop a hill and watched the nearby city for some movement, for the Shadowers to come. But between the hill and the gate lay emptiness, and the land around held no signs of life.

Namid's eyes burned with the tears she fought back. How could they all be gone? Pretty much everyone she had ever cared about in Rhadanthus. Despite her efforts, a few bitter tears slid down her cheeks as she remembered Thes' ready grin, Dar's guidance and hints at ways to improve, the raucous jokes that circulated through the Shadowers, and the wild celebrations after a good haul.

All gone.

Just within the fog-enshrouded city, Namid saw shapes piled on the ground at the gate, those who had been so close to escaping. She stared at the grim sight.

"There's no one there. I'm sorry," Enric murmured as he unwrapped the bandage from his head and touched the sore spot. Elnathan, the Shadowers' Healer, had done a decent job and Enric's wound looked as healed as if a few days had already passed.

"I had hoped someone found their way out through

another gate and circled around to meet us," Namid said.

"None of the Shadowers made it," Aahmes snapped, but his voice sounded rough and he turned away.

Namid had no response to that. She rubbed her forehead, trying to banish her fatigue. Enric gave Aahmes a disgusted look.

"It occurs to me that I've not had the pleasure of a formal introduction to this fellow," Enric said.

Namid's lips curved in a slight smile. "Well, in that case, I have the misfortune to introduce Aahmes." She turned to Aahmes. "This is Enric."

"Enric Raphahan," the young noble said, watching Namid.

She shrugged. "It's your life." She looked at Aahmes, curious to see what he would do with this information.

"Yes, it is," Enric said. "And if I must defend it, I'm not unprepared."

"A little fancy," Aahmes said. "But well said. I have nothing against the Raphahans in particular." He looked at Namid. "And now I know what you were doing with Fellin back at Shadow Keep."

Namid just nodded and frowned at the reminder of the Shadowers.

"Why did it stop at the edge of the city? This killing fog," Enric said, gazing at Rhadanthus.

"I think I remember hearing the spell was supposed to have been limited to a certain-sized area," Namid said.

"And Rhadanthus is that size," Aahmes said.

"Maybe," Namid said. "Seems like it, anyway."

Namid glanced toward the sun. It was near midmorning, maybe even past.

"All right, they didn't make it out. This gate, anyway," she said. "But maybe they made it to one of the others. They could be injured and waiting there."

"We should at least investigate that possibility," Enric said as he stood.

"We?" Namid said.

Enric looked sheepish. "I cannot simply leave you in this predicament." He gave her a hand up to her feet.

"It's not your problem. Go follow your quest or whatever," Namid said. His offer touched her and irritated her at the same time.

"Yeah, we can do fine without your help," Aahmes said.

Now Namid looked at him. "We?"

And she wondered if Dar's last message had meant she should not trust anyone else other than herself, even Aahmes, another Shadower, albeit former. Of course, he also saw the message….

Or did it mean that the two of them should not trust anyone else, other than each other?

Aahmes shrugged. He pushed his hair back from his face with one hand and looked at his feet. "I used to work with them, too. Remember."

Namid studied the two determined-looking men and shrugged. "Well, then if *we* are going to do this, we should be about it."

Enric glanced back at Rhadanthus and turned away again. "There's no reason to remain here longer. I propose we make our way to the next gate and see what survivors might've escaped that way."

Namid and Aahmes agreed and they again mounted the horses. Aahmes pointed out that the West Gate was almost as close as the North Gate to the Shadowers' base and perhaps some of them had gotten out that way. They started to circle the city to the West Gate, traveling roughly parallel to the curved city walls.

~ ~ ~

Somewhat over a candle-mark later, they approached the West Gate. The sight that met them was much like that at the North Gate: no sign of anything alive and plenty of signs of the dead. However, the killing fog seemed thinner.

From her vantage atop the horse, Namid saw what

looked like a pile of skeletons, rather than bodies, near the gate. The skeletons looked stripped clean. She suppressed a shudder at the sight.

"Should we return to the city?" Enric said.

Aahmes glanced over his shoulder at him, then stiffened.

"What is it?" Namid said, trying to twist around to see.

"I think we have company." Aahmes turned the horse so Namid could see back the way they had just come. Looking where he pointed, she spotted a faint dust cloud, not too distant.

"Coming fast." Aahmes said.

"Perhaps they're more survivors," Enric said.

Namid shuddered as uneasiness washed over her. Somehow, she knew Enric was wrong.

"I have a feeling not," Aahmes said, as he urged their horse away from the city. Enric followed.

"It does look like they're coming around the city, too." Namid said.

"They must have escaped like we did, and we just missed them somehow," Enric insisted. "Let's go talk to them."

Aahmes caught the reins of Enric's horse as the noble turned toward the dust cloud. "Let them come closer so we can see, before we show ourselves."

Enric looked at Namid, who nodded her agreement with Aahmes' assessment. "I feel I'd rather know who it is first," she said.

Aahmes dismounted and motioned Namid to join him. "Take the horses further down the hill so they can't be seen," he told Enric.

"I don't take orders from you!" Enric shot back.

"We don't have time for this," Namid said as she dismounted.

"Are you good at hiding and spying, your lordship?" Aahmes said. "No? Then leave it to those who are."

Enric glared at Aahmes and Namid, then grabbed the horses' reins and led them down the hill away from the city gate and away from the dust cloud.

"I can't believe my ears," Namid said as she and Aahmes squirmed their way into the grass at the top of the hill. "Did you actually say I'm a good Shadower?"

"Hah! You're still little more than a tyro. Stay here and watch and learn."

With that, he left her at the top of the hill and wriggled down the side toward the approaching dust cloud. Namid soon lost sight of him in the grass.

She smiled to herself as she waited. She had not realized before that she missed the time when he had been a Shadower, missed their frequent raillery.

But still, Dar had said to trust no one else. She wished she knew whether that included Aahmes, since it was so easy to fall into the pattern of working with him.

After several long breaths-of-time, she began to make out the figures causing the dust cloud. She counted three, on horseback.

"City Warders," a voice said in her ear. She jumped. Aahmes chuckled.

"Tyro," he said with a grin and slid back down the hill toward Enric and the horses. Namid watched the three figures until she could see the City Warder uniforms they wore, then she followed Aahmes.

When she joined her two companions, they were already embroiled in another disagreement.

"—talk with them," Enric said. "They're Warders, after all. They'll be able to aid us."

"You really don't know Rhadanthus, do you?" Aahmes said. "The Warders can be just as bad as any dark-alley cutthroat."

"I imagine you would know all about that, wouldn't you?" Enric said as he mounted his horse. "*I* will speak with them." He urged his horse into a canter.

"Wait!" Namid called out to him, but he didn't seem to hear.

"Let him go," Aahmes said.

"Shouldn't we—"

"You want to be taken in? They'd as soon chain us up and haul us off as look at us, you know that." Aahmes mounted his horse and held a hand down to her. "Come on, let's get out of here."

"We've managed Warders before. He hasn't. They're only three and they can't pin anything on us out here." She gave him a knowing look. "And I just can't imagine that you'd want to miss out on a chance at that stuffed pouch he's hauling around. Not to mention the rings…."

Aahmes seemed to ponder that, then scowled at her. "All right, come on."

He helped her up behind him and they followed Enric. They caught up to the noble as he met the Warders, three grim-faced men who rode ready to draw their swords.

"Identify yourselves," the Warder in the lead ordered. Namid studied his face and did not recognize him. Odd. She thought that she at least knew the faces of all the Warders.

"I'm Enric, a newcomer to this area. These are my traveling companions."

Namid found herself the object of intense scrutiny from the two men who had not yet spoken.

"And their names are?" the Warder prompted Enric.

Something felt wrong here, but Namid could not decide what. She started to caution Enric. Too late.

"Aahmes and Namid," he said.

"Ah, traveling companions, is it?" the Warder said and shared a knowing look with his comrades. "You'll be returning with us to Rhadanthus."

After a moment of stunned silence, Enric said, "But what about the killing fog?"

"Clever question," the Warder said. "As you know, it affected only half the city." He turned to his men. "Take them."

"Hang on!" Aahmes yelled as the two silent Warders lunged for them. Namid barely had time to secure her grip around Aahmes' waist before the horse did something she had never seen before. It whirled, jumped almost straight up in the air and kicked out with its hind legs. Its hooves just caught one of the men in the chest. He fell with a cry.

When the horse landed, it reared and caught the other man with its forelegs and knocked him to the ground as well. Namid started to slide but stayed on the horse by clinging to Aahmes like her life depended on it.

The horse spun around again and Namid saw the first man struggling to pick himself up. He looked angry. And his clothes now looked unlike any kind of City Warder uniform.

Like it had been under some glamour, his uniform changed as she watched. More than anything, his clothing now resembled a loose, dark green-gray robe. She caught her breath as she remembered the last time she had seen a robe like that — a part of her past she had not thought to see again.

"We need to get out of here!" she yelled in Aahmes' ear.

He gave her the Shadowers' hand signal of acknowledgment and urged their horse toward Enric. Aahmes grabbed the reins of Enric's horse, then turned his horse away from the city and the false Warders and gave it its head.

As they shot away from the struggle, Namid thought she heard Aahmes mutter something. She felt the faintest hint of Power but could not tell where it came from. She looked back at the false Warders, worried what they might be forging with Power. Instead, the three Warders began to yell and curse as they tried to control their suddenly wild horses.

~ ~ ~

Aahmes kept them moving at a fast gait for close to a candle-mark before he let the horses slow, then stop. Namid had kept watch behind them but had seen no sign of pursuit. She slid off the horse to sit on the stationary ground. She was surprised that her hands were shaky. She tucked them in her lap.

"So, what was that?" Enric said as he eased himself to the ground and let his horse free to graze. "Did either of you notice something strange about their uniforms? Did they seem to change?"

"I don't think they really were City Warders," Aahmes said. "I didn't recognize any of them."

"Oh?" Enric said. "You can't tell me that you know all the City Warders."

"Know them? No. But I do know all their faces," Aahmes said. "Or did."

"A likely story," Enric scoffed.

"It's true," Namid said. "For us, it's necessary to be able to recognize who's a Warder."

Enric's expression still held doubt. "Maybe they hired more people to help out with the current situation."

"Pretty fast work, if they did," Namid said.

"And why would they have some disguise glamour on their clothes to make them look like Warder uniforms?" Aahmes said. "I never heard of the Warders employing mages."

"All right then. So now what?" Enric said. "Perhaps we should return to the city by another route and investigate."

"I have a feeling we'd just be walking into a trap," Namid said. Aahmes nodded.

"If they're not City Warders, how did they know you two?" Enric said.

Namid and Aahmes exchanged looks and Aahmes shrugged. "Even if they were Warders, our names shouldn't have been known to them.... Perhaps someone sold us out...."

Namid tilted her head and stared off into the distance. "I suppose that's possible, but it doesn't make sense that someone would have sold out both of us. I'd expect one or the other, but not both."

Aahmes shook his head. "Who knows. But I don't plan to just walk back in there. Even if they were telling the truth about half the city surviving."

Namid agreed.

"But my quest!" Enric said. "I need to find out about Nazextas."

"Didn't you say something about needing a guide?" Aahmes said.

"Yes. Someone who knows Yiruny."

"I might be available."

"You?" Namid scoffed.

"I've traveled," Aahmes said. "I can find my way around Yiruny."

"Do you know where Nazextas is?" Enric said.

"I don't even know *what* Nazextas is," Aahmes said. "But I know who to ask. 'Sides, I don't exactly have anything I need to do right now. About payment...."

Enric studied Aahmes with narrowed eyes, then nodded and pulled three navns out of his pouch. Aahmes' eyes widened as the noble dropped the gold coins into his hands.

"You'll receive the same amount when we find Nazextas."

Aahmes nodded, for once wordless. Three navns was generous payment for a service, and even more so for a simple guide.

A flash of reflected sunlight from one of Enric's rings caught Namid's attention.

"You'd better not wear such baubles openly," she told him, waving a hand at his rings. "Even out here. You'll just be killed for them."

"And there's no guarantee we'd interfere," Aahmes said with a slight grin. Then, at a look from Enric, "I'm just your guide, not your bodyguard."

Enric frowned but stripped off his jewelry and dropped everything into his pouch. Then he turned to Namid. "It would please me if you would consent to accompany me on this journey. You would be most welcome."

Aahmes started laughing.

Namid glanced at him and enjoyed seeing his jaw drop as she stood and gave Enric a small curtsey. "I believe that

I'd be honored to join you."

No reason not to, she thought. Perhaps it would help her avoid brooding about the loss of Dar and Thes, and the other Shadowers. And she needed to get far away from Rhadanthus. That false Warder's disguised robe.... If the robe was identical to those she remembered from a grim time years ago — if it signified the man's allegiance to those people she had escaped.... Namid shuddered.

Time to flee again.

CHAPTER 4

Around midday, they retrieved the horses and rode on. This time, Namid rode behind Enric to give the other horse a rest from carrying double. They rode at an easy pace, leaving Rhadanthus behind.

"I propose we hasten to the next city and there obtain information and better horses," Enric said.

Both Aahmes and Namid stared at him.

"How well do you know this area?" Namid said.

"I viewed a map once."

"He viewed a map once," Aahmes imitated.

Enric tossed him a disgusted look.

"Listen," Namid said. "The closest people around outside Rhadanthus are bands of outlaws. And they could be anywhere."

"Outlaws," Aahmes said, with a hint of mischief in his eyes. "Sounds like my kind of people."

"And how would you find them?" Namid said. "It'd probably take weeks. Of course, that wouldn't matter, because by then you'd have starved to death, anyway."

"I have no intention of putting myself into the hands of such rabble," Enric stated.

Aahmes opened his mouth to comment but, at Namid's glare, settled instead for an innocent grin.

Namid's stomach chose that moment to rumble. Aahmes and Enric both looked at her, Aahmes stifling laughter.

Namid shrugged it off. "And obviously we're going to have to find something to eat."

"I can hunt," Enric offered. "I hunted often in my family's preserve."

"You can hunt?" Aahmes scoffed. "Hunt what? Our horses?" He made a sweeping gesture at the ostensibly barren grassland around them. "You are no doubt the expert hunter in prairie like this."

Enric flushed and glared down his nose at Aahmes.

After further discussion, they decided to try to find some of the farms supposed to be outside Rhadanthus, in the hope of getting some food. And they turned southwest, expecting to join the West Road before long. As they traveled, they looked for any animals or birds that they might catch for food but spotted nothing of the sort.

The land they crossed was dry with autumn, gentle hills covered in knee-high grass that had turned a gold-brown color. From the higher points, the view extended for leagues in all directions. No trees grew in the stony soil of this vast prairie, only the grass and frequent clumps of low bushes. The almost-constant breeze chilled them, but not too much with the sun shining.

During the afternoon, they found a couple of long-deserted farms, no surprise since much of the land in this western portion of the realm of Paronia had proven unsuitable for growing food, although people had tried. At each farm, they searched for anything that might be useful, but found nothing worthwhile. The farms had all been deserted long enough that anything of use had either already been taken or had rotted away. They drank what water they could from the wells and watered the horses. Namid and Aahmes cleaned the bloodstains from their clothes the best they could. Then, lacking a way to take any water with them, they moved on.

About mid-afternoon, Aahmes stopped once, dismounted, and peered at the ground. Namid wondered if he had found something, tracks maybe, or signs of some animal they could catch for food, but he only picked up a few rocks and mounted again. At her puzzled look, he grinned.

By dusk, they still had not come to the road, so they stopped atop the tallest hillock nearby and settled as well as possible for the night. They spoke little. Namid stayed wrapped up in her own thoughts. Hunger and thirst combined with the cold of night to make her sleep uneasy at best, despite her fatigue, and she saw the others also often awake. They started out again in the light of dawn, under one moon in the sky: Gopan, the smallest of the five moons. Namid again rode with Enric.

Sometime around midmorning, Enric broke the silence that had wrapped itself around them. "What a lonely place this is," he said to Namid.

She nodded. "But it has its own beauty, too. I'd forgotten how it was to travel, 'though usually I was better provisioned."

"I'm truly sorry about your people," he said.

"I can't help hoping, even now, that maybe some of them got away too."

"I'm sure some did." He sounded confident. "They appeared too experienced to be caught like that."

"I'd like to think so," Namid said.

"I'm glad that you're coming with me," he said, maybe hoping to cheer her.

Namid heard an unfamiliar sound from behind them. She strained around to look, in time to see Aahmes, standing a short distance away, release one end of a strip of cloth he was whirling around. A rock flew high and something fell.

Aahmes crowed in delight as he mounted and galloped ahead. He returned moments later, holding up some largish bird.

Namid grinned, and her stomach rumbled at the thought of roasted meat.

"We're certainly not going to eat it raw!" Enric said.

"Certainly not," Aahmes mimicked as he dismounted.

"We can collect some of these bushes to burn," Namid said as she also slid to the ground.

Enric peered at the nearby dry bushes. "They'll burn too rapidly, I think."

"Then we'll just have to get a lot of them," Aahmes said.

Enric nodded. "We'll get the bushes while you clean the bird," he said to Namid.

"Oh, no," Namid said. "Aahmes caught it, he'll clean it."

Aahmes chuckled at the expression on Enric's face.

Namid poked at Enric's arm. "The two of us'll get the bushes."

It took much longer than she had expected to collect enough dry bushes, break them into suitable sticks, clear a spot on the ground, and set up for the fire.

"So, which of you carries the tinder box?" Enric said.

Namid and Aahmes exchanged a glance, shook their heads, and looked back at Enric.

"I was to travel with caravans, and stay in the finest inns," he said.

"Raw's better than nothing," Namid said.

Enric looked somewhat queasy at that. "I shan't be able to stomach raw bird."

Aahmes sighed and began pacing around, studying the ground. Namid and Enric watched curiously. Aahmes paused three times to grab something from the dirt. When he returned to them, he carried two fist-sized stones and a bit of fluff that looked like it came from some rodent's nest.

He positioned the fluff and some dry grasses on a larger stone near the place they had prepared for the fire and piled some smaller sticks at his side. Then he struck the stones together, once, and again, working to direct the sparks to the fluff and dried grasses, while at the same time trying to block the wind with his body.

After long breaths-of-time of watching Aahmes, and trying to help block the wind, Namid sighed to herself. She avoided using her Power openly. Past experiences had taught her that was best. But they needed to eat, and she would rather not get sick from raw meat. And it was uncertain when, or even if, Aahmes would be successful at getting a flame. Although difficult with just the three of them around, Namid hoped she still might be able to hide her use of Power. She decided she had to try.

She edged closer to Aahmes, hoping to give the impression that she still simply tried to block the wind. She narrowed her eyes, ducked her head to try to hide her concentration and focused on the stones and the fluff. She called on the hidden reserve within and directed the Power toward the striking stones. She pictured extending a glowing finger, then released a tiny bit of Power.

A bright spark leapt from the stones to the fluff and grasses and began smoldering there. Namid glanced up to a strange look from Aahmes, who turned away to nurse the spark into flame and transfer the fire to the sticks.

"Better get the bird over there, too," Namid said, hoping to forestall questions.

Soon they feasted on the hot meat, licking grease from singed fingers. Namid kept catching odd looks from Aahmes, but he said nothing.

After they had finished the bird, Aahmes walked off, muttering something about trying to find more birds.

"You've traveled much?" Enric broke the silence.

Namid shrugged. "Some." Her travel had been a matter of compelling necessity and self-preservation, not choice. She hoped he would catch the hint that she preferred not to discuss it. She glanced at the clear sky. "I don't think he's going to find any more birds."

Enric followed her gaze and shrugged. He stretched out on the warm ground and soon dozed off. Namid envied him. A nap did sound good, but her aches from riding kept her from settling down. After all, it had been several years since she had last ridden so much, and she was no longer accustomed to extended time on horseback.

Namid poked a stick a few times at the almost-dead fire then clambered to her feet and walked around, hoping to ease the cramps in her legs. She checked on the horses and brought the one Aahmes had ridden closer to the other. Just like his rider, the horse seemed determined to have his own way and ambled off again. She glared at him a moment, then shrugged. The horse did not seem to want to go too far.

She walked to the top of a nearby hill and scanned the land around. It looked much the same in all directions, even toward where she knew Rhadanthus to be. She did not see Aahmes but was unconcerned that he would have any problem finding his way back. She had noticed in the past that he seemed to have an uncanny ability to find his way almost anywhere.

Namid sat and her thoughts drifted to Aahmes. She did not dislike him, she realized, at least not most of the time. He irritated her, and others too from what she had seen over the years, always ready with a mocking comment, appearing always ready for a fight. Namid stretched out, stared at the sky and felt the sun start to bake her. Her mental description of Aahmes sounded somewhat familiar....

Somewhere in her musings, she fell asleep. The next she knew, Aahmes was shaking her.

"Thought you might be interested in eating some more." He gestured toward two birds roasting over the fire.

Namid nodded and saw that she had napped into evening. She peered at the fire as she followed Aahmes back. How had they gotten it started again? It must not have burned out, she decided. That explained it.

After they finished their meal, they settled for the night, leaving three more birds that Aahmes had caught to smoke over the remains of the fire.

Namid's nap earlier, however, had left her without any immediate need for sleep, so she prowled around their camp. The second time she passed Enric, she heard his voice out of the darkness.

"So, you're also not sleepy." He joined her.

"That's what comes from napping in the afternoon."

They paced in silence then for a long time.

"Somehow you don't belong," Enric said.

"What?"

"You don't belong in a place like Rhadanthus. You're different somehow. Too urbane. I can picture you in the court of some Earl or Duke, but not as part of that city's rabble."

"Really?" Namid laughed but cringed inside. She had worked hard to blend in well enough with the Shadowers and their sort so that no one would suspect her origins. And yet this noble had come too close to the truth.

"That's interesting," she hedged. "Maybe you're just not used to dealing with our type."

Enric gave her a strange look. "Maybe," he said after a time, sounding not at all convinced.

By mutual consent they returned to the camp. Namid rolled up in her cloak, and eventually fell asleep.

~ ~ ~

Sounds of frantic activity woke Namid. She sat up, blinking to try to focus her eyes and spotted Aahmes wrapping the smoked meat in some cloth, the fire already covered with dirt. She heard Enric's voice from some distance away. He stood silhouetted against the bright morning sky.

"There it is again!" he called.

"We saw a cloud of dust earlier," Aahmes explained as Namid stood up. "He thinks it might be some caravan, or something, on the West Road, and demands we go see." She ignored the exasperation in his voice and joined Enric.

She looked where he pointed and, by squinting, was able to make out what had excited him. After a long look, she had to agree with Enric. It looked like enough dust to be a caravan, or a similarly sized group, moving out there.

"They're headed for Rhadanthus," Aahmes said.

"Not the false Warders, then," Namid said.

"We'd better warn them, then!" Enric said as he ran to the horses. Namid and Aahmes followed.

"Why?" Aahmes demanded. "They should take care of themselves. Everyone in Rhadanthus lived by that."

"And died by it," Enric said. "We should have tried to help, instead of riding past!"

"And joined them in death?" Aahmes said. "No thanks! And those people out there will find out what happened soon enough. I say we just get down to that road and be on our way. Besides, for all we know, they're the ones who sent Sy'shythys."

"Maybe," Namid said. "How about we just look them over first, then decide if we want to let them know we're here?"

Enric nodded with a smile, and Aahmes agreed with a shrug. They mounted the horses, Aahmes and Namid again sharing one, and started toward the dust cloud, eating as they rode.

Around noon, they came to the place from which they thought the dust had risen. And found nothing there. No dust, and no road. Only thin grass and dry earth.

They munched more of the smoked meat as they rode up the nearest hill. From the summit, they scanned the countryside, and located the dust cloud without trouble.

"It's just as far away as before. If they're really headed toward Rhadanthus, we should be catching up to them," Aahmes murmured.

"It might only seem that they're just as far away," Enric said. "I'd guess that distances here can be deceiving. Come on." He rode down the hill at a canter.

"This doesn't feel right," Namid said as they followed Enric.

Aahmes nodded. "And didn't it look like the dust was

now moving west, away from Rhadanthus?"

Namid squinted at the sun, but it was too near noon. "I can't tell. Have you ever heard anything about this prairie maybe being haunted?"

"No. But I wouldn't be surprised."

They chased the dust cloud through the afternoon, pausing at deserted farms long enough to drink from the wells while always keeping the dust cloud in sight. But they never got any nearer. In the late afternoon, they stopped atop a small rise.

"It's still there," Enric said.

"And as far away," Aahmes said. "There's no point in continuing this mad chase. It's just some trick. So, continue on? Or make camp here?"

"I say camp here," Namid said. "The horses could probably use the rest, and I know I could."

"Did city life make us a little soft?" Aahmes taunted.

Namid just punched him in the side and slid off the horse.

They set up a meager camp, ate, and rested for what was left of the day.

In her dreams that night, Namid raced from Sy'shythys, but this time knew she would not escape. Closer it came, tendrils like long fingers reaching for her…. They caught in her hair… grabbed her arm… pulled her back….

Then she found herself sitting upright in the cool night, shivering. She stood up, wrapped her cloak around herself, and started to pace, hoping to calm down. She was startled when she realized that she was not pacing alone.

"We might as well continue on," Enric said.

"Especially since none of us can sleep," Aahmes added from her other side.

Namid agreed. Four moons were visible, the four smallest: Gopan; Tursa and Trisi the twin moons, so-called for their similar oval shapes and reddish colors; and Nidvi, the largest of the four. They provided enough light for traveling.

"And no more chasing after dust clouds," Aahmes said.

As she mounted behind Enric, Namid heard him say something under his breath.

"What was that?"

He half turned to look at her and his teeth flashed in the moonlight as he grinned. "I was just asking Vlatas for patience with your brother. Is he always this contrary, or do I just bring it out in him?"

"He's not my brother," Namid told him. "And, usually, he's worse than you've yet seen him."

"Wonderful. How long have you known him?"

"Ever since I came to Rhadanthus, a number of years ago. I remember I felt lost, and a bit frightened, and the Shadowers took me in."

"The Shadowers?"

"That's the rabble she helped lead," Aahmes said, as he moved up to ride next to them. "They used to be an official guild in Rhadanthus' better days, ages ago. They'd hire out to various nobles as spies, and sometimes as assassins. Of course, the assassins' league didn't like that. Anyway, now the Shadowers are hardly more than petty thieves." He urged his horse into a trot and moved ahead of them.

"Don't forget sellswords," Namid called after him. "We were that, too," she added under her breath.

"You two certainly clash often enough," Enric said. "Do you hate each other so?"

"Aahmes was a Shadower when I joined, and we've been at odds almost since that very day. He left the Shadowers when Dar—the leader—asked me to be one of his Seconds."

Enric pondered this for a while. "He thinks you took the place that should have gone to him?"

Namid shrugged. "What about you? How'd you get involved in this quest for Akavos' blade?"

"I've had this for a long time." He tapped the hilt of his dagger. "With various blades, of course. All Raphahan children are entrusted with an important item, one each, a family heirloom of sorts. As youngest, this was mine. But about four weeks ago, I found out the truth about it. During one of my father's lavish feasts, a strange priest came to the gates of our manor. As the youngest, I had been granted the dubious honor of admitting him and seeing that his wants were satisfied. Despite all else my father does, he *does* act civil toward the priests.

"So, ever obedient to my father's commands, I left the hall, and collided with the priest in the hallway! Somehow, he had entered through our locked and guarded gates. I was about to demand an explanation, but something stopped me. Somehow, I felt that my questions had become unimportant. He beckoned me to a small room, where he said we could talk. I remember how his height struck me. He was taller than Aahmes. And he wore a long robe and cloak of some silvery cloth. He kept the hood of his cloak pulled forward, so his face was shadowed. He looked unlike any priest I had ever seen. He said his name was Myung. He told me that the hilt to my dagger—I wore it at the time—was actually part of Akavos, a sword of Power. He said that it had fallen to me to reunite the hilt and blade. He told me my quest must begin in Rhadanthus."

"Why Rhadanthus?" Aahmes said, having moved closer again.

Enric shrugged. "Maybe he knew I could find a guide there."

"Did this Myung also tell you about Nazextas?" Namid said.

"Yes, but only the name. And he said something about Yiruny, which I didn't hear because just then a great noise came from the hall. I excused myself to investigate. When I returned just a few breaths-of-time later, Myung had vanished."

"And just on his word, you started off on this mad quest?" Aahmes said.

Enric looked down at the ground and rubbed the back of his neck with one hand. "Well, I needed to do something—"

"He needed to do something," Aahmes mocked.

"It's a tradition in my family!" Enric snapped. "We're all expected, upon reaching a certain age, to undertake some activity which will prove our worth… something like that."

"That's rather scanty information to start a quest," Namid said.

"Rather!" Aahmes said. "And now I'm tangled up in this fool's quest—"

"Which somehow seems appropriate," Namid said.

"I just realized something!" Enric said. "When Myung first spoke to me, he used the secret language of the god Vlatas. But only Vlatas' initiates are supposed to know it!"

"Maybe that's what he was," Namid said.

"No. We don't wear anything like what he wore."

Namid had no answer to that, so just watched Aahmes ride ahead again.

So, Enric was an initiate of Vlatas, Namid mused. She wondered how his family felt about that, since everyone knew his father was critical of the gods and their priests, even if he did treat priests well. And who was this Myung?

"And what's his interest in the sword?" Namid said. "Why couldn't he just find the blade himself, instead of sending someone else off on some wild journey?"

It seemed that Enric was about to answer, but Aahmes shouted at them from the top of the large hill they had been climbing. He waved, urging them to hurry, and disappeared over the top.

Enric and Namid galloped up the hill and halted, awestruck. In a vast depression below them stood the most beautiful city Namid had ever seen. It spanned leagues, covering the entire valley and extending up the slopes of the surrounding hills. Much like Rhadanthus, it was circular in shape. But this city shimmered and glowed in the darkness and lit the entire valley, although not the nearby countryside. So only the moons lit the spot where she and Enric stood. Namid glanced at the sky and saw by the stars that it was close to midnight.

She peered down the slope of the hill and saw Aahmes making his way toward the city. Without warning, his horse stopped and refused to go any further. Enric and Namid soon reached Aahmes' side, and their horse also refused to go any closer to the city.

"Do you see it?" Aahmes whispered.

"Yes," Namid murmured.

She shivered from the singular prickling in the air that marked a substantial amount of Power nearby. Then the city demanded her attention again. She watched, fascinated and troubled at the same time, as it collapsed in on itself. The outer walls rushed inward, driving luminescent buildings before them like sheep. At the center, for a moment, she glimpsed a tower. Then everything blurred and flowed together in a sky-high pillar of all the colors imaginable. A frightful shrieking filled the air, grew louder and pierced her ears. The light intensified. Two eyes, full of malice, peered from the pillar of light. She felt they searched for her. The eyes focused on her for an instant and a chill ran through her.

Glowing wisps reached out from the city, headed for her. She leaned away, wanting nothing more than to run, certain they meant her harm. The eyes vanished, and the wisps snapped back as the pillar started to rotate, ever faster, until it resembled one of the tornadoes that sometimes roared across the prairie. The shriek sliced through her. Namid thought she heard a single mournful bell toll midnight. With a flash, the funnel vanished, leaving the night deathly still. As the silence lengthened, she realized how tightly she had wrapped her arms around Enric's chest. She jerked back, and he took a deep breath.

"I begin to wonder about the wisdom of this undertaking," Enric muttered. "Killing fogs, will-o'-the-wisp dust clouds, and now demon cities."

"Demon?" Aahmes said. "No, the city was torn from the ground, sucked up into the storm cloud. Just for an instant, two evil eyes looked at me, then it all faded away."

"I saw eyes, too," Namid said. "But not the rest." She described what she had seen, then Enric told what he had seen. Enric had not seen the eyes at all, only she and Aahmes had.

They stared at the enigmatic valley for several long breaths-of-time.

"Anyone feel like making a camp here?" Namid quipped. Enric just shook his head. Aahmes glowered. Namid sensed the two men felt more uneasy with Power than she did. Not that she felt at all at ease about this strange city.

"Let's get going." Aahmes suited action to words.

They skirted the valley, rather than ride through it. Namid felt relieved after that place vanished into the hills behind them. She would have wagered that the others felt the same.

They rode the rest of the night until, as dawn approached, they found a sheltered area that boasted a small trickle of water. They decided to stop there. As they had traveled, the land had changed. The hills had gradually grown taller, some of them lofty enough to be called mountains. The low bushes and prairie grass had given way to soil too rocky even for such miserable plants, forcing the horses to forage for sparse clumps of vegetation.

They dismounted, ate half of the small amount of meat that remained and poked around the cart-sized boulders surrounding them to find crannies that looked likely to be shaded most of the day. Despite the hard, rocky ground underneath, Namid fell asleep soon after she crawled into her cranny.

However, her sleep proved anything but restful. Visions of that accursed ghostly city, and the eyes, filled her dreams. Other images stole in: Dar's face twisted in death and yet he kept trying to tell her something, her father's face twisted in anger as he found out about her Power, then a man who looked not unlike Aahmes, but somehow sinister. The latter seemed to speak to her in welcome. Then she raced in fear through a familiar cavern, eyes shielded from some nameless horror. She could not cover any distance! And he kept getting closer....

Namid bolted upright, wide awake, her clothes wet with sweat. She gazed at the unfamiliar surroundings, confused. After a moment, she remembered where she was.

It seemed to be early afternoon.

"Rest well?" Aahmes said, his voice heavy with irony. He lay stretched out nearby in a patch of shade, legs crossed at the ankles, feet propped on a small rock. He watched her as she stood up and shivered a moment in the breeze.

Namid noted the dark smudges under his eyes. "You're a good one to be asking," she said. She joined him in his patch of shade, wanting to be near someone familiar, even if it had to be him.

"Why, this is so sudden." He grinned as she settled herself.

"Stuff it." She gazed off into the hazy distance. She debated with herself for several long breaths-of-time and decided to broach the topic.

"Dar," she said in a quiet voice, and tried to push aside the sudden pang of grief that stabbed through her. She heard Aahmes shift around but did not look at him.

"Yes?" he said after a moment.

"You saw his last message?"

From the corner of her eye she saw Aahmes nod.

"So...." She paused for a long time, then continued when Aahmes did not jump in to say something. "So... think he was talking to both of us?"

Aahmes was quiet long enough that she wondered whether he would answer at all. She peeked at him. Now *he* stared off into the distance.

"Could be either way," he said finally. He grinned and met her gaze. "Would you trust me? Should I trust you?"

Namid studied him for a long time, then said "Hmm."

He chuckled. "Exactly."

Then he looked past her. "I think our young noble will

be joining us soon." He waved a hand toward Enric's twitching form, then looked back at Namid. "Did you dream about that city?"

"Yeah. You?"

He nodded. "Particularly those eyes. I think I'd like to get my hands on this Myung. Maybe I'll borrow your poison." He tapped her armguard.

Namid pulled the arm away. "Perhaps."

He gave her a wicked grin.

Enric groaned and sat up as abruptly as Namid had. He blinked in the glaring sunlight and focused on them.

"I see you had similar fortune with sleeping," he said as he stood. He pulled out the last of their food and joined them. They ate in silence.

"What now?" Enric said, looking at his last bite of meat.

Namid looked at Aahmes. "More birds?"

He shrugged. "Haven't seen any."

"Perhaps we'll find the road soon," Enric said.

"That doesn't guarantee food," Namid pointed out.

"There might be other travelers."

"Like that dust cloud?" Aahmes said. "Right."

He left to check on the horses and returned a short time later.

"Looking at the land here, I'd say we crossed into Yiruny sometime last night," he said.

"So, now all we need to do is find some people and inquire of them about Nazextas," Enric said.

"I don't know if that's such a good idea," Namid said. "I get a feeling that this Nazextas is something special, maybe secret. By asking just anyone about it, we might only find trouble."

"Seems likely," Aahmes said. "We *could* just find someone, and have you read their thoughts, or something like that."

"Read their thoughts?" Namid said, her eyebrows raised. "What *are* you talking about?"

"Well, after that trick you pulled with the fire," he said.

"Why not?"

So, they knew of her use of Power. Uneasiness crawled down her back, but she could not undo what she had done.

"I can't do anything like reading thoughts. That's straight out of children's tales!"

"I say we settle this question when we actually find someone," Enric said. "We have some candle-marks of daylight left. Let's ride." He headed toward the horses.

"It's better than trying to sleep," Aahmes said. He gave Namid a look that said the question of her Power had not been settled. She returned one that said she agreed.

"Would my lady be willing to ride with her humble servant?" Aahmes said and gave her an exaggerated bow.

"Don't you start."

They again rode, angling further south of west, still hoping to meet up with the West Road.

CHAPTER 5

The long afternoon gave way to dusk. After the sun slipped below the horizon, some heat wafted up from the ground, but otherwise the air cooled rapidly. The cooler temperature seemed to agree with the horses, who picked up their pace and even frisked.

They rode leisurely and let the horses choose their own path for the most part. Enric whistled some melancholy tune, while Aahmes and Namid rode in silence.

"Did you hear that?" Enric said, breaking off his whistling.

"How could we hear anything over that noise you were making?" Aahmes said.

"That happens to be a famous composition by a celebrated bard!"

"I'm not arguing with that," Aahmes said. "It's the performance I object to. If you must whistle, at least do it on key."

Namid wondered how Aahmes knew it was off key. She had never before known him to show any knowledge of music. Then she heard a hint of a sound in the night behind their banter.

"Shhh," she said.

They both turned to her.

"So sorry to disturb you," Aahmes said. "Do you want us to take our discussion somewhere else, so it won't upset you?"

"Will you hush? I heard something," Namid said. "But I can't tell what it is if you keep talking."

Enric gave Aahmes a smug look. "I told you I heard something."

"Shhh."

They listened to the night for some time before the sound repeated. It seemed close.

"Oh, it's only a bird." Enric sounded disappointed.

"What were you hoping for?" Aahmes said. "A winsome maiden who's been waiting all her life for you?"

"I doubt it's a bird," Namid said. "We haven't run across any songbirds since we left Rhadanthus."

"And in case you haven't noticed, it's nighttime," Aahmes added.

Namid slid off the horse. "Let's see who or what our singing bird is."

"I'll come with you," Enric offered and started to dismount.

"No, you stay with the horses. I'll go." Aahmes joined her on the ground.

"Why—"

Namid cut Enric off. "Remember, we've had more experience at this kind of business."

"You're not a good enough sneak," Aahmes said.

"Back in a few breaths-of-time," Namid said, and she and Aahmes slipped into the night.

A few paces away from Enric, the two paused to listen. The soft sound came again, off to the right. They consulted using the Shadowers' hand-talk, having to spell everything on each other's hands. It was too difficult to distinguish the subtle signals otherwise since no light from the moons penetrated the clouds. They decided to split up and try to circle around the 'bird', to come in from both sides.

Aahmes disappeared into the dark, skulking straight ahead from where they had stopped. Namid sidled to the right and kept low. She found it challenging to hold her steps silent as she crossed the rocky ground.

She heard the sound again. It now sounded somewhat like a hummed tune getting louder, then softer again. It seemed to come from beyond a rock outcrop ahead of her. She moved toward it and found Aahmes crouched next to it. By hand-talk, he told her he could not get through the way he had tried, and he agreed that the sound came from the other side of the rocks.

They crept around the boulders. As they moved, one of the moons appeared through a break in the clouds and supplied some minimal light. The humming stopped.

"I've been waiting for you," came a voice from in front of them. Both Namid and Aahmes jumped.

"Come on around," the voice added. "No reason to stay in hiding."

Aahmes and Namid approached, still cautious. Namid saw that Aahmes had one of his daggers in hand.

They rounded the last rock and discovered a young woman, perhaps Namid's age or a bit older, lolling at the base of the rocks. She had short dark hair, very curly, and skin darker than theirs. Kohl lined her eyes. She wore a light-colored vest, laced down the front, and a full, matching skirt that reached to her calves, with pantalets beneath it. The moon was not bright enough to distinguish the colors. She was barefoot. Her clothes and manner marked her as a Prazny.

Inveterate wanderers, the Praznies usually traveled in large family groups and roamed the various realms at will, trading a variety of goods, for the most part. But it was an open secret that they stole when trading did not work. In certain circles, by an unwritten understanding, they were treated as the rulers of the roads. They owed no allegiance to the Monarch nor to any lesser noble in the Six Realms.

The young Prazny returned their scrutiny.

"The two of you are really very good, for outsiders," she said as she stood. "I almost did not notice you coming." Praznies were known for their ability to move anywhere unseen and unheard, if they chose.

"I am Inezha, of Staehw's van. You, and your friend with the horses, will accept our hospitality?" She phrased the last as a question, but Namid knew she meant it more as a command. Prudent travelers did not refuse such invitations, as the alternative was, at best, rough treatment at Prazny hands. Of course, most prudent travelers tried to avoid ever meeting the Praznies at all.

"Of course," Namid said.

"We'll just go get Enric—" Aahmes said.

Inezha stopped him with a hand on his arm. She gave him a broad smile. "No need. The others are already guiding your friend to our camp. Follow me."

Inezha led them through the tangled maze of boulders to a clearing lit by a fire in its center and bordered by several Prazny wagons. At the far side of this area, a gap showed in the surrounding boulders, almost large enough for two of the wagons to drive through side by side. Several horses, including theirs, were picketed near this opening.

Inezha hurried toward a large man who stood near the fire. Aahmes and Namid followed at a walk, taking the time to look over the camp. They shared glances at the second looks many of the Praznies gave them as they passed.

They had nearly reached the fire when Inezha rejoined them. The large man followed her. Namid felt dwarfed next to him. He was bulky, solidly muscular and tall, taller than anyone she had met before. The top of her head just reached his shoulder. He moved with an air of authority that any ruler would have envied. His face was round, bearded, and his dark hair was shorter than Inezha's, with small curls that clung to his head. His skin was darker than Inezha's. He wore white trousers and a loose, bright green shirt that gapped open in front down to his wide, brown belt. Like

Inezha, he was barefoot.

Inezha introduced him as Staehw, the leader of the van, then hurried off to tend to something. Aahmes and Namid introduced themselves to the large Prazny. As so many of the other Praznies had, he gave them a quick second look, comparing them one to the other.

"Welcome almost-Praznies," Staehw said in a deep voice. "You are nearly unheard."

Namid knew that this represented the highest praise an outsider ever received from them. The Praznies prized stealth. Namid thought back to the brief time she had spent with a Prazny family years ago and hoped she remembered their customs.

"You honor us," she said. "Coming from one both unheard and unseen."

Staehw smiled. "You know something of our ways. Come. Join us at our repast. But first, you will want to refresh yourselves. You carry a whiff of the killing-mist about you."

Aahmes and Namid glanced at each other.

"Ah, yes," Aahmes said. "Your senses are sharp. We've come from Rhadanthus, where the mist now rules." Aahmes imitated the Praznies' manner of talking with ease.

"A tragedy, that," Staehw said. "You must have a share of the wisdom of the road." In other words, they knew when to leave a place, another talent Praznies admired.

Aahmes and Namid both agreed.

Staehw laughed and draped his arms around their shoulders. "Come, my friends. Your companion is no doubt already relaxing under our expert care."

"No doubt," Namid murmured.

"I am certain you are eager to join him," Staehw said to Aahmes. And to Namid, "Inezha has prepared a delight for you." He called the Prazny woman over.

Namid wondered what he meant by delight as she watched the two men walk to one of the wagons, engrossed in conversation. She suspected Staehw was doing most of the talking. She felt a light, cool touch on one arm: Inezha.

"Come with me," Inezha urged. She seized Namid's hand and tugged her to another wagon. "We now have a washing basin large enough to climb into and stretch out!" she said with a large smile. The washing basin must be the delight, Namid decided.

"And Staehw complains that now we are all too clean!" Inezha continued. "But the women love it. And, sometimes, the men can be persuaded to join us."

"I would imagine that would make it a little crowded," Namid said with a slight smile.

"Oh, yes." Inezha grinned. "Here." She pushed open the door to the largest wagon and led Namid inside.

The bright colors that Praznies seemed to love decorated the wagon's interior, which was lit by several candles along the walls. A large basin dominated the room, a bath in reality, large enough to stretch out in, as Inezha had said. Such a luxury was rarely enjoyed by even those who could afford to purchase such a thing. Namid doubted that the Praznies had purchased it.

Inezha stepped over to an urn that sat next to the bath and lifted its lid. Steam puffed out of the opening and, as she opened two other urns, began to fill the wagon.

"It's ready for you."

"My thanks." Namid removed her cloak and belts and dropped them on a small table. She removed one armguard, started to unlace her overtunic and caught a strange glance from Inezha.

"Is that all you have to wear?" the Prazny said.

"We left in something of a hurry," Namid said with a wry grin.

"If you wear those we might lose you in the night. You have nothing more festive?"

Namid shook her head as she tossed her tunic atop her sword.

"After we've poured the water, I'll find you something brighter to wear. More suited to a guest at our repast."

Together, they shoved the urns closer to the basin and poured out the water. Namid unbraided her hair, letting it fall loose over her back, and finished undressing. Inezha gave her another strange look when she settled into the water without removing her second armguard, and her gaze also lingered on Namid's dagger necklace, but she did not comment. After she made sure Namid did not need anything else, Inezha left to find some more-festive clothes.

After Inezha had gone, Namid removed the armguard and set it on the floor next to the basin. She took a deep breath and slid under the water. She sat up again a few breaths-of-time later and pushed back her hair. A faint floral scent rose from the water, and its warmth relaxed her cramped muscles. Just as she started to doze off, she noticed a small chunk of soap on the edge of the basin. The idea of being clean won out over laziness. She grabbed the soap and subjected herself to a thorough scrubbing, something she had not been able to do to her satisfaction in far too long. It felt wonderful. The piece of soap had grown noticeably smaller when she finished. She felt one tiny twinge of guilt about that—such soap being even rarer than baths—then laughed at herself. If anyone could acquire more, it was the Praznies.

The water had cooled, so she looked around for something to use to dry off. She was just considering using her overtunic, dirty as it was, when Inezha returned, her arms full of clothes. She set them down and pulled a towel out of the pile and tossed it to Namid.

"Thought you might be looking for that soon," Inezha said with a grin.

Namid squeezed most of the water out of her hair. As she stepped out of the basin, she wrapped up in the towel. She flipped her hair back over her shoulders and had just started to comb it out with her fingers when she realized her mistake. In her pleasure over the bath, she had forgotten to cover the small tattoo she bore on her forehead at her hairline. Namid started to pull her bangs back down over it, but Inezha had already seen it. She stopped Namid's hand and stepped closer for a better look. Her eyes widened, and she dropped her gaze to Namid's right wrist and noted the tattoo visible there.

"Forgive me, Lady Mage-Initiate," Inezha whispered, her head bowed. "I did not know you." She made a sign that Namid recognized, that of one follower of the god Ilenii to another.

"There's nothing to forgive." Namid rearranged her bangs and laced the band around her wrist as Inezha watched her, looking concerned.

"There is danger here for you," Inezha whispered. "Few in the van still follow Ilenii."

Namid frowned, disturbed. While most people maintained only a casual connection to their god or gods, the Praznies had always been devout followers of Ilenii. According to legend, Ilenii had shown special favor toward the Praznies, and they, in turn, had vowed to be hers. Forever. So the old tales said, anyway.

"Who do they follow now?" Namid said as she finished drying off.

Inezha started to answer, but a knock on the door interrupted her. A woman's voice called something to her in another tongue, and she replied in the same.

"I must go. I am needed." Inezha paused at the door. "You can put your things inside the wagon next to this one while we feast. And get away from Staehw! This night, if you can." Then she was gone.

Namid dressed in the red vest, skirt, and pantalets Inezha had brought for her, and slipped on a pair of sandals. She also strapped on her other armguard and rebraided her hair. The apprehension from Rhadanthus had returned. Namid felt she should heed Inezha's advice, but also felt there might be something to learn here. She would just have to stay alert, and maybe find out more from Inezha later.

Namid retrieved one of her daggers to use for eating and bundled up the rest of her things. She ducked into the wagon Inezha had mentioned and set her things in a corner. The lightest touch of the Power ensured they would remain undisturbed.

When she stepped back outside, Namid found Aahmes and Enric waiting for her. Enric still wore green, but had exchanged his own clothes for a Prazny's, right down to a pair of sandals. Aahmes wore blue, also Prazny attire, and had kept his boots. Where his shirt gapped open, Namid saw he no longer wore the bandages from Rhadanthus.

"Just like a female," Aahmes said with a mock frown as Namid joined them. "Keeping us waiting. All of us." He gestured toward the fire, where it seemed all the Praznies had gathered, many looking toward the three.

Namid started to snap back at Aahmes, then noticed the humor lurking in his eyes. She settled for giving him a stern glower.

"A woman of quality always takes her time preparing for a feast," Enric told Aahmes, who just shook his head and looked away.

Enric offered Namid his arm. "You look stunning. Since they're ready now, shall we join them?"

Namid gave him a smile. "My thanks for the compliment." She took his arm, then also Aahmes' hastily extended one, and they walked to the waiting Praznies.

Staehw made room for them next to him. He seated Aahmes to his left, and Enric and Namid to his right. The dishes were arranged so that two people shared the same plate. Namid shared with Enric, and Aahmes shared with Inezha. Staehw, however, shared with no one.

The Praznies served a hearty meal of a variety of vegetable dishes and sauces, bread, and the sticky pastry that was their favorite. The meal also included a sweet drink called Cielila, made from the ila fruit. The juice from the ila fruit, even in modest amounts, was known to be intoxicating.

Aahmes and Enric both consumed a couple cups of the Cielila during the course of the meal. Their hosts drank even more. Namid found it too sweet, and so just sipped it.

Once they had finished the business of eating, the Praznies told stories and outrageous jokes, growing louder as they passed around more Cielila.

"This is quite a fest!" Enric said.

Staehw leaned around Namid. "So, you like it my friend? Good, good." He poured more Cielila for Enric, and also refilled Namid's cup. She felt strange but tried to ignore it. She did not pick up her cup, however.

"You look like you could be one of us," Staehw said to Namid. "Prazny clothes suit you well."

"They suit you well, too," she said, and they laughed. She caught a glimpse of a scowl from Aahmes at her words. And Inezha looked annoyed. Namid was surprised to realize that she meant what she said. She blamed it on too much drink, something the Prazny encouraged, no doubt. But he did look quite fine….

Staehw seemed to sober somewhat. "Alas, that I must dim this joyous fest. But we must talk a little."

"By all means," Aahmes chimed in from beyond the Prazny leader. "Talk away. The sooner it's spoken, the sooner it can be forgotten."

Staehw's face darkened a moment. Then he laughed and clapped Aahmes on the back, seeming to take Aahmes' words as a joke. Aahmes winked at Namid and she knew better. She hoped he did not push the Prazny too far.

"Exactly, my new friend," Staehw said to Aahmes. "So, you understand why I must speak of the dangers of the road."

"Your concern is most kind," Enric said, "but we can deal with any problems jus' fine. We're well protected, what with—"

Namid poked him in the ribs, hard, to keep him from revealing anything about her Power.

"Of course, my friends," Staehw said. He seemed unaware of Namid's action. "I do not cast doubt on your abilities. As you know, though, safety can best be found when traveling with a large group of friends, such as us."

Enric spread his arms in an expansive gesture. "What a wonderful idea—"

"A generous offer," Namid broke in as she ducked under one of Enric's arms. "But we would not force you from your path to ours, just for our safety." With Inezha's warning in mind, she did not relish spending any length of time with Staehw and his van.

"Our paths might not differ as much as you think," Staehw said. "You travel to Foroughi, do you not?"

At the name, Enric looked up in delight. "Yes, exactly!" Namid started to speak but held her tongue at his quick look of warning. Perhaps he was not as drunk as he sounded.

"I suppose you just happen to be traveling to Foroughi too," Aahmes said.

"Why, yes, my friend," Staehw said with a smile. "And we always welcome traveling companions." He looked at Namid, then. "And some are far more welcome than others!"

No doubt. Since Namid had traveled with Praznies once before, she felt able to handle whatever might occur. But she knew that if they accepted his offer—not that they had much choice—some sort of payment would be required before they all parted. Namid suspected she knew what form Staehw would like that payment to take.

"How far are we from Foroughi?" Namid said.

"A fair distance," Staehw said with a serious look. "Three days travel, at least."

A lot could happen in three days. Namid glanced at Aahmes, who shrugged. She already knew Enric favored the idea.

Namid turned to Staehw. "It seems that we're all agreed then."

"Traveling with your van these next days will be the highlight of the journey," Aahmes said and saluted Staehw with his cup. Namid hoped no one else noticed his sarcastic tone, although she saw Inezha give Aahmes a sharp look.

Staehw nodded, looking too pleased with himself. "You will be honored members of my humble van for the length of our travels together," he said. He turned his attention to the dancing that had begun during their conversation.

Namid waited until he and Inezha joined the dancers and turned to Enric. "Why Foroughi?"

"I know one of the lords there. He might be able to tell us something."

"Friend of your father?"

"No. Mine."

The festivities ended late, as such things tended to. However, the van started out shortly after dawn. Staehw had given Namid a beautiful black gelding to ride. She worried what the reckoning would be at the end of all this.

Enric looked less than enthusiastic about the early morning, and Aahmes taunted him mercilessly about it. But when Aahmes' horse stumbled, he winced, and it was his turn to be on the receiving end.

They traveled rapidly that day, particularly after they picked up the West Road. Staehw hovered most of the time at Namid's side, talking about his travels and various times that he had gotten the better end of a deal. He seemed to need no response from her, so she said little and watched the Praznies around them. After a time, she even stopped listening to Staehw, which deterred him not at all. Namid noticed that Aahmes and Enric each acquired a female Prazny companion during the course of the day, both women as talkative as Staehw. She did not think it a coincidence that these arrangements kept them from talking alone together. She did not see Inezha at all during the day.

The land they rode through changed and became less rocky. As they descended from the mountains, thick grasses began to reappear.

At dusk, they left the road to make camp. While some of them, including Namid, tended the horses, others prepared the dishes for that night's fest. Namid felt relieved when Staehw said he had some matters to attend to and left her.

She spotted Aahmes and Enric nearby and joined them.

"You two are sure getting close," Aahmes said as Namid walked up.

"And you seem to get along very well with your companion, too," she countered.

"All mine talked about was getting a husband," Enric complained. "And she eyed me strangely."

"Interesting," Namid said. "They usually don't marry someone who's not a Prazny."

"Did you notice that there are far fewer Praznies here than you'd expect for a van of seven wagons?" Aahmes said, lowering his voice.

Namid nodded. "And a good number of them very old, or very young."

"Really?" Enric said. "Is this normal?"

"No," Namid said.

They were not given more time to talk together. Staehw came to take them to the fest.

The meal that night rivaled the first for both variety and quantity of foods, but it did not last as long. Namid allowed herself to be persuaded to dance with the Praznies, so when they all staggered off to sleep, she felt bleary and somewhat footsore.

She entered the wagon Staehw had designated as hers and found Inezha waiting, perched on a small stool. The Prazny's eyes were reddened, looking like she had been crying, but she smiled when she saw Namid.

"I'm glad to see you," Namid said. "I need some answers...."

"You cannot remain with the van!" Inezha said.

"I'm beginning to realize that myself. What happened to the others, the rest of the van?"

Inezha shifted her feet and avoided looking at Namid. "They were called into service."

"By whom? I thought Praznies owed allegiance to no ruler...."

"By their god!" Inezha almost spat the last word.

"Calmly. Who is their god now?" Namid had a strong feeling she was not going to like the answer.

Inezha glanced around, maybe fearing eavesdroppers. She leaned close and whispered, "Sesaisyd."

Namid stared at her. This was worse than she had suspected. "How can that be? The other gods killed him. Are you sure?"

Inezha nodded. Namid plopped down on a second stool and tried to absorb this.

"You know that we fled from Sy'shythys," Namid said after a few breaths-of-time.

Inezha looked at her in horror. "Then the Dark Prince's minions already pursue you!"

Namid shook her head. "I don't think it's us personally. We just happened to escape the possession of Rhadanthus."

"Staehw does not intend to let you leave the van when we reach Foroughi."

"Does he know I follow Ilenii?"

Inezha shrugged. "Even if he does, that is not why he would require you stay."

Namid recalled the way he had been eyeing her and nodded. "I understand."

Inezha gave her a stern look. "Leave while you are able," she said. Then her tone changed, and she raised her voice. "Let me take your things and clean them up." And Namid heard someone outside.

Namid agreed and released the Power that guarded her possessions long enough for Inezha to take the clothes. Then the Prazny was gone.

CHAPTER 6

Vague fears and warnings troubled Namid's dreams that night and left her on edge, expecting some trouble. But the next day passed much as the previous one. Staehw rode at Namid's side and talked, as before. He looked pleased whenever his gaze fell on Aahmes and Enric and their Prazny companions. They saw more people traveling the road, but the other travelers did their best to ignore the van and hurried toward their destinations.

As the day wore on, the glimmer of an idea to get them away from the van came to Namid. Staehw was not going to like it. But she felt he would not like anything that ran counter to plans he had made, and she decided that she did not care about that. And anyway, she saw no other way to solve the problem.

She had the advantage of knowing some of their ways better than Staehw might think. Namid just hoped that he would still honor traditional Prazny customs. She viewed the approaching evening with some anxiety.

Toward sunset, clouds gathered in the sky and a chill breeze sprang up. The van stopped earlier than the previous day, but still they held the evening fest. And by the time they finished eating, the wind had died down. But Namid felt a heaviness in the air that kept her on edge. Her plans to deal with Staehw did not help her state of mind any.

The usual storytelling and drinking followed the meal, but Staehw talked and drank little. After most of his people cavorted near the bonfire, he turned to Namid and her companions.

"Alas, my friends, by this time on the morrow we shall have arrived at Foroughi and you shall be wanting to follow your path alone."

Aahmes tried to look sorrowful as Enric responded. "It's truly an unfortunate occurrence. You've been exceedingly generous to allow us to travel with you. It's a shame we must part so soon."

"Yes, indeed. But there's one small matter to be resolved before we can part," Staehw said.

"A small matter?" Enric said.

Several members of Staehw's van moved to positions surrounding Namid and her companions. Namid wished she had not eaten so well, as her stomach tried to tie itself into knots. She forced herself to sit still and see what Staehw's move would be. That might determine how she applied her idea.

"A minor thing," Staehw told Enric. "Just a small matter of trade."

It was as Namid had remembered. When they allowed travelers to join them, the Praznies required some form of payment from their 'guests' in return for allowing them to go their own way after. And the payment sometimes meant slavery for their former guests, particularly if they had no goods. Like Namid and her companions.

"I am afraid we have nothing to trade," Enric said. "We're not traders—" Namid could tell that he knew nothing about Praznies and their ways. Staehw probably could also.

"What he says is true," Namid interrupted. "We're not traders. But perhaps we can reach some agreement that will be pleasing to us both."

Staehw gave her a look that she could interpret all too well. But then he surprised her.

"I have heard that you carry several fine blades," he said, looking from Aahmes to Namid, and back.

"We can hardly trade our blades, travelers as we are," Aahmes said. "Others we meet might not be as friendly as you." His tone of voice showed just how friendly he felt Staehw was.

Staehw frowned, but his tone stayed pleasant. "How very true, my friend. It was not my meaning that you part with all your weapons. And there are blades sold in Foroughi, some perhaps even better than those you now carry, and well-priced."

"If that's the case, why don't you get yourself some blades there? Especially if they're better than ours," Namid said with an overly sweet smile.

"The blade I am interested in is an unusual one," Staehw said. He leaned toward her. "The sword you carry…."

Namid stared at him for a long time. This she had not expected.

"That's important to my family," she said. "It's not a blade to be traded."

Staehw looked amused. "Think on it." He turned to watch the dancers while his people backed off somewhat. But they still surrounded them. Namid studied the Praznies but could see no sure way to get free of their circle.

A short time later, Staehw returned his attention to Namid and her companions. "Have you thought on this matter?"

"No amount of time will change this," Namid said. "The blade stays with me."

Faster than she would have thought possible, Staehw seized her wrist. "Then, my delight, you shall remain with me, along with your unusual sword, while these two fine fellows proceed with their business."

Enric sat stunned, but Aahmes was already halfway to

his feet, dagger ready, in spite of Staehw's people.

"Loose her," he ordered.

Namid was startled, and a part of her secretly charmed, that Aahmes would leap to her defense.

"You're in no position to make such a demand," Staehw said, without even looking at Aahmes. "Be grateful that I choose to be so generous."

Aahmes started forward, but Namid signaled him to wait. He was clearly incensed, but he stopped.

"It's true that we're not in a position to make demands," Namid raised her voice to attract all the Praznies' attention. "But we *are* still in a position to bargain. I offer Oyanzaynye."

She enjoyed watching Staehw's expression transform from self-congratulatory to astonished. Then he scowled at her, fuming, knowing she had bested him. And, because she had made it a public declaration, he was bound to follow the Praznies' code. She hoped.

In her previous travels with Praznies, Namid had learned that they even demanded trade among themselves. But when several bands of Praznies met, they traded entertainments, rather than any material goods. They called this Oyanzaynye. They considered it acceptable for non-Praznies to do this too, but, of course, they never informed their unwitting guests of this.

"You know our ways too well," Staehw said with frown and released her. His people started murmuring to each other.

"I once lived with a Prazny van for a time," Namid said. Aahmes darted a glance at her, but she ignored him. "Do you have a tambour and someone who can keep a beat on it?"

"I'll play it," Aahmes said, before anyone else offered.

You? Namid asked by hand-talk.

Of course, he returned. Somehow, he even managed to make hand-talk sound smug.

Staehw sent someone for the tambour while Namid

prepared herself. The Praznies all settled themselves in a large ring around the bonfire. Inezha helped her clear the area of small rocks and other debris.

"Do something he's never seen," Inezha whispered. "Or you might not see the morrow." Then she was gone again.

Namid slipped off her sandals and left them near Enric.

"What are you going to do?" he said.

"Watch."

Aahmes joined them, carrying a brightly colored tambour. He tapped it and it gave a pleasant thrum.

"What rhythm?" he asked Namid.

"Have you heard of the Veils Dance?"

He nodded but gave her a hard look. "You're not going to dance that, are you? With the way Staehw looks at you already…."

"Of course not." Namid said. "But that's the rhythm I want. But start out slower than usual. And try to keep time with me."

Aahmes looked solemn. "You'd better know what you're doing," he whispered. "Staehw's already furious, and he doesn't look like the forgiving sort."

"Trust me." She gave him an impertinent grin.

He frowned at her and sat next to Enric.

"Whenever you're ready," Aahmes said.

As Namid turned back toward the fire, a flash of lightning lit the sky. Wonderful. She had always wanted to dance for her life in rain and mud!

As if he had somehow heard her thoughts, Aahmes grinned at her. She nodded back and, in the hostile silence around the fire, began to dance.

She concentrated on dredging from memory the dances she had seen and learned. She tried to work their motions into her own dance, tried to ignore the knot of apprehension in her stomach. She shook with pent-up energy, which ruined her balance and she stumbled through several steps. She caught the sound of the tambour's thrum and tried to move around the beat. She whirled around the circle, trying to pull the Praznies into the dance, to make them one with it, but she did not remember the dances as well as she had thought, and she stumbled again. She felt the Praznies slipping away from her, Staehw in particular.

A sudden crack of thunder sounded, and she jumped. Despair washed over her. She was not going to be able to do this. She looked at the clouds and sent out a silent plea.

Ilenii, help me!

A flash of lightning seemed to release her from some restraint. She felt Ilenii's touch and glimpsed an image of the god in the clouds.

Dance, initiate.

The storm burst around her, wrapping her in its furor. And Namid flowed into a timeless state where she no longer noticed her audience. She moved into a dance she had never seen or learned. And she drew them in.

The tempo increased, and Namid no longer knew or cared if she led the tambour, or the other way around. The fire flared into her eyes and made her one with it. A memory came of Ilenii's temple, where she had experienced her first true awakening to Power. She wove the wonder from that time into her dance and unwittingly included a trace of Power in her gestures.

The storm rolled overhead with its violent flashes and rumblings, and its Power joined with her. The fire on the ground and the fire in the clouds danced with her and gave the impression that she commanded them. The tambour beneath Aahmes' hands thrummed, ever faster and louder. A wind sprang up and flowed howling into the dance, to twist around the fires then soar away, drawing her senses with it. For an instant, Namid felt meshed with the wind, caught up in its wildness.

The tambour called her back. Four solid beats, like the tolling of a bell, slow and definite. The Power melted into the night, the storm roared away, and Namid slipped dazed to the ground near an ordinary, dying fire. One last thrum from the tambour, and the night fell silent.

After a timeless moment, Namid looked up to stunned expressions on the faces of her audience. From the corner of her eye she saw Aahmes wipe the sweat from his face. She became aware of her sticky, sweaty clothes, labored breathing and throbbing feet, and she realized she had no idea how much time had passed. She stood with difficulty—taking a moment to catch her balance—and her movement seemed to free the Praznies, who shifted positions and stretched muscles held long in one place. Namid frowned as she realized what a dangerous thing she had done, playing with a storm's Power as she had. She had not meant to, but it was too late now to change that.

Namid faced Staehw across the remnants of the fire. He had not yet moved, and she did not like what she saw in his face.

"Trade," she said. Her voice sounded stronger than she felt.

Staehw glared at her as his people started murmuring. Several times Namid heard the phrase 'Aytivsardz shirav'. It meant something offered in trade that had a value that could not be matched.

Staehw halted the talk with a sharp gesture. "Sleep this night in our van," he said. "And take yourselves from us on the morrow." He looked at Namid, and she felt a sudden chill at the anger and enmity that burned within his eyes. "The horse is yours."

He walked away. The others followed his example, except for one dignified, elderly man, who watched as Namid sat next to Enric, then joined them.

"As a child, I heard of that dance from my grandmother. But I never thought to see it, Daughter of Ilenii," he said, and smiled at Namid's startled reaction to the title. Enric stared at her. Aahmes glanced at her, then looked away into the night.

"Quietly, please," Namid said. "I've been warned that Ilenii is not served here. I would not have my position become known."

"Most no longer follow her, that is true," he said. "I do. You are safe from me. But that dance has already declared to all that the god Ilenii favors you. You could only have knowledge of it from her. But I carry another warning for you. Use no more magic here. Staehw feels it, can even use it some, and he is not your friend." He gave them all a long look, then followed the other Praznies.

Without a word, Aahmes walked toward the wagon he shared with Enric. Enric and Namid watched him, then Enric turned to her.

"I'll help you move your belongings to our wagon," he said.

"I don't think that's necessary," Namid said.

"But what if Staehw decides to move against us? We'd be safer if we were all together."

"He can't make a move now. We've already traded. 'Sides, I can take care of myself." Namid smiled at him and limped to her wagon.

Inside, she slipped out of the Praznies' clothes and back into her own, which she found folded and stacked, waiting for her. Inezha must have finished cleaning them and left them for her. Namid checked to make sure her blades were all in their proper places, then flopped on the mattress on the floor, keeping her sword by her side. She pulled a blanket over her feet and fell asleep.

CHAPTER 7

A sharp ring of metal on metal disturbed Namid. She bolted upright, half-asleep, holding the hilt of her unsheathed sword. She heard another clash and realized it came from somewhere outside.

Namid buckled on her sword belt over her other belt and sheathed the sword, grabbed her boots and hurried outside. Enric met her and pointed to a shouting cluster of Praznies.

"What's going on?" Namid said as they ran closer.

"It's Aahmes and one of the Praznies. Something about the Prazny's sister!"

Namid groaned.

Staehw reached the crowd at the same time as Enric and Namid. One look at his expression and the Praznies scurried out of his way. Namid heard a cry of surprise and pain, then Staehw stepped in the midst of the combat. He grabbed the Prazny and yanked him away from Aahmes, who crouched beyond, holding a bloodied dagger. The Prazny had a deep cut on one arm.

Namid dropped her boots and strode toward Aahmes.

"By the gods, what do you think you're doing?" she

hissed at him in fury.

He straightened and looked down at her in surprise. "Doing?"

"That's what I said!" Namid lowered her voice even further, so the whole camp would not hear. "Do you know the danger you've put us all in with this crazy stunt? Do you want them to declare feud?"

"Declare feud?" he repeated, angry in his turn. "I was the one attacked. If anyone—"

"Quiet," Enric said. "Staehw comes."

They all turned to face the big Prazny and Enric made certain that he stood between Aahmes and Namid. Staehw stopped just out of reach of Aahmes' dagger.

"An unfortunate happening," he said. "One forgotten as you leave us." He gestured toward the horses.

Aahmes opened his mouth to protest, but Enric gave him a sharp jab in the ribs with his elbow.

"Most unfortunate," Enric agreed as he gave Staehw a slight bow. "And gladly will we leave, but we cannot ride away without gear and some provisions."

Staehw's expression darkened. Before he could reply, Inezha hurried up and spoke to him in their language.

Namid turned on Enric. "Are you crazy, too? We'll be lucky to leave with our lives, and you want gifts of food?"

"Provisions," he said. "We don't know that Foroughi is only a day away, as he told us."

Namid turned away, not wanting to admit aloud how right he was. But she doubted that Staehw would give them anything.

When Inezha finished talking, Staehw glowered at her a moment, then made a sweeping gesture with one arm, which forced her to duck. Two men ran over to a wagon and started unloading gear for the horses. Staehw turned his back on the three and walked away. Inezha lingered a moment longer.

"Hurry," she urged in a whisper. "Go now." She scurried after Staehw.

Enric and Aahmes returned to their wagon to get their own clothes — they still wore Prazny attire. Namid retrieved her boots and put them on.

Namid ached from her performance the night before and had developed a headache from too little sleep. She headed toward the horses, frowning when the Praznies avoided meeting her eyes. Still, Namid persuaded two Praznies to saddle the horses by pointing out that it would allow them to leave even sooner. They also loaded some provisions that another Prazny brought over.

Namid had just assured herself that they had not prepared any nasty surprises, when Enric and Aahmes returned, carrying their bundled clothing. They still wore the brightly colored Prazny clothes, and Enric told Namid that Staehw had said he would only burn them if they left them behind. Namid debated whether she should also grab the clothes that she had worn and decided to leave them. She doubted she would wear them again anyway. None of the three spoke further as they mounted and rode away from the van.

They rode most of the day in morose silence and ate on horseback. The one time Namid asked, Aahmes declared he had nothing to say about the knife fight. As afternoon wore on toward evening, Namid found herself glancing back at the road behind, worried at the intense feeling of being watched. She felt certain that someone followed, although she saw no one.

"Something wrong?" Enric said, breaking the silence and startling her.

"No," she said, but she did not sound certain, even to herself.

"There's nothing there," he assured her.

"I don't know," she said. "I have a feeling—"

Aahmes snorted. "The day I trust a feeling of one of Ilenii's—"

"You have something against Ilenii's followers?" Namid interrupted him.

Aahmes pulled his horse up. "Sly… sneaky… shifty," he said, emphasizing each word. "Can't trust the—"

"Really?" Namid said. "This coming from *you*?"

His eyes widened momentarily, then narrowed.

And she remembered something he had said in Rhadanthus, on the roof of Shadow Keep. "Belaraketh, is it?"

Now she understood better. Belaraketh was Ilenii's brother and bitter rival. It was said that their devotees were destined to hate each other, even as the sibling gods did.

Aahmes dropped one hand to the hilt of his dagger. With a slight flex of her left wrist, Namid brought her stiletto into her hand.

Before she knew what happened, Enric snatched her sword and positioned his horse between her and Aahmes.

"This is the most insane display I believe I've ever witnessed," he shouted and brandished the sword.

At that moment, a bolt of red lightning split the air. It struck less than a pace in front of Namid's horse. A branch of lightning touched the naked blade Enric held. All their horses reacted violently, rearing and bucking. Namid saw Enric thrown before her horse charged off away from the others.

By the time Namid controlled her horse again, she could no longer see the road or the men. And she was shaking as much as her horse. A glance at the sky confirmed what she had suspected. Even if the lightning had been the normal color, it could not have been natural. She saw no clouds at all. And, when she took the time to notice, she felt the lingering remnants of Power, like a bad aftertaste.

She turned her horse in the direction she hoped led to the road. After a few steps, for no apparent reason, the horse stopped and would not be moved. Namid peered ahead to see if he had detected some threat.

Without warning, she could see nothing at all. It seemed that she should be afraid, but she felt strangely calm. A faint light appeared in front of her, so faint at first that she doubted she even saw anything. The light brightened and took on the shape of a woman, one whose features Namid recognized. Namid knew that protocol demanded she kneel to her god, but she was unable to move.

"You need not kneel before me, my initiate," Ilenii said. "Belaraketh's man must be tolerated. He will be needed, as will you."

Needed?

"Yes," Ilenii answered Namid's unspoken question. "Further explanation now will only increase your danger. But do not mistake the danger you're in. Look not to your companions for the source. Be wise using your Power. Go with my blessing…."

Namid blinked. She felt as if she had just awakened from a deep sleep, but she knew she had not dreamt the god. Her tiny dagger felt cold on its chain around her neck, but she forgot about it when she looked up. The road lay a few paces in front of her, Aahmes and Enric waiting at its edge.

Aahmes greeted her with an expressionless face and curt nod, but Enric hurried over to her.

"You are uninjured?" he said.

"I'm fine," Namid told him. As they resumed their journey, Namid felt reluctant to speak of what she had experienced. She wondered if the men had spoken with their gods, too. She decided not to ask.

"We were fortunate," Enric said. "I've never known a storm to move so rapidly."

"That was no storm," Aahmes said. "I'd call that an attack. And I don't think it was supposed to miss."

Enric paled. "Who?"

"If it was an attack, that's the question, isn't it," Namid said.

"Wonder if it's got something to do with that Myung," Aahmes murmured. He ran a hand back through his hair.

"Do you think so?" Enric said.

Aahmes just shrugged.

They rode in silence for a long time. Then Aahmes

produced another suggestion.

"Could've been Staehw."

Enric glanced behind them. "It wouldn't surprise me if that were the case."

"He's probably our closest threat," Namid said. "Look. That must be Foroughi."

Namid felt relieved when they put the city walls between them and the open road. The gates closed for the night behind them. She found herself in the lead as they rode up the street and hunted for a good inn in the failing light. Enric had insisted they wait until the next day to see his friend.

A lot of people moved through the streets, but they ignored the three or noticed them only enough to go around them. Therefore, Namid was unprepared for the two rather large, obviously self-indulgent women wearing brightly colored gowns who planted themselves in front of her. They all had to stop to avoid riding over them.

"How much for the night?" one said, looking at Namid.

"What?" Namid said.

The woman sidled over to Aahmes. "I like his looks. How much you charging for the night, dearie?"

Namid could tell by the look in his eyes that Aahmes was livid, but he kept his mouth closed. Enric, on the other hand had let his mouth fall open in shock. He looked like he would be catching flies soon if he wasn't careful....

"Uh, we're not—"

"We'll pay double whatever his usual is. But we must have him tonight!"

"But, I'm not—"

She interrupted Namid yet again. "All right, triple. We must have another escort for our party!"

Clearly, she was not going to let Namid explain that they were not what she thought. "Can't. One of those uptown ladies..." Namid said and shrugged, secretly enjoying Aahmes' expression.

Both women looked crestfallen, but then they noticed

Enric.

"How 'bout him, then. He's yours too, ain't he?"

Enric blushed and studied his hands.

Namid shook her head. "Still learnin'...." She gave them an exaggerated wink.

"Oh, of course," said the woman who had not spoken before. She shared a knowing look and grin with her companion. Then something toward the gate caught both women's attention, and they hurried off.

"Perhaps later," the first called back over her shoulder as they rounded a corner and were gone.

The three continued on in stony silence.

"Was that absolutely necessary?" Enric said a short time later.

"Would you rather have gone with them?" Namid countered. "I'll always take money...."

"Let's just forget that it happened," Enric said.

Namid shrugged and glanced at Aahmes. The look he gave her said that he would *not* forget, *and* he would be looking for a way to pay her back.

As if she had planned it.

I had no choice, Namid told him by hand-talk. He turned away.

Enric spotted an inn ahead and they rode over. Enric paid right away, not even bargaining over the price for rooms for them and boarding for the horses. A meal in the common room was included as part of the deal. The inn was a busy place, with a lot of customers, and Namid felt uneasy in the room with too many strangers to watch.

Maybe she had been in Rhadanthus too long.

After they ate, they each enjoyed a mug of Karinthe. Namid noticed a few of the other guests eyeing them, but it seemed no more than curiosity.

Aahmes left after a while. To wander around the city in search of some amusement or another, Namid assumed.

Enric refilled her mug. "You said that you once lived with a Prazny van for a time...."

Namid nodded.

"That must have been exciting. Traveling wherever you wanted, no restrictions."

Namid smiled. "It's true that very few will interfere with a Prazny van. But I'd wager that you've traveled."

Enric grimaced. "Yeah, you'd think so, wouldn't you?"

"Oh?"

Enric gulped his drink and poured himself some more. He poured more for Namid too, although she had barely touched hers. "Fourth sons don't count for much. Got to follow father's orders, always keep in mind our place below the heir, and the other older brothers, but above everyone else. Act this way, comport myself that way…." He stared into his mug a long breath-of-time, then drained it again. And refilled it again.

"Travel was always strictly ordered and involved a score or more of servants and aides. I practically had my own version of a Prazny van." He laughed without humor. "But not nearly the freedom. Had to adhere to the schedule…."

He shook his head and stared down at the table.

"And now I must prove myself to that man by undertaking a *noble* quest to piece together a magical sword," he muttered after a moment. "Prove I can go find something." He gave a short laugh. "We hire people to do that."

"But at least you're on your own for it. Free of the servants and aides and schedules."

He smiled at that.

"And who knows, maybe you'll find something more than a magical weapon," Namid said.

Enric shrugged. "I think I'll be happy with the magical sword. Maybe its magic can help…. I've seen some of what my father's done, like what he did to your Shadower. And how he's treated the family, especially my brothers. At least I've been mostly ignored, as the fourth son. But could I become like him? He wasn't always like this."

"Oh?"

Enric thought a moment. "It was about twelve years ago, I think. I remember he was always strict, but not vicious and cruel like he is now. But something happened. Some horrible betrayal. By a close friend. I don't know what. The adults kept the details from reaching us children. And then… he just snapped."

Enric sighed. "The family's tried to stop him, but he's too powerful. Too many follow his whims blindly. We've managed to save a few. Undermine his atrocities in some areas. Some have even whispered of assassination to stop him…. Such a harsh, horrid solution. You probably think horribly of me…."

Namid shook her head. "I think I can understand why there'd be talk of such a thing."

"Your Shadowers used to be assassins, right? That's what Aahmes said?"

Namid looked around to make sure no one was paying attention to their discussion. "That's not the type of thing to discuss openly in some random inn." She lowered her voice. "And yes, *used* to be. But not anymore. Not for a long time. I can kill if I must. But not for hire."

"How do you know? That you can kill if you must? Have you?"

"Yes," Namid said in a flat voice.

Enric looked away from her cold gaze. "Sorry. Passing thought. An ill-advised one. I'd really prefer another solution, anyway. If we could just undermine him further…. Ah, well. I apologize. Too much Karinthe, I think. I didn't mean to burden you with family difficulties."

Namid shrugged. "Maybe being away from there, from him, you'll be able to figure out your other solution."

"I can hope." With an effort, he smiled. "At least I'm away from anyone pestering me to be nice to this family or that one because they're looking for a noble son to marry their daughter."

"There a lot of those?" Namid said, with a grin.

Enric's expression relaxed into a more genuine smile.

"You have no idea. It's enough to drive a fellow to…." He shrugged.

"To run off on a quest?"

He laughed and nodded. He called for another bottle of Karinthe and again filled his mug. He sipped his drink, lost in thought, and seemed to have forgotten she was there as he stared off into the fire in the fireplace across the room.

Namid had not drunk much Karinthe, but all of a sudden, her vision started to blur. As she looked about the room, a kind of glow appeared around each person there, an aureole. She saw several different colors, but a single table in one corner drew her attention. A disturbing, impenetrable darkness clung to the people seated there. The aureole vanished and left her looking at three hooded figures. Men or women, she could not tell.

Namid realized that Enric had spoken.

"What?"

He grinned. "And I thought that I'd probably had too much to drink. I said: I think I'll go up to the room now and get some sleep. We'll visit my friend tomorrow. Oh, and I talked the innkeeper into a separate room for you. It's near ours."

"Thank you."

He gave her a shy smile. "Good night, then."

He made his way to the stairs and disappeared up them.

Namid sat in the common room until midnight, nursing a final drink and keeping a furtive eye on the table in the corner. The three there did nothing suspicious, however, and after they left, she went up to her room.

It seemed only moments after she stretched out on the bed that a frantic pounding on her door interrupted her sleep. An unpleasant odor, one she could not immediately identify, filled the air. Namid yawned and had started to get up to see who pounded at the door when it burst inward. Enric stood in her doorway, shirtless, and framed by a flickering orange light.

She sheathed the stiletto she had unconsciously drawn.

"Fire!" he said.

She grabbed her sword and ran into the hall. As they lunged for the stairs, Namid realized she had left her boots in the room. Thank Ilenii she had been too tired to undress further.

Just before they reached the stairs, a wall of smoke and flame erupted before them. They retreated from the heat, choking.

"Where now?" Enric shouted over the roar of the fire.

"Window!" Namid shouted back.

She coughed from the smoke as she grabbed his arm and they ran back. They ducked into the first room they came to and closed the door behind them. Namid smashed the single window with the hilt of her sword. They climbed through the opening onto a narrow ledge outside and jumped down. They both landed hard but did not break anything, then hurried around to the front of the inn.

There they found a crowd of onlookers. Aahmes stood there, too. He was barefoot and wrapped up in a blanket. His expression promised a horrendous fate if anyone commented.

"My dagger!" Enric exclaimed and started toward the flaming inn. Namid grabbed his arm to stop him.

Aahmes pulled the dagger that was part of Akavos from beneath his blanket and handed it to Enric. "I grabbed it after you ran for Namid."

"You have my thanks."

Aahmes nodded and turned back to watch the fire.

"The horses?" Namid said.

Aahmes shook his head, his attention still on the flames roaring in the predawn stillness. "Gone. Stolen maybe." He gestured at the crowd near them. Only people, Namid realized, none of the horses from the stable.

A lone figure at the edge of the crowd caught Namid's attention. It was the innkeeper, watching his livelihood burn with an anguished expression. She felt a surge of sympathy for the poor man and, looking into the fire, realized that she might be able to help. Such a small use of Power should go unnoticed.

She closed her eyes and called on her reserve of Power—safer and harder for someone to detect than if she called Power from the area around. She guided the Power to the fire and laid it over the flames like a blanket, willing them to subside. The heat on her face lessened and she heard the crowd muttering. Then she encountered opposition… Power counter to her own… willing the inn to burn. The flames shot up as she staggered from the intensity of that will, her concentration shattered. And she knew, somehow, that the fire had been meant for them.

When she recovered, she caught strange looks from Enric and Aahmes.

"I'll tell you later," Namid murmured, trying to clear her head. She felt the beginnings of what promised to be an incredible headache.

"It seems we'll be visiting Baron Zelimir a little earlier than I had thought," Enric said.

"Baron Zelimir?" Aahmes said.

"If you plan to visit Baron Zelimir Dytel, good people," a new voice broke in, "perhaps we can travel there together. Forgive my eavesdropping. I also wish to be a guest of the good Baron."

Namid spotted the speaker: a man somewhat over twice her age, and about her height, with lighter skin. He was smoke blackened, as she felt sure they all were, and across his back he carried a case which could only contain a lute. Beneath the smoke residue, his dark hair and beard showed streaks of white. His clothes had been brightly colored, before getting smudged. And she knew him. From a time before Rhadanthus.

"Das?" she blurted in surprise.

His eyes widened as he focused on her. He started to speak but stopped when she shook her head. He nodded but his lips formed the word 'later'.

"You know this man?" Aahmes murmured.

"We've met," Namid said.

"Troubadour Odasoro, at your service," the newcomer said as he bowed low to the three of them and swept the ground with an imaginary hat.

"And I thought he talked too fancy," Aahmes said, cocking a thumb at Enric.

"Your blanket's slipping," Namid said with a wicked grin, then caught the end of Enric's introductions.

"—and it seems you already know Namid. She's graciously agreed to accompany me on at least a portion of my journey."

Odasoro took Namid's hand, bowed low over it and brushed it with his lips. "A pleasure, of course" he said. "And a surprise to encounter you in Yiruny."

Namid shrugged. "It's good to see you again."

"I'd enjoy the chance to talk together, exchange stories," Odasoro said.

Namid gave him a sharp look but could not read anything from his expression.

"—common sense," Enric was saying to Aahmes. "Unless you would rather sleep out here in the streets."

He turned away and started up the street. In the direction of the Baron's dwelling, Namid assumed. After a moment's hesitation, Aahmes followed.

Odasoro took Namid's arm and they followed at a slower pace.

"This is quite a long way from your father's banquets," he said in a quiet voice.

"Yes. And you remember why."

He nodded.

"You plan to take service with this Baron?"

"If he will have me. If he judges my poor tunes worthy…."

"Modesty? From you?"

He smiled and shrugged. They caught up with the others, who had stopped to wait for them. The crisp night away from the heat of the burning inn chilled Namid. She hoped Enric's friend was not too far away.

"You were going to tell us something," Aahmes urged Namid.

"No doubt it can wait," Enric said, with a significant glance at Odasoro.

"I believe we can trust to the troubadour's discretion," Namid said, staring down Aahmes' incredulous look.

Since her knowledge of Power had become an open secret between them, she described what she had felt through the Power. She kept to herself the attempt to quench the fire. She had no desire to share everything about her abilities with the Power.

"Staehw?" Enric wondered.

"The Prazny?" Odasoro said. "He's an excellent one to avoid."

"We found that out," Aahmes said.

"Is it much further to your friend's?" Namid asked Enric. The frigid cobblestone streets felt rough on her bare feet, although the cold was well on its way to numbing them completely.

"Just ahead," Enric said.

Many breaths-of-time later, they stood before the decorative gates to a small palace, although it loomed larger than many of the temples in Rhadanthus. Enric tugged on a rope that hung next to the gate and a bell rang inside.

A guard appeared at the gate, a torch held out to light the visitors. Namid smiled, imagining the picture they must present… smoke-stained, half-clad, and shivering from cold.

Enric stepped closer to the gate. "We wish to see the Baron."

The guard looked them over, his nose wrinkled like he smelled something fetid. "His Lordship is unavailable at this time. Come back after noon."

"Kindly inform the Baron that Lord Enric Raphahan is here," Enric said loftily.

With a sigh, the guard vanished back into the darkness.

Moments later they heard running footsteps, and a young man in rich clothes appeared at the gate. He had dark brown skin, a neat beard, and wore his nearly black hair in finger-long coils. He looked much too awake for that time of morning. The guard followed close behind.

"Enric! It *is* you! Open the gates."

The man took the torch and fidgeted while he waited for the guard to open the gates. Then he and Enric embraced like long-lost brothers, pounding each other's backs, and barely avoiding getting burned by the torch. Namid assumed this was Baron Zelimir.

"It's grand to see you again!" said the man when they stopped beating each other. "But look at you! What happened? Did you finally burn down your family's house?"

Enric blushed. "No. A local inn burned. And it was not my doing."

Zelimir gave the rest of them an exaggerated wink. "Of course not. But come in. Too icy to stand out here gossiping."

He ushered them into his home. Enric made the introductions. Zelimir's gaze lingered on Namid with a look of half-recognition, but then he shrugged and turned to Odasoro.

"Well met, Troubadour, though I had not looked to see you until the morrow."

Odasoro bowed. "My lord, it is the morrow." He waved a hand toward the faint glow of sunrise visible through the tall windows.

Zelimir chuckled. "That it is. Although I prefer to receive my guests at a more decent time of day."

"For such an indecent time of day, you're remarkably alert," Enric said.

Zelimir shrugged as they turned down a wide hallway. "Diplomatic affairs to attend to."

Namid paid little attention to the conversation, as she became increasingly concerned with getting somewhere to rest soon. The numbness in her feet had given way to sharp pangs, making walking almost impossible.

"You're bleeding," Aahmes said.

Namid looked back and saw bloody footprints on the shiny stone floor. Before she could say or do anything else, Aahmes had swung her up into his arms, and carried her down the hall. Namid was too relieved at the sudden easing of the pain to object. Then she remembered that he was also barefoot.

"Your feet aren't cut," she said, resentment tingeing her voice.

"Tough skin."

"Do you want me to hold up your blanket for you?" she teased him, as his makeshift covering started to slip.

He gave her a bland look that dissolved into a wicked grin. "That's up to you."

So Namid held up Aahmes' blanket, while he, carrying her, hurried to rejoin the others. As they approached, one by one the others turned to stare at them, and Namid felt her face grow warm.

"What's the matter?" Enric said, his face and voice expressionless.

Namid tried to retain some measure of dignity, all the while being shaken by Aahmes' silent laughter.

"Looks like I cut my feet on the walk here," Namid said. "And Aahmes kindly offered to carry me so I wouldn't bloody the floor any further."

Zelimir looked concerned and circled around to look at her injuries.

"As soon as I show you to your rooms, I'll wake my Healer," he said.

"Are they that bad?" Namid asked Odasoro, who had also stepped to the side to see.

"Difficult to say. There's a fair amount of blood. I'd say the Healer's a good idea."

"Can't hurt," Aahmes said.

"They already do," Namid said.

Zelimir led them to lavish rooms, suites really, fit for

nobility. Two rooms made up each suite: a small sitting room with a bedroom behind. Aahmes set Namid in one of the plush chairs in her sitting room and headed to his own rooms. The Healer arrived moments later and clucked over Namid's feet as she washed them off.

"Well?" Namid said while the Healer dug in her bag for something.

"You're lucky, m'dear," she said as she slathered Namid's feet with some kind of balm and added a touch of Power to aid the healing. "Just cuts you've got here. A few large ones and many tiny ones, scratches really. You'll be able to walk a bit after you've rested." Her expression grew stern. "As long as you don't go about barefoot."

Namid smiled. "No fear of that."

The Healer wrapped Namid's feet in soft bandages. "To keep them clean," she assured her and helped her clean up from the fire. She pulled out a sleeping shift and robe for Namid, then left with an admonition to rest.

Namid had changed into the shift and robe and was hobbling over to the door to the bedroom when someone knocked on her outer door.

"Come."

Enric and Zelimir entered, stopping just inside the door.

"Are you all right?" Enric ventured.

"Fine. Just some scratches, really."

"I must apologize, Lady," Zelimir said. "I should've seen that you were injured."

"Don't let it bother you. I didn't even realize that I'd broken the skin. Your Healer assures me there's no serious damage."

"For which I'm grateful," Zelimir said. "I've already told Enric… I had planned a banquet and dance for two days hence…." He smiled. "And I'd be pleased if you would agree to join us. If you feel up to it."

"Dancing?" Namid repeated. After the dance she had tried to put together for the Praznies, she wondered if she would be able to perform any dance steps well enough. Her feet might not have healed enough by then, anyway. Even if they had, if she made too many missteps, she could always blame her injured feet. Either way, she could at least enjoy the music.

She shrugged and gave Zelimir a nod. "Why not? It sounds delightful."

"I'll have a dressmaker attend you, so she can adjust some gowns for your selection. If that meets with your approval? Before you rest?"

Namid nodded. The Baron left, but Enric settled himself in a chair. Namid's feet started to ache again, so she limped to another chair and sank down with a small sigh.

"How long are you planning to stay here?" Namid said.

"I think just a few days. Zel will be disappointed, but he understands about quests. That is, of course, if we can learn anything about Nazextas."

"Yes, if."

The dressmaker arrived and Enric retired.

After the dressmaker finished taking Namid's measurements and left, Namid headed to the bed. She stretched out with a small sigh, finally able to resume her interrupted sleep.

CHAPTER 8

A tapping sound encroached on strange dreams. Namid peered over the coverlet at the door, noting how dark it was in the room.

"Yes?"

The door opened a little and Enric peered around it. "Did I wake you?"

Namid sat up, wrapping the covers around herself. "Yes. But I would've gotten around to it myself, at some point. How long have I slept?"

"The better part of the day. Would you like to come eat?"

"How soon? I really ought to dress."

"Whenever you're ready, Zel said. He also said the clothing in the closet is at your disposal. Shall I call a servant to assist you?"

"No. I can manage."

Enric looked dubious. "Then I'll await you out here."

After he closed the door, Namid pulled herself from the bed, surprised and pleased to find that her feet only felt stiff. She lit a single candle that sat on a small table by the bed. In the closet, she found several dresses, all elegant enough for a lady at court. Looking closer, she saw where they had all been adjusted, no doubt to fit her. Surprising that she had not heard whoever hung them up for her. She must have been exhausted.

She chose the simplest dress: a beautiful gown of dark red velvet, with thin silver trim. She liked the color, and the sleeves would cover her armguards well. She found a pair of matching slippers that fit over the bandages. She planned to remove the bandages later.

Namid changed into the dress, having a little trouble with some of the lacing. But she did not want to call a servant, so she managed. She ran a comb through her hair and left it loose. She blew out her candle and joined Enric.

The hall where Zelimir awaited was small, allowing for intimate dining, and lit by several elaborate candlesticks. The tapestries that adorned the walls depicted various scenes of lords and ladies in gardens, at banquets and at celebrations. The air carried the faint scent of flowers, although none were visible. When Enric and Namid arrived, Odasoro stood examining one of the tapestries, while the Baron supervised the servants setting out the food. Aahmes watched this last, looking like he might pounce on the food at any moment.

Aahmes looked comfortably aristocratic, Namid thought. The several days' growth of beard was gone, as were the soot and grime from the fire. He had pulled his hair back and secured it at the nape of his neck. He wore a blue velvet doublet and darker blue trousers. The doublet suited him, accentuating the breadth of his shoulders. He prowled the length of the table with a feral grace. Namid wondered if that came from having been a Shadower, or if it was just his way. She decided it was most likely natural. In the next moment, she chided herself for noticing. She was *not* interested in any kind of entanglement, and certainly not with him. He also seemed younger than he had back in Rhadanthus, and Namid wondered just exactly how much older than her he was.

Enric and Zelimir also looked distinguished, the former in green again and the latter in pale blue. Odasoro wore the bright colors typical of troubadours. But Namid's gaze kept straying to Aahmes.

When he noticed her noticing him, she looked away. Even across the room, she heard his chuckle. At the sound, the Baron looked up, then hurried over to greet Enric and Namid.

"You're improved, I trust?" he said and offered Namid his arm to escort her to the table.

"Yes, thanks."

The next candle-mark or so they all enjoyed the excellent meal. When they could eat no more, Zelimir led them to another room to sit and talk. A servant brought a light wine.

"So, you've started on your quest," Zelimir said to his friend.

Enric nodded. "You knew I would eventually."

"But why for the blade belonging to this sword?"

Enric told him about Myung and his visit to the Raphahan holdings. When he finished, Zelimir frowned.

"I don't like the sound of this."

Enric shrugged. "So far it hasn't been too bad."

Aahmes snorted. "You don't call being chased out of Rhadanthus by Sy'shythys bad?"

The Baron seemed perplexed at Aahmes' comment. Namid thought that he might never have heard the actual name of the killing fog.

"And Namid thinks the fire at the inn could have been deliberate," Odasoro added.

Namid felt Zelimir's gaze on her and gave him a questioning look.

"Why do you believe this? Did you see something suspicious?" Zelimir said.

Namid glanced at Aahmes and Enric, uncertain how much she wanted to share.

"You can trust my friend's circumspection," Enric said.

Namid nodded and related what she had seen in the inn's

common room, and what she had sensed. She still said nothing of her attempt to quell the fire.

Zelimir fell silent for a long while after that, then spoke again in a quiet voice.

"So, you have magic?"

"Some," Namid admitted. "Why?"

He shrugged. "I merely entertained a fleeting thought that you might be able to help, but I begin to doubt anyone can. There've been some disturbing happenings recently. Small groups of people in dark green-gray robes have shown up in the city. People call them Dark Priests, and these priests are gathering followers all over the city. Normally another sect would not be a cause for concern, but I think these Dark Priests are using magic to control people, to compel them to join with them. But I cannot prove it."

Namid met Odasoro's gaze, remembering a shared past that involved Dark Priests. He shrugged and looked away, indicating that *she* must decide how much to reveal.

"Something similar happened a number of years ago in northeastern Paronia," Namid said. "In the capital city. It's rumored that even members of the nobility came under their influence. And all children who had reached a certain age were required to serve the Dark Priests at least one year in a kind of hidden stronghold."

"Interesting coincidence that these Dark Priests are showing up," Enric said. "Could they be connected to Sesaisyd?"

"Sesaisyd?" Zelimir exclaimed. "How could that be possible?"

Namid shrugged. "It *was* Sy'shythys, the killing fog, that consumed Rhadanthus. There's no mistake about that."

Zelimir's eyes widened at that.

"Perhaps Sesaisyd did not truly die at the hands of his fellow gods?" Odasoro said into the silence that followed her statement.

"We all know the story of his defeat," Zelimir said.

Nods all around. It was a well-known tale: how long ago

the evil god Sesaisyd had made a bid for ultimate power and had been stopped by a temporary alliance of several of the other gods. And how, when they caught up to him, there had been a tremendous battle of Power that had changed the face of the land. And Sesaisyd had vanished from memory.

Namid came out of her thoughts to catch Zelimir's response to something Enric said.

"—not in honor of your visit." A smile touched the Baron's lips. "I am celebrating my betrothal."

"Really?" Enric exclaimed. "Wonderful! I congratulate you. Who is the lady?"

As the two nobles settled into what sounded like a rehash of old capers, mixed with speculation on the merits of various ladies for Enric's benefit, Namid's attention wandered. Maybe attending this party of Zelimir's was not a good idea. After all, such events belonged to her past. And just now, discussing the Dark Priests' activities had brought back a number of other, unpleasant memories. She had lived in the capital when their activities had reached a peak—

She jumped at a touch on her arm.

"Dreaming away, huh?" Aahmes said. "Not surprising. But you look like you'd welcome a distraction from your thoughts. Care to spar? That match we've put off for so long?"

Sparring sounded good. It had been too long since she had faced anyone whose skill was so close to her own. Or possibly better, Namid had to admit.

She smiled slightly. "Now? In this?" She brushed the skirt of her gown.

He frowned at her. She countered it with an innocent look.

"Change," he said. "I don't need the advantage anyway, to defeat you."

"Even with the advantage, you won't," she said. "In the dark?" she added.

Aahmes grinned. "Isn't that the best way?" At her glare,

he added, "There are torches all over. And the variety of blades in his armory…."

Namid smiled to herself, unsurprised that Aahmes already knew the contents of the armory. She looked at the others, but they were involved in conversation and probably would not even notice they had left. So, she agreed.

Back in her rooms, Namid wasted no time changing back into her usual shirt, overtunic, and trousers. She noted in passing that they had been cleaned and the numerous small tears repaired. She left off her undertunic. She did not need the extra layer. She found some low, soft boots to replace the slippers, and braided her hair. She debated about bringing her stilettos. After all, this was going to be a friendly contest. She found that she looked forward to it, something better than sitting around talking about Dark Priests and quests. Or noble ladies.

She decided the stilettos would come, as always, but remain sheathed, of course. She felt especially uneasy about leaving her poisoned weapon lying around too far from her.

Namid opened her door just as Aahmes had been about to knock. He had also changed clothes, but left his hair tied at the nape of his neck. He now wore dark gray, like she did. His looked like a Shadower's customary clothes. Probably he had gotten one of the Baron's people to make them for him, since all his things had burned at the inn, she felt certain.

"You do know the way to the armory from here, I assume," Namid said.

His look asked how she could think otherwise.

They traveled down several corridors, avoiding the main ones out of the habit of being Shadowers, rather than from any real desire to pass unseen.

The armory was more impressive than Namid had imagined, and the single guard at the door admitted them without question. Namid glanced at Aahmes at this, but he just shrugged and grinned. About twice the size of the hall where they had dined, the room held examples of weapons from all the realms, and even some from places unknown. Aahmes and Namid spent some time just browsing.

They eventually met by some shelves that held a wide variety of knives. Aahmes indicated a matched pair with blades nearly as long as Namid's forearm, and black hilts. Namid grabbed one and studied it. The knife's guard was larger than was common on knives she had used before. She tried a couple of different grips and smiled at the extra protection the oversized guard gave her hand and fingers, no matter which grip she used. She nodded her approval and looked up to find Aahmes watching her with a small smile. With a nod, he took the matching knife and led the way to a large practice arena.

Torches spaced along the walls supplied the illumination in the room. A bench ran the length of the wall opposite the door, and the floor consisted of packed dirt. Namid looked up, expecting to see the night sky, and instead saw a ceiling high overhead. She also noticed a kind of platform perched high on one wall. For spectators, she assumed. The room felt cool, but she knew she soon would not notice.

"You like it?" Aahmes said.

"Impressive." Namid faced him. "But we're not here to look at the Baron's architecture."

"True. Are you planning to use that?" He indicated her right armguard, no doubt meaning the stiletto underneath.

"Got you worried?" she taunted.

"I sometimes have a feeling that poison of yours is after me," he said as he rolled up the sleeves of his shirt, baring sinewy forearms that showed faint scars from previous knife fights.

"Really?" Namid studied his face, surprised to see that he was serious. "Curious."

She *had* gotten the poison from Ilenii's temple in Rhadanthus. Could it have been made specifically against Belaraketh's followers? Even if so, how would Aahmes have a sense that it was after him?

With a shake of her head, Namid dismissed these

thoughts to concentrate on the bout. She rolled up her sleeves as well, unlaced both armguards and set them on the bench. No need to worry here about hiding that small tattoo. Aahmes already knew the things it signified about her allegiance to Ilenii, at least the gist. He glanced at the tattoo but said nothing. Then they faced each other, each taking a knife-fighter's stance.

"'To first blood?" he suggested.

"Sure…." She gave him a mischievous grin.

He laughed, then lunged and nearly caught her off guard. He moved faster than she had expected. She darted away and sliced at him with her knife. He dodged, then rolled and tried to come up behind her. But she was not there, having spun to face him as he stood.

He grinned, and she knew that this match would be a lively challenge.

This time Namid attacked. As Aahmes shifted to avoid her, she also shifted, her blade headed for his unprotected shoulder.

A hurried twist let him avoid her blade. Their blades rang as they happened to tap each other, and they were apart again.

Aahmes immediately came at her.

She brought her arm up to block him. Then he held his blade in his left hand. Namid spun aside and elbowed him in the midsection where he had been cut days before. He only grunted. Probably the Healer had seen to his injury as she had hers. Aahmes snatched at her braid, but she whipped it out of reach.

She saw an opening and stabbed at his side. He barely avoided the stroke and backed off a short distance.

"Not bad," he said. "For a tyro."

If he hoped to upset her with that, as when they were both younger, he failed. She just laughed.

"Too much for you," she said.

He smiled again. "No."

He moved in again, knife held low, back in his right hand

again. Namid watched as he closed, timing it, then trapped his knife and spun to get a clear cut at him.

But he spun away from her and back in. Namid twisted to avoid his blade, but one foot came down on something on the floor—maybe a small pebble—sending a pain shooting through her foot that ruined her balance and brought her to her knees.

Aahmes' dagger came down as hers came up. Namid found herself staring at a slice across her wrist. It began to bleed.

"The bout's mine!" Aahmes gloated.

Namid looked at him and slowly smiled. "Is it?"

His gaze dropped to the bloody line her knife had drawn across his forearm. He looked back at her, astonishment in his eyes. Then he sat down in the dirt, shaking his head. Namid laughed at the picture he made.

At the unexpected sound of applause, they both turned, on guard at first, then relaxing as they saw who it was. Enric stood in the doorway, flanked by Zelimir and Odasoro. Odasoro stopped clapping when the two Shadowers looked at them.

Enric glared. "Quite the spectacle you two put on," he snapped. "You could have murdered each other!"

"Highly unlikely," Namid said.

"No chance," Aahmes added.

The Baron clapped his friend on the shoulder. "Don't be so serious." He came toward them, hands outstretched.

"An impressive exhibition," he congratulated them. "I've not seen its like, though I hadn't thought to need to have a Healer attend you again."

Namid accepted his help to stand, although Aahmes did not.

"There's no need for that," Namid told Zelimir. "They're only scratches."

"As we agreed," Aahmes said and walked away.

Enric stopped him, however, as he reached the door. Namid collected her armguards and put them back on, earning strange looks from both Odasoro and Zelimir. They joined the others. Enric continued to scowl.

"We came to tell you that Myung is here—"

"Myung?" Aahmes interrupted. "So, he finally decided to show his face."

Enric hushed him and glanced around like he feared Myung might overhear. "Come on," he said and led them from the arena. "He has something to tell us."

The priest waited for them in the room they had used for their meal. He looked exactly as Enric had described him.

Namid saw Myung stiffen when she and Aahmes entered, and his hood turned from her to Aahmes and back again. She wondered at the more-than-usual reaction. Myung motioned everyone to seats.

"Is Akavos with you?" the priest asked Enric in a soft voice, not waiting for the nicety of introductions.

"No. I left it in my rooms."

"Retrieve it."

Enric hesitated, then did so. When he returned, Myung held out his hand for the dagger. As Akavos touched the priest's hand, the blade vanished, leaving him holding the ornamented hilt.

"As I thought," he murmured and looked at each one of them in turn. When he turned toward Namid, she strained to see within his hood, but it was too shadowed.

"You need not remain here," Myung told Zelimir. "They will not be harmed."

"They're my guests. I'll hear what you have to say."

"Brave. And perhaps foolish. But so be it."

"Why don't you start with telling us who you really are," Aahmes said.

"I am Myung—"

"Lovely," Namid said, irritated already with the mysterious posturing, and in complete agreement with Aahmes. "Enric told us as much. If you're so interested in the blade to that thing, why don't you get it yourself?"

"I may not." The hood turned to her. "Karile na'ak eh zandh. Ophele tez za seidalar."

Namid stared at him, stunned. How could he know the secret speech of Ilenii's initiates? She knew he was not one of them. Then what he had said penetrated. If he could be believed, it meant that she now held the rank of Initiate-Priestess, one rank higher than before, should she choose to claim it. She had gained the position at the loss of Karile, a friend and teacher.

Namid felt someone's scrutiny and turned to find Odasoro giving her a concerned look. "Are you all right?"

Namid managed a nod and looked back at Myung. "All right, I'll listen."

The hood bowed to her. "I am Myung, as I said, servant of Roivah-neheb."

Aahmes whistled. Roivah-neheb was the acknowledged head of the pantheon of gods. The god's priests were said to be more Powerful than most.

"My time is limited, so I'd appreciate no more interruptions," Myung said. At their silence, he continued.

"In addition to the blade of Akavos, the sword's proper wielder must be discovered. Time is short in which to do so. Baron Dytel, while this does not directly involve you, I'm certain your guests will appreciate any aid you can offer...."

"Of course."

"What are you planning to use this sword for?" Aahmes said.

"I'm not the one to use it. It must be joined to its blade because it will be needed to oppose a great evil that's gathering Power."

"A great evil," Aahmes repeated. "And how does this involve us?"

"Have any of you looked at the moons recently?" Myung said.

"What's that got to do with it?" Namid said.

"In three weeks' time, shy three days, they will all be dark—" Odasoro said.

"At the same moment," Myung broke in.

Odasoro threw a look of challenge Myung's direction. "The last time that occurred was thousands of years ago," he said.

"Truly?" Enric exclaimed in delight. "Incredible! And we shall witness it."

"Indeed. But, it's not a cause for celebration," Myung said. "With the moons' waning comes a time of Wild Power, a particularly dangerous Power, especially in the hands of the unscrupulous or poorly trained."

"Yeah, right." Aahmes scoffed.

"And we're supposed to make Akavos whole by then, so you say," Namid said. "But you still haven't said why. And why us?"

Aahmes nodded. "This sounds more like something the gods should be concerning themselves with. And what if we refuse?"

Myung looked at each of them in turn: Enric, Odasoro, Aahmes, then Namid. "You four are chosen of your gods. There are others who will join you soon. The gods can no longer directly participate in events in this world. They've retreated from it, leaving it to us."

"But I've seen Ilenii," Namid said. "And we've talked."

Myung seemed startled at that. "That was but an image of herself, that she sent to communicate with you," he said after a moment. "She, and the others, can do no more than this."

After a period of silence as they pondered this, Odasoro spoke up. "How does one oppose a great evil?"

"That's the task of Akavos and its wielder. Know that there are those who will try to stop you, so this must be accomplished as swiftly as possible." He froze then, his head tilted like he heard some sound the rest of them could not.

"What is it?" Enric said.

"I must go before they track me to you." He rested one hand on his chest near his throat, gathered Power and vanished. Akavos dropped onto the empty chair.

105

"Wait!" Namid called, but he had gone.

"One cannot go against one's fate," Odasoro murmured.

"So, you believe this *Myung*. You think this is fate, or something?" Aahmes sneered. "Some heroic tale of prophesies and destinies?"

Odasoro shrugged.

"Well, I make my own way," Aahmes said. "I mistrust this cryptic priest's scheming."

"But quests are supposed to involve mystery, and evil, and destiny," Enric protested.

Aahmes looked at Namid. *Well?* his hands asked.

I agree with you, she answered in kind. *Yet….*

Yeah. Yet.

"Well, I'll still help you find out about Nazextas," Aahmes said. "But afterward…." He shrugged.

Enric looked at his friend. "I'm afraid this means we shan't be able to attend your celebration tomorrow."

Zelimir nodded. "I quite understand."

"Why not?" Namid said. "We still have no idea where or what Nazextas is."

"We'll have to find out—" Enric started.

"Namid and I will find out," Aahmes broke in. "We can do it better than you. I'm your guide, remember? You and the troubadour here go to the party. You'll probably do that better."

Namid felt secretly relieved at his idea. Her uneasiness at the thought of this celebration had been growing. While unlikely, she dreaded encountering someone less circumspect than Odasoro who might somehow recognize her from the past. Gathering information would be a much more desirable task. After everyone agreed to this plan, they separated to see to their own pursuits for the rest of the evening.

CHAPTER 9

Namid woke early the next morning. She found a bowl and pitcher of cool water outside her door and bathed as well as she could. The slice from Aahmes' dagger itched, and the water helped ease the discomfort.

She also found a pair of sturdy boots, gray to match her usual attire. They fit perfectly, and even contained hidden sheaths. Perhaps Aahmes had a hand in that part? And she realized that her feet felt fine. The Baron's Healer had done an excellent job.

After breakfast, Namid searched for the others. Odasoro and Zelimir had disappeared somewhere, but she found Enric and Aahmes outside watching the Baron's guards in the practice yard. With many wide gestures, Enric described some sword techniques to Aahmes.

"That's no good if your enemy comes in low inside your guard with a dagger," Aahmes said, as she joined them.

Enric looked shocked. "Impossible! That would not be an honorable move."

"Have you ever fought in a battle or war?"

"No, of course not."

"Then you can't really say what would or wouldn't be

possible."

"If your enemy *does* come at you like that," Namid said, addressing the original topic, "you simply swing like this and he'll bother you no more." She demonstrated the stroke, using an imaginary sword.

"You know the sword?" Enric said.

"I'd be pretty stupid to carry one if I didn't," Namid said and patted her sword, which hung at her side.

"Ready to go find out about Nazextas?" Aahmes asked her.

"So early?"

"Could take some time. I doubt people here'll be as willing to talk as in Rhadanthus. After all, they don't know us."

"I'm sure you plan to remedy that. All right." Namid unbuckled her sword belt and handed it to Enric. "Take care of this for me, will you?"

"Won't you want it with you? In case of trouble?"

"No," Aahmes answered for her. "It'd only mark her as wealthy. They'd probably rather rob her than talk to her."

Namid nodded her agreement and headed for the gate with Aahmes. Once outside, they hiked through a maze of streets to reach a poorer section of the city, an area Aahmes said should have someone who could help them. After they agreed to meet at a certain crossroad at sundown, they separated.

And Namid spent an ineffectual day first finding the people in the area who 'knew things', then speaking with those who would talk to her — only to learn that no one could tell her anything.

Sometime after midday, as she paced a random intersection while she tried to eat an overripe apple, an old woman called to her.

"Lady! Lady!"

Namid turned. "You mean me?"

"Yes, pretty miss. You be wantin' to know somethin'. Me sister'll tell you. She's got the Sight, she has. Come."

Namid studied the woman a moment, and decided why not? Wary of danger, she followed the stranger into a cramped, crooked side street, to a small red tent set right in the street. The woman beckoned her inside but did not join her there.

The flimsy tent walls meant it was bright inside, although with a red tinge that Namid found sinister. The woman's sister sat facing the door. Namid saw that she was blind.

"See your future? Only cost you one korz."

Namid dropped the copper coin in the bowl next to the woman. "The korz is yours, but I'm not here for my future. I'm not even sure you can help. Your sister—"

Namid stopped as the woman's face began to alter. The flesh began to melt and run—much like Dar's as he fell to Sy'shythys—leaving a bloodied, bare skull, which turned toward her. Namid shuddered. The jaw of the skull in front of her dropped open.

"Soon…" a hollow voice said.

A skeletal hand that dripped with gore reached out for Namid. She could not move. It seized her wrist, sending a flare of agony exploding up her arm, but fracturing the spell that held her frozen in place.

Namid twisted her arm to break the skeleton's hold and fled. Mocking laughter chased her back to the main street. Once there, she collapsed against a wall and tried to regain her composure. No one seemed inclined to get involved, so she was left alone.

Nearly a quarter candle-mark later, when Namid felt steadier, she found the closest tavern, downed a mug of Karinthe, and started on another. They did not help. Still, she stayed there until dusk, starting at any sudden sound and more disturbed than she wanted to admit, then left to meet Aahmes.

Namid found the proper crossroad just as a lamplighter finished there and moved on. She leaned against the lantern's supporting pole and waited. The darkness around her small circle of light seemed alive with whispers. She periodically turned to check the shadows but saw nothing.

Just as Namid started to wonder if Aahmes had encountered some trouble, a group of rough-looking men ambled by. They made ribald comments as they passed, but otherwise did not bother her. A short time later, she definitely heard a sound behind her, but when she looked, she still saw nothing there. However, when she turned back, five of the men who had walked by earlier stood in a semicircle around her, just at the edge of the lantern's light.

"Well now m' boys," one said. "What's this?"

"Looks like a girl," another said, and they all laughed.

Namid just tilted her head and gave them a withering look. At the same time, she wondered what she had been thinking. Idiot move, she told herself, standing on display in the brightest part of the street. Their laughter had an ugly sound that sent a shiver of warning through her. Five-to-one odds… not good. Not good at all.

"Bet she's lost."

"Bet she's a new girl."

"Not much business on this street."

"'Cept for us."

"And since we weren't told about any new girls…."

"We get a free taste!"

They edged closer. Namid put her back against the post to take advantage of what little protection it offered.

"You've got it wrong, boys," she said. "I'm waiting for someone."

"Sure it's not us, dearie?"

"C'mere and show us what you've got."

"We'll show you what we've got."

A slight twist of her wrists and her stilettos dropped into her hands. The men hesitated.

"So, she wants to play rough," the first one said.

"We like playing rough."

They laughed again.

From somewhere in the darkness came the clear sounds of footsteps approaching, hard boots on the cobblestones.

The men melted into the shadows, leaving Namid alone, but she still felt them out there, watching.

Namid stepped to the edge of the light and peered into the darkness. She finally detected a familiar shape.

"You're late!" she said. Aahmes made a quick hand sign, telling her to go along with what he had in mind. Namid gave him a suspicious look. Seeing he held no weapons, she sheathed her knives as he stepped into the circle of light.

"Had to finish setting things up," he said, louder than necessary. Was he playing to their hidden watchers? "You know how she is about payment…."

Namid glared at him, suspecting, and not at all liking, the form this charade seemed to be taking.

"Don't worry," he continued. "We've got the entire night."

He stepped in close and rested his hands lightly at her waist. He leaned down to her ear and whispered, "If you don't play along, your 'admirers' might just kill us both."

She draped her arms around his neck, acting the part, as he had asked. "I might just kill you anyway," she murmured. "We can take them."

"I heard about this gang earlier," he whispered. His breath on her neck sent a thrill of shivers down to her toes. "Serious trouble, and too many more friends, too close. And some are even this place's city warders."

Namid growled under her breath.

"You're even prettier than they said," Aahmes said louder again.

He leaned close, looking deep into her eyes. For a long moment, they stood that way. Then he kissed her, gently, tentatively, but with a poorly concealed ardor that surprised her. Namid felt herself responding in kind, and almost lost herself to the sensation. But then she realized what was happening, remembered where they were, and started to pull away. Aahmes let her go.

When they parted, Namid noticed a strange look in his eyes. Then he looked away.

"Mm, as good as promised." He still spoke loudly. "But I know a better place...."

Aahmes draped a possessive arm around her shoulders and guided her away from the light and the still-waiting men.

Once they had strolled far enough away, Namid pushed him off, confused at her own reactions and incensed at his audacity. To her surprise, he didn't resist, but he did give her an equivocal look.

"You enjoyed that, didn't you?" she snarled.

"That settles us for that little incident when we first entered this city."

Namid glared.

"It worked, didn't it?" Aahmes said. "I found out today that the local brutes won't interfere in 'business'. They leave people alone if their services are already paid for."

"Services? Paid for?!" Namid clenched her fists and turned away, then whirled back. "You know very well, that 'incident' when we arrived wasn't my doing. But this... this... you deliberately—" Namid almost hit him then, but something in his expression stopped her.

He shook his head in denial. "I didn't plan—"

She flung a hand out in repudiation and settled for stomping away toward Zelimir's residence. She realized Aahmes had matched her pace only when they arrived together at the gates. Somehow, during the trek, much of her anger had slipped away, replaced by a confusion of other feelings.

"Interesting method of rescue," she murmured, remembering his touch, the kiss.

Aahmes replied with a noncommittal grunt. And he would not meet her gaze. He muttered something that sounded like "Not the first kiss I would have—" and brushed his hair back from his face with one hand.

"What?!"

Had she heard him correctly?

"Nothing. Let's go in."

Odasoro and Enric waited just inside, both dressed in

celebration finery and looking worried.

"What did you discover?" Enric said.

"You were gone a long time," Odasoro added.

"It was unavoidable," Namid said. Then to Enric, "Nothing, no one I talked with had even heard of Nazextas."

"One old woman I spoke with knew something," Aahmes said. "She didn't know what it is, but she did say where we can find out." He paused. Probably for effect, Namid thought.

"You're not going to like it," he added.

"Out with it, Aahmes," Namid said, still irritated after their earlier exchange. She had no interest in catering to his usual banter.

Aahmes glanced at her. "Seems the Praznies are the ones who know about Nazextas," he said.

Enric groaned.

"And how much would you wager that Staehw's van is the only one close?" Namid said.

"Staehw again, eh?" Odasoro said. "Shall we confront him in the morning and see what he says."

"We?" Enric repeated.

"I've already spoken with the Baron about temporarily excusing me from his service. Myung *did* indicate that I am involved in this, too. Besides, you'll need a proper chronicle of your quest, and no one does such a thing better than a troubadour."

Aahmes laughed and clapped Enric on the shoulder, while Enric looked pleased and embarrassed all at the same time. They started down the hall, but Namid held Odasoro back until the others were beyond hearing.

"Das, please tell me you're not just doing this to watch out for me."

Odasoro gave her a small smile and shook his head. "I'm worried about you, of course, Your Highness, especially considering what happened before. I can't deny that's one of my reasons. But the others I mentioned are just as valid."

"You believe this supposed priest, then? And please don't call me that."

Odasoro nodded his acknowledgement of her request. "Nothing yet seems to repudiate his claims. And some things seem to support them."

"But, really! Destinies and quests? And I'm foreordained to play a part? Me?" Namid made a cutting motion with one hand and frowned. "My belief in such tales was crushed when the Dark Priests came."

Odasoro nodded, his expression somber. "I remember."

CHAPTER 10

After a quick, early breakfast, the four met in the courtyard and headed out into the city to learn the location of the Praznies. Namid wore her sword this time, but still carried Zelimir's dagger. When he saw them off that morning, the Baron had told Aahmes and Namid to keep the daggers, and welcome. Namid kept an eye on Aahmes, ambivalent about the events of the previous night and any difference they might mean to their adversarial accord. But he acted no different, and she soon relaxed.

After less than a candle-mark of asking around, Odasoro learned from a merchant that the Praznies customarily camped just outside the south gate. The four headed there, hoping to catch the van before they took to the road again.

Their path took them through a part of the city that looked even worse than the area Namid and Aahmes had visited the day before. The buildings were little more than piles of old bricks, combined with pieces of wood and cloth tied together, sometimes nailed. The muddy paths that served as streets smelled like sewage. The people there peered at them, their expressions suspicious, at best. And most showed them open hostility. The little group picked their way through all this and stayed away from the buildings and as close to each other as reasonable, hands near weapons.

Without warning, a scream tore through the air. Namid whipped around, wondering if they were under attack. The scream came again.

"Down there," Enric said, pointing to a side street. He started down it at a run.

"Wait!" Namid called. "It could be a trap."

But he was gone, with Odasoro close behind him. Namid looked at Aahmes, who shrugged. So, they also followed, but at a slower pace.

Further down the street, Namid heard the sounds of fighting. Then another sound came, an ululating screech that froze her in place. As it died away, Namid felt her heart pounding. Beside her, Aahmes drew a deep breath.

"The Vlenorx," he said.

"What?"

"Vlenorx. They're slavers, from somewhere to the south. Beyond the Kazkalar Sea, I think. They don't care how they acquire their slaves."

Their gazes met, then Namid ran toward the sounds, sword ready. Aahmes ran right behind her. They rounded a corner and plunged into a melee in a small market square.

The wiry Vlenorx were fierce fighters, about Odasoro's height, with dark, dark skin and hair. Namid took several cuts as she fought to reach Odasoro, who wielded only a single short dagger. He gave her a grateful look when she handed him her much longer knife. Then she charged back into the fighting.

After a battle that felt interminable, Namid faced no additional foes. She cleaned her sword on the cloak of a fallen Vlenor and looked around.

Five other people remained upright in the gory square. The Vlenorx either lay dead, only a very few, or had run off when the battle turned against them. Namid saw her companions had taken only minor wounds, as she had, so she studied the two strangers.

One was a girl who seemed young, younger certainly than Namid, with long red-gold hair and skin even paler than Enric's. She crouched near the center of the square, shuddering, her hands covering her face and her hair flowing loose around her. Her once-fine yellow gown was torn and dirty.

The other person was a large man in a habergeon and leather leggings, a warrior, nearly as tall as Staehw. His hair and beard were a dusty brown, his tanned skin a few shades lighter. He leaned over the girl, apparently trying to comfort her, his great-sword propped against his side.

Namid sheathed her own sword and moved toward the pair. As she approached, the man looked at her with narrowed eyes. His hand found the hilt of his sword.

Namid held up her hands, empty, and stopped a short distance away, close enough to feel dwarfed by his bulk. She noticed with surprise that his eyes were as green as Enric's.

"Can I help?" Namid said. "Shall I find a Healer?"

He studied her, suspicion clear in his expression. After a moment, that expression softened as he seemed to decide to trust her.

"Your assistance was timely," he said. "You and your friends are formidable. The lady will not need a Healer. Just a moment to recover from this fright."

"Naturally," Aahmes said as he joined them. "The Vlenorx do seem to prefer young girls, when they can get them."

The girl looked up at that, her pretty face grimy and tear-streaked, and dominated by large blue eyes.

"Those filthy beasts should be hunted and exterminated like the vermin they are!" the girl spat.

"We have a feisty one here," Aahmes said to Namid.

The girl stood, ignoring the warrior's extended hand and glared at Aahmes. Namid realized then that the girl was older than she had first thought, probably about Namid's own age. She stood almost eye-to-eye with Namid.

"I'll have you know that you are addressing a favored daughter of the Earl Navele," she told Aahmes.

Namid peered at her. The realm of Navele was far to the east, on the other side of Paronia. Why was this favored daughter so far from home?

Aahmes gave the Earl's favored daughter that languid, infuriating look that he had so often used with Namid.

"Oh," he said after a breath-of-time.

The warrior put a gentle hand on the girl's arm as she started toward Aahmes, fists clenched. Namid noticed painful-looking rope burns on her wrists. She would not need a Healer? Probably 'the lady' did not want to be sullied by the touch of any low-born Healer that Namid might find.

"Please, Lady. Without the help of these people, you might very well be a prisoner still," the warrior said.

The Earl's favored daughter gave him an adoring look.

"I'm confident that you would have shortly destroyed them all yourself."

For a moment, he looked ready to correct her view of the situation. But he bowed instead.

"Your confidence is flattering," he told her. He turned to Namid. "I am Haeith, guardian to Lady Cameni Jiang."

Before Namid could say anything, Enric stepped up and bowed to Cameni.

"We're honored to have been of assistance to you," he said. "I am Enric Raphahan. My companions Odasoro, Aahmes, and Namid."

Cameni ignored the rest of them and fixed her gaze on Enric. "I'm most grateful to you. You saved my life!"

Enric blushed.

"If I might make a suggestion, Lady Cameni," Enric said. "You should not travel with only one companion. No insult intended to you," he added, giving Haeith a nod. "But where two people alone might be considered easy prey, a group often passes unmolested."

"A sensible observation, my lady," Haeith said. He hefted his sword and began cleaning it.

"Quite," Cameni agreed, but Enric held her attention. "Tell me Lord Raphahan, are you adventuring?"

"Please call me Enric. And I'm on a quest."

"Really? How wonderful! Tell me about it."

"Perhaps in a better place, at a better time," Namid said. "Remember, Enric, we have someplace we need to be."

Cameni gave her a venomous look and took Enric's arm. "If you must go somewhere, I shall accompany you and you can tell me all about your quest."

"Of course," Enric murmured, as they started to pick their way through the mess in the square.

"Is she always like that?" Aahmes asked Haeith as the latter finished cleaning his sword.

"To people she deems beneath her station," Haeith said, then hurried to catch Enric and Cameni.

Aahmes, Odasoro and Namid followed.

"Beneath her station?" Aahmes repeated. "Interesting how she just decides—"

"It's the names," Namid interrupted and wondered how he could not know that. She thought everyone raised in the Six Realms knew the custom. A suspicion entered her mind, but she did not take the time to examine it just then.

"She and Enric both have the two names," Odasoro said. "Which marks them as members of the nobility."

"While we poor inferior wretches have only the one," Namid added.

Aahmes snorted. "Crazy system. But at least we'll be able to get rid of her soon."

"Don't be too sure," Namid said.

"She's not coming with us...."

"What if those two are a couple of the others Myung mentioned?"

Aahmes looked horrified. "I hope not."

"Yeah," Namid said, and he chuckled. "But it's certainly odd to come across them this way. I wouldn't expect to find a 'favored daughter' out traveling with just a single guard."

Aahmes nodded.

They caught up with the others at the south city gate. Enric pointed at the Prazny camp outside the walls.

Namid took a deep breath. "Come on, then. Let's get this over with."

They strode toward the camp, apparently unnoticed until they came within a few paces of the nearest wagon. Then there was a hubbub and Staehw appeared, a wicked-looking dagger held ready. He stopped beside one of the wagons and glared at them.

"You are unwanted here," he said.

"And I don't particularly want to be here," Namid said. "Nonetheless, here we are. We need some information."

"I give you nothing."

"I see."

"Leave now, while you are able."

Namid clenched her fists and took a deliberate, deep breath. "If I were to bind you…" she said, calling on yet another Prazny tradition.

Staehw's eyes widened. That particular tradition was seldom used, but said to be potent, involving Power as it did. Staehw's expression hardened.

"Bind me then, if it's in your mind," he snarled. "I give you nothing."

Staehw's expression showed that he doubted she would go so far. Maybe she shouldn't. But she somehow felt this needed to be done. Perhaps some prompting from Ilenii led her to it, although it would reveal her abilities with the Power even more.

She raised her voice, so all could hear. "In that case, the consequences of thy actions be upon thee." She waved a hand toward the wagon near him. A dagger appeared, burned into the wood by her Power. More Power flowed to her without any need to call it.

"With this," she continued, "I bind thee in thy coming and going, in thy loving and hating, waking and sleeping, and in thy living and dying, and beyond, until such time as thou art willing to render unto me that which I require.

"Further, I declare and promise, in the hearing of these gathered, that upon that day when thy knowledge is freely given unto me, any claim of recompense for Aytivsardz shirav is fulfilled and thou shalt not be subject to any further demands that I might place upon thee, claiming thy repayment of Aytivsardz shirav was incomplete. But let it also be known that if this knowledge is withheld, misfortune shall dog thy footsteps, driving family and friends from thee, until the day of thy death, and cling to thy spirit until the ending of all days, may such time be long in coming!"

Namid waited, feeling silly at how pompous she had sounded. Why had she done it that way? How had she known the phrasing?

She cast out around her but felt no outside Power directed at her. Just as when she had danced for the Praznies, however, she seemed to be doing things not entirely of her own volition. What was going on?

Namid looked at the silent Praznies, trying to hide her uneasiness, and noted their fearful and awe-filled expressions.

"Wasn't that a little drastic?" Aahmes murmured in her ear.

"Maybe," Namid whispered back. "We'll just have to see."

"And no doubt you enjoyed it," Aahmes whispered.

She shrugged.

Staehw stared at her for several long breaths-of-time, then tucked the dagger into his belt.

"What is this knowledge that you need so desperately?" he said, without indicating any willingness to give it.

"Nazextas."

The name produced an immediate response from the Praznies, who all stared at them as if they had just grown tails and second heads. The Praznies edged away, agitated and murmuring.

"You demand too much," Staehw said.

"We know that you can tell us about Nazextas—"

"You mustn't speak the name," Staehw interrupted Namid.

"You know of it," Aahmes said.

"All Praznies know of Spirit-City," a woman said and shrank under Staehw's gaze.

"You know where it is?" Enric said.

"You're not thinking of going there!" another woman said.

"Tell us what you know of this Spirit-City," Namid said.

"No." Staehw turned his back on them and entered one of the wagons. The other Praznies followed his example, leaving them standing alone.

"That was certainly unprofitable," Odasoro said as they started back to Foroughi.

"Maybe," Namid said. "I think he'll tell us."

"That seems highly unlikely," Enric said.

"Particularly after you acted so rudely," Cameni said. "If anyone were that rude to me—"

Namid turned on her. "You'll live happier, and longer, *Lady*, if you wait to speak until you know what you're talking about."

Cameni stared at Namid, her eyes wide. Namid waited, expecting to be slapped at the least, certain that Cameni would at any moment. But Enric took Cameni's arm and guided her away, talking in a soft voice. He gave Namid a nasty look over his shoulder.

When they reached the city gates, a lone Prazny stood there, apparently waiting for them: the old man who had warned them against Staehw days ago.

"You live a dangerous life," he said to Namid.

Namid shrugged. "I'm still alive."

"For now," Aahmes said.

"Can you tell us about Nazextas?" Enric asked the old man.

The Prazny looked at him long and hard.

"If you would, we'd appreciate it," Namid said. "I know you risk Staehw's displeasure...."

The Prazny laughed, and at that moment seemed much younger. "Staehw's displeasure doesn't concern to me. I see that you need to know this thing. As you heard, Nazextas is Spirit-City."

"It's haunted, then?" Cameni said.

The Prazny laughed again. "Not exactly, young beauty. The city itself is said to be a spirit. It appears in different locations on different nights soon after sunset and vanishes at midnight, taking with it anyone caught within its walls."

Namid, Enric, and Aahmes shared a look.

"I think we've already seen it," Aahmes said.

"Is this truth?" The Prazny studied each of them in turn.

Namid nodded. "But we didn't know what it was." She described what they had seen.

The old Prazny listened thoughtfully, while both Odasoro and Cameni looked intrigued. Haeith studied their surroundings and gave the appearance of ignoring the tale. When Namid finished, the Prazny nodded, but said nothing.

"Well?" Aahmes said. "Are you going to tell us how to find it again?"

"I'm not certain I want to find it again," Enric said. "I'm still a bit leery of dreaming."

"You will not feel thus after you have been within," the Prazny said. "The city is said to be extraordinarily beautiful."

"That doesn't account for Staehw's reaction," Namid said.

"Staehw is a fool," the old man said.

"Of course. Surely you see that, Namid," Aahmes said.

"You're better qualified than me there," Namid said.

"How often does this wondrous city appear?" Cameni said.

"No one knows for certain. But it is believed that once someone has seen it, it will not again appear to them."

"Great," Aahmes said. "So, we can just forget about this whole quest thing—"

"However," the Prazny interrupted. "These are strange times — unusual happenings in the south, in the realm of

Izrediuz…. For you young ones, I feel Nazextas will appear again."

"Where?" Haeith said, joining the conversation.

"I will take you there this day."

"You?" Aahmes laughed. "No thanks. We'll find it ourselves, and probably do better, too."

"What if we can't?" Enric said. "According to Myung, we have little time."

Cameni placed a slender hand on the Prazny's arm. "How can you doubt such a nice old man?" she demanded of Aahmes. "I feel he will lead us truly to this amazing city."

"Us?" Aahmes repeated. "Who said you're coming?"

"Your leader! Lord Enric—"

"Our leader, Lord Enric?" With a dangerous look in his eyes, Aahmes turned to the young noble.

"It is my right," Enric informed him loftily.

Wrong thing to say, Namid thought.

In one swift motion, Aahmes drew his dagger and lunged at Enric. Cameni gave a small shriek, but Namid had already jumped in Aahmes' way, having guessed what he might do.

She grabbed his arm and threw her weight against him to ruin his balance and turn aside his attack. That trick would not have worked if he had expected it. Then Haeith grabbed Aahmes and lifted him away with little effort.

"He can invite her along if he wishes," Namid told Aahmes. "It doesn't matter. We have important things to tend to."

Aahmes stared at Namid a long moment, then relaxed and allowed her to take his dagger.

What was that? Namid asked him by hand-talk.

Aahmes gave her a slow wink. *Reminding him we're all part of this,* he responded. *He doesn't decide for us.*

"You can put me down now," Aahmes told Haeith, who set him on his feet. Namid returned his dagger to him, over Cameni's protests.

Aahmes glared at Enric. "You should've talked it over

with the rest of us first."

"I... I will, if the situation ever again arises," Enric stammered.

"If you children are quite finished," the Prazny said, "you had better collect your belongings and return here. We have a distance to travel before dark."

He turned away, like a king dismissing his subjects, settled down in the sun and leaned against the wall. He closed his eyes and seemed to go to sleep.

As they hurried back through Foroughi, Namid was surprised to find Cameni walking next to her.

"You want something?"

Cameni spoke without looking directly at Namid. "I must commend your actions. You acted quite valiantly, stepping in to stop your brother."

"He's not my brother," Namid said and shrugged. "I couldn't let Aahmes injure, or even kill, Enric. Which he easily could have."

"You feel something for *Lord* Enric?" Cameni said.

Namid smiled to herself at the emphasis. "I like him well enough," she said, then noticed Cameni's expression. "He's a friend."

"Oh." Cameni smiled at that.

"Now a question for you. How did you come to be a captive of the Vlenorx? Someone of your rank doesn't just travel about with only a single guard."

Cameni gave her a quick, penetrating look. "True. But we, Haeith and I, received an unquestionable mandate from the High Priest Myung to travel to this city. Then we ran afoul of those horrible creatures while trying to follow the High Priest's directions to an important meeting. I'm certain it was to meet Lord Enric."

Myung again.

"I think I was destined to meet him," Cameni said in a quiet voice, with a dreamy smile.

Myung? Oh... Enric.

Namid sighed.

CHAPTER 11

Baron Zelimir expressed sorrow at learning that they had to leave so soon. He gave them all the assistance they could have asked for, including clothes and cloaks, horses, and supplies enough for a couple of weeks. He also arranged for the retrieval of Lady Cameni's and Haeith's belongings and horses from their inn. Enric and his friend spoke together briefly as everyone assembled in the courtyard, then the six all mounted and headed out. In passing, Namid noted that Cameni wore a more practical gown than the fancy one she had worn earlier that day. And it looked like she'd gotten those rope burns Healed. Probably only the Baron's Healer had been good enough for the favored daughter.

Haeith rode in the front as they left the Baron's courtyard, with Odasoro behind him. Cameni and Enric rode together next. Namid followed them and Aahmes brought up the rear.

"How can you tolerate them acting so recalcitrant?" Cameni asked Enric as they rode. Although Cameni's voice was quiet, Namid still heard her.

"What do you mean?" Enric said.

"Those commoners," Cameni said and waved a hand

back toward Namid and Aahmes. "They don't defer properly to you, they speak out of turn...."

"Well.... I'm not their overlord, or anything like that. They aren't even from an area my family rules."

"But we're nobility. It doesn't matter if they're *our* subjects or someone else's. They owe any of the nobility their obedience and homage. They should be treating you with deference and seeing to our needs. It's *your* quest, after all." She laid a hand on Enric's arm.

Enric shifted in his saddle. "It's not just my quest. We're all in this together, as Aahmes so pointedly reminded me earlier." He gave Cameni a long look. "I think we're all going to need to work together for this."

"Oh. I see." She sounded thoughtful.

Enric started to tell her about what Myung had said two days before. Namid stopped paying attention at that point. And she started when Aahmes tapped her shoulder.

She glowered at his chuckle. "How do you do that? Even on horseback?"

He just grinned at her. "Think it's going to end up 'them' and 'us'?" he said.

Namid gave him a surprised look. She had not realized his hearing was that sharp. Something to remember. "I don't know," she said. "Not sure it's going to matter."

"I'll not follow their lead, if they try to throw their titles around. They have no idea what it's really like here outside their safe little castles. And I'm not kowtowing to her," he said. "Or him."

Namid grinned. "Somehow, I'm not surprised." She looked at the two nobles in front of her and considered Cameni's words. Once, long ago, she might also have looked at things that way. She turned back to Aahmes. "Me neither."

Aahmes grinned at her. "Good. 'Don't trust anyone else', right?" he said and dropped back to ride behind her again.

Namid looked over her shoulder and watched him for a

moment, then turned back. What had Dar been trying to tell her with that message? Or tell both of them? And did she trust Aahmes? With their common background in the Shadowers, she was inclined to. More than she trusted anyone else in the little group, except for Odasoro — she had known *him* well before meeting any of the others. But *should* she trust Aahmes? Well, she felt no qualms about having him behind her, so she obviously trusted him some or she would be the one at the back. But she was not. Perhaps *he* did not trust her behind him....

The small group kept to the wider streets through the city and, before long, rode through the south gate and reached the spot where they had last seen the old Prazny. But he was nowhere in sight.

"Trust him, the *lady* says," Aahmes muttered.

Without warning, the ground beneath Cameni's mount's nose seemed to heave upward. Her horse reared and squealed in alarm. Somehow, Cameni managed to hold on. As she fought to bring her horse under control, Namid saw the problem: the old Prazny. Apparently, he had been seated and had risen abruptly.

Cameni still fought her nervous mount, with Enric trying to help, when Aahmes rode over to them and placed a hand on the horse's nose. He spoke a few words under his breath and the animal quieted. Aahmes gave everyone a smug look and guided his horse to a position behind the old man.

"And here's our faithful guide," Aahmes scoffed. "Come to show us the way to our doom."

"The doom we might encounter will not be yours," the old Prazny assured them. "I will lead you true. But you must heed my words about Spirit-City. Or the doom might just reach out to clasp you also."

Cameni shivered, although the air felt warm enough.

"If you're taking us into some danger, speak of it plainly," Aahmes said, one hand on a dagger's hilt.

"I cannot speak more plainly of it, as I do not know its

nature. And call me Tamanend, if you feel compelled to speak to me at all." He turned away from Aahmes, showing that he had no desire to speak further to him.

"Are you certain you're able to find the city?" Enric said.

"I'll find it. Now, we should travel far from Staehw before resting. This night you will need to be alert."

"So far, he makes sense," Aahmes said. He turned his horse and headed away from the gate.

"Do you have a horse?" Odasoro asked Tamanend.

"I would not have been able to leave the van if I'd taken one of Staehw's herd," Tamanend said.

"You can ride with me," Namid offered. "I don't think we'll be too much for this fellow."

The Prazny bowed to her with great dignity, which made her smile.

"You honor me, Revered One." He used the form of address reserved for Ilenii's High Priests. He swung up behind Namid.

"As you do me," Namid said as they followed Aahmes. "I've not been granted so high a station. I'm not sure I'd even be considered devout...."

"Perhaps not in human sight," Tamanend said in her ear. "But as the gods see it.... Ilenii *did* grant you that dance...." She felt him shrug.

They caught up to Aahmes and continued at a gentle pace, following Tamanend's directions. The day turned hazy, eventually masking the sun, but Namid thought that once away from the city, they traveled northward. They rode single file most of the time, except for Cameni, who stayed at Enric's side. They ate as they rode and shared a skin of Cielila that Tamanend had brought along. Cameni made sure she and Enric drank first.

When Cameni passed Namid the skin, she lingered nearby. Namid glanced at her as she drank.

"Tell me, is he always so... so irascible?" Cameni said.

Namid passed the skin over her shoulder to Tamanend. "He? Who?"

"Him. The one who's not your brother."

"Oh, him. Aahmes, you mean. Irascible? I guess you could put it that way. I think suspicious and dangerous would be more accurate, though. The last few days have been... unsettling. But it's mainly due to his home city, I think. A treacherous place, where you must always be on your guard."

"And if you're not?"

"You're dead."

Cameni looked appalled. "How horrible!"

"Talking about Rhadanthus?" Aahmes said as he rode up on Namid's other side.

"Rhadanthus? That slimy, filth-ridden pool of iniquity?" Cameni exclaimed and peered at Namid in distaste. "Is that where you hail from as well?"

Namid shook her head. "But, up until recently, I lived there." She gave Cameni a wicked grin.

"And he's a native of the place?" Cameni said, peering around Namid.

"Yes."

"No."

Namid looked at Aahmes in surprise. "No?"

He grinned and shook his head. "No. It was just in my best interest to let everyone think so."

"So where are you from?" Cameni said.

His eyes took on a distant look and Namid wondered if he would answer. Then he shrugged.

"I was born in the north, the far north," he answered Cameni, but looked at Namid.

"So, you're one of the barbarians?" Cameni said.

Aahmes gave her one of his cold looks. "Only some of the clans are what you'd call barbarians. Ours was not. We were somewhat nomadic, raising horses."

No wonder he's so good with horses, Namid thought.

"Were?" Enric said as he rode closer.

"Yes." Aahmes' voice turned bitter. "Shortly after I reached my eleventh winter, a leadership dispute suddenly became an undeclared war, and my entire clan was destroyed."

"All killed?" Cameni said.

"Assassinated," Aahmes said.

"That term implies a position of power," Enric said. Namid saw him shoot a quick glance at Cameni, who seemed to miss it.

Aahmes smiled. "Yes, it would imply such a thing. My clan had held the high chieftainship for the last couple hundred winters, or so."

"Are you the only one to survive?" Namid said.

"The only one I know of." He urged his horse into a canter and moved further ahead. After that, they all rode in silence for a while.

~ ~ ~

"If the city always appears in a different place each night," Enric ventured about midafternoon, "how are you going to be able to find it?"

"Be assured he has his ways," Aahmes declared, back to his normal self.

Tamanend glanced over Namid's shoulder at Aahmes, then turned to Enric.

"I do not truly need to find it," he said. "I already know where Nazextas will be this night. It is simply a matter of getting there in time."

"You already know?" Haeith sounded dubious.

"Yes. The gods betimes grant me glimpses of things to come. And I have seen where the city will be this night."

"Are we going to be there in time?" Odasoro said.

"Without a doubt," Tamanend said.

"So, you've seen this too?" Aahmes challenged.

"I have."

Aahmes snorted and again distanced himself somewhat from the others.

As they rode, and the afternoon wore on, the haze

thickened into honest clouds and the breeze turned cold. They traveled uphill and Namid realized that they had been doing so for a while. The air had a strange feel to it that she doubted came from the weather.

Namid guessed it was a couple of candle-marks until sunset when Tamanend suggested they stop and get some rest. While they hunted for a good place to settle, Namid noticed Aahmes glance over his shoulder several times. She realized that she had also been trying to watch in all directions, unable to shake a feeling that someone watched them. Aahmes pulled up to ride next to Namid, while the others rode ahead.

"You feel it too," Aahmes said.

Namid nodded. "We have a shadow."

"Shadowers' shadows," Aahmes murmured.

"You two are as good as Inezha told me," Tamanend said. "They're Prazny."

"From Staehw's van, I'll wager," Namid said.

"How long have you known we were being followed?" Aahmes said.

"Several candle-marks," the old man said.

Namid twisted around. "Why didn't you say something?"

"No reason. They only follow."

"Great," Namid said in disgust. "Now we'll have to set a guard while we rest."

Odasoro called to them. They had found a place to stop: a small cave, but large enough for their purposes. They fed the horses and tethered them at the cave's opening.

Aahmes took a spot near the entrance. His expression dared anyone to object. Tamanend looked like he might, then seemed to think better of it. However, he also sat there. While the others found spots for themselves, Namid moved toward the back of the cave and picked a relatively rock-free patch of ground.

Cameni settled next to Enric, all the while complaining about sitting on the ground, even after Enric helped her spread her cloak to sit on.

"Minstrel, play us something soothing," Cameni ordered after she had settled.

Namid glared at her. "He doesn't—"

"I don't mind," Odasoro broke in. He pulled his lute from its case and began to tune it.

Enric leaned over and whispered something to Cameni, who frowned.

"Please," she said in a flat voice.

"My pleasure," Odasoro said and began to play softly.

Namid and Aahmes exchanged glances and he shook his head. Namid noticed Haeith watching them. He gave her only a slight nod when she gave him a questioning look.

Namid wrapped up in her cloak and stretched out on her piece of cave floor. She drifted off to sleep to the familiar sound of Odasoro's lute.

The next Namid knew, she was sitting bolt upright. An odd, bluish glow stretched into the cave from outside. Namid squinted against the light, just able to make out Aahmes and Tamanend still sitting at the cave's entrance. Everything was still, even her companions. Then Aahmes turned toward her. She started to question him, but he stopped her with a finger on his lips.

Come over slowly, he instructed by hand-talk. *We're not alone.*

As Namid followed his suggestion, she made a slight questioning motion toward the others. Aahmes shrugged.

Look outside, his hand-talk told her.

Namid knelt next to him and froze, awed. Just outside, their horses stood motionless, more like statues than live animals. But what caught and held her attention were the small creatures that hovered around the horses' feet. She counted six of them, each surrounded by a bluish glow. Their forms shifted as she watched them. At times they resembled tiny people or small, shining birds, but most often they formed indistinctly shaped glowing figures.

Namid had never seen anything like them, but she had heard of them. And like so many others, had thought them only childhood stories. Those same stories said they indicated the gods' special attention, whether for good or ill was not always clear. However, Namid had never heard of six of them together.

Namid glanced at Aahmes and saw an expression on his face that she had never seen there before. He watched the creatures raptly, enchanted. He exchanged glances with her, and they both looked back outside, to find the creatures gone, the horses moving restlessly, and the first stars showing in the darkened sky.

Their companions awakened in the same instant, looking dazed. Tamanend gave Namid and Aahmes a knowing look and nodded. His smile seemed to speak of some secret insight.

"We must go now, if we're to catch Nazextas at the right time," the old Prazny said as he moved out of the cave.

"They will be happier left here," he added, when Haeith started toward the horses.

"Then you do plan for us to return," Aahmes said.

"Unless you do something foolish," Namid murmured.

He frowned at her.

Namid grabbed her sword from her pack as she passed her horse. She intercepted a curious glance from Haeith as he grabbed a small bag and a waterskin from his pack. Enric retrieved an ornate sword from his kit. He also tucked the hilt of Akavos into his tunic.

"Nice sword," Aahmes said.

"Gift from Zel. Since Akavos no longer has a blade."

They followed Tamanend through a confusing maze of large rocks. As it became dark enough to begin to make the trip hazardous, they rounded a last boulder and faced a huge, open vale, large enough to hold a city at least the size of Rhadanthus. The largest of the five moons, Itieka, pulled free of the clouds and the ghostly walls of Nazextas took shape before them.

"It's beautiful!" Cameni exclaimed.

"Just at the proper time," Tamanend murmured, and

hurried toward a gate in the wall that faced them.

The rest of the group followed at a slower pace. Namid glanced at the others, able to see them clearly in the glow from the city. Enric, Cameni, and Haeith seemed enthralled by the apparition before them. Odasoro's lips moved, like he was already composing a ballad to describe the city. Aahmes' gaze met Namid's and he gave her a saucy grin. Then he turned to Enric and they spoke. Namid saw a glint of gold change hands as Aahmes collected on the payment Enric had promised him several days earlier.

When Tamanend reached the gate, it opened before him without a sound. He paused to motion them forward, then he hurried within.

They all increased their pace, but as they came to the gate, they slowed again, almost in unison. For no apparent reason, Namid began to feel that this was not a good idea. However, she entered the city along with the others. Namid was unsurprised to hear the gate close behind them. The others did not seem to notice.

They found themselves on a wide thoroughfare that ran straight ahead. On both sides of the street stood small buildings that, in any other city, would have been shops. Namid saw no other streets from where they stood, but Tamanend was nowhere in sight. Everything around them, street, buildings, wall, and gate, all glowed a shadowy blue-white, just solid-looking enough to avoid transparency. Namid reached toward the wall of one of the buildings, expecting her hand to pass through it. She was surprised to feel a smooth, almost glassy surface, nothing like the rough wall she saw. It felt cold.

"It doesn't matter what Tamanend thinks," Enric said. His voice sounded a long way away. "I'm going to get the horses."

He turned back toward the gate and made a strangled sound. They all turned to see the problem and found themselves looking down a street. The gate had vanished, and there seemed no end to the street.

"Oh, no!" Cameni said. She moved closer to Enric, her hand reaching for his. He gave Namid a helpless look.

"Which way?" Aahmes said. He made a gesture that seemed dreamlike in its slowness.

Namid indicated the way they had originally faced.

Haeith made a strange sound. Namid turned to see that he stared in the direction she had indicated, at nothing that she could see. And he seemed to be listening. Then he drew his sword and charged down the street.

"Not this time!" he shouted.

The others all hurried to follow him, but while they seemed to be running as if they were in deep water, he moved swiftly and vanished into a blue-white fog further down the street. They slowed, then stopped. Namid felt that even had they continued, they would not have caught him.

"We can't just desert him!" Cameni cried. "He could be in trouble!"

"Trouble?" Aahmes scoffed. "From who? This place is deserted."

"I don't know. Ghosts, maybe!"

Aahmes started laughing.

"You?" Enric said, looking in the direction of one of the buildings. "What do you—" And he walked through a wall that had looked solid before. It felt—to the others when they tried to follow him—just as solid as it looked.

"This is taking a disturbing pattern," Odasoro said.

Namid nodded. "The rest of us had better— Cameni, no!"

Cameni disappeared through another wall, one that felt just as solid as the previous one, when Namid tried to follow.

"Something's wrong here," Aahmes murmured.

"Yeah," Namid said. "Let's continue down this way and see if we can at least find Haeith."

They had passed a few buildings when Aahmes, who was a little ahead, stopped. He put his hands up and seemed to be trying to push empty air.

"What is it?"

Aahmes shrugged. "Some kind of barrier. Feels like glass."

Odasoro touched it and yanked his hand back. "It's icy!"

Namid walked away from them, toward a building at the side of the road. She kept one hand brushing the wall that blocked their way. The wall extended all the way to the building and as high as she could reach.

"No way around it here," she told the others.

Odasoro had imitated her across the street. "Nor here," he said.

Aahmes glanced over his shoulder and froze, an expression of horror on his face.

"Come on!" he shouted. "We have to get out of here!" He turned back toward the unseen wall and ran down the street.

Odasoro and Namid tried to follow but ran into that cursed wall.

"Aahmes!" Namid yelled.

He kept running, apparently oblivious to her voice, and disappeared into haze, just like Haeith.

Namid looked over her shoulder, even as Aahmes had, and saw nothing.

"What do you imagine he saw?" Odasoro said.

Namid shrugged. They headed back the way they had come.

"I don't like that someone seems to be splitting us up," Namid said as she studied the buildings they passed. "Chipping away at the edges of our group until we're each alone. Ow!" She ran into another invisible wall.

"I'm also getting the impression that we're caught in some sort of maze," Odasoro said.

"I suppose we could try the buildings," Namid said without enthusiasm. "Maybe we can find a way through one of them."

They each picked a side of the street and tried the doors and windows of each building as they worked their way back toward the first barrier. At every building, they met the same smooth, unseen wall blocking the way.

Namid was ahead of Odasoro, so she came to that part of the street that had been blocked before he did. Before she realized it, she had walked past what had been the invisible barrier. When she saw where she stood, she turned to tell Odasoro and saw him stopped at the barrier that she had apparently passed through. Namid called to him, but he did not seem to hear her, and he acted like he could not see her either. When she tried to go back, she found the way blocked.

Namid tried waving her arms, hoping she might somehow get Odasoro's attention, but he looked right past her. He seemed to be shouting something, but she heard nothing. After a few breaths-of-time, he turned away and started trying doors on the buildings across the street. The second one he tried opened for him and he disappeared inside.

Namid waited several moments. When he did not reappear, she headed down the street the direction Aahmes and Haeith had gone.

As she walked, she strained to hear some sound beyond her own footsteps. But all around was complete silence. Namid started humming to herself, which she decided was better than talking to herself. It helped some. She gazed at the buildings that she walked past. They now looked more like houses than shops.

Namid glanced behind and thought she saw the gate. She stopped for a longer look, but the glowing fog grew thicker. She started back that direction, hoping to catch another glimpse of the gate and ran into another invisible barrier.

She cursed to herself, liking this less and less.

She felt a tentative touch of Power and froze, even holding her breath. Namid closed her eyes and sent a thin tendril of Power outward, trying to follow that faint touch. She brushed the gate, but could not go beyond it, so she extended her awareness into the city, hoping to locate her companions somehow. Instead, she plummeted into all the Power she could ever have dreamed of having, much more than she could harness.

Why had she not sensed it before?

The question was swept away as, in her expanded awareness, the city seemed to take on color and substance, with people moving about. Namid was drawn toward the center of the city, to a beautiful crystal tower that rose high above the surrounding structures.

She felt motion within it and strained for a closer look. Suddenly, a blinding white aura wrapped the tower and she felt a surge of Power leap out from it. She pulled away as fear punched through her — she had no chance at containing such an immense amount of Power. She could not let it trace her thin path of Power back to her body. If it did, Namid knew she would flare up like a bonfire.

She hauled back her extended senses, fleeing the wave of Power just beyond. Faster it came, and she panicked. She wasn't going to make it!

Her thoughts exploded into light and she was back.

She opened her eyes and, for an instant, saw the street as she had seen it in her vision, full of normal people hurrying about their tasks. Then the Power exploded in her face. She hit a wall, hard, and fell. As she fought to stay conscious, she heard a faint, beautiful sound of pipes in the distance. Then everything went dark.

CHAPTER 12

Namid struggled up from the lightless mere of pain. She decided if she hurt that much, she must still be alive, so she eased her eyes open. Not a handspan in front of her face, she saw the hem of a pale blue robe, with one white-clad foot peeking from beneath it. She realized she lay on her left side, with her sword beneath her. Not the most comfortable arrangement and one that explained at least some of her discomfort. She started to move and moaned as pain shot through her entire body. She closed her eyes again and tried to will away the soreness, or even some of it, without success.

"Have you decided yet if you'll live?" The voice sounded like Aahmes', and when she looked up, Namid saw him standing over her. The owner of the robe and white shoe was nowhere in sight. A breeze started up and Aahmes' form dissolved into smoke and blew away.

"I'm reserving judgment on that for a while yet," Namid said to the remnants of the smoke.

She struggled into a sitting position and leaned against the wall. In front of her, people walked in the street and stepped around her without looking at her. They looked like the people she had seen before the Power had hit her. But as she watched them, they faded, and she could see through them. Whispers came to her.

"Priestess, why so long away from the temples?"

"I'm really only an Initiate-Priestess, at best," Namid muttered. "And I didn't really belong there."

"—foolishness, to challenge the magic here. Were you taught no better?"

"That's not what I was doing," Namid said.

"You should have entered the city when first you saw it."

"Time is short."

"When first we saw it, we didn't know what it was!" Namid snapped. She disliked being scolded when in agony, especially by people invisible to her. "Show yourselves!"

The hazy people just kept going about their tasks.

Namid wondered how long she had been senseless.

"Time has little meaning here."

Are you answering my thoughts?

She received only silence.

Namid struggled to her feet and caught herself on a ledge on the wall nearby as her left leg gave out and she nearly blacked out again. She stood a moment and concentrated on breathing through the pain. Sounds of fighting drew her attention and she looked up.

Beyond and through the transparent people, she saw a cluster of struggling figures, the flash of weapons. The city wavered and dissolved into a mountain road. Somewhere unfamiliar to her. She edged toward the conflict, and her vision, or the world around her, flickered. One man fell to the ground, grievously injured, surrounded by dead who all wore clothes like his. The attackers, dressed in unrelieved dark green-gray, laughed and ran off.

Namid tried to run after them and stumbled as her leg gave out again. She heard the distinctive whoosh of a heavy blade slicing through the air and looked up as a great-sword stopped a finger-length from her face.

"Haeith?"

"You're real?" he said.

Namid reached up and touched the blade with a finger. It was solid and felt normal. "You are, too."

He nodded and reached out to help her up. She realized that his clothes resembled those she had seen on the dead. And the injured man had been him.

The mountain road flickered….

And they now stood on the street with the transparent people going about their lives around them.

Namid clung to the warrior's arm as darkness threatened to overwhelm her vision again.

"Here." He held a small packet out to her. It looked like folded parchment. "This should ease the pain for a time. What happened?"

"A bad encounter with a wall," Namid said. She swore he almost smiled at that.

She opened the packet. It gave off an herbal scent and held a light-brown powder mixed with tiny bits of crushed leaves.

"It's better mixed with hot water but can be swallowed with a drink of just about anything." Haeith said. He held out his waterskin. "Water in here, just not hot."

Namid looked up at him, wondering about trusting him. As if he knew her thoughts, he took a pinch of the leaves and powder from the packet and put it on his tongue, then swallowed some water from the skin. He handed both the packet and the waterskin to her.

With a nod, he urged her to go ahead. She did, and the pain began to ease its grip right away. Namid started to feel sleepy.

"The drowsiness will soon pass," Haeith said. "Have you seen any of the others?"

"Not since we all got separated," Namid said and straightened up, with a smile at the lessening pain. "What happened to you?"

He gazed down the street. "Ghosts and memories."

Namid started to turn and a bright fog engulfed them.

Flicker....

The fog faded away, leaving them standing in the middle of a different street.

Now the people of the city, still transparent, hurried along, not taking time to chat with each other. Namid saw fear on their faces, but when she looked around, she saw nothing to cause it. For a moment, she thought she saw horses at the end of the street. But when she squinted, trying to see better, she saw only glowing fog.

"Do you see all this, too?" Haeith said. He held his sword ready.

"What do you see?"

"Fearful citizens scurrying from an enemy, trying to decide what to do. A city besieged."

Flicker....

She and Haeith stood atop one of the city walls. From that vantage, they saw hundreds of campfires, a vast army that darkened the horizon. Namid thought she heard the far-off thunder that multitudes of men and horses make.

And the whispers returned.

"—army from the south—"

"Dark Priests come for Akavos—"

Haeith and Namid exchanged looks. "The noble's sword was once kept here," Haeith said.

"Good, you hear them, too," Namid said. She turned to look back into the city.

Flicker....

She found herself standing outside a flower shop. And Haeith was gone. She cursed to herself.

"Namid?"

She looked around and spotted Cameni a short distance away. The noble wore an elaborate gown and headdress. She peered at Namid, her expression quizzical.

"Should I help her? She looks hurt...." Namid heard Cameni's voice, but her mouth had not moved. She had not said anything.

"But she's only a commoner. Their place is to help us, not the other way around..." the voice came again as Cameni stood looking at her. And like a faint echo, Namid heard Cameni's voice once more. "They keep telling me empathy—"

Namid took a step toward Cameni and a swirl of fog swept between them.

Flicker....

Namid stood near the base of the great crystal tower she had seen before. The transparent people who hurried by looked frantic. Except for one man, somewhat less transparent than the rest....

"Tamanend?"

The Prazny did not respond or react. Namid saw a young girl break through the crowd and run to the old Prazny. Tamanend lifted her high and they both laughed with joy. As Namid watched, the old Prazny grew younger, and more transparent, until he seemed no older than herself. Clutching the girl to him, Tamanend stepped into the crowd and Namid lost sight of him.

The city flashed white and the transparent people all vanished. But she still stood in the same place.

Namid turned back to the tower and her gaze was drawn upward.

"Boudra will save us," a whisper said.

From the tower, Namid heard ominous rumblings and saw strange flashes. Then she saw a growing glow, coming from deep within the building. Silhouetted on the tower's high balcony stood a young mage.

"Boudra," the whispers said.

She watched as he gathered Power, raised his arms high, and sent a huge spear of Power flying out beyond the city walls. Attacking the invading army, Namid assumed.

Flicker....

She stood on the wall again. Namid heard faint, martial music and looked around. Odasoro sat nearby, playing his lute.

The tune became a dirge and he now sat weeping into his hands, the body of a woman lying at his feet. He looked up at Namid. His face became Dar's.

"Don't trust anyone else."

Then no one sat there.

Namid shivered, then fought to stay on her feet as the ground shook beneath her. When the shaking stopped, she turned to look again at the attacking army. Boudra's spear of Power flew over her head and struck the invaders' encampment. With a flash like a lightning strike, they vanished. A breeze whisked the smoke away and Namid saw a vast hole in the ground where the invaders had been. But no sign of the army.

She heard faint cheers from behind her, in the city. She turned—

—and stood again at the base of the tower. She saw no sign of Boudra. The transparent people were back, this time running away from the tower. As Namid watched, the tower began to pulsate with an ever-increasing blue glow that brightened into white. She felt the Power rising again and wrapped her own around herself for protection. She hoped it was enough. She would not be able to run fast enough to get away.

Unbound Power swept out from the tower into the city, faster than a horse could run. The Power staggered her, but at least this time she did not slam into any walls. As she watched, the city itself glowed yellow, then white, ever brighter. She closed her eyes against the glare and thought she heard a single mournful bell.

She opened her eyes to darkness. Someone crashed into her. She rolled away and gasped at the renewed pain. Namid felt the Power of the city. Somehow the city *was* Power.

She touched it, the lightest possible touch, ready to withdraw at the slightest hint of danger. And she again saw the city as it had looked when they first entered.

"What's going on here?' she whispered. "Is all this real?"

"Real?" the whispers echoed her. "Is…. Was…."

Namid sat in the middle of the street, alone, with wisps of fog floating around and past her.

Far down the street, figures emerged from the fog, one an older man who looked like a noble. At his side, a younger Enric seemed to be pleading with him. Namid heard no sounds. The older man shook his head. He backhanded Enric and knocked him away, then nodded to his left. Namid saw nothing there, but in the next moment screams of agony came to her from that direction.

Flicker....

The faint sound of pipes came to her again. And the whispers started again.

"Akavos—"

"The shepherd's pipe—"

"Eight, made seven, six to Power, then nine—"

Namid heard what sounded like fighting but muffled. She edged toward the sounds, peering into the fog. She fought a wave of dizziness and fatigue that washed over her and kept walking.

The sounds grew louder and drew her around a corner into a side street. Ahead, she saw indistinct figures in strange clothes struggling together. She looked down and saw blood splattered on snow.

"No!"

That was Aahmes' voice.

The fog cleared. Aahmes stood in the bloodied snow amid tens of dead, head down, shoulders slumped. His daggers dropped from his hands.

"Aahmes?" Namid spoke softly.

From the corner of her eye, Namid saw a shadow move at the side of the street.

"Aahmes, look out!" she shouted.

"There you are!"

That was not one of the whispers.

From the shadowed fog at the edge of the street, Staehw charged at Aahmes, dagger ready.

Namid tried to run, to get there in time, but her injuries

slowed her. She scanned the fog as she ran. Tamanend had said they had been followed. So where were the other Praznies?

At the last moment, Aahmes dropped to the ground, without ever having turned to face Staehw. The enraged Prazny overshot his target but spun around faster than Namid expected. Aahmes stood, clutching both of his daggers.

And Staehw spotted Namid.

"I will have the magical sword!" Staehw shouted and charged her this time.

Namid twisted her wrists to release her two stilettos from their sheaths, then held the blades ready.

Aahmes leapt for Staehw, but the Prazny dodged just enough that Aahmes' blades only left shallow cuts. Then Staehw was on Namid.

She ducked and twisted away from his blade and saw an opening.

But her leg crumpled under her. It was all she could do to roll away from Staehw's blade.

She tried to stab him in passing but missed. She realized she had almost gotten him with her poisoned blade. She re-sheathed it. She did not mean to use it here.

She rolled away from Staehw's attacks and pulled a dagger from her boot to use instead of the poisoned stiletto. The tip of Staehw's dagger caught her shoulder and drew a bloody line partway down her arm. She retaliated as she moved, but only scratched him.

This was bad. With her injuries slowing her, she did not think this would end well for her.

Then Aahmes was on Staehw and Namid was able to struggle to her feet.

Motion in the fog caught her attention. Namid saw another figure racing toward the battle.

"Inezha?"

The young Prazny leapt into the air and landed on Staehw's back. She wrapped both arms around his neck and squeezed, grimacing with the effort.

Staehw staggered a couple of steps, but still blocked Aahmes' attack. The Prazny leader now bled from numerous cuts and scratches, but Namid did not think any of them were deep. He staggered again, Inezha's weight pulling him off balance. Fog engulfed the two Praznies.

And they were gone.

For several breaths-of-time longer, Namid and Aahmes remained poised for an attack. When none came, they began to relax. But both kept their weapons out. Namid noticed the bodies she had seen earlier were now gone, as was the snow.

"We need to get out of here," Aahmes said.

"Good, you're real."

Aahmes gave her a half smile.

"I think I saw the horses," Namid said.

"Horses—" the whispers said.

"Oh, stop that," Namid snapped.

Aahmes chuckled, and they walked down the street. "I've glimpsed the horses, too. And the others—"

Flicker….

Namid caught herself just in time to avoid going over the side of a balcony. Aahmes was nowhere in sight, but the young mage stood next to her. He chanted something in a language she had never heard. And the whispers came to her over his chant.

"Akavos—"

"—the pipe—"

"—the sword whole—"

"Is the shepherd's pipe what we need here?" Namid said.

Boudra turned to her. "Get it and go!"

Power swept out from him. It threw her back against the balcony's rail and over. She screamed.

Flicker….

Namid struggled up from darkness and pain. She again lay with her back against a wall. She wriggled her way into a seated position and checked all her blades. Good, she had not lost any. She looked around.

This time she was at the edge of a small open space, like a town square. It was ringed with small buildings that looked like shops, all closed. Five roads came from various directions and converged in this place. And she heard something. Voices. Some of them the whispers she had been hearing. But some not.

Namid shifted her position to one she hoped would let her move quickly if she needed to. She tried to suppress a groan as her injuries protested the change of position. Cameni stepped into the square from the street to Namid's right.

"Are you injured?" Cameni said.

The look Namid gave her apparently answered her question, as she looked abashed.

"What happened?" Enric said as he joined them from the street to Namid's left.

"—challenged the magic—" a whisper said.

"From what I've seen here, that doesn't seem too smart a move," Aahmes said, coming up behind Enric.

Namid started up. "I didn't challenge—" Sudden, sharp pain stifled her protest and brought darkness to the edges of her vision. She eased back to lean against the wall.

Enric knelt next to her, concern obvious in his expression. "Will you be all right?"

"Now there's a stupid question," Aahmes said.

"I'll live, I think," Namid said.

"Where's Haeith?" Cameni said, looking around.

"Here," Haeith said. He emerged from a street across from them.

Odasoro emerged from a different street and joined the small group.

"That's all of us," Namid said. "Except Tamanend…."

"I don't think he'll be leaving the city," Odasoro said. "From what I saw."

Namid nodded, remembering the old Prazny growing younger, then transparent like the others in the city.

"I saw those other Praznies," Cameni said. "The ones you were so rude to. They chased me."

The others had seen them, too, but with differing versions of their encounters with Staehw and Inezha.

"Has anyone discovered why we needed to come here to Nazextas?" Enric said. "Myung told us to come here. There must be some reason."

"Maybe for this?" Cameni pulled a golden shepherd's pipe from somewhere within her skirts.

Aahmes eyes widened at the sight of the golden gleam.

"Is it truly made of what it looks like?" Aahmes said. He held his hand out for it.

Namid watched him as he examined it and smiled to herself at the delight she saw in his expression. She then studied the pipe itself. It looked to be etched, a design of vines and leaves, she thought.

"That must be what I heard, once before I passed out, and then again later. Was that you playing?" Namid asked Cameni.

"No. I tried to, naturally. But it made no sound."

"And yet I heard it," Namid said.

"Just as you passed out," Aahmes said.

"Yes," Namid said.

"Probably hearing things then. After what's happened," Aahmes gestured to her general injured state. "It's no wonder—"

"Don't patronize me! I know what I heard."

"Everything I've seen and experienced here, except for us, was from the past," Odasoro said. "Perhaps you heard it played from the past."

Namid considered that and nodded. "Perhaps."

"—run—" said a whisper.

They all looked around but spotted no threat. Not even any transparent people.

More whispers joined in.

"South—"

"Nazextas has moved—"

"—before it moves again—"

"Leave... go south—"

Everyone exchanged looks.

"I think we have what we were supposed to find..." Enric said.

"And I'm inclined to get out of this place," Namid said. "Even without being urged."

With some difficulty, she made it to her feet.

"But our horses!" Cameni said.

"—horses—" a whisper said.

Flicker....

And the small group now stood on what seemed to be the street they had first walked. In the direction they faced, just visible in the fog, stood their horses. And some distance beyond them, a gate.

"Helpful. But troubling," Aahmes said.

"Let's go!" Enric urged.

They jogged down the street. Aahmes still carried the golden shepherd's pipe.

Namid glanced back at a sound. "It's Staehw!" she shouted.

"Go!" Odasoro said, and they broke into a run.

Namid soon lagged, however, as Haeith's herbal concoction wore off without warning and the pain tore through her. She wondered why the herbs had not lasted longer.

The others reached the horses. They had started to mount, when they realized that Namid was not with them. At that moment, the whole city flashed a brilliant white and the horses danced, tails twitching.

"Namid!" Enric called.

"Go!" she shouted back, now unable to manage anything more than a slow limp.

Enric followed her command, but at a walk, his face turned back toward her. Aahmes gave Enric's horse a slap on the rump to send it off and flung himself onto his own horse. He galloped back to Namid and pulled her up in front of him, then spun back around and charged for the gate.

"Keep down," he instructed her, which she found easy to do as the pain increased. They dashed after the others, slowing slightly for Aahmes to grab Namid's horse's reins.

As they raced for the gate, Namid felt Power gathering, pulling in, and she remembered what she had seen when the city disappeared. Aahmes bent low over her and held her on the horse. The ground shook. The horse stumbled but kept going.

The others reached the gate and passed through. Enric lingered in the opening and urged Aahmes and Namid forward. He backed out of the way as they came closer.

Then the gate bracketed them on either side. An unnerving tug tried to prevent them from leaving. The horse stumbled again but kept to his feet. And they broke free.

Aahmes pulled the horse up a few paces beyond the others and turned back toward the city.

But it had vanished.

Namid started to shiver, even in her cloak. She clung to the horse as waves of fatigue washed over her. And her stomach clenched in hunger. To her surprise, snow covered the ground around them, and several large trees grew scattered nearby.

"What's wrong?" Aahmes said when Namid stayed flat on the horse's neck.

"I was slammed into a wall and the stuff Haeith gave me to help with the pain has worn off."

"Can you still ride for a ways?"

"If I don't have to change from this position—and don't have to do anything—it shouldn't be too bad."

"I'm starving," Cameni said as Aahmes and Namid joined them. "We should eat."

"The whispers did say the city had moved," Enric said. "I'm hungry, too. And tired."

"I'd say the city moved twice, taking us along," Odasoro said as he studied the sky. "Judging by the moon phase."

"So then, where are we?" Cameni said.

"Much further north than before," Haeith said. He handed Namid another packet of the herbal mixture and his waterskin.

"We're in the clans' territory," Aahmes said in a quiet voice. "And we need to find shelter before we rest. There's a storm coming."

Cameni looked at the sky. "Really?"

Namid glanced that way and saw the stars and Nidvi, the second-largest of the moons. No sign of storm clouds.

"My people know the weather in our own lands. There's a storm. We can eat while we ride."

Aahmes guided the group through the rest of the night and kept Namid from falling off the horse. Even with Haeith's herbal mixture, her pain felt worse than before. Toward dawn, as the wind picked up and snow began to fall, they came to a deserted structure, a small stone hut, it looked like. They dismounted and entered, urging the horses inside, too. Namid relied on Aahmes' help, as she could barely move.

Inside they found two rooms, with a fireplace set into the wall dividing them. A modest stack of wood sat next to the fireplace. They settled the horses into the second room while Haeith got a fire going. Namid leaned against one wall, unable to move without risking collapse. She paid little attention to what the others were doing. Instead, she tried to use her Power to lessen the pain, closing her eyes to focus better.

Sometime later, Namid felt a light touch on her arm. When she opened her eyes, she saw Cameni's concerned face a handspan in front of her. Her initial thought was surprise that she hadn't fallen over while lost in concentration.

"I called you several times, but you didn't answer," Cameni said.

Namid managed a weak smile. "I was concentrating."

"On eliminating the pain?"

"Yes."

"And did you succeed?"

"Not really."

Cameni studied her. "I can possibly be of help. I've had some training in the god Jelth's traditions."

Jelth? So, noble Cameni was a Healer. Nice of her to mention it, Namid thought, then sighed to herself. Even her thoughts turned caustic when she hurt.

When Namid nodded, Cameni told her to close her eyes again and she placed a gentle hand on Namid's forehead. Several moments passed and the pain eased. Namid opened her eyes and steadied Cameni as she staggered.

"That was more difficult than I thought it would be," Cameni said.

"How many years of training do you have?"

Cameni looked down. "Less than one."

"You're quite talented then to be able to do so well with so little instruction."

Cameni blushed at the compliment. "It should have been easier. There was something making it more difficult." She narrowed her eyes at Namid and dropped her gaze to her throat. She touched the chain Namid wore.

"What is this?"

Namid pulled it out from beneath her shirt, revealing the tiny sheath that hung from the chain, and the tiny dagger it held.

"How exquisite!" Cameni breathed. "Did you know it has Power?"

Namid tilted her head and sent a light tendril of Power toward the tiny dagger. Cameni was right, it did have Power, a Power that felt odd, turbulent. And somehow familiar. "Interesting. I hadn't felt Power from it before this."

"Where did you get it?"

"It's something I acquired a few years ago," Namid hedged, unwilling to elaborate.

"How?"

Namid was saved from having to answer when Odasoro announced that breakfast, or whatever they wanted to call it, was ready.

Although they had eaten while riding, Namid was hungry. The meal tasted better than anything she had eaten in a long time, barring the recent meals at the Baron's house. Better certainly than Namid's own cooking, which she would be the first to admit was not the best, but at least edible.

"Now that's food!" Aahmes said. "Not like what you cook," he added with a glance at Namid.

"Which is still infinitely superior to what you cook," Namid returned.

"She's feeling better," Enric said to no one in particular.

"Do you know how long this storm might last?" Odasoro asked Aahmes, after they had all listened several long breaths-of-time to the wind howling outside.

Aahmes shrugged. "All day, at least."

"We might not have enough wood," Haeith said.

They all looked at the woodpile, trying to judge its quantity against the raging storm outside. Namid felt certain that Aahmes would feel the need to come up with a smart remark. He did not disappoint.

"We shall all just have to get a little better acquainted then and huddle together for warmth, won't we?" he said.

Namid pretended not to notice his quip. No one else responded to him, either.

They spent the rest of the day trying to save as much of the wood as possible against the colder night. They even waited until the fire was almost out before adding the next piece. The room grew colder and they wrapped themselves in extra clothes and blankets to help keep warm. And still the wood stack dwindled. At one point, Aahmes ventured outside muttering about an axe and green wood, but he returned empty-handed.

Sometime after what would have been sunset, if it were visible, the cold intensified. They brought the horses into the same room, hoping that it would be warmer with all of them there. Namid used her Power to try to spread the heat from the fireplace further through the nearby walls, with limited success. Still, she tried again periodically. Even a little bit would help. They were finally obliged to huddle together close to the fire.

Namid found herself crowded between Aahmes and Cameni. The Earl's daughter seemed unable to stop shivering. From her other side, Enric shared his cloak with her to help keep her warm.

"Fun, isn't it?" Aahmes murmured in Namid's ear. She tried to disregard the tickle of his breath, the warmth from his body, her awareness of how close he sat.

"Ha!" she said.

He chuckled, something she felt more than heard.

The wind continued to howl, and it grew colder. They huddled together even closer and Namid felt a soothing torpor come over her. She thought she leaned against Aahmes' shoulder before she fell asleep.

CHAPTER 13

The sounds of people and horses moving around pulled Namid from a peaceful slumber. She forced her eyes open, awake, but barely registering that her companions stirred also.

Their shelter seemed to have been invaded by a multitude of men and women, all strangely dressed in cloaks of heavy cloth woven in a crossbarred pattern of various shades of gray, yellow, red and brown. Namid had never seen the like before. The trousers and boots the strangers wore beneath their cloaks—which they wore belted at the waist—looked much like Namid's, although some wore trousers of the same crossbarred pattern as the cloaks. When Namid sat up, the strangers ringed the huddled group. They grew deathly still when Aahmes sat up. Where his arm touched hers, Namid felt his tension.

"So, you did survive," one of the men said to Aahmes. "Everyone wondered when your body wasn't found."

"Yes, I survived," Aahmes said. "No doubt to your clan's regret."

The man shrugged. "The old chief is dead. Now Lann rules. And I think he'll be pleased to see you."

The strangers prodded Namid and her companions from their huddle and easily relieved the cold-stiffened little group of their weapons and got them onto the horses. With the clansmates surrounding the small group, they set off.

The storm had ended and Namid saw the faint glow in the east that meant dawn was not far off. The frigid air numbed her exposed face and the horses struggled to get through the drifted snow.

They traveled several candle-marks like this, horses struggling, and riders squinting against the bright sun on the snow, bundled up against the cold.

"How much longer?" Cameni said, shivering.

"If the old hub is still used, it's not much further," Aahmes said.

"No talking," one of the guards growled.

Aahmes gave him a sour look but said nothing further.

Namid caught Aahmes' attention and mimed playing a shepherd's pipe, giving him a questioning look. His smile answered her, and he stretched out one leg to show her the silhouette of the pipe hidden in his boot.

Namid glanced at the rest of the group and noticed how miserably cold Cameni looked. She guided her horse over to one of their guards. He watched her with narrowed eyes but let her approach.

"You could at least give her another cloak," Namid said.

The man scowled. "No need. We're here." He indicated a large mound of snow that lay ahead.

"This is it?" Enric said.

"Much of it's underground," Aahmes said. "It helps to keep it warmer in the winter."

"Silence!" ordered the man Namid had spoken to.

"Why?" Aahmes challenged. "Do you so fear talk—"

"Just take 'em in," another of their guards interrupted. "Lann'll deal with them."

"Yes," Aahmes said. "Let's talk with Lann."

"Who's this Lann?" Namid asked Aahmes as their guards ordered them to dismount at the entrance.

"A cousin," Aahmes said with a frown. "Distantly."

"Now I'm concerned," Enric quipped. If Aahmes heard, he chose to ignore it.

Right inside the entrance, they descended several stone steps and followed a long stone hallway. Elaborate lanterns lit their way. At intervals, smaller hallways led off the main one. Namid wondered at the size of this underground complex. More walking brought them to an ornate door, the only wood they had seen so far in this complex. The door seemed designed to set off a part of the complex from the rest.

Beyond the door, elaborate hangings decorated the rock walls and the dirt and rock floors hid under smooth, polished wood. Namid thought it must be where the clans' lords, or princes, or whatever they called their rulers lived. Somehow, she was not surprised that this was where they would find cousin Lann.

As the guards led them through this area, Namid noticed Aahmes' expression harden and take on a trapped look. As Enric had said, she now felt concerned. She moved her wrists slightly, reassured by the feel of her stilettos, but could not shake a sinking feeling as she realized how small those weapons were against a whole clan, or more. Then their guards ushered them into a large audience chamber, one any ruler might have envied, and Namid had no time for such thoughts.

A man wearing rich furs sat at the far end of the chamber and watched them approach. Namid saw his eyes narrow when he spotted Aahmes, but he made no other move. Studying his features, she saw no family resemblance to Aahmes. They shared similar coloring, of hair and skin, but nothing else. Lann's face had a pinched look, and his thin mustache curved down over the corners of his mouth. Other clansmates they had seen so far had all been clean-shaven. Namid decided she disliked his eyes. They looked too calculating, too accustomed to hiding plots and vicious secrets. One of the guards stepped to his side and spoke in his ear.

"So, you yet live," the fur-clad man greeted Aahmes.

"And you sit in a place that's yours through murder, Lann," came the cold reply.

Lann's expression changed to one of pain and disappointment. Namid wondered irreverently if he practiced the look. "The murder was not my deed, nor was it condoned," he said.

"Then return to my clan what belongs to it."

"I'm afraid that's impossible, as you know," Lann said, with the air of one stating the obvious when he should not have to. "A clan that's no more cannot claim the chieftainship. And one man is not a clan. Even if you managed to dig up some bastard, half-breed wench of a sister…." He focused on Namid.

Aahmes glanced where his cousin looked and clenched his fists, his eyes narrowed in fury.

He wants to make you mad, Namid told Aahmes by handtalk.

She returned his cousin's look, and laughed deliberately, secretly pleased at the frowns she got from many of the clansmates. She took a step toward Lann and stared him down. "Not some lost member of one of your clans. Not a bastard. And not his sister. You'll have to do better with your insults than that."

Lann's gaze slid away from her challenge and returned to Aahmes.

"We'll have to continue this interesting discussion later, I'm afraid." He ordered one of his men to show them to their chamber.

Namid did not like the emphasis he put on the word chamber and had a sudden premonition of what it would be. With so many of Lann's clansmates around, they had no choice but to go where they took them. And, as Namid had suspected, their 'chamber' turned out to be nothing more than a large room with one door, wooden and thick, that guards locked behind them.

For the next several breaths-of-time, Aahmes treated them to a string of curses that only a former resident of Rhadanthus could have produced. Cameni covered her ears, but clearly still heard too much, because she looked shocked. Namid just grinned and enjoyed his creativity as his curses got more elaborate and imaginative.

"I doubt Lann will return to you what's rightfully yours," Enric ventured after Aahmes' cursing got quieter and he shifted into another language. The clans' tongue, Namid guessed.

"Of course not." Aahmes growled. "He's going to kill us."

"Kill?" Cameni echoed, her eyes wide and frightened.

"Which is why we're getting out of here now," Aahmes continued as he turned toward the door.

"But how?" Enric said.

Namid wondered the same, but moments later she knew the answer. She felt the heady rush of gathered Power and realized with surprise that it centered around Aahmes. The Power washed through her and she saw what he planned. She knew somehow that a display of Power was only going to make matters worse.

"Wait!" Namid launched herself toward Aahmes at the same time he released his attack on the locked door.

She found herself between him and the door and was forced to use her own Power to shunt his attack away and around. It was harder than she had expected. His Power probably matched hers. She caught a brief glimpse of the horrified look on his face, then the collision of their two forces lit the room with a blinding flash.

And all went still… except for the sinister laughter that came from the black-edged hole where the door had stood.

"So… I was correctly informed," Lann said as he entered. Fifteen or so of his clansmates followed him into the room and spread out.

Lann continued, "I had hoped to prompt this little confirmation elsewhere. Wood's so precious here." He gave

Aahmes a strange look. "I'm surprised to find a clansman dealing in such things. The girl I knew about."

"Informed?" Namid said.

He gave her a sickly sweet smile. "Yes. I've had word of you. And now that I'm certain I have the right ones, I'll be sending you south. You have a rendezvous that I'm sure you'll not want to miss. But first, we must take one small precaution."

He motioned to a grizzled old man who stood just outside the shattered doorway. The man hurried to his leader's side and handed Lann a beautiful ceramic goblet.

"I'll need one more dose," Lann said as he took the cup.

"Immediately, Chieftain." The man bowed and whispered something to one of the younger men that sent him running.

Lann held the cup out to Namid. "I have been assured that the wine's flavor is not affected."

Namid shivered, not from the cool air in the room but from the thought of what lurked in the wine. She backed away and tucked her hands behind her back. "By what? What else is in there?"

"Don't drink it!" Cameni called out, before a guard's hand clamped over her mouth to silence her.

Namid realized then that all of Lann's clansmates now held naked weapons. Enric had stepped toward Cameni, to be stopped short by the points of two swords at his throat.

"I really must insist," Lann said and stepped closer even as Namid backed up again. Another step and she backed into Aahmes, who had not moved. He clasped her hands where she held them clenched behind her.

"If you drink it willingly, it will be much more pleasant than if I must have someone pour it down your throat," Lann said.

Can't argue with that, Namid thought, having once had the disagreeable experience of being forced to drink something. She would prefer to avoid doing that again. But she feared what they had put in that wine.

"Oh, and sure you could just blast us with your magic." Lann said the last word like it tasted disgusting. "But you'd kill your friends, too. That's if you've even got anything left after your little display." He indicated the ruined door.

"You haven't answered the question," Aahmes said while he spelled into Namid's hands a desperate plan to break away from there. The plan did not seem feasible. The clansmates had them too badly outnumbered, with all of them armed and ready for their captives to try something. Namid shook her head slightly, hoping Aahmes would get the message and not try anything rash.

"About what's in it? Not poison, I assure you. That wouldn't do at all. Merely a little concoction that will guarantee no magical difficulties while you journey."

"There's no reason I should believe you," Namid said.

Lann shrugged and made a slight gesture. His men moved to surround them, to cut them apart from each other. As two grabbed Aahmes' arms, he twisted, breaking free of them, and made a grab for one of their swords. He never made it. They closed in on him and beat him to the ground.

"All right!" Namid shouted.

The skirmish ceased. Aahmes struggled to a sitting position, his face already bruising. But he had wounded several of his guards, Namid noted with satisfaction. Aahmes gave her a look she could not interpret but acted docile enough as the men surrounding him hauled him to his feet. He made no sound, but a look of pain crossed his face.

Namid took the goblet from Lann and peered into it. The deep red wine had a pleasant aroma. She surreptitiously used a small amount of the little Power she still commanded after blocking Aahmes' blow to try to see what they had put in the wine, without success. But she *was* able to tell that it was not poison, or at least not a poison she was familiar with. That did not reassure her. The cup felt colder than she expected. She burned nearly all the rest of her Power to throw up a ward within herself, to counter any poison. She hoped.

"Namid, no," Odasoro said.

Namid spared him a glance, then looked into Lann's eyes. She remembered that she had heard once that most of the clans were supposed to be superstitious. So, she decided to add a little something, on the off chance it might help.

"I'll drink your concoction. But I give you fair warning…. If I die of this, ill fortune will haunt you and yours all the rest of your days. And I can ensure that they'll be many." She let a hint of Power flash in her eyes. She did not know if she could follow through on her threat, but she tied the last of her Power into her words, just in case.

Lann fell back a pace and fear showed in his expression. Several of his clansmates made signs with their free hands, probably to try to ward against her Power. Then they closed in on her again, anyway.

Before they touched her, she lifted the goblet in a salute to Odasoro, glanced back at Aahmes and gave him a wink, and drank.

The wine tasted sweeter than she expected. When she had finished it, she detected a slight, bitter aftertaste that must have been Lann's concoction.

Namid looked up to find Lann studying her.

She felt vague, detached from everything. Then her hands and feet went numb. The crash of the goblet on the floor was the first clue she had that she had dropped it. She turned, the motion making her dizzy, and Aahmes' eyes were the last things she saw clearly. Roaring haze swept around and through her, her knees buckled, and she fell into the dark.

CHAPTER 14

Unfamiliar voices floated through her darkness, arguing, fussing about too much of something, about losing someone. Or perhaps she dreamed it. She dreamed of other things, bright flashes of lights and glowing towers, a sword and Power.

And she dreamed of a man who looked like her and Aahmes. But she knew somehow that his age far exceeded either of theirs, although he did not look it. He seemed asleep, but despite that, Namid felt that he was trying to say something.

For a time, she drifted in a state of semi-awareness, punctured by more voices, some half-familiar, the feel of a horse beneath her, or the cold hardness of the ground. Finally, she was able to open her eyes and focus on something.

It was a tree.

Namid looked around without otherwise moving and guessed the time of day as shortly after sundown. A short distance away, several men and women gathered around a fire, clansmates from their attire. Closer, between her and the fire, some long bundles lay on the ground. Her companions, she assumed. Asleep maybe.

She lay on her side, inadequately wrapped in a cloak. Her wrists and ankles were bound, though not well. Her head throbbed, and she felt dizzy, and she knew then how the concoction guaranteed 'no magical difficulties'. No ability to concentrate meant she could not even attempt to control any Power. And she still hurt from what had happened in Nazextas, although much less than she last remembered, before the doctored wine and the darkness. But she had somehow acquired some new hurts, she suspected from being thrown over a horse.

She gritted her teeth and tried to will away the throbbing. No luck. But after a long time, it eased somewhat, enough to let her again take note of her surroundings. The sky was fully dark, although Itieka, the largest moon, gave a feeble light through thin clouds. Namid heard the laughter of the clansmates by the fire as they passed around a wineskin.

Cringing against another onslaught of pain, she rolled over to her back and discovered another bundle next to her. She rolled further and nudged aside a corner of a cloak.

Beneath it Aahmes lay, ostensibly unconscious, wrists and ankles bound like hers. Namid guessed that he had also been forced to drink that concoction. As she started to drop the cloak, he opened his eyes.

"Welcome back among the living," he greeted her in a quiet voice, with a hint of a smile.

'What?" came Enric's whisper from beyond Aahmes.

"Namid's back with us."

"Namid?!"

"Shhh."

Namid propped herself up on an elbow to look beyond Aahmes.

Enric smiled when he saw her. "We feared—"

"That'll wait," Aahmes interrupted. "Are you going to free us?"

"Uh, yeah." A flex of her wrist and her stiletto dropped into her hand. Why hadn't her stilettos been taken from her?

She easily dealt with her bonds and freed Aahmes. He did the same for Enric and returned her stiletto. She hesitated in sheathing it.

"What about the others?"

"We'll free them when we're ready to move," Aahmes said.

"Oh?" Namid invited him to explain.

"We have to escape now. They haven't said where they're taking us, but I did hear one mention Staehw."

Namid groaned. "Him again?"

"Yes. And we can't let you get another dose of Lann's concoction."

"Don't expect anything flashy from me," Namid said. "Or really anything Powerful at all."

"I might come up with something," Aahmes said. At her questioning look, he added, "I *have* had some of that stuff, and more recently, but much less than they gave you."

Namid nodded and regretted the movement.

"So how are we going to manage this escape?" Enric said. "I'll remind you that there are twice as many of them as all of us."

"Watch," Aahmes said.

Namid sensed him gathering Power from the night around them. The Power felt peculiar, more chaotic than normal, more agitated. Maybe just an aftereffect from that concoction? She shrugged to herself, dismissing the whole thing, and looked where Aahmes had indicated.

At first, the darkness remained unbroken. Then a faint, bilious green patch of light formed and hovered a few handspans above the ground. It expanded into a sickly haze that pulsed lighter then darker and snaked through the trees toward their captors. Namid caught glimpses of hand-long fangs and longer claws within the writhing murk.

The clansmates fell silent, their attention fixed on this eerie apparition. The haze thickened and crept closer to them. It paused at the edge of the firelight, then lunged toward them. All without a sound.

The clansmates remained frozen in place a breath-of-time longer. Then one man screamed, a high, shrill sound of such pure terror that it chilled Namid to the bone. More clansmates screamed then and they all fled into the surrounding darkness. The haze split and surged after them.

After the last sounds of this macabre hunt faded into the night, Aahmes sank back, his eyes closed. Namid noticed that his hands shook.

"Magnificent!" Enric said.

"See if you can find some wine for him," Namid said. When Enric turned away to search for untainted wine, she leaned closer to Aahmes. "I do have to agree with him.... Impressive! Are you going to live?"

He looked at her through narrowed eyes and gave her a sardonic, but weak grin. She took that as her answer.

Enric returned with the wineskin their captors had been so happily emptying and nearly spilled the remaining contents in his haste. Namid rescued the skin and gave Enric her stiletto.

"Better cut them free," she said and nodded at the squirming forms of their companions, who seemed to be trying to see what had happened.

While Enric freed the others, Namid held the skin for Aahmes and after a couple of swallows, he was steady enough to hold it himself. She pulled her cloak over to her as the others joined them.

"What happened?" Cameni demanded as Enric returned Namid's stiletto.

"You can blame it on him." Namid jerked her thumb in Aahmes' direction.

"Tell you later," he said, lowering the wineskin. "They might be able to return when the illusion fades and I, at least, don't plan to wait for them." He stood. "Let's get our weapons back. And see if the clansmates left anything interesting." He led the others toward the dying fire.

Namid stayed where she sat, unwilling to attempt standing, with the dizziness and pain that lurked at the edges of her awareness. Odasoro remained with her.

"Why are you hovering?" she asked him, sharper than she intended.

"Would you like some support?" he said and extended an arm.

Namid waved him off. "I'm just resting. I'm fine."

"You've been skirting closer to oblivion than you might realize. You drank that concoction a full seven days ago." His voice softened. "And while you moved around well enough the last few days, and ate and drank, it was clear you were wits-wandering. We feared you would not truly return to us."

Namid looked away and suppressed a shudder. "Aahmes hides it well," she said, then wondered why she had mentioned him.

"He's reserved," Odasoro said with an enigmatic smile and walked over to help the others.

Namid watched her companions sort through their captors' possessions and decided it was time to attempt standing. Getting to her knees was easy, no pain in her head and no disorientation. She used a nearby tree to steady herself and soon stood upright. Without warning, everything started to spin, and waves of nausea pulsed through her. Namid wrapped her arms around the tree to remain upright and squeezed her eyes shut against the whirling.

Haeith found her that way many long breaths-of-time later. She felt a gentle touch on her arm and groaned a question.

"Namid, what's wrong?"

She opened one eye but closed it again when she saw the world still spinning.

"Nothing, obviously. I've just fallen madly in love with this oak tree here."

"It's an alder."

"Oh."

"Here. I'll steady you."

Slowly she released the tree and tried to use his arm for balance. But when they started walking, she was forced to cling to him.

"Perhaps I should carry you instead?"

"No, please. I'll be fine. Just guide me." Namid had no intention of opening her eyes yet.

So, bit by bit, they approached the others. Namid heard their half-formed questions, but Haeith apparently waved them off. After a long eternity, he told her they had come to the fire. He helped her settle herself on a log and she opened her eyes. The small fire made her eyes ache, but only for a few breaths-of-time. She smiled at Haeith, who crouched nearby, scrutinizing her.

"Thank you."

He gave her an abrupt nod. "Your courage and perseverance would make you a good Flame Warrior," he said.

Namid looked at him in surprise. Most people considered Flame Warriors just a legend from the tribes far to the east. Flame Warriors were reputed to be extremely loyal to their friends, fearsome to their enemies, and capable of fighting on even after taking wounds that would have killed most lesser warriors.

"You're a Flame Warrior?" she said.

He stood, his gaze fixed on the ground. "Was." He turned to go. "Rest here a while. I'll bring your horse to you when we're ready to leave." He turned away.

A short time later, Enric joined Namid on the log. "We're nearly ready to depart," he said.

"Good. I'm ready to leave this place. Preferably before Lann's clansmates return."

"Indeed. Have some wine?" He held out a skin.

"Yes, thank you."

"No!" Aahmes strode up to them.

Namid glared at him but did not drink. "No?"

"Not while you're still dizzy. Unless you'd like to pass out again. I learned that a couple of days ago." He held up two small pouches and another skin. "But Cameni found some herbs that'll at least let you walk by yourself. And some water and food might help, too." He tossed her one pouch and the skin, which held water, and started to spoon out some sort of soup from a pot that sat over the fire.

"I can walk just fine," Namid declared.

He gave her a skeptical look over his shoulder.

"It's just standing that's giving me problems," she added.

Aahmes started to laugh, and Enric joined in.

"Well," Namid grumped, with feigned irritation. "Bunch of crazy, hovering nursemaids."

~ ~ ~

Later, however, as they rode away from the campsite, Namid was grateful for the herbs, and the food and water. The nausea had vanished, and the spinning made its presence known only if she moved her head suddenly. As they rode, Namid continued to munch some bread and cheese they had found and wondered where they headed now. No one spoke as they followed Aahmes through the forest.

After dawn began to color the sky a rosy gold, they came to the edge of the forest. To their left, perhaps a hundred paces away, a road ran to the south. Namid followed it with her eyes and saw a city in the distance.

"Does anyone know where we are?" Cameni said.

"Yes," Odasoro said.

A catch in his voice caught Namid's attention and she had a sinking feeling.

"That's Kilaadi," she murmured, unsure she was right, and at the same time certain she was not wrong.

"At last!" Cameni exclaimed. "The capital. Civilization!"

"And a center of activity for the Dark Priests," Odasoro said. "Remember, Namid spoke of that many days ago."

Cameni frowned. "We can't take Akavos there, then."

"I think we might have no choice," Namid said in a quiet

voice. "I feel we need to go there."

Aahmes snorted but made no further comment.

"I feel so also," Haeith said.

"Me, too," Enric said.

"Do you dare risk it?" Odasoro asked Namid, and she felt everyone staring at her.

She gazed back at Odasoro. "As I said, I think we have no choice. And that all happened years ago. I've changed, and likely no one is left there who will recognize me."

"Except for—" He stopped at the stern look she gave him.

"We won't be going there, so it's of no concern," Namid said.

"What happened 'years ago'?" Aahmes said.

She did not answer right away, but studied him, considering. Then she said, "It's how I ended up in Rhadanthus. The Dark Priests were consolidating their hold on Kilaadi, and I... let's just say that I was forcefully uncooperative. And soon afterward, I realized that I had better run if I wanted to stay alive."

Her companions said nothing for several breaths-of-time.

"Then we cannot ask you to again enter that city," Enric said.

"You're not asking me. I feel the pull, just as you do. I'll be careful." Namid held his gaze. "Very careful."

He gave her a bow from the saddle. "Let's go then."

~ ~ ~

They reached Kilaadi's gates before noon. In addition to the normal, bored-looking guards, two men in dark green-gray cloaks stood near the gates and studied each person who entered the city. Namid kept her own cloak wrapped about her, with the hood pulled forward. The air felt cold enough that this drew no undue attention. She studied the Dark Priests even as they studied the small group. She was pleased when they paid the small group no more attention than they paid anyone else.

After they moved out of sight of the gate, Namid heard soft exclamations of relief from her companions.

"Now where do we go?" Cameni said.

"I feel pulled this direction," Enric said. He pointed toward the Monarch's citadel.

"To the citadel?" Cameni breathed, her eyes wide.

"Is this pull from the sword?" Aahmes said.

"I think so."

"I think we should locate an inn and get some rooms," Odasoro said. "We're all going to need rest again soon…."

"And a base to work from," Aahmes added.

Cameni turned to Namid. "Do you know a good inn?"

"Yes. But I think we should stay elsewhere—"

"Some filthy slum, no doubt," the Earl's daughter interrupted.

"No. But it's bad enough that we won't be marked as people of wealth. And they won't ask awkward questions."

"No need to worry about being mistaken for people of wealth," Cameni said and wrinkled her nose. "So long out in the wilds… I'm sure a decent innkeeper would take one look at us and throw us out anyway!"

"That's the spirit!" Aahmes grinned and turned to Namid. "Where's your inn?"

"This way."

Namid led them through several twisting side streets, to one of the poorer parts of the city.

"You're not taking us where I think you are, are you?" Odasoro said as they emerged from a tiny alley into a street that was little wider.

"Probably." She smiled at him.

"Do you remember what happened the last time we were there?"

"We, nothing! I wasn't in the thick of it."

"What happened?" Cameni said.

"A bit of a misunderstanding," Odasoro hedged and

looked somewhat embarrassed. Namid nearly choked on her laughter.

"Perhaps you had better elaborate," Cameni said, with a stern look.

"Later," Namid broke in, no longer feeling amused. "Look."

Further down the street, flanking the door to the inn where Namid had planned to stay, stood two more of the Dark Priests. Their hooded heads turned toward the small group as they paused in the street.

"They've seen us," Aahmes said in a quiet voice, one hand stealing toward a dagger.

"Wait," Enric said. "We cannot afford to draw attention to ourselves."

"We'd better do something soon, then. I believe sitting in the middle of the street draws attention," Haeith said.

"We'll try the inn anyway," Namid said and rode toward the building so she would not have to hear all the objections. A moment later, she heard the others follow.

The small group stopped by the inn door and dismounted. A boy came running to take the horses but stopped in his tracks when he saw the Dark Priests. When they made no move, he sidled closer.

"Care well for them," Haeith said as he handed the boy a vikl, the silver coin of the Six Realms.

"Aye, sir." The boy scurried away, leading the horses.

They turned to enter, but found their way now blocked by the two Dark Priests.

"What is your business here?" one demanded.

Odasoro took a step toward him and bowed. "Good sir, we seek only a place to rest and some food."

"You're strangers to the city?" the other said.

"Yes. Is there some reason we may not enter?"

"Where have you come from?" the first said, ignoring Odasoro's question.

"The north."

As they stood there in the cold, Namid felt the little

strength she still had dwindling. Odasoro continued speaking with the Dark Priests, but she lost the sense of the words. When she felt herself starting to fall, she grabbed Enric's arm. He stood closest. He looked at her in concern.

And her motion attracted the attention of the Dark Priests. As one came closer, Namid tilted her head to put her face in shadow. She doubted any of them would recognize her, but she did not want to take any chances. She began to think that trying to bluff their way in was a mistake, but it was too late to run now.

"Your companion's injured?" the Dark Priest said. Namid thought she heard anticipation in his voice and wondered if they had been told to look for someone who was supposed to be injured.

"She's only ill," Aahmes said. "Bad water, maybe." Namid stifled a laugh at that.

The Dark Priest stood near her a moment, close enough to touch, and she felt a fleeting sense of Power. She held herself still, trying to give no reaction, and soon he moved away.

'There's no reason for you not to enter," the Dark Priest answered Odasoro's earlier question. "Welcome to our fair city."

They all murmured appropriate thanks and escaped inside, where the innkeeper hurried to get them rooms. He gave them two that overlooked the stables and left to bring the food they requested. They all gathered in one of the rooms.

After the innkeeper left, Namid collapsed onto one of the beds with a sigh, not bothering to take off her cloak or boots.

"Are you all right?" Enric said.

"Haven't we heard that stupid question somewhere before?" Aahmes muttered.

"Mostly just tired," Namid said. "But food is welcome." She started up with a sudden thought. "By the way, I'd recommend that no one use any Power while we're in

Kilaadi. Healing included." Namid held Cameni's gaze until the Earl's daughter nodded, then she laid back down.

The others stayed in the room and talked quietly until the innkeeper returned with the food. Namid heard him ask if 'the ill one' needed anything else but did not hear the answer. When he had been sent on his way with some coins, Namid sat up again, glad to take the plain hot stew and fresh bread that Enric handed over.

When she could eat no more, Namid set the bowl on the floor, stretched out again and listened to the others speculating on why they had been drawn to the city. And the curiosity that several of them all felt that pull.

Suddenly someone shook Namid.

"Namid! Please wake up!"

"What? Why?" Namid opened her eyes and, with difficulty, focused on Cameni's worried face. It occurred to her that Cameni often looked worried. "What now?"

"The Dark Priests have surrounded the inn!"

CHAPTER 15

Their door opened, admitting Haeith.

"They're not letting anyone leave," he reported. "And they're searching everywhere."

"Where are the others?" Namid said.

"They went out earlier," Cameni said. "To follow the sword's pull." She glanced out the window at the late afternoon sun. "I imagine they'll return soon. Are the Dark Priests looking for us?"

"Maybe," Namid said. "I didn't think we did anything to arouse any suspicions. It might help if we knew what they're after. But I don't dare go…. Haeith, see if you can find out what they're looking for. Carefully! Don't give them any cause to take you."

Haeith looked a little startled at Namid's easy assumption of leadership but gave her a slight bow.

After he had gone, Namid turned to Cameni. "Gather all the valuables you can—yours, Enric's, anyone else's—the gems and money, and bring them all here. Hurry!" Cameni nodded and ran to the other room. Whatever the Dark Priests were searching for—and Namid had a bad feeling she knew what it might be—she planned to make sure that they found nothing worthwhile with them.

While Cameni was gone, Namid took her sword and the rest of her blades, except for the stilettos in their armguard sheaths, and concealed them within the rushes of the mattress. She had a suspicion that appearing so well armed would pique the Dark Priests' interest. And it was possible that one of them might even recognize her sword.

Cameni returned with a small velvet bag. "These are all I found. I put everything together. Is that all right?"

Namid nodded as she took the bag. She glanced inside and whistled softly. It held more than double what she had seen in Enric's pouch back in Rhadanthus.

"There's quite the fortune here," she said and tucked the bag away with the weapons. She pulled a chair up next to the bed.

"Sit."

Cameni looked surprised at Namid's order but obeyed. "What?"

"I'm supposed to be sick," Namid explained as she pulled off her cloak, boots, and tunics and dumped them atop her pack, leaving her wearing only her shirt and trousers. "You stayed to watch over me. We don't know where the others went, they didn't say. We don't have much money, which is why we're staying here. When the Dark Priests come here, they'll treat you like you're worthless. Don't take offense. Act a little afraid, and very respectful, like your servants might if they thought they'd angered you. Say as little as possible. We'll be fine."

Namid crawled back into the bed and found a position that did not put her directly on top of the weapons and other valuables. She pulled the covers up to her chin.

"How could you know how my servants would act—"

"No time. Don't act like I'm dying," Namid said. "I'm just ill and need to rest. You might get away with a little indignation if they get too loud. I do need my rest, you know." Namid grinned at her.

"You don't really look ill anymore," Cameni said.

"Then, I'm just recovering. But I could have a setback, which is why I need rest."

Cameni jumped at a knock on the door.

"Go answer," Namid whispered and closed her eyes, feigning sleep. But she listened closely.

She heard Cameni open the door and ask, "What is it?"

"We're here to search your room," said a man's voice.

After a pause, Haeith said, "I told them we have a sick woman here—"

"I would advise you not to get in the way," said the stranger, a Dark Priest, Namid assumed.

"I... I beg you to search quietly," Cameni said. "She's resting."

She gasped then, and Namid pictured the Dark Priests shoving the door open. She heard several heavy footsteps, loud enough that they would certainly have disturbed her if she had been asleep. She sat up partway and acted as if she had just been awakened.

"What's going on?"

One Dark Priest came over to the bed, while the other three pawed through their possessions. When the one near Namid spoke, she knew he had been the one who spoke at the door a moment ago.

"Where are your friends?" he demanded.

Namid glanced at Cameni and Haeith where they stood against one wall.

"I don't know," she said. "They went out."

"Where?" he said. He twined his fingers in Namid's hair and pulled her toward the edge of the bed. His strength surprised her. He did not look that strong. Cameni made a small distressed sound, but Namid could not turn her head to see her. She winced as he tightened his grip, twisting his fingers further in her hair. "Well?"

"I really don't know! They didn't say."

"You expect me to believe you would allow your friends to leave you, to go wandering about a strange city, without you knowing where they were going?" He gave Namid's head a rough shake.

"Believe what you like!" Namid snapped, starting to lose her temper, and her patience. "They have their own business. Some of us don't go around prying into others' business."

He stared at her a moment and Namid feared that she had gone too far. She had hoped that their little act would convince the Dark Priests that the small group was not worthy of their time. However, she had a feeling that instead this was going to end badly. But, to her surprise, he released her.

"Why do you want them?" Haeith said as he stepped further into the room.

"All strangers must be accounted for," was the uninformative answer.

Namid felt warmth at her throat and too late remembered her dagger necklace. She felt that the Dark Priests should not have it, should not even see it. Although she made no move, the Dark Priest turned back toward her. The expression on his face changed from irritation to exultation as he reached for the necklace. Namid pulled back from his cold hand on her neck, trying to think what to do.

Just before his reaching fingers touched the little dagger, the Dark Priest gave a soft moan, then slumped to the floor. In the same instant, his fellows likewise crumpled. As the warmth faded from her necklace, Namid felt a surge of Power far to the south.

That can't be good, she thought.

Cameni, Haeith, and Namid stared at each other a moment, speechless. Then Namid jumped up, trying to ignore how the room swayed, and began stuffing everything back into the packs, stepping over and around the fallen Dark Priests to do so.

"Get the rest of our things," Namid ordered Haeith and Cameni and pointed at the door. "We're leaving!"

"But—"

"Go!"

They went.

"I thought you said to avoid using Power here," a quiet voice said from the direction of the window. Somehow, his presence there did not surprise her.

"Yes, I did, Aahmes."

Namid continued gathering their things and heard the soft thud as he dropped inside. "It's convenient of you to return just now," she said. "It saves us searching."

"I've always had good timing," he said as he repacked another pack. "The others are getting the horses. Here are your tunics."

"Thanks." Namid pulled on both tunics, then her boots. "How long have you been there?"

"Long enough." Then something in his voice changed. "I think I know why you had to leave here."

Namid looked up at him. He gazed back at her with a calm expression.

"Oh?"

He shrugged and changed the subject. "Do you have the feeling that we don't really know what's going on? That we're being herded around?"

Namid froze, struck by his observation. "I hadn't really thought about it, but things *do* seem rather contrived. Any ideas?"

He shook his head. "More a lot of questions than anything else. And then there's Dar's warning…. I get a feeling that all this involves us, you and I, more than the noble and his broken sword." He took Namid's hand, holding it lightly. She could easily pull away if she wanted. She didn't pull away.

"Because of your cousin's obvious interest in us and none of the others?"

"That's part of it. Cameni has Power, too, but you notice that they didn't bother drugging her."

"We're stronger in Power than she is…."

"More practiced, at least. But there could be another

factor…." He just looked into Namid's eyes, and she felt that she teetered on the verge of seeing some grand plan.

"We clearly have a shared ancestry, somehow," Aahmes said. "It's obvious to everyone who sees us. And—"

The door banged open behind Namid as Haeith and Cameni returned. Namid snatched her hand from Aahmes' grasp and felt her face grow warm. He gave her the familiar, irritating grin, but said nothing. Namid bent to pull the group's fortune and her weapons out of the mattress.

"We have everything," Cameni said as she dropped the packs she carried on the floor.

"Out the window," Aahmes said.

Namid buckled on her sword, grabbed her cloak, and helped dump the packs out the window. As Haeith helped Cameni over the sill, Aahmes and Namid checked the downed Dark Priests.

Aahmes whistled. "Looks like they'll be out for candle-marks. What'd you do?"

"Later. Let's go."

A ledge outside the window slanted down to the stable roof. From there it was an easy drop to the ground. As Aahmes and Enric saddled the last two horses, Namid heard a commotion from the inn.

"That's it," she said and mounted her horse. "Let's go!"

After tightening the last straps, Aahmes and Enric also mounted. The others already sat on their horses.

"This way!" Odasoro called from the mouth of a tiny alley.

"I hope you know where you're going," Namid called to him after long breaths-of-time riding single file through the stinking alley.

"Trust me," was his reply.

Moments later all the bells in the city began to ring.

"And there's the alarm," Enric said.

"They'll be closing the gates," Haeith said.

"Not the one we'll use," Odasoro said.

"Why am I suddenly uneasy about this?" Enric said.

"Only just now?" Aahmes said.

The tiny alley ended, and they rode down a strangely deserted street, one unfamiliar to Namid.

"Do you know where we are?" Cameni asked Odasoro.

"Yes."

"Are you going to tell us?" Aahmes said.

"I don't think so. I doubt any of you would like it."

On the heels of that statement came a probe of Power so insistent that it overpowered Namid's senses. When it vanished just as abruptly, she noticed that it had also affected Aahmes and Cameni... and Haeith! Enric glanced at his pack then, as from within, Akavos sounded a clear, bell-like tone.

"Now we have problems," Namid said.

Aahmes grinned at her. "And we didn't before?"

Namid ignored him. "How much longer?" she asked Odasoro.

"A quarter candle-mark, or so... if we gallop whenever we can."

"Which would draw attention to us," Enric said.

"We're already rather obvious," Aahmes said, with a gesture at the empty street.

"I don't think—" Cameni was interrupted by a shout from behind them. One look at the Dark Priests on their horses made their decision easy.

"Follow me!" Odasoro shouted and urged his horse into a gallop. The rest of them stayed right behind him.

Within a few paces, they again found themselves in the twisting alleys that seemed common in this part of Kilaadi. They tried to hold their pace but were forced to slow around the many corners. Without warning, Odasoro pulled his horse to a halt, causing a few worry-filled moments as they all tried to avoid colliding with him and each other.

"Trapped," Aahmes said as another group of Dark Priest came toward them from ahead. Their fellows clattered up behind, blocking that route.

Namid edged her horse past the others until she was

next to Odasoro. The others crowded in behind them.

"Surrender to the Dark Prince's authority," ordered one of the men in front of them.

"So, they *are* adherents of Sesaisyd," Enric murmured.

The Dark Priests eased toward them as Namid turned to Odasoro.

"Be ready to move fast," she murmured and rode toward the Dark Priests before he could try to stop her.

"I would speak with you, Priest," Namid addressed the man in front.

He raised a hand and his comrades held their places. Then he rode toward her. Namid had a half-formed idea of hitting them all at once with whatever Power she could, but it suddenly became unnecessary. With strident shrieks, dozens of people dropped from the roofs around them onto the startled Dark Priests.

"I had hoped for something like this!" Odasoro said as he moved up next to Namid. "The last time I traveled through here, this area still resisted these priests."

The short battle ended with all the Dark Priests unconscious on the ground. One of the group's benefactors approached them.

"Straight that-a-way, Lord, takes you out o' the city," he said to Odasoro and pointed the way the group had been headed. "They'll bother you none, now."

Then he seemed to notice Namid for the first time and his eyes widened. He bowed. "We'd looked for your return, Lady." He smiled, then. "But I'd say we'll be waiting yet a mite longer. The gods go with you, Lady." He moved aside so the group could pass.

They rode past the downed Dark Priests and saw their benefactors searching them. One elderly woman looked up as they approached and walked up to Aahmes.

"Here, m'dear. These might stand you in good stead." She handed him several pendants and turned away. He glanced at them and tucked them into his tunic.

Just beyond the site of the ambush, the alley curved and

widened, then ended at a stone wall.

"Trust him, he says," Aahmes grumbled.

"No faith, that's your problem," Namid said.

"Not really. Just an overabundance of experience."

"That man who so kindly helped us seemed to know you," Cameni said to Namid.

"He did seem to, didn't he?" Namid avoided looking at Aahmes. She did not want to see his expression.

With a low rumble, a section of the wall in front of them swung outward. Namid looked around in time to see Odasoro replace a small stone in the wall to the left of the opening. The instant the opening stretched wide enough, Aahmes rode through it.

"All clear," he reported, and they followed his example. The door rumbled shut behind them.

"Where are we now?" Enric said as he peered out into the dusk.

"Outside the city, of course," Aahmes said.

"I know that!" Enric snapped.

"Let's get under the trees and you can chatter all you like without giving us away," Namid said.

After they had ridden well within the woods, and some distance from the city, Enric resumed the discussion.

"I meant where outside the city," he said. "East, or west, or what?"

"Then why didn't you say so in the first place?" Aahmes said with a wide-eyed expression. The corners of his mouth quirked up.

"We're east of the city," Odasoro said.

"Are we going to stay the night here?" Cameni said.

"We'd better ride a bit yet," Namid said. "We're probably still too close here."

"South, still?" Cameni said.

"Yes." Enric was the one who answered. He turned to Namid as they all guided the horses through the trees. "You know we followed the pull of the sword?"

"Cameni told me."

"Where did it lead you?" Haeith said.

"To a library," Aahmes said, sounding disgusted.

"A library? The Royal Library?" Namid said. She felt Aahmes' gaze on her but refused to look at him.

"Yes," Odasoro said. "It's still open to anyone, but few dare enter now with the Dark Priests in control."

"Not much longer and it will soon be too dark to ride through here without some light," Aahmes said.

"Not a problem," Namid said. "I can guide us. I can see in the dark."

"That does explain a few things…" he muttered.

"I intend no insult," Haeith said. "But are we not far enough into the trees that we could risk a torch?"

Aahmes chuckled.

"I think we can risk a light," Namid said. "But not a torch. Someone might smell the smoke. Keep a tight rein on the horses. This might startle them."

Namid followed her own advice and called up a minuscule bit of Power. Again, the Power seemed more chaotic than normal. There also seemed to be more than she had expected. With some effort, she gathered it into a fist-sized orb of reddish light that hovered in front of them a handspan above the ground. It provided illumination for a couple of paces around. The horses acted skittish when it first appeared, then settled down.

"Will that do?" Namid said.

"Yes," Haeith said and urged his horse toward it. He smiled as the orb glided forward at the same pace. They all continued on, then.

"What did you find out at the library?" Cameni asked Enric.

"You didn't tell anyone about the sword, did you?" Namid said.

"Of course not," Enric said. "We found, or rather were drawn to an ancient scroll. Fortunately, Odasoro could read the language." He paused. "I think we have a problem. According to that scroll, Akavos was the sword used by the gods to defeat the Dark Prince—"

"Should mean it's good enough for Myung's 'great evil', right?" Namid said.

"Yes!" Enric sounded exasperated. "But that's not the problem. The problem is that this scroll said that the sword will be needed again. For *exactly* the same purpose!"

Silence followed this announcement. Namid imagined they all thought the same thing....

Sesaisyd still lives.

We're supposed to defeat a god?

CHAPTER 16

Somewhat before midnight, they decided to stop. None of them could push themselves or the horses any further. They set up a rough camp in a small clearing and ate by the light of the orb. Although exhausted, no one seemed inclined to go to sleep right away.

"Are you going to let that burn the rest of the night?" Aahmes broke the silence after they ate and cleaned up.

"Huh? No, I guess not." Namid released the Power and the orb vanished. Although filtered by the trees, moonlight from all five moons lit the camp. "Anyway, it doesn't burn."

"Did that scroll say anything else?" Haeith said.

"Yes," Odasoro said. "It said the sword had not been allowed to remain intact because its magic could be too great a temptation for the unscrupulous. One piece is supposed to be in a city called Corentris, in Izrediuz. This piece is a black jewel...."

Namid masked her surprise at hearing of Corentris. She knew the place and wished otherwise.

"Corentris?" Cameni mused. "I've never heard of it."

"A jewel? As I remember, there's no place a missing jewel would go," Namid said to Enric.

"That's correct."

After a moment, Cameni said, "Just how many pieces is the sword in?"

"The scroll mentioned only the three," Enric said. "The hilt, blade, and this jewel."

"Corentris," Aahmes repeated. "I just realized why that name's familiar. Do you remember your Shadowers initiation Trial, Namid?"

"I'm not likely to forget it," Namid said. "You're thinking of the Star of Corentris?"

"What's that?" Cameni said.

"A statue," Aahmes said. "Roughly star-shaped. With a jewel in the center. But not a black jewel. The statue belonged to a mage."

"A mage?" Cameni repeated.

"Yes," Namid said. "My Trial was to obtain the statue from him."

"Steal," Aahmes said with a grin.

"Steal?" Cameni said. "From a mage?"

"There wasn't really much risk," Namid said.

"But there was supposed to be," Aahmes growled good-naturedly. "You weren't supposed to manage it, you know. Or at least not without getting caught."

"That's awful!" Cameni said.

Namid shrugged. "I accepted the challenge. It was my choice."

"And, of course," Aahmes continued, "at the time, I didn't know that Namid was a mage herself."

"Nor I, you," Namid said. "When I required you return it."

"I'm afraid I don't understand," Cameni said. "You required that he return the statue? I thought when thieves took valuable objects, they kept them."

Aahmes laughed. "Or they sell them, of course. But this statue could too easily be found by that mage, once he knew it was missing."

As they had talked, the dagger at Namid's throat had

grown warm, like it had in Kilaadi. Namid touched a fingertip to it and, at that same moment, a faint bell-like tone came from Enric's pack.

"Really?" Namid said.

"Again?" Aahmes said, as Enric dug the hilt of Akavos out of his pack. It glowed faintly and Namid's dagger grew warmer.

"Enric, would you bring me Akavos?" Namid said and pulled her tiny dagger from its sheath on the chain around her neck. The dagger also glowed faintly.

Enric complied and dropped the hilt into her hand. She held the dagger in her other hand.

"What's that sound?" Cameni said.

"This," Namid said. She brought Akavos and her dagger close together and Akavos hummed. The sound grew louder as she brought them even closer to each other. The others crowded around for a better look.

"Where did you get that dagger?" Enric said.

"From the Star of Corentris. When I first approached it, with every intention of grabbing the statue and running, it moved, leaning toward me. I don't know why, but I put out my hand and this little dagger dropped into it. Then the statue resumed its normal shape and stayed that way."

"So long...." Aahmes murmured.

Namid nodded, catching his meaning. The link to something that happened years earlier could not be by chance....

"What happens if you touch them one to the other?" Odasoro said.

"Let's see."

She touched the hilt with just the tip of the dagger and was blinded by a sudden flare of light as pain shot up her arms. She heard someone cry out. The light vanished as suddenly as it had appeared, and she was left sitting empty-handed, in complete darkness until her eyes adjusted.

"I'm all right," she reassured the others. She shook her hands and cursed under her breath. "That hurt!" She flexed her hands and decided there was no real damage. Certainly, they looked just fine. No burns at all.

"Wonderful idea…" Aahmes said.

"But look!" Cameni said.

On the ground in front of Namid, in a patch of silvery-red light from all the moons, lay the hilt and a beautifully etched blade. There was no sign of Namid's tiny dagger.

Odasoro leaned over and touched a finger to the hilt, then the blade. "They're quite cool."

"I think we've found the blade," Aahmes said. But when he tried to fit it to the hilt, the two pieces just fell apart again.

"Maybe," Enric said and retrieved the hilt.

"Probably," Odasoro said. "The scroll did say the jewel was also needed to make the sword complete."

"What more did this scroll say?" Haeith said.

"Nothing terribly coherent," Odasoro said. "Something about a prophecy, which, by the way, mentioned that six are needed to fulfill it."

"Six? Six people?" Cameni said.

"What do you think?" Aahmes said. "Six horses?"

"You never know," Namid said.

He glared at her. "Maybe 'asses' is the more appropriate word." He stood, ignoring Cameni's shocked expression. "I'm going to sleep."

"There's one good idea you've had," Namid said.

"I'll take the first watch," Haeith said.

"Wake me next," Enric said. He took the blade from Aahmes and looked it over, then held it out to Namid. "Will you keep this yet awhile?"

"Of course." Namid wiped it clean, wrapped it in an extra tunic, and tucked it in her pack.

Everyone but Haeith, of course, settled in to get some sleep. Namid wrapped up in her cloak and stretched out, but, as Enric's watch began several candle-marks later, she still lay awake. That surge of Power to the south that she had felt earlier disturbed her. And, unlike her companions, she knew about Corentris, more than she would have liked.

It was the true center of the Dark Priests' activities, a city they controlled absolutely. And it lay to the south.

Namid had been to that city, years before, as a prisoner. The memories still haunted her. She rolled over, telling herself that she needed sleep, and met Aahmes' gaze. They stared at each other in the light from the two moons still in the sky, then he used hand-talk to say they should talk. Namid considered refusing but knew she could not put this off forever. So, she walked out into the night with him. Enric did not notice them because they wanted it that way. They stopped out of earshot of the camp and she turned to Aahmes.

"What?"

He looked away from her and shifted his feet, then brushed his hair back from his face with one hand. "In the library, I poked around a little while the others figured out that scroll. In a back room, I found some dusty paintings of the Monarch and his wife and their family. One included their children, their sons and daughters, young, but nearly grown…." His voice trailed off and he gazed at Namid.

She tried to meet his gaze but felt too uncomfortable. Instead she stared off into the darkness and tried to decide what to say. She finally just started speaking, instead of trying to think it through.

"I've kept the secret long enough now that it's hard to speak of it. The Dark Priests came to Kilaadi about twelve, thirteen years ago. The Lady Royal, the Monarch's wife, was little involved in ruling, but the Monarch eagerly welcomed the Dark Priests' advice. Before too long, that led to their guidance, and eventual control. One of the first things the Dark Priests did was take every child of ten years or older to their city to 'teach' them…."

Namid closed her eyes and tried to banish the pictures her memory threw up of that time, images of cruelty and torture, terror and death. She felt Aahmes touch her arm. After a moment, she was able to continue.

"So many children never returned from that place, and

most who did were firmly under the Dark Priests' control. The royal family's older daughter died there. The younger daughter had learned a little about Power while she was in their city, and she had discovered that she had some command of it. She returned to Kilaadi somehow free of the Dark Priests' control and determined to try to free her parents and city. She failed. Many deaths and many weeks later, the Dark Priests compelled the Monarch to declare her a witch and banish her from the city. For some reason, they did not execute her...."

"A witch?" Aahmes said.

Namid nodded. "What they call someone they say uses the Power for ill, but they haven't actually caught the person doing it...."

Namid sighed. "Oh, what's the use of pretending.... After they exiled me, I came to Ilenii's temple and studied there about a year, learning to control and use the Power. Then I traveled to Rhadanthus, part of the way with a Prazny van. You pretty much know the story from there."

The silence stretched, and she finally looked at him. At his look of commiseration, her eyes burned with tears she tried to blink away.

"Are your parents still alive?" he said. "And what of your brothers?"

Namid shrugged. "I think my parents are still alive, but I don't know what state they're in, under the Dark Priests' control all this time. I suspect they're prisoners in their own citadel, at best. The Dark Priests rule the city, as you saw. My brothers had already left the city before the Dark Priests came. I've heard nothing about them."

"The troubadour knows you from that time?" Aahmes said.

"From before, although he knew what happened later. He used to perform at family banquets."

"So, you've been all alone."

Namid nodded. She took a deep breath as she remembered what had happened during that horrid time, remembered watching her sister die of the Dark Priests' treatment of her. And she let the tears fall, unable to stop them.

Aahmes tentatively extended a hand toward her. He made no other move, simply waited. She looked at his hand, then slowly up at his face. She placed a hesitant hand in his and stepped toward him. He pulled her close and folded her into the warmth of his cloak, wrapping his arms around her. Namid buried her face in his chest and felt safe, strangely, a feeling she realized she had lacked for far too long. They stood like that for a long time and eventually her sobs quieted. Aahmes loosened his clasp and she looked up at him but didn't back away.

He gave her a slight smile, unlike his usual teasing ones, and brushed one finger down her cheek, tracing the tear tracks.

"So, what's this audacious royal daughter's real name?"

Namid looked away, suddenly shy for some reason. "Tanyala Sainamid Shartov."

"That's quite a mouthful." She looked up to find him grinning.

"Blame her parents." Namid smiled wistfully. She leaned back, the better to see his face, and her smile widened into a grin. "Your turn. So, what was that fight in the Prazny van all about, anyway?"

Aahmes looked surprised at the change of subject, then chuckled. "I'd told the man's sister 'no'. She decided to take offense. And then *he* took offense."

Namid chuckled with him. "And *then* he made the mistake of engaging you in a knife fight. You should've seen your face when I chided you." She leaned her head against his chest again.

"I'd thought you would've left this quest of Enric's after we found Nazextas..." she said after a moment.

"I really *do* think that we're entangled in this somehow, something beyond Myung's word and being in the wrong place at the wrong time. Something to do with who we are.

Possibly even the Power we wield."

Namid nodded. "Yeah. We have this Power. We can help, do things others can't. So, shouldn't we? Someone needs to oppose these Dark Priests. I *know* they're evil, whether or not they're Myung's 'great evil'." She looked away, trying not to dwell on all the connections to her past.

"We should get back," she said after a time.

He nodded and released her, but she kept hold of his arm as they headed back to the camp.

"Aahmes."

"Yes?"

"What about you, O Heir-to-a-Chieftainship? Is Aahmes your name?"

"I'm not heir. While the chieftainship was in my clan, it wasn't even in my family line. Hasn't been for... I'm not sure how many winters. And what Lann said is true, no one who's clanless can be high chieftain."

Namid poked him in the ribs. "Quit dodging the question. Name?"

He sighed. "It's not my full name. Mine's as much of a mouthful as yours, perhaps more so. Aahmestharq Fathir Harunsson, of the clan Naalin."

"Oh! I don't know that I'll be able to remember all that," Namid teased.

"Remembering it is something you might want to do?"

She gave him the noncommittal answer, "Hmm." Then at a sudden thought, she giggled.

"What?" he said.

"Better not tell Cameni. She'd never get over knowing your name's longer than hers and so she isn't more important than you in her world!"

Aahmes chuckled. "We wouldn't want that."

They walked in silence for a time, then, "Aahmes?"

"I won't say a word to anyone of what you told me."

CHAPTER 17

It was nearly noon before they headed out again. Namid felt somewhat uneasy around Aahmes after the previous night's talk, and yet she caught herself watching him. The times he caught her looking at him, he gave her a slight smile. Enric provided the morning's excitement when he missed his money and gems. He accused Aahmes and that led to a shouting match. Everything was resolved when Cameni and Namid explained what they had done, and why. Then, of course, the gems and money all had to be sorted out again and returned to their proper owners. Aahmes watched this with a familiar glint in his eyes, but when he noticed Namid noticing his interest, he shrugged and started getting the horses ready.

"It would be nice if we could arrange to travel during the day and sleep at night," Cameni said as they plodded through the trees.

"This is day," Aahmes said. "And it looks to me like we're traveling."

She gave him a sour look.

"And what do you have against night travel?" he continued. "It can be much more interesting."

"Maybe. But it's definitely dangerous," Cameni said. "And when we stay in an inn again, we'll be quite obvious if we sleep during the day."

"Someone might think we're trying to hide our activities if we're only out and about at night," Enric said.

"We *are* trying to hide our activities," Aahmes pointed out. He moved his horse closer to Namid's. "By the way, you haven't told me what you did to the Dark Priests back at the inn."

"Nothing at all. I think the dagger did it." She tapped her dagger-less necklace. "It did have Power you know." Namid gave him an evil grin.

"Really? I never would have guessed." Aahmes matched her grin with one of his own.

"Since you're answering questions," Cameni said. "What about that man who knew you?"

"I told you, I once lived in Kilaadi."

"He called you 'lady'," Enric said.

"That's how he knew me."

"I think that you are, in fact, an important citizen of the city. Maybe a member of the nobility in hiding, pursued by evil," Cameni accused. "Not just a common thief."

"If you wish." Namid hoped they would drop the subject soon. She had no desire to share what she had told Aahmes, but they seemed determined to dig it out of her.

"What's wrong with being a common thief?" Aahmes said, coming to her rescue. "And what makes uncommon thieves? Are they the same as exceptional thieves?"

"I would expect better of even you," Cameni snapped. "You are, after all, a prince of your people!"

Aahmes laughed. "I'm no prince. And I'm thrown out, anyway. Remember? Maybe even under death sentence. And who looks for a prince among 'common thieves'?"

"Who indeed?" Cameni said and gave Namid a strange look.

"What's that for?" Namid said.

"You're not being overly cooperative in imparting

information," Cameni said.

"True," Namid agreed.

Cameni looked shocked. Aahmes chuckled.

"You're not getting anything from her that she doesn't want to give," he told Cameni. He winked at Namid. She gave him a cool look in return.

"If you're done pestering me, perhaps we could decide on our next course of action," Namid said.

"We're traveling south—" Cameni began.

"Incredible," Aahmes murmured.

"To find Corentris," Cameni continued and glared at him. "At the next city, I think we should get a map."

"That's a good idea," Namid said. "Except it won't help. Corentris isn't on any map. I do, however, know how to find it, given certain landmarks, the first of which is the roadway that runs south out of Kilaadi."

"Remember what happened the last time we tried to find a road," Aahmes murmured ominously, and was ignored.

"It should be to our right," Enric said.

"True," Namid said. "But if I remember correctly, some distance south of Kilaadi the road curves far to the east because of Lake Kundu."

"You do remember correctly," Odasoro assured her.

"So, we just keep going the direction we already are," Enric said.

"At least the forest is better than hot, empty grasslands," Aahmes said.

"I'm not sure I'd mind the hot," Cameni said. "Questing through snow doesn't sound appealing or wise."

"Who in this company has shown any sign of wisdom?" Aahmes said.

"There are wolves in this forest, aren't there?" Cameni said.

Namid nodded. "But they usually avoid people. They're shy creatures here."

"You say that like you know it personally," Aahmes observed.

"Have you ever shape-changed?"

Aahmes gave her an incredulous look. "Of course not. It's impossible."

"Is it? I think I liked the shapes of the wolf and the hawk best. Although I make a pretty large hawk."

Aahmes snorted.

"Truly?" Cameni breathed. "What's it like to fly?"

"Incredible. Words can't describe riding the wind high above the land. But if you start to think too much about what you're doing, you often find yourself not doing it anymore. I once saw someone revert to her normal shape in midair. Fortunately, she was only a little way above the ground at the time, so she only broke a few bones."

"Did you ever run into any trees?" Aahmes said.

"I thought you didn't believe it," Enric said.

"It makes a nice story," Aahmes said.

"I've not run into anything," Namid said. "But I did scare a few acolytes at Ilenii's temple once."

"You studied at Ilenii's temple?" Odasoro said.

"Yes. I thought you— What is it?"

"Do you remember which gods confronted Sesaisyd?"

Namid thought back to dim childhood memories of tales told by firelight. "Was Vlatas one of them?" she ventured.

"Yes. The scroll listed them all... Ilenii, Belaraketh, Vlatas, Narqir, Shiara, and Jelth. And it said that one day they would return to finish off the Dark Prince for good."

"They can't, according to Myung," Enric said.

"Shiara? Isn't she the god of troubadours?" Namid said.

"Yes," Odasoro said.

"My people honor the warrior god Narqir," Haeith said.

"And the training that I've had in the use of Power I received in the temple of Jelth, god of Healers," Cameni said.

"So, the gods are returning after a fashion," Enric said. "Through us."

"Which god do you follow?" Cameni asked Aahmes.

"The god of liars?"

"No," Aahmes said without rancor. "But you're close. Belaraketh."

"He's the trickster god," Odasoro said. "Patron of thieves. Also magic."

"And you follow Ilenii," Enric said to Namid. "What is she god of?"

"Mages."

"Secrets and mystery, too," Aahmes added.

"You're unlike any mage I've ever met," Cameni said.

"How many mages have you met?" Aahmes challenged.

"What were those pendants that woman handed you?" Namid asked Aahmes, hoping to avert yet another argument.

"I don't know." He dug them out of his pack and passed them around. "She gave me six of them. There's a faint sense of Power about them. Vile…."

Namid examined the pendant he gave her. It was smaller than her palm, circular, and made of dark green-gray metal. Unfamiliar runes covered both sides and it hung from a black silk cord. "The Power feels like that of the Dark Priests. Not unexpected…" she said. "But I can't tell what the Power's for or supposed to do."

"It's faint enough it's probably hard to sense even a short distance away," Aahmes said.

"Can anyone read the runes?" Enric said.

"No," Namid said, and the others shook their heads. "But I've seen something like them before," she continued. "I *think* they're used as passes to let people into otherwise restricted areas of the Dark Priests' temples."

"Terrific," Aahmes muttered.

"They might be useful," Odasoro said. He hung one around his neck and tucked it under his shirt. Haeith and Enric followed his example, while Cameni tucked hers away in her pack.

"I don't like it," Aahmes said as he studied his. "It's too convenient."

"What's the Shadowers' main rule for staying alive?" Namid asked him.

He smiled. "Use whatever comes your way."

"Right."

She returned his smile and tucked her pendant in a pouch secured to her belt. After a moment, Aahmes imitated her.

~ ~ ~

"I think the trees are thinning," Enric said many candle-marks later, near sunset.

"I hope that means we're close to the road," Cameni said.

Namid called a halt and dismounted. "If we are, we'll want to make sure it's empty before we come crashing out of the woods."

Aahmes grinned. "Wouldn't want to be taken for common thieves, would we?" He also dismounted.

"Right. We'll take a look ahead," Namid said. "Wait here."

Aahmes and Namid slipped into the underbrush and, after a short distance, lost sight of the others. They did not have far to go before they came to the edge of the forest. Some scrubby bushes extended from the trees to the edge of the road. Just beyond the road lay Lake Kundu, afire with the reflected sunset.

They had just turned to go back when Namid heard horses coming from the direction of Kilaadi. She glanced at Aahmes to see if he heard them too and he nodded. They both dropped to the ground and scrambled under the bushes, getting as close to the road as possible to see who rode with such haste.

Moments later a small company of Dark Priests reined in almost directly between them and the setting sun. Namid counted ten of them.

"Are you sure this is the right place?" one Dark Priest

said.

"This is where His Eminence said that man would meet us."

Another looked toward the sunset. "He'd better get here soon, then. We do have other duties, too."

"There he is," a fourth pointed down the road to a lone rider headed toward them.

When the rider came closer Namid stifled a groan. Aahmes' hand clamped around her wrist and she felt his tension through the contact. The lone rider was Staehw. He stopped a couple of paces away from the Dark Priests.

"How…" Namid murmured.

"When Nazextas moved, he must have been able to leave the city near here?" Aahmes whispered, with a shrug.

"Could be." Namid whispered back.

"There's something I need to know?" Staehw asked the Dark Priests.

"Yes. A holy relic stolen long ago has reappeared. It's now in the hands of thieves."

"This concerns me?"

"These thieves have escaped Kilaadi. If they know anything about what they carry, and His Eminence is certain they do, they'll be traveling south. You must find them."

"I have my own search."

"They coincide. She you seek is one of the thieves."

"In that case, gladly will I search for you."

"When you find them, they are to be brought before the Lord of Corentris."

"She's mine."

"They are to be brought before the Lord of Corentris," the Dark Priest stressed.

Staehw glared at the Dark Priest, then inclined his head. "As the Lord commands." He wheeled his horse about and galloped back the way he had come.

"It's a shame we must work with his ilk," one of the Dark Priests said.

"Not for much longer, though."

They turned their horses back toward Kilaadi and spurred them onward.

Aahmes and Namid stayed in their leafy hideout for a time, just to be certain the Dark Priests would not return. Even before the dust in the road had settled, however, Aahmes began cursing under his breath. He still kept hold of Namid's wrist, and she felt him shaking with some barely restrained emotion. Or perhaps that was her.

She leaned close and whispered, "What's upset you so? I'm the one they seem focused on."

"I despise that man. We're going to have to do something about him," he said, his voice as low as hers.

They slithered back out of their hiding place.

"How about go around him?"

"I'd prefer something more painful and permanent," he said as he finally released her wrist. He had gripped it so tightly, Namid wondered if he left the mark of his fingers through her armguard.

"I thought that's what you meant, but that'd delay us," Namid said, still in a quiet voice, after they returned to the relative safety of the trees.

"We can take the time," he said, speaking just as quietly.

"I'm not so sure."

When they rejoined the others, they told them about the meeting on the road, but said nothing about Aahmes' solution to the problem.

"Has anyone kept track of the days since Myung spoke with us?" Namid said when they had finished discussing what they had just witnessed.

"Why?" Cameni said.

"At that time, we had three days shy of three weeks to make Akavos whole, so it could oppose a great evil," Enric explained.

"Tomorrow will be the fifteenth day since Myung spoke with us," Odasoro said.

"Still about seven days away, then," Namid muttered.

"So?" Aahmes said.

"Didn't you hear the Dark Priests? They mentioned His Eminence and also the Lord of Corentris. His Eminence is the First High Priest, the highest rank. And the way they talked about the Lord made it sound like he's no longer spellbound…." Namid trailed off as she realized what she had been saying, realized that she had just opened herself to questions about things she had not wanted to discuss. Now she was probably going to have to. And probably should.

"His Eminence is the First High Priest of these Dark Priests?" Haeith said.

"Yes," Namid said.

"How do you know all this?" Cameni said, right on cue, suspicion clear in her tone.

Namid exchanged glances with Aahmes, who shrugged. She knew he had not said anything but was uncertain what he was telling her with his gesture. She sighed.

"Remember I said I was in Kilaadi when the Dark Priests gained control?" Namid said.

Cameni nodded.

Namid chose her next words with care. "I was also among those they took to their hidden stronghold. Corentris. I learned a lot about them during that time. They often spoke of their Lord of Corentris, who supposedly had been under a spell of the gods for centuries. Remember back in Kilaadi, we all heard that they *do* follow the Dark Prince. I'm thinking this spellbound Lord *is Sesaisyd*. When the moons are dark, Myung said, all this Wild Power will be available, but I think it might already be loose. The Power's felt strange recently. Turbulent. What if the spell has weakened, maybe enough for him to break it with this extra Power available? And from the way those Dark Priests back at the road were talking, it sounded like this Lord's already awake. But if he's the 'great evil', he wasn't supposed to be a threat until all five moons were dark. And that's still several days away."

"But now he might already be free," Odasoro said.

"Then we've failed," Cameni said.

"No!" Enric exclaimed. "We have these pendants. We can sneak into this city and find the jewel. Then, when Akavos is whole, we can destroy Sesaisyd!"

"You sound very sure of this," Aahmes said. "But don't forget, Myung also said we'd have to find the person to use Akavos."

"We will."

"But we still have to get past Staehw first," Namid pointed out.

"We could stay in the forest, travel parallel to the road and go by night," Haeith suggested.

"Except he would likely still notice us," Aahmes said. "You don't have any experience with Praznies, do you?"

"No. So then if they're as alert as you say, we will have some difficulty."

Aahmes smiled. "You could say that."

What Enric had said gave Namid an idea. "We'll travel on the road," she said. "This night, right past Staehw. As Dark Priests."

CHAPTER 18

About a candle-mark later, they inspected their disguises by the light of a small orb of Power. Aahmes had created a minimal glamour around everyone to help them look little like themselves and more like the people they pretended to be. And also to give their dark clothes that dark green-gray color seen in the Dark Priests' attire. All of which meant that they carried a faint hint of Power about them, but that was nothing unusual for Dark Priests.

To help the glamour, and so Aahmes could use the least amount of Power possible, they all made every possible mundane attempt to look their parts. Haeith, Aahmes, and Namid dressed to imitate Dark Priests and openly wore their pendants. Odasoro, Cameni, and Enric wore dark tunics and trousers they had recovered from their clansmate guards' gear. They darkened Enric's hair with dirt and used a subtle application of some of Cameni's cosmetics to modify all their features. Namid braided Cameni's hair, similar to her own, and both women tucked their hair down their backs under their clothes and pulled their hoods forward to help with concealment.

Aahmes and Namid would carry torches and use them

to help shadow their faces within their hoods. Namid thought they all looked convincing enough in dim light but doubted it all would hold up to serious scrutiny.

They wrapped all their valuables, the gems, Odasoro's lute, Namid's sword, and the hilt of Akavos, in extra clothing and concealed them all in packs underneath food and clothes. Haeith wore his own sword since it proved too unwieldy to hide or for any of the rest of them to carry convincingly. Aahmes and Namid carried their daggers, concealed but within reach. Cameni and Odasoro also carried daggers. Enric wore the sword his friend had given him, with its hilt and scabbard wrapped in cloth and leather strips so that it looked well worn. They reviewed their story one last time and headed for the road, having decided that Haeith would speak for them, if needed.

Once on the road, Aahmes lit the torches and Namid released the orb of light. The torches burned with a lot of smoke and fortunately, clouds hid the moons, which gave them plenty of shadows. They headed in the direction Staehw had gone earlier. Haeith hunched down in the saddle to try to disguise his size.

The road curved back around the southern edge of the lake and turned south again. At this bend, they saw Staehw's camp set off the road. It was much smaller than before, with no wagons. They continued as if to ride right past, but a sentry stopped them to tell them the van's leader wanted to speak with them. Haeith ungraciously agreed to speak with him. Namid thought his act of arrogance and self-importance was convincing. She studied the camp while they waited. On the far side of the camp, Namid saw a stripped tree branch had been driven into the ground as a pole. And they had tied someone to it. Inezha.

Namid glanced at Aahmes, but he had already seen. He nodded at Namid and spoke quietly with Haeith, who nodded.

After they had waited many long breaths-of-time, Staehw sauntered over to them.

"What is the meaning of this delay?" Haeith demanded, sounding irked by the wants of these lesser beings. He spoke with a quaver and in a pitch unlike his usual voice. Namid smiled to herself.

"My man merely wished to allow me the pleasure of offering my assistance in whatever endeavor you pursue," Staehw said. He looked them all over but gave no sign of recognition.

"Your assistance is not required in this matter, Prazny. We travel to Corentris."

They had argued about mentioning this, since they *were* going there, but no one thought of any other reasonable destination for Dark Priests traveling at night. And they decided it might be more suspicious if they did not declare a destination to a supposed ally.

"And what of these, Priest?" Staehw indicated Cameni, Odasoro, and Enric, dimly visible in the light from the smoky torches.

"They travel with us," Haeith said with the air of a man who impatiently stated the obvious. Then he changed the subject. "What's wrong in your camp?"

Staehw looked confused a moment, then recovered. "You mean the girl?" He waved a hand at Inezha. "She's been causing problems, acting against the will of the Dark Prince."

"What has she done specifically?"

"She's tried to counter me at every turn, even attempted to run off to find the thieves I seek. To warn them, no doubt."

"A serious offense," Haeith agreed in a solemn voice. "She will come with us. His Eminence will want to deal with her. You'll provide a horse, so she doesn't slow us."

Staehw looked unhappy about this but sent his man for the horse.

"My people will get the girl," Haeith said as the Prazny started toward Inezha.

Staehw stopped in his tracks. "Certainly."

So, Aahmes and Namid rode through the camp. They avoided the bonfire and stuck to the shadows as much as possible without being obvious about it. They reined in a pace away from Inezha and dismounted. Aahmes handed Namid his torch as they approached her. Inezha looked up and Namid cringed at the beating she had taken. Her face was badly bruised, her lower lip split, and both of her eyes were swollen almost shut. Through the rents in her clothes, Namid saw bloody cuts and scratches and more bruising.

"No," Inezha moaned.

Namid took a position right in front of her while Aahmes worked to untie her from the post.

"It's all right," Namid assured her in a quiet voice.

Inezha peered at her, her expression odd. "What—"

"Hush. We're getting you out of here."

"Do act like we're what you see, though," Aahmes advised. "Or we're all in trouble."

So Inezha objected and struggled weakly as they got her onto the horse Staehw's man brought over. Aahmes secured her hands to the saddle and ran a rope beneath the horse's belly tied to her ankles. He mounted his horse and held both torches as Namid mounted, then returned a torch to her. Staehw's man handed Namid the reins to Inezha's horse. Inezha continued to mutter protests.

When they rejoined the others, Staehw advised them to slap her if she got too noisy. Haeith thanked him coldly and started past.

Staehw seemed to look too long at Namid as she passed him, but she felt certain he saw nothing of her face within the hood.

They kept their pace steady for the next candle-mark or so, then stopped to untie Inezha. After quick introductions, Odasoro passed her some water and food while Cameni dug out a cloak for her.

Namid retrieved her sword from the pack, feeling much better to have it back. They resumed riding but kept the pace slow while Inezha ate.

"I thank you," she said when she had finished. "I'd not thought to see you again. You know they're looking for you?"

"We know," Namid said. "Are you up to a short gallop?"

"I think so. As long as it *is* short."

"Just long enough to put a good distance between us and Staehw," Namid said.

They gave the horses their heads and flew down the road. Several leagues further on, they slowed again. Ahead stood a closed gate set into a wooden wall that looked large enough to surround a large town. The road led to the gate.

"We'll camp off the road," Namid said. "Then enter the town tomorrow when they open the gate."

"I'd prefer to sleep in an inn," Cameni said.

"They won't let us in looking like this," Enric said.

"Particularly you," Aahmes said. "Your makeup's smeared."

Enric glared and Cameni giggled.

They turned off the road and rode well into the trees before stopping. There they shed their disguises, cleaned up as well as they could, and became again their usual selves. They also dug out some clothes that fit Inezha well enough, to replace her torn ones. And Cameni tended her injuries.

The torches had long since burned out, but they decided not to build a fire and risk being seen. So, it was a cold camp for them.

Namid took the first watch, which passed without incident, although the air turned noticeably colder before she woke Aahmes for his watch. After she was sure that he was awake, she wrapped up in her cloak, and some of the spare clothes for warmth, and fell asleep.

Namid was not surprised to wake stiff and cold. The rising sun sparkled in a light dusting of snow that covered the ground and coated those who had not risen yet. Inezha and Haeith were already walking the horses around to warm them. Inezha looked better for some sleep and Cameni's Healing. Odasoro, Cameni, and Enric started to stir as

Namid stood up.

"Where's Aahmes?" Namid asked Haeith.

"Checking if the town gate's open yet."

"And it is," Aahmes said as he returned.

"Then let's get going," Namid said, eager to find some place to get some hot food.

"Wait," Aahmes said. "I saw two Dark Priests enter the town just after the gate opened.

"Great," Namid murmured.

"So, I suggest we split up," Aahmes continued.

"Split up?" Cameni said. "Won't that leave us more vulnerable?"

"If we enter as two groups who seem to know nothing of each other," Odasoro said, "that might provide us a measure of protection and keep us inconspicuous. If they're looking for us, we can hope they're looking for one group of six people, not two or more smaller groups."

"Seven," Enric corrected him.

"Possibly," Odasoro allowed. "But we can hope that they don't know that Inezha's with us."

"Couldn't we just go around this town," Enric said.

"That might be the wiser course—" Aahmes said.

"No!" Cameni exclaimed. "I must have a hot meal."

"And we should probably get some better winter clothes. Cloaks, at least," Namid said. "The road could be bitterly cold without them."

"And the horses would do well with warmer blankets," Inezha spoke up.

"It's decided, then," Namid said. "So, how shall we divide up?"

"Haeith and Enric will stay with me," Cameni said.

"Fine with me," Aahmes said.

"I also," Odasoro said. "We would be appropriate companions for a young lady of quality out on a journey."

Cameni smiled.

"And I'm not," Aahmes murmured.

"Obviously. Me neither," Namid said, with a small smile.

"So, I'll go with you."

"You flatter me."

"You flatter yourself. I'm there to make sure you don't do something foolish." She gave him a big, ingenuous grin.

Cameni tried to stifle a laugh. Aahmes glared.

"I will travel with you also," Inezha said to Namid. "Perhaps as your guide, if anyone asks?"

Namid nodded. "And we'll meet outside the southern gate, out of sight down the road in, say, three candle-marks? Is that enough time to get what we need?"

At everyone's nods, it was settled. Cameni slipped off to change into clothes better suited to her role, a gown she had packed that was well-made without looking too rich. Then she and her companions in the venture headed for the town gate. Aahmes, Inezha, and Namid would wait a quarter candle-mark or so after the others entered before entering themselves.

In that time, Namid changed out of her normal gray clothes into some of the clansmates' clothes. They were large on her, but that let her keep another layer of clothes beneath to help stay warm. Then they backtracked to come out on the road out of sight of the gate.

The lone guard at the gate seemed preoccupied and barely glanced at them as they rode up.

"Your pardon," Inezha said and he focused on her.

"Yeah?"

"Can you tell us of a good place to get a hot meal?"

This time he looked at them closer, then shrugged. "Popular request this morning. Keep following the main road. 'Fore the center of town, there are a few good places."

"Our thanks."

Just as the guard had said, they found a few inns and taverns that looked promising. Outside one, their companions' horses stood tethered, so they picked a different one.

The innkeeper was a sour-faced man, inattentive, but he brought them food soon enough after they had shown him that they could pay. The few other customers occupied two tables on the far side of the room.

"Have you noticed anything strange here?" Aahmes said about halfway through the meal, keeping his voice quiet.

"You mean the people we've seen?" Namid murmured.

"They've all looked to have their minds elsewhere," Inezha said. "And they're almost rude."

"I've seen it before," Namid said.

"Those controlled by the Dark Priests?" Aahmes said.

"Yeah. But if we tread carefully, we should have no problems."

A shadow fell across their table. Looking up, Namid saw a familiar figure clothed in his silvery robe, face shadowed by a hood. Myung seated himself across from her.

"Might've known you'd show up again," Aahmes said.

"I wouldn't think this would be the best place to meet up," Namid said.

"I bring you grave warning," Myung said, ignoring their quips.

"The Lord of Corentris has broken free before he should have been able?" Namid said.

"You know that?"

"We figured it out. And we also know exactly what it is we're about."

"Oh?"

"The sword led us to an ancient scroll," Aahmes said.

"Ah. Even so. I'll still warn you, however. The Dark Priests and their Prince know what you're attempting to do. They hunt you. And you're running out of time."

"We know."

"Then why do you sit here calmly eating breakfast?" For the first time, Namid heard a trace of emotion in his voice. He sounded exasperated.

"We have to eat," Aahmes said.

"And we need certain supplies if we're to survive the weather in order to accomplish this 'quest'," Namid added.

Myung looked from one of them to the other. His gaze

touched briefly on Inezha, who gave him an inscrutable look in return. Neither of them said anything.

"It might still work," Myung muttered after several breaths-of-time.

He turned to Namid. "New obstacles lie between you and Corentris. At your current pace of travel, you will be unable to enter the city before the Wild Power is fully loosed. And then it will be too late."

"But, no doubt, you've come up with a fantastic solution to this problem," Aahmes said, sarcasm thick in his voice.

Myung turned toward him with a frown. "I have," he said. "There's a way of traveling faster…. It's known to a few northern clansmates."

Namid looked at Aahmes. "Why didn't you say anything about this? Do you know how it's done?"

"I know how it's *supposed* to be done," Aahmes said. "But I've never used it myself. It's not without its… difficulties."

"But can you do it?"

"He has no other choice," Myung said. "I must continue to lead them as much as possible away from you. The gods go with you. And remember the golden pipe." Then he was out the door and gone.

"Golden pipe?" Inezha said.

"Do you still have it?" Namid asked Aahmes.

"Of course. Shall we get going?"

Namid nodded and gulped the last of her meal. They left the payment on the table.

Outside, they untied their horses and led them down the street. Namid noticed their companions' horses still waited outside their inn.

"I wonder if we should warn them," Namid muttered.

"They should know to be careful," Aahmes said.

"You're right. And, of course, we don't even know them."

Aahmes chuckled.

It took them some time to find a shop that sold heavy-enough cloaks, but once they found it, they discovered that it also sold blankets, even horse blankets. Inezha opted to wait outside with the horses while Aahmes and Namid went inside.

The shopkeeper glared at them as they entered, then suddenly smiled. He was the first person in the town to offer them such a welcoming expression.

"Greetings and welcome to this humble shop," he said. "You're obviously new to our town. Please look around. Were you thinking of something in particular?"

One thing in his little speech caught Namid's attention.

"We're obviously new here?" she said.

The shopkeeper glanced around and lowered his voice. "Of course. Those of us left know how to tell others who are yet free. And I know everyone left free in this town."

"Free?" Aahmes said, his face expressionless.

"Yes, free. You know. Untainted by the Dark Priests."

"Ah."

"You're certainly uninhibited about saying such things," Namid said. "How do you know we're not spies for them?"

"A friend saw you speaking to the silver-robed priest," he said, as if that explained everything. Perhaps it did.

"We need warm cloaks," Aahmes said. "And blankets, some for the horses, too."

"Cloaks that are good for any rough travel and weather we might encounter," Namid said. "Unlike these lovelies." She made a sweeping gesture at the fancy velvet cloaks the shop displayed to advantage.

"Then you're not going to stay in town. Good." The shopkeeper disappeared into a back room and returned a moment later with his arms full. He piled everything onto a table and started to sort through it. After a few breaths-of-time, he held out several heavy woolen cloaks in a variety of bright colors.

"Just the things," he said. "Try these."

Namid smiled. "Beautiful. But we'd do better with something a bit less festive."

"Oh? Hmm, yes. Let's see. Ah, these should do." This

time he held up two heavy woolen cloaks, both dyed a blue so dark it almost looked black.

"Those are good," Aahmes said. "We'll need another like the shorter one."

While the two of them haggled over the price for the cloaks and blankets, Namid drifted over to the window. From there, she had a perfect view of Inezha, the horses, and a good portion of the street. And the person she saw approaching on horseback caused her to start in surprise: the all-to-familiar figure of Staehw.

Inezha saw him, too, for she bolted behind the horses to put them between her and the other Prazny. By happy chance, her horse—the one that had belonged to Staehw—already stood behind the other two horses.

Namid kept Staehw in sight and, to alert Aahmes, whistled the code the Shadowers used for danger. Aahmes joined her at the window, and the shopkeeper did likewise.

When Aahmes saw Staehw, he cursed under his breath.

"Ah, you're familiar with that one?" the shopkeeper said. "Seems he's their eyes and ears. A bad one, that."

As Staehw turned down a side street, Aahmes handed Namid a large bundle. "Horse blankets," he explained. He draped one of the cloaks around her shoulders. He already wore one. He carried a cloak for Inezha and more blankets.

The shopkeeper stopped them as they headed for the door. "One word, my friends. Travel any direction but south. It's said many Dark Priests travel south."

Aahmes and Namid just looked at each other.

"And a word for you," Aahmes said to the shopkeeper. "You've not seen us."

"Of course." The shopkeeper stood in the doorway and watched them as they gathered the horses.

"I thank you for the cloak," Inezha said and hugged it close as she mounted.

Namid nodded.

They headed for the south gate, avoiding the Dark Priests who roamed the town.

CHAPTER 19

Nearly all three candle-marks had passed by the time Namid, Inezha, and Aahmes left the town. A short distance past the town walls, the road curved, just enough to get them out of sight of the guards at the gate. Here they rode a short distance into the woods and settled down to wait unseen and watch the road.

They waited in silence. As the time for their companions to join them passed, they edged through the woods to a spot that would let them see the gate. Just a few moments later, they heard a commotion that direction. Three of their companions galloped out the gate, with the fourth horse, riderless. Aahmes slipped back through the woods, Namid assumed to intercept the rest of their group out of sight of the town. Inezha and Namid followed at a slower pace, with the horses.

When they joined them, they found Cameni crumpled on the ground, sobbing, while Aahmes held the horses and Haeith and Odasoro stood nearby, looking uncomfortable. Namid gave Aahmes a questioning look. He shrugged.

"What's happened?" Namid said. "Where's Enric?"

Cameni cried harder and hid her face in her hands.

"The Dark Priests have him," Haeith said.

"We were buying cloaks," Odasoro said. "And Enric had stopped in another shop. He would've been only a few breaths-of-time. Through the window of our shop, we saw them taking him away. There were too many of them…."

"It's my fault!" Cameni cried. "He wouldn't have been in that shop but for me!"

"Oh?" Aahmes invited her to explain, his eyes narrowed.

"It doesn't matter how it happened," Namid said. "It's not your fault. If you hadn't been in different shops, you might *all* have been taken. And then we wouldn't know what happened. Right?"

After a moment, Cameni nodded. She tried to stop crying.

"I suggest we move further from the town," Odasoro said as he handed Cameni a cloth to dry her eyes. "Then we can discuss what to do."

"There's really nothing to discuss," Namid said as they headed away from the town and further into the trees. "We have to free him."

"That'll be risky at best," Aahmes said.

"Afraid?" Namid taunted.

"Any smart person would be," he said. "But I'm going with you anyway."

"We all are!" Cameni said.

"No, my lady," Haeith objected. "This'll likely require special talents that I believe these two have. You do not. And the fewer people involved, the better chance they have to slip through unnoticed."

"You mean that I'd be in the way," Cameni said in an emotionless voice.

"You would," Aahmes said.

"Stay out of it," Namid hissed at him. He grinned.

"Do you presume to tell me what to do?" Cameni demanded of Haeith.

"Lady Cameni. You're not trained in any form of combat. Nor as a scout. The danger for you would be too great. I speak as the one who is supposed to protect you."

"And he speaks wisely," Odasoro said. "You'll remain with us?"

Cameni glared at each of them in turn and gave a sullen nod. Then she turned to Namid. "You *will* find him, won't you?"

"If anyone can, we will."

They all retreated even further into the trees where Aahmes and Namid prepared for their excursion. The others set up a camp and otherwise settled in to wait.

"They're likely to be alerted to something like this," Aahmes said as he stashed knives of diverse sizes about his person. "Particularly after they all charged out of there like a whole army was after them."

Namid dropped her cloak on her pack. It would only get in the way. "Yeah. It's not going to be easy."

Aahmes handed her a couple of knives to add to her collection, and also a small packet. Inside the packet, Namid found a set of lockpicks. She looked up at him in surprise.

"Figured you'd lost yours back in that inn fire," he said.

She nodded. "Thanks." She tucked them into one of the hidden pockets in her boot.

He gave a slight shrug and pulled a coiled rope out of his pack. He also shed his cloak and now wore all gray as Namid did, the usual garb of a Shadower. "Ready?"

Namid grabbed her sword. "Yes… no, wait." She walked over to Odasoro, who was working to get a small fire started. She heard Aahmes following her. Namid handed the sheathed sword to Odasoro, who gave her a questioning look.

"Just hold this for me," Namid said. "And if something happens—"

"I'll hold it for your return," he interrupted and gave her a seated bow.

"Right," Namid said.

"Let's go," Aahmes said.

They slipped away without alerting the others. Even

Inezha did not seem to notice them go. They hurried back through the trees and avoided piles of dried leaves as much as possible. They stopped again near the spot from which they had first looked out on the gate and watched the activity, while staying well back in the shadows. The guards now looked more alert and spoke with everyone going in or out.

Aahmes touched Namid's arm to get her attention. *Daytime is bad for this*, he told her by hand-talk.

She shrugged. *No choice*, she answered the same way. *Time is probably short.*

He nodded. *Over the wall?*

Namid nodded and followed him away from the busy gate and around the wall to the west. She studied the wall as well as she could while on the move. She did not see anyone on top of it. The wall was wood and crudely built. Perhaps they had nowhere on top for patrols. As she and Aahmes moved further away from the gate, the trees grew closer and closer to the wall until, standing beneath them, they could almost touch it. At this point, Aahmes stopped.

"Let's try a tree and see if we can save the rope," he whispered and jumped to catch a low-hanging branch. He pulled himself up and climbed higher, toward a branch that overhung the wall. Namid followed, moving slower. She had not climbed trees since she was much younger. So, it took her a while to catch up to where he perched, looking over the wall. He said nothing when she joined him. She followed his gaze.

This part of the town held houses, small and unimportant to the powers in the town. The buildings were shabby at best, and in some cases falling apart. But she and Aahmes seemed to be in luck… no one around.

After several breaths-of-time of watching, Aahmes crawled out along the branch and dropped into the town on the other side of the wall. Namid stretched out on the branch so she could just see him and waited.

He stayed poised in a crouch for several long breaths-of-time, probably listening. Then he motioned her forward.

Namid joined him on the ground and they glided into the shadows of the buildings. Then they looked around.

The buildings looked no better up close, and a foul odor permeated the air. Namid tried to breathe through her mouth as much as possible, but then she tasted it.

Sometimes you just can't win, she thought.

Where now? Aahmes asked by hand-talk.

Center of town? Namid responded. *Where the center of power is?*

He shrugged. *In towns I know, yes…. Remember, I'm not from nearby.*

Namid grinned. *Right. Let's check the center of town.*

They stuck to back alleys and shadows and headed toward the town's center. As they got closer, the number of people around increased and Namid noticed that many of them were Dark Priests. The Dark Priests did not seem to be looking for anyone, but just the fact that they wandered around was cause for concern. Aahmes and Namid eventually reached an area that looked like a market, bustling with the last of the harvest coming in. They stopped at the edge.

"Ideas?" Aahmes said.

"Go shopping?" Namid grinned.

Aahmes gave her a strange look, studied the people in the market for a few breaths-of-time, then looked back at her. "Who knows. Maybe the tale-bearers have already heard something." He moved away from the market, pulling her with him.

"We match too well. That a Shadower tunic?"

Namid nodded, knowing what he was saying. They both stripped off their overtunics and turned them inside out. All Shadower overtunics were gray on one side and a different color on the reverse, for those times when a quick change was needed. Namid's was blue and Aahmes' was a deep green. Namid smiled to herself at this proof that Aahmes had gotten Baron Zelimir's people to recreate his Shadower clothes. Namid slipped her overtunic back on over her undertunic and shirt and waited while Aahmes slipped his on and rolled up the sleeves of his shirt, presumably so that they looked even less alike. While Namid unbraided her hair and tousled it so it hid a good portion of her face, Aahmes grabbed some dirt from a dry patch on the ground and rubbed it into his trousers to change their gray to a faded brown.

He took her arm. "Let's go."

They wandered around the marketplace, separately but near each other, and pretended to look at the wares for sale while listening to conversations. After close to a candle-mark of catching bits and pieces of talk, Aahmes bought some food and steered Namid to a quiet corner to sit.

"Not much talk of use…" he said and bit into an apple.

"I heard talk of a ruckus with the Dark Priests earlier. Probably Enric," Namid said.

"Someone mentioned their temple on the east side."

"Could be he's there."

"Have to try it."

So, they left the market and walked toward the east side of town, changing back into their gray tunics on the way. Here the buildings were in much better shape and the carvings on pillars and curtains in windows indicated some wealth. Namid felt certain they looked out of place, but no one seemed to care. They had no trouble telling where the temple sat. Few ordinary people lingered in that area and far too many Dark Priests. The temple itself was small for such a structure. It looked like it might have once been someone's house.

They stayed among the surrounding buildings and circled the temple, examining it from all sides. It had two entrances that Namid saw, and a large number of windows, the latter seemed covered with dark drapes. Namid counted thirteen Dark Priests walking around outside. They looked more alert than those in the rest of the town. And many of these Dark Priests also carried swords beneath their cloaks.

After they had circled the building, Aahmes and Namid slipped away and stopped at a shop window, acting as if they were examining the goods on display.

"Doesn't look good for a closer look," Namid whispered.

"No, but I think he's there."

"Oh?"

"Open yourself up a little to the Power and see what you feel."

Namid glanced at him to see if he was serious with so many Dark Priests so near. He nodded, so she let her thoughts go still and tentatively opened herself to the Power. She worked to keep her touch passive to avoid alerting anyone.

Aahmes was right. Namid felt Akavos' Power from inside the temple. And she felt a fainter hint of Akavos' Power, like an echo, separate from the Power that clearly came from the hilt. Although she had sensed no Power about Enric when they first met, Namid felt certain that echo must be him. A little of Akavos' Power seemed to have become part of him and she wondered if the Wild Power had something to do with it. She had never before been able to find a specific non-Powered person through the Power, so she hoped her assumption about the echo was true. That meant the Dark Priests had both him and the hilt.

Namid pulled away, careful to avoid leaving any ripples of Power to betray her presence. She nodded at Aahmes.

"So now what?" he said.

"We *could* try to get in," Namid said.

"Hmm. Unlikely that would end well. There's no telling how many Dark Priests are inside. I felt their Power in there but couldn't tell their numbers. I'd guess at least as many as we see outside."

"Yeah. I didn't really think we could. Ideas?"

He clasped his hands behind his back and stared down at his boots for several breaths-of-time, then shrugged. "Nothing that won't get us caught or worse. You know these Dark Priests better than I. What will they do with him?"

"They'll definitely question him…."

"I thought so. Will they keep him here?"

"I doubt it. They'll take him to their city. They have better 'facilities' for questioning people there."

Aahmes frowned. "I can imagine. So, his life is safe for a while, then."

"Relatively, but—"

Aahmes shushed her and pulled her into an alley. Then she heard what had alerted him: the sound of several people approaching from the direction of the temple.

Aahmes and Namid pressed back against the wall in the shadows as five Dark Priests walked down the street.

"Word is he was one of those with the witch in Kilaadi," one of them said as they passed.

"Maybe," another said. "But it's certain he'll tell us everything after they work on him in Corentris."

"And if she's here now, we'll find her," a third said.

Namid looked up at Aahmes and caught a strange expression on his face, a mix of determination and protectiveness. When he noticed her looking at him, his expression became merely grim. "That's it then," he said. "We have to get out of here."

CHAPTER 20

Their journey back mirrored their path in, except Namid and Aahmes progressed even more cautiously, if that was possible. As a result, it took almost twice as long to get back to the tree outside the wall as it had taken them on their way in.

They rejoined the others, both exhausted from the several candle-marks of close calls and hide-and-seek with a large number of Dark Priests.

"Well?" Cameni demanded. She glared at Aahmes first, then Namid, as they both slumped to the ground.

"We found him," Aahmes said.

"But we couldn't get to him," Namid added. "They're holding him in their temple. For now. My guess is they sensed the presence of Akavos in the town." Namid paused, wishing she did not have to say the rest.

"They're going to take him to Corentris," she said after a moment.

Cameni gasped and turned pale. Odasoro supported her as she sank down next to a tree.

"We have to rescue him!" Cameni said. "No matter how many of them there are!"

"That'd be foolish," Aahmes said. "As well as ineffectual. And would probably just get all of us killed, him included."

"But we can't just leave him with them. And he had the sword, so now it's in their hands, too!"

"Not quite," Namid said. "Enric asked me to keep the blade. So, they have only the hilt."

"That jewel the scroll spoke of is in Corentris," Odasoro pointed out.

"But they might have no better idea of its exact location than we do," Namid said.

"But what if they change their minds somewhere along the way?" Cameni demanded. "And decide to kill him, instead?"

Namid shook her head. "That won't happen."

Cameni still looked skeptical, so Namid reluctantly explained further. "Remember, I know something of their ways. They need him alive to question him about the rest of us. And that's a remarkably good reason to get there as fast as we can." Here she looked at Aahmes.

"Question?" Cameni echoed.

"Use your imagination," Aahmes said. Then to Namid, "I need rest before I can channel the Power for that swift travel."

"How long?"

"I think until dark. It'll be easier to travel at night, anyway. Some hazards are decreased."

"What is this?" Odasoro said.

"A way of traveling faster," Namid said. "Depending on how the Dark Priests choose to send Enric to Corentris, it might even get us there before them."

"They could get him there faster?" Aahmes said.

Namid nodded. "Possibly. I don't know how they do it, but I do know that they can move people in haste, if they want."

"What good will getting there first do us or Enric?" Cameni mumbled.

"Maybe no good!" Namid snapped, irritated with her. "But we might be able to save him from being subjected to the more unique techniques they employ to get information. I assume you'd consider that desirable?"

Cameni stared at Namid in surprise. Namid wondered if it was because of what she had said, or the rather callous way she had said it.

"I... I didn't realize," Cameni stammered.

"Now you do," Aahmes said. "The rest of you might also want to get what rest you can, since I can make no guarantees of survival if you fall asleep later and fall off your horse." With that cheerful announcement, he wrapped himself in his cloak and, to all appearances, fell asleep.

After she checked the horses, Inezha followed his example. Cameni lay wrapped in her cloak, but stared at nothing for a long while before her eyes fluttered shut. Haeith and Namid sat and listened to Odasoro softly play his lute. Namid nibbled some food and Haeith worked on his sword. Namid thought, too, that all three of them also kept at least half their attention on their surroundings in case the Dark Priests should come upon them there.

After a while, Namid also drifted off. The next thing she noticed was a sore back from the tree she leaned against and a stiffness in her muscles. She stood, stretched, and looked over her companions. Haeith still sat on watch, but all the others slept, except for Aahmes, who sat tailor style, with his hands resting on his knees and his eyes unfocused. Namid saw a faint glow surrounding him that was unrelated to the fading sunset.

Namid nibbled some more food from their supplies as she checked on the horses and surveyed the road, finding the first half-dozing and the second empty. When she returned to the camp, the others were stirring.

Everyone stretched out the stiffness from their short naps and ate a little as Namid had, except Aahmes, who did not move. The rest of them saddled the horses and made all the other preparations for travel. Mindful of Aahmes' comment about falling off the horses, Namid made certain that all their gear was securely fastened. Then they waited on Aahmes.

"How long will he sit thus?" Inezha said after many long breaths-of-time of waiting.

"I shouldn't think much longer," Namid said. "It won't get much darker." Then she felt a sudden gathering of a great amount of Power, including some from her since she had not been prepared to shield herself. As she steadied herself with a hand on a nearby tree, she grumbled to herself that he might have warned her. Then she heard his amused chuckle.

"Next time I will," he said.

"How—"

"I have talents you are unaware of," he said. "However, keeping a light while speeding our travel is not something I should try at this time, so if you would...."

From her own reserve of Power, Namid created a small, dim orb of light.

"Enough?" she said.

"Should be," he said. "Now we just need to get back to the road and mount up. I'll take care of the rest."

"Wonderful," Cameni murmured, sounding skeptical.

Namid glanced at Aahmes to see if he had noticed Cameni's imitation of his normal skepticism, but he seemed oblivious. Or maybe he just chose to ignore it.

He met Namid's gaze and gave her a tight smile but said nothing. Namid saw that his eyes were nearly all pupil. She saw little of their usual gray-brown color. For the Power to have affected him so, he must be holding onto a lot of it. Namid hurried the others to the road, worried about straining his limits if they delayed too long.

Once they left the trees and mounted again, Aahmes instructed them to walk the horses down the road and stay close to him. He stretched one arm out to the side, fingers spread wide, and spoke some words in an unknown language. For a moment nothing happened, although it seemed to Namid that they all held their breath.

Then something yanked at the world around them and bent it out of shape and focus. Everything flipped over and spun around, and a moment of nausea assaulted her. They were left with a blur of gray fog all about them, at the edge of the light cast by Namid's orb. The night was still, with no sounds at all, not even the horses' hooves or anyone's breathing. Then Namid's horse snorted.

"We can have as much light as we want now," Aahmes said, his voice echoing slightly.

Namid increased the light and noticed that it failed to penetrate the fog that surrounded them.

"You can still talk while maintaining this?" Haeith said, gesturing at the fog-blur.

"Some," Aahmes said. "But I still must concentrate."

"The horses dislike this," Inezha said as she tried to calm her mount, which kept mincing away from the rest of them.

"Stay close," Aahmes warned. "The area affected is necessarily small."

Namid noticed then, as her horse also shied, that the horses still moved at a walk. This was certainly an extraordinary use of Power.

"How long can you keep this up?" Namid said.

"Some candle-marks, I think," Aahmes said. "Setting it up is hardest. Holding it is easier. So far."

"Why is it easier to travel this way at night?" Odasoro said.

"Empty road, or nearly. Fewer things to avoid."

They traveled in silence for a long while. The horses seemed to grow accustomed to this way of traveling, although they rolled their eyes from time to time. Finally, Odasoro took out his lute.

"Since the horses don't seem to require much guidance," he answered Namid's questioning look.

"Can anyone hear us as we pass?" Cameni said.

"No," Aahmes said.

"Good," Odasoro said, and launched into a popular

tavern song. Cameni looked shocked when Haeith joined in but seemed resigned when Inezha and Namid did also. Fortunately for her refined sensitivities, the song was one of the least ribald ones. Namid knew Odasoro also knew some of the other kind.

After he finished that song, Odasoro started a lengthy ballad that had been known to go on for candle-marks at some feasts. It told the mixed-up tale of a baker who fell in love, somehow, with a dragon, and what happened to them after. They all listened and laughed at the lovers' imaginative, bumbling attempts to remain together.

And so, the night passed.

Several candle-marks later, while Odasoro played only idle snatches of songs and the rest of them nodded with fatigue, Aahmes warned them to keep a firm rein on their mounts. They would be stopping soon.

"But it's still dark," Cameni said.

"Not much longer," Aahmes said. "And we're all tired. Also, we might want concealment before dawn. Reason enough?"

"I suppose," Cameni said.

Aahmes glanced at Namid, and she dimmed the light. The world spun, and they found themselves in the real night again.

The horses took the change rather well, shying only a little, probably too tired to do much else. They did stop walking, however.

By the dim light, Namid saw that they had left the forest behind them. They now stood amid low grass-covered hills, and still on a road. The same one, she hoped. She saw the faintest glow to the east, just below a layer of clouds.

"Where are we?" Cameni said.

"East and a little south of Rhadanthus," Aahmes said.

Now Namid was sure they were still on the same road, the right one.

"It would have taken us days to get this far, and that's if we pushed the horses to their limits!" Inezha said.

"Impressive," Namid said to Aahmes. "And the first time, too."

"The first time?" Cameni repeated. "You've never done that before? Why didn't you inform us?"

"It would've served no purpose," Namid answered for Aahmes. "Besides—"

"Shhh," Inezha broke in. "I hear horses."

"Just what we need," Namid muttered. She released the orb, which plunged them into near darkness. After her eyes adjusted to the little moonlight that seeped through the clouds, she saw well enough.

"Let's at least get off the road," she whispered. "They might pass us in the dark. Follow me."

"I can't even see you," Cameni hissed.

"I've got her reins," Aahmes said. "Go."

Namid led them off into the tall grass along the side of the road, which rustled as they passed. She hoped the sound was inaudible more than a pace or two away. She stopped them in the largest clump of taller grass that she found.

"Don't go any further," a voice called out of the night.

CHAPTER 21

Namid whipped around. Dark figures came toward them from all directions, people on horseback. Namid guessed that some use of Power had made the voice sound so close. She let one of her stilettos drop into her hand.

"You'll all be handin' over your weapons, now," a man's voice said as the figures approached to within a couple of paces of their position.

"I know that voice," Aahmes said.

Namid also knew it and had not thought to hear it again. "Thes?"

After a moment of silence, one of the strangers lit a torch and rode closer.

"Namid? Is it really you?"

In the flickering torchlight, Namid saw it was indeed her old friend, somehow alive. She sheathed her stiletto and urged her horse closer to Thes, heedless of the weapons leveled at them. And she embarrassed him by hugging him while their horses danced around each other. When she felt him start to lose his seat, she let go.

"Thes! I can't believe it! We'd thought you dead."

"Now m'dear," he said and waved his companions back.

"You know I'm harder t' kill than that! But we'd thought the same o' you…."

"This the one you was tellin' us about?" one of the other men said.

"Aye, this is Namid."

"We'll take them to the camp with us, then. Come on."

Thes leaned down to snuff out the torch in a patch of bare earth, then rode next to Namid.

"Where are we going?" Cameni said, and was ignored.

Namid had some questions of her own. "What are you doing here? And how'd you find us?" she asked Thes. "We didn't make that much noise."

He chuckled. "True enough. But we've banded with someone who's got some o' that magic—"

"Thes…" another man said, the warning clear in his voice.

"I hear you. Not t' be spoken of. Don't worry, you'll like Wesh."

"The leader of these men?" Namid said.

"Aye. And myself now."

"How'd you escape? We waited for you…."

"We waited for *you*, just outside the North Gate, like you said," Thes said. "Those o' us that made it." He laid a hand on Namid's arm. "We never saw Dar again…."

Namid looked away. "We did. He's the reason we escaped. But he didn't make it. And we waited near the North Gate…." She looked at Thes.

He held up a hand. "I swear. We were there. Don't see how we all missed each other." He peered at her. "You said 'we'?"

"Yes. Aahmes is still with me."

Thes glanced around at Namid's companions, and spotted Aahmes toward the back of the group. "Are you crazy?"

Namid laughed. "Probably. Did all of the others escape, too?"

"Most o' the Shadowers made it. But now we're with

233

Wesh." He sounded apologetic.

"I'm glad you all found a new place for yourselves." Namid laid a hand on his arm to keep him from interrupting. "I've got something else I'm doing right now. And when it's done… I don't know that I'll return to Rhadanthus. Thes, all I want is to go my way. Please don't delay us."

Thes studied her for several breaths-of-time.

"You're different somehow," he said. "You'll have t' see Wesh. But I'll try t' get him to send you on your way without delay."

"Thank you."

"Interesting thing," Thes said as they rode. "Wesh asked quite a bit about you when he first found us outside Rhadanthus." He gave Namid a sidelong look. "No one told him much, just about you in the Shadowers."

"Me specifically? Not just leaders in the Shadowers?"

"Aye. For some reason, I didn't think much o' it then, but now it seems odd. Thought you should know."

The rest of the ride passed in silence, except for some murmuring from their escorts. Perhaps as much as half a candle-mark later, they descended into a large depression below a ring of low hills. Within, a camp was set up, with one low fire burning in its center. Even for that early time of day, the camp bustled with activity.

Their escort stopped them at the camp's edge and one man rode to the largest tent. Inezha stretched elaborately while they waited, attracting the attention of many of the men of their escort. Namid smiled to herself. Inezha winked at her in the gray light. Namid yawned suddenly, earning a smile from her and an amused glance from Thes. While they still waited, several former Shadowers came up to greet Namid. Many long breaths-of-time passed before the man returned from the tent.

"He wants to see them all," he told the escorts.

"Go on," Thes urged Namid. "We'll see t' the horses." Namid got the impression that, while he made it sound like an offer, they had no choice in the matter.

So, they dismounted. Before she left her horse in Thes' care, Namid grabbed the pack that contained the blade of Akavos. They followed the man toward the tent, Cameni holding tightly to Odasoro's arm. Whether for support or reassurance, Namid could not tell.

"Thes seems changed," Aahmes said.

"Because he didn't insult you?" Namid said. "Maybe he's saving it for later."

"If we have a later," he murmured.

At the tent, one of their escorts held aside a flap for them to enter but did not follow them inside. A single candle in an elaborate candlestick lit the tent's interior. The candlestick looked to be gold. Expensive rugs covered the ground, and a large one hung before them, partitioning off the back part of the tent.

"Exquisite," Cameni said, examining a filigree necklace that she found on a small table to the right of the entrance.

"My thanks, my dear," said the man who came around the hanging rug from the hidden part of the tent. He stood only a little shorter than Haeith, but was thinner, with jutting brows, lightly tanned skin, and dark hair and eyes. He was dressed all in black. Namid felt she had seen him somewhere before.

He looked them all over with mild interest. Namid noticed he paid no special attention to how closely she and Aahmes resembled each other. Unusual for someone just meeting them.

"You must be Wesh," Cameni said.

"I am. And you are...."

"Cameni," she said, for once not proclaiming her noble status. "These are my companions, Haeith, Odasoro, Inezha, Aahmes, and Namid."

Namid studied Wesh during Cameni's introductions, trying to figure out why he seemed so familiar, so she saw his sudden interest when he heard Aahmes' name.

"Aahmes?"

"Have we met?"

Wesh lit a pipe that he picked up from another table, watching Aahmes all the while. "I've heard the name before," he said.

He studied each of them in turn, but when he came to Namid, his eyes narrowed, and speculation crossed his features. And Namid caught her breath as she remembered where she had seen him before.

"You're Namid?" he asked her and held her gaze.

"Yes. But your name's not Wesh," Namid said.

He gave her an enigmatic smile, bowed and looked at her companions. "Perhaps you all might be more familiar with me under the name of Chendrukhar."

Aahmes cursed under his breath, but the others gave no indication of recognition.

"You mean you haven't told them of your daring?" Chendrukhar asked Namid.

"I didn't mention your name," Namid said. Then to the others, "Remember the story of my Trial and the Star of Corentris? This man is the mage who owned it."

Cameni gasped and shrank away. The men looked worried but held their places. Inezha looked confused.

"I'll tell you about it later," Aahmes told her.

"And you used this man's name," the mage said to Namid.

"Well, it *was* his idea to steal the statue," Namid said, with a grin for Aahmes.

The mage turned hard eyes on Aahmes, who met his gaze without hesitation. After a few breaths-of-time, Chendrukhar smiled.

"Yet another one with Power," he said. "Well, I assure you that I consider the theft of my statue a thing of the past, unworthy of further mention. But you might have Aahmes here tell you sometime how he returned it to me."

Namid gave Aahmes a questioning look, and he looked almost sheepish.

"Later," he muttered.

"If you know he returned it, you must have figured out that a Shadower stole it in the first place," Namid said. "But you didn't come after us—"

"Namid…" Aahmes said, warning clear in his tone.

Chendrukhar gave them a slight smile. "Of course I knew it had to have been a Shadower. No others in the city would have been capable of the theft. And I did come after the Shadowers. But your leader met with me, and we reached an agreement to stay out of each other's business from then on. Dar even became a friend."

Aahmes and Namid exchanged glances. "You know what happened to Dar and Rhadanthus?" Aahmes said.

Sadness crossed Chendrukhar's face as he nodded and looked down. "At least I was able to save most of his people…."

After a moment, he looked back at them. "Enough of that sort of talk. I trust you are not visiting me for the same reason as the last visit." He gave Namid a pointed look.

"We would not have been here at all, except your people brought us," Namid said.

"Ah, yes. There is that small factor." He puffed on his pipe, then set it aside. "So, you're Namid…. One of Dar's Seconds. My compliments on your Shadowers."

"Thank you. Are we free to leave?"

"Perhaps a bit of rest first? All of you look like you could use it."

"Why should we rest here?" Aahmes said. "What do you want from us?"

The mage shook his head in mock sorrow. "What a low opinion you have of me," he lamented.

"You were part of life in Rhadanthus," Aahmes said, like that explained it. Which it did, when Namid thought about it.

"True. I admit to some interest in what you are doing here. And in how you got so close before we discovered you."

Namid decided to see what he would do with an

enigmatic bit of information. "Perhaps you'd share what you know about the origin of your famous statue?"

He gave her a thoughtful look. "You would seek out Corentris? Why? Do you hope to find a match for the Star? And what makes you think Corentris lies in this direction?"

Namid kept her expression blank at his probing questions.

Aahmes shrugged. "It would be nice to have a statue that we could keep."

"Or sell," Namid added, hoping to maintain their Shadower facade in the mage's eyes.

Chendrukhar chuckled.

"It's all well and good to talk of keeping and selling statues we don't even have," Cameni said. "But now we're very tired.... So, if you'll allow us that rest you offered...."

"Of course, my dear. We can talk later. You ladies are welcome to the use of my tent if you wish."

"That is an offer I feel we can't refuse," Namid said, ignoring the strange look Aahmes gave her. "You are most kind."

He inclined his head and opened the flap for the men.

"I'll have someone bring you the rest of your things," he told them and left.

"I don't trust him," Cameni said after he had gone.

"Good," Namid said and peered into the second room. It was furnished with plush cushions atop a thick rug that covered the ground. "But then why did you accept his offer to rest here?"

"We need to rest, so why not take advantage of the opportunity offered here? And I'm tired of camping." Cameni peered around Namid into the other half of the tent. "And he does know how to furnish a tent."

"You realize of course that all this was probably stolen," Namid said. She sat on a large red cushion and tucked her pack beneath her feet. The cushion was comfortable and a welcome change from the ground.

"Stolen? More of your type of people, no doubt."

Namid shrugged. "The type of people I've dealt with recently, anyway."

Someone called Namid's name from outside the tent.

"That'll be the rest of our packs."

"I'll get them," Inezha volunteered and disappeared beyond the rug. When she returned, she dropped their things on a smallish cushion and crawled over several others to a large purple one near the wall of the tent and curled up on it. Namid and Cameni both watched her.

"None of her injuries was too bad, was it?" Namid said.

"No," Cameni said. "And I Healed those she had. Maybe she's just catching up. I doubt she slept well in Staehw's camp."

"True enough," Namid said.

"Do you think we'll be safe enough in here?"

Namid shrugged. "I'll arrange it so no one can enter without waking us." Namid placed a light touch of Power around the tent so she would know of anyone trying to enter.

"Good. Then I'll follow Inezha's example." Cameni made her way to a large pink cushion and settled down on it. "How I hate riding so much."

"Hmm, yes." Namid leaned back on her cushion, but despite her yawns earlier, sleep eluded her. Something that had nagged at the edges of her thoughts finally came forward and refused to be ignored. What was Chendrukhar doing out here waylaying random travelers? He did not seem the type to turn to such banditry, or to lead such a band. He was knowledgeable and experienced in the use of his Power. He shouldn't need to resort to theft to advance himself or to survive.

And this seemingly chance meeting with the rest of the Shadowers was just one coincidence too many for her. This whole quest seemed to be a string of improbable predicaments and events, like someone was guiding it all, as Aahmes had surmised. But who? And why?

And how had she and the Shadowers missed each other

outside Rhadanthus? Could some glamour have kept them from seeing each other? If so, again why?

So far, they had merely reacted to events, without time to stop, to think things through. Perhaps the time had come to act, not react. But what action to take? And how to be sure that it had not already been anticipated?

These thoughts kept Namid awake long after her companions drifted off, whirling through her mind, bringing up images of strange happenings since meeting Enric. She realized she was not going to sleep anytime soon so she spent some time searching the tent. She found plenty of treasure, but nothing that seemed important or related to their journey. And no papers or books, either. Nothing that might have useful information. One brooch tempted her larcenous side, but she resisted and instead went outside.

She saw some activity still in the camp, but less than earlier. Namid suspected many had gone to wait for unsuspecting travelers, a common activity for outlaw bands such as this one. She spotted Chendrukhar on the far side of the camp, striding about in his black cloak. She watched him for several breaths-of-time before he noticed her.

As he approached her, Namid wondered why she was not doing the sensible thing and resting, like her companions. Even if she only managed to doze, that would still help. But she felt too restless to sleep. She realized the restlessness had been building for some time, separate from all the questions that plagued her.

Chendrukhar bowed when he came close. "Is there something you require?"

"No. I just couldn't sleep."

"Would you care for something to eat, then?"

"Hot?"

"If you like."

"Then yes."

He accompanied her to the fire and made sure one of his band served her as much as she wanted. He watched her as she ate, apparently oblivious to her small use of Power to make sure no poison was hidden in the food before she took the first bite.

"Aren't you going to have something?" she said when she finished eating.

"I've already eaten," he replied. "Do you remember the offer I made you?"

"Offer?"

"Those many years ago. To instruct you in the Art. Shortly before you took the Star."

"Oh. Yes, I remember."

"The offer still holds."

"Ah. Thank you. That's very generous. But I'm involved in something just now that I should complete before I consider other offers."

"I understand." He took her empty dish and carried it to a pile near the fire. She followed.

"You do?"

"Perhaps better than you might know. Six of you, traveling through this area, with Corentris on your lips, the waning moons, an ancient prophecy. When you six came to this camp, I suspected you were part of that."

"Oh?"

"Yes, indeed. And I respect your need for secrecy in this matter. I won't hinder you."

"Such solicitude. Why are you looking at me that way?"

Chendrukhar had been studying her through narrowed eyes. She felt a fleeting, feather-light touch of Power.

"I think you have no need of instruction, after all. And I'm uncertain you needed it even when I first offered."

She shrugged.

"So, you've also felt the Power building south of here."

Namid nodded and realized that might explain her increased restlessness.

"Disturbing to say the least. I myself have slept no more than a third of the night for many nights now. Are you prepared for what you might find in Corentris?"

Namid gave him her best bland look and countered with

a question of her own. "So, you're saying Corentris is this direction? Are there more statues there like yours?"

He returned her look for a long moment, then smiled. "If you'll excuse me, I have some things I must attend to." He headed back across the camp. Namid watched him for a few breaths-of-time, then turned back toward the tent.

She felt his gaze on her the whole way back to the tent. Once inside again, she plopped down on her cushion and wondered what it was about him that set off warnings in her mind, other than the combination of too much curiosity and too much knowledge about things he should not have heard of. Namid leaned back and tried to clear her mind. She suspected she would need all the rest she could manage. She closed her eyes against the bright daylight and tried to think soothing thoughts.

CHAPTER 22

The next she knew, Namid crouched by the hanging rug with her sword in her hand, wide awake. She realized someone had lifted the flap into the other half of the tent.

"Namid?" came a quiet voice. Aahmes. She sheathed her sword as she pulled back the rug. Haeith and Odasoro stood there with Aahmes, all their gear at their feet.

"What is it?" she said.

"Come look," Aahmes said, then followed her to the tent flap and they both peered through the slit where it did not close completely. At the far side of the camp Chendrukhar stood talking with Staehw. From their gestures, the conversation seemed heated.

Namid cursed under her breath and sent Odasoro to wake the others.

"How long has he been here?" she asked Aahmes.

"Just a few breaths-of-time. We saw him ride up, so we ducked in here."

"How could he have gotten here so fast?" Namid wondered. "Do you think he knows a way of swift travel like yours?"

"I thought only some of my people knew it. But...."

Aahmes shrugged.

"He does have a little Power, but I've never seen him use it for anything that needed fine control," Inezha said as she and Cameni joined them.

"Where are our horses?" Namid asked the room at large.

"I believe they put them with our host's horses," Odasoro said.

"Great."

"They're still talking," Aahmes said.

"That won't last," Namid predicted.

"We have to get out of here!" Cameni said.

"Obviously," Aahmes said.

"Out the back?" Haeith suggested.

"Let's go," Namid said.

One by one, they crawled under the back wall of the tent and pulled their packs after them, then slipped through the camp, behind tents whenever possible. It was early afternoon. Namid noted, with a sinking feeling, that the horses stood no more than ten paces away from Staehw. If he looked at them closely, he might recognize Inezha's. And, of course, the horses were unsaddled. Namid hoped everyone could ride bareback.

"I'll get the horses," Aahmes said. "Just need a diversion."

Inezha muttered something in the Praznies' language, sounding more annoyed than anything else, then said, "I'll do it. And don't wait for me."

"Wait!" Namid said, but Inezha was already gone.

They watched as, a few breaths-of-time later, Inezha stepped out of Chendrukhar's tent and ran over to the mage and Staehw. And started what looked like a three-way argument.

"She's got their attention," Aahmes said. "But we're going to need more…. There're still the others in camp…."

Namid considered for a moment, then nodded. "Go."

She called Power from her reserve and sent it sliding through the grasses near the camp on the side far away from where they hid, rustling them as if a large number of people were trying to sneak through. She vaguely noticed the bandits' surprise and frantic activity, but most of her attention was taken with controlling the Power.

Her concentration was broken when her horse nuzzled her hand. The grasses fell still, and she saw Chendrukhar start to turn toward them.

Namid grabbed her horse's mane and mounted. Aahmes tossed her pack to her and jumped on his own horse.

"They're coming," Haeith said.

"Let's ride!"

They galloped through the rest of the camp, headed south. Staehw shouted something unintelligible at them and swung up on his horse. Then they cleared the last tent.

"I'm going to start the swift travel," Aahmes said.

"But what of Inezha?!" Cameni said.

"We should honor her request to go. If we wait, her actions will have been for nothing," Haeith said.

"This close to them?" Namid asked Aahmes.

"Sure. I've heard it feels like the Power is being used somewhere else. And he's coming after us."

Namid glanced back and saw Staehw atop his horse, trying to get free of Inezha, who slowed him by dragging on the horse's reins. Namid felt Aahmes gather Power, then the familiar disorientation and the world around them blurred.

A few breaths-of-time later, the world came back into focus. Aahmes slowed, which forced the rest to slow also to avoid riding over him.

"Why are we stopping?" Cameni said.

"We're far enough away for now," Aahmes said. "And I couldn't hold the swift travel any longer with no preparation and the horses going at that pace. And they couldn't have held that pace."

"But what if that Prazny can do this swift travel spell and catch up?" Cameni said.

"At least it'll just be him, and not a camp of bandits, too," Namid said.

"And a mage," Aahmes added.

"That, too" Namid said.

Cameni did not look cheered by that. "I wish we hadn't left the saddles behind. And poor Inezha."

"It was Inezha's choice," Aahmes said. "And as for a saddle... just put a blanket between you and your horse."

Cameni gave him a nasty look but slid off her horse and started digging in her pack.

"Of course, then your blanket'll smell horsey," Namid teased, also dismounting.

In the end, they all used blankets to substitute for the lost saddles. They would be fine if they traveled no faster than a walk. Namid hoped they would not need a faster pace.

"Do you know how close we are to Corentris?" Aahmes asked Namid as they started riding again.

"Another night's ride like the last one should take us far enough south. Then we'll have to ride normally so I can look for landmarks."

He nodded. "I'd like to ride normally until dark."

"Won't that just waste valuable time?" Cameni said. "I thought we needed to get there swiftly. And what about Enric?!"

Aahmes scowled at her. "The time won't be wasted. It'll allow the horses, me too, more relief from the swift travel."

"Oh," Cameni said.

"Could you not teach another this spell?" Odasoro said. "To allow you to rest."

"Yes!" Cameni said. "How about Namid?"

"Me?"

Aahmes studied Namid and she felt a feather-light touch of his Power. "It might work. You've got the Power and control."

Namid gave him a doubtful look. "Thanks, I think. What do I need to do?"

"Have you ever used thought-speech?"

Namid shook her head. "I've heard of it but was told

that knowledge was lost long ago."

"Not entirely." He gave her a smug smile. "Clear your mind of distractions."

"Easy enough for you to say," Namid muttered and tried to empty her thoughts.

~*Yes, it is,*~ said his voice in her head.

She glanced at him in surprise, then grinned.

"All right. Just give me a breath-of-time."

Closing her eyes helped eliminate outside distractions. After a few breaths-of-time, in the darkness behind her eyelids, images formed and showed her how he shaped the Power for the swift travel and how, while within it, he still knew the direction of travel and guided them around any obstacles. At one point, Namid wished the images would go slower, and they did. She caught a faint echo of Aahmes' amusement at her surprise.

All of a sudden, her concentration failed, and the images splintered like broken glass.

~*Enough,*~ came Aahmes' voice, and he was gone from her thoughts.

Namid opened her eyes and wondered if the headache teasing at the edges of her mind was going to pounce. It held off.

"Well?" Cameni said.

"Don't rush her," Aahmes said. "She'll need time to take in what she's seen and gather Power before she tries anything."

"Yes," Namid said, and was surprised at how soft her voice came out. She sounded tired, too.

"Then we might as well ride," Cameni said. "At least we'll still be getting closer."

So, they rode normally until dusk. Even as Namid sorted out what Aahmes had shown her and slowly gathered Power, she kept alert for any sign of pursuit. She imagined the others watched also.

As the sun slipped below the horizon, Aahmes moved his horse next to Namid's.

"Any questions about how it's done?" he said.

"I don't think so," she said.

"Ready to try it then?"

She gave him a sharp look. "I don't know…."

"Try it. I've never heard of any disastrous results from difficulties with learning this use of Power, only sometimes when people tried to stretch its use. Unlike others I could mention."

Namid did not bother to answer, but instead concentrated on what she had learned. She gathered a little more Power, then shaped it as Aahmes had shown her. For a breathless instant nothing changed, then she felt the now-familiar whirling and the world around them began to blur. And almost at once solidified again.

Namid slumped across her horse's neck, too drained even to remain upright.

"It's no good," she said.

"Maybe with more practice…" Odasoro suggested.

"We don't have the time to waste," Cameni snapped. "Cast your spell," she ordered Aahmes, who ignored her, while already gathering Power for the swift travel.

Sudden anger banished Namid's fatigue as if it had never been. "Listen, *Lady*, your precious Enric will be well enough until they get him to Corentris. And even then, they won't want to render him useless to their purposes. We're just as concerned about him as you are, but there are limits to what can be done with the Power. And limits to how much Power any one person can safely control when tired, distracted, or injured. I would have thought you would have learned that in your training! So just back off!"

Cameni stared at Namid, shocked, and started to say something. But Odasoro spoke first.

"Softly, Namid. We've come this far without major conflict." He looked at Cameni. "But we must remember we are all allies in this. No one's rank makes a difference in this venture." He held Cameni's gaze until she gave a slight nod, then he gave her a confident smile. "We'll get to Enric in time. Namid, is there some way you can tell where he is now, maybe even how he is?"

"Could you?" Cameni said, giving Namid a contrite look.

Namid's anger drained away. "I can try. After I've rested a bit."

"Will you? Please."

Namid gave Cameni a tired smile. "All right." Others might be able to locate them if she did that, but she decided not to mention that. It might not matter, anyway.

"If you're done," Aahmes gave Namid a mock glare. "I'll go ahead and start the swift travel."

This time, the whirling sensation was immediately followed by the blurred world. And it stayed that way.

~ ~ ~

When the attack came, it caught Namid by surprise. She had been drifting along in a pleasant daydream, then something ripped the peace from her. Sudden pain in her head blinded her, and she only realized that her horse had thrown her when she hit the ground. This second pain, however, helped clear the first a little, at least enough so she could focus her eyes. She still felt disoriented, then the swift travel dissolved, and normal night returned.

All around, her companions and their packs lay scattered, thrown from their horses as she had been, from the look of it.

Namid sat up and gasped as pain shot up her side. By the curses and exclamations, she knew her companions found themselves in similar straits. She looked around for the horses but saw no sign of them.

"What happened this time?" Cameni's voice carried above everyone else's.

"I don't know," Aahmes said and struggled to his feet. "Namid?"

"I'm here," Namid said.

"Can you call up some light?"

"Yes. Just give me a mo—"

Without warning, an overwhelming Power crashed into Namid—into all of them, she thought—and everything went insane. Namid could not see or hear, and although she believed she still sat on the ground, she could not feel it beneath her. She felt that up and down had somehow been lost. She could not tell which was which. Then an intense pressure crushed her, squeezing her breath out. She tried to fight, to gather Power from the night, but she could not reach it. She struggled against the attack, pounding against it with the little Power she had in reserve.

Then she dropped into a cold, dark world and the insanity disappeared as quickly as it had started.

"Namid?"

Something touched her. Or Namid thought something touched her. She was uncertain of everything at that point.

"Namid? Can you hear me?"

Namid opened her eyes to a night that again looked normal. Aahmes helped her sit up.

"What happened?" she whispered. Her throat felt raw and even that short question hurt.

"I'd hoped you would know. The horses are no doubt long gone, I can tell you that. Can you give us light?"

Namid tried to concentrate and only succeeded in giving herself a raging headache.

"Forget it," Aahmes said after a moment. "Maybe a torch.... Cameni! Come sit with Namid while I find a torch."

Namid watched Cameni crawl over to them, surprised that she obeyed him. From her motions, it was clear she only found them by following their voices. With clouds blocking the moonlight, it was certainly too dark for her to see anything. When Cameni touched Namid's arm, she started to ease her pains, which came as a great relief.

"I found a torch," Odasoro said. "But perhaps we shouldn't light it just yet. It might attract more unwanted attention."

"But how can we find our possessions without light? We can't just crawl all over feeling for them," Cameni said.

"I can see all our packs lying around here," Namid said.

"Right, you can see…" Cameni murmured.

"I've heard that the ability to see in the dark is fairly common among those with magic," Odasoro said. "Although it works better for some than for others."

"Unfortunately for me, I fall into the latter group," Aahmes said. "Where's Haeith? He hasn't said anything."

"Go forward about four paces, and a little to your left," Namid told him. "I think that's him."

Aahmes followed the directions. "Haeith?" He knelt next to him.

"Well?" Cameni demanded. "Is he all right?"

"I'm not sure. He seems to just be kneeling here, but he's not responding to me. Namid, I think we do need light."

"Save the torch," Namid said, and laboriously called up a small reddish orb. It appeared next to Aahmes and gave barely enough light.

"He seems almost entranced," Aahmes said. "But I don't sense any more attacks."

"Maybe he's doing it himself?" Cameni said.

Aahmes concentrated for a moment. "I think he is," he said. "And if he's doing what I think, it's keeping the hostile Power away from us."

"Don't disturb him then," Cameni said.

Aahmes stood and the light followed him. "Of course not," he growled. "I don't need you to tell me what Power workings to leave undisturbed."

He turned away and started collecting packs.

Something drew Namid's attention to her own pack, lying where it had fallen, a pace or so away from where she sat. She felt the faintest touch of Power as she saw a reddish glow start to grow around it. She lunged for the pack and its precious cargo of Akavos' blade, bowling Cameni over in the process. At the same time, Haeith cried out and collapsed and Namid's small light vanished, snuffed out by another surge of Power, another attack.

Namid pulled all the Power she could manage into herself, headache be damned, this time easily dragging it from the night around her. She vaguely perceived it was mostly the chaotic Power she assumed was Wild Power that rose and responded to her call.

Just before she reached the pack, the glow around it shot upward and formed a spinning column of red light, with growing sparks of flames within. Namid slammed Power around herself for as much protection as possible—no time for the niceties of setting it up properly—and dove into the maelstrom. She felt an instant of excruciating pain but shunted it aside as unimportant as she turned all her attention and will toward keeping the pack from vanishing.

Long moments passed while she dug through the pack, trying to find the blade. The whirling flames filled her sight and blocked out all else. Their roar deafened her to any other sounds. She felt the first flutters of panic as her strength began to fade and her control slipped. The unbelievable heat from the firestorm began to leak through her defenses and she knew she needed a few more breaths-of-time than she was likely to have.

Without warning, the heat receded as she felt a familiar presence and Aahmes added what remained of his Power to her own. Namid's searching fingers found the blade of Akavos. She clasped it close and released her hold on the pack. With a clap of thunder and a searing explosion of heat that she felt even through the double layer of defense, pack and maelstrom vanished. Namid sank to the ground in the sudden silence, her ears ringing.

Gradually, over the throbbing in her hands, she became aware of a lot of voices talking all at once and of someone repeating her name over and over. Gentle hands took the blade from her and turned her hands over to reveal the scorched palms. Fortunately, the pain seemed a distant thing. And, as if from many leagues away, a touch of Healing brought a soothing coolness flowing over the burns. Namid started to slip into a welcome sleep, but the next moment she fought off the impulse and looked up into Cameni's reproachful gaze. Aahmes crouched nearby, a flickering torch in one hand.

"I'll sleep later," Namid told Cameni.

For a moment, Cameni looked like she would argue, but instead she just shook her head and stood. She walked over to Haeith, who sat holding his head.

Namid glanced at Aahmes, who had not moved.

"Are you going to continue doing things like that?" he said, his face and voice both suspiciously expressionless.

Namid studied her hands, noting the smooth pink blotches that marked the palms after Cameni's Healing. Her hands still felt scorched inside, though.

"Someone has to," Namid said. "The stakes seem to be getting higher every time we turn around." Then she grinned at him. "Besides, I seem to be getting good at it."

That got a laugh from him, one not too forced. "I'm not sure I'd call it 'good'. Now what?"

Namid shrugged. "Well, obviously, we're going to be walking. We should at least get some distance from this place. Then rest until light."

"And then?"

"We'll have to take stock and see."

So, they gathered up their packs, or rather Namid's companions did. Everyone refused to let Namid lift or grab anything. They found their way back to the road and followed it for a few leagues. When they later moved off the road again and stopped to rest, Namid's hands had begun hurting again.

"The damage was pretty severe," Cameni told her as they all settled. "And Powerful, as you know. You can see I Healed the surfaces rather well, but the insides are still damaged. I can't Heal them all at once. And I'm not certain they'll ever heal completely. But I can do a little more now. And I can block the pain for a time."

"Please do."

CHAPTER 23

The midmorning sun in Namid's face woke her. She felt the weight of an extra blanket over her. Her hands throbbed, but at least the pain was less than it had been. She stretched out her fingers.

Yes, definitely better.

The others were already up, talking in quiet voices.

"Why didn't someone wake me?" Namid said and struggled out from her tangle of blankets.

Aahmes glanced at her. "Her Ladyness wouldn't allow it."

"You needed the sleep," Cameni said. "Truly, we all did."

"We don't really have the time," Namid said as she tried to roll up the blankets with her less-than-cooperative hands. Odasoro gently took the blankets, bundled them up, and stuffed them into a pack. "Especially not if we're going to have to walk the rest of the way," Namid added.

"Oh, I'm sure that Aahmes can work that travel spell on us as well as horses," Cameni said with a nonchalant wave of one hand.

"Can you?"

"Probably," he admitted. "But we'll still travel slower than if we had horses."

"Any chance of finding them?"

"I looked through Power out as far as I dared," Aahmes said. "They're nowhere within leagues of us. Not even a hoofprint at the spot where we lost them."

"Hmm. Well, considering who our adversaries are, I guess we shouldn't be surprised at any way they'd use Power," Namid said.

"There seems to be an increasing number of those adversaries," Odasoro said. "Any way to tell who was behind the attacks last night?"

"The Power of the first attack had a different feel to it from the attacks that followed," Haeith ventured after a moment.

Aahmes nodded. "I think the first was Staehw...."

Namid nodded. "I think so, too. But the others *did* feel different. Sort of like the Dark Priests...."

"But not, at the same time," Aahmes finished.

"Since we're talking about Power, are you sufficiently recovered to try to find Enric, Namid?" Cameni said.

"I did say I'd try, didn't I."

Namid sat and closed her eyes to help block out distractions. She cast out with her senses as far as she could, but remained passive in the Power to try to avoid detection, looking for that faint echo of Akavos' Power that she thought was Enric. She touched the spot of the attack the previous night. As Aahmes said, no sign of the horses. But the area glowed still with residual Power to her other-sight.

Extending further, she found no sign of Enric or even Akavos. But she did brush the dangerous gathering of Power to the south that must be Corentris. And, to the north, she sensed another familiar threat. One far closer than it should have been. She broke her light trance.

"I couldn't find Enric," Namid said and gave Cameni a sympathetic look. "Or the horses, either, although I've never much been able to use Power to sense animals. But I did encounter someone. Staehw is still on our trail and catching up."

Aahmes grimaced. "I'm beginning to think that man's going to track us all the way across the Six Realms and back."

Cameni shuddered. "How close is he?"

"Too close. He must have a fast horse. It's even possible he's using Power somehow to keep it going."

"Just what we need," Cameni said. "More complications."

The misgivings Namid had back at the bandits' camp returned with Cameni's words.

"Yes, we do seem to have had a lot of bad luck on this journey…." Namid looked at Aahmes, who nodded.

"What are you saying?" Cameni said.

"You think all that has happened has been other than coincidence?" Odasoro said.

"You mean one of us is working for them?" Cameni said.

Namid shook her head. "No, not at all. But Aahmes and I have wondered recently whether we are truly acting freely in this."

"Someone would control us?" Haeith said.

"Possibly, but I don't think it's quite that heavy-handed. I think maybe just prodding us along. Maybe also putting obstacles in our path. Or maybe someone else is doing that." Namid shook her head. "It's confusing. But, they do seem to have had a good idea of our location all along."

"The fire at the inn," Odasoro said.

"Lann and his clansmates expected us," Aahmes said.

"The Dark Priests in the capital," Haeith said.

"And Sy'shythys," Namid added and looked at Aahmes. "We would not have left Rhadanthus, particularly together, but for that."

"Makes me think of that one Shadower," Aahmes said. "You remember him, Namid? Short fellow who used to set up those elaborate schemes, deceptions within deceptions."

"Oh, you mean Macai," Namid said. "As I remember, he was hanged because of his elaborate schemes…."

"Well, that really wasn't his fault—"

"You mean that all along someone has been controlling our path?" Cameni interrupted. "Someone's set up some elaborate scheme?"

"Isn't that what we've been saying?" Aahmes said.

"It seems possible," Namid answered Cameni, ignoring Aahmes. "It seems that they've known somehow what we've been doing."

"Perhaps we can change that," Haeith said.

"You have an idea?" Aahmes said.

"A possibility. We could create a semblance using the Power. Something to mislead any who watch us."

"What kind of semblance?" Odasoro said.

"I believe a combination would work best," Haeith said. "Something that I was once part of involved the semblance of people where they weren't and another of nothing where they were."

Namid gave him a thoughtful look and wondered if this was something from his time as a Flame Warrior, but she would not ask. When he had mentioned the Flame Warriors days ago, she had gotten the distinct impression that he did not wish to talk of his involvement with them and why he no longer belonged to that elite group.

"That sounds good," Aahmes said. "But to keep it going for any length of time will require more than one of us holding them."

"Could one person hold each semblance?" Odasoro said.

"I'll hold the semblance of nothing where we actually are," Haeith said. As they all turned to stare at him, he gave them a small smile, and added, "I've done so before."

"I think I could hold the semblance of us where we aren't," Namid said.

"You're our guide. Can you hold this semblance and still get us to Corentris?" Cameni said.

Namid took a quick assessment of her own reserves of Power and the Power in the area, including the Wild Power, which began to flow to her when she took notice of it. "Yes, for quite a while, I think. Once it's set up, I imagine I won't have to keep my full attention on it. And Aahmes'll be busy, anyway. We still need him to do the swift travel, which I think we all agree he does much better than I." Namid grinned.

Cameni gave her a tentative smile of agreement and the others nodded.

Don't try to do too much, Aahmes said by hand-talk when Namid looked at him.

I won't, she replied.

"How long will this take to set up?" Cameni said.

"Perhaps a candle-mark," Haeith said. "Namid and I will need to make sure our semblances are well meshed to begin with. That might be the most difficult part since we have not worked together before."

While the others resumed their places on the ground, Haeith pulled Namid aside.

"Are you sure this'll work?" she asked him, keeping her voice quiet to avoid worrying the others.

"I've seen it work before, and used it, several times. This thing was one of my responsibilities as a Flame Warrior, and it's one of the things that's contributed to the Flame Warriors' legend. And I've seen your Power and control." He smiled one of his rare smiles. "I think we've nothing to worry about."

He knelt on the ground and pulled Namid down next to him.

"Then I defer to your greater experience," Namid said. "I've done a few small, simple illusions before, but nothing like this."

"I'll guide you. Here." He picked up her left hand and placed it at about eye level and palm to palm with his right hand. Namid felt a tickle of Power as their hands touched.

~First you need to picture each of us in your mind, one by one,

and wrap a sliver of Power around each image to hold it until you call for it.~ He smiled again, no doubt at her expression as she realized that he had not said that last aloud, but rather directly into her mind.

So, Aahmes was not the only one to know the so-called lost secret of thought-speech.

Namid pushed aside her wonder at that for a later time and attempted to do what he said. She found Aahmes' image easy to form and hold, she almost did not even have to think about it. For the others, Haeith included, she simply studied each of them until the image seemed to burn its way into her thoughts, then she wrapped the Power around it.

But for herself, she just could not get it to work. After several tries, Haeith called Aahmes over and asked him to give her an image of herself.

"Do I really look that bad?" Namid asked the two men after she wrapped the Power around that last image.

Aahmes gave her a wicked grin. "You could do with some cleaning up, certainly!"

Haeith shook his head. "Away with you now." He shooed Aahmes back toward the others, never once letting his palm leave Namid's. "We have work to do."

Aahmes continued to grin as he rejoined the others.

Haeith turned back to Namid. "Now this part could be difficult. We've each been trained in different disciplines of the Power, but we must mesh our Power together for this to work."

Namid nodded. "What do I need to do?"

Haeith looked thoughtful. "If you'll permit, perhaps it will be easiest if I control the initial creation. Can you relinquish control to me temporarily?"

Namid studied him for several long breaths-of-time. A small chill of fear ran through her at his words. By giving him control, if he wished to do anything to her, she would be helpless before his Power.

But she knew the reputation of the Flame Warriors, and she got a sense of him through the Power. Although she feared doing this thing, she knew at the same time that no harm would come to her from him. So, she nodded. And forced herself to relax, because if she tensed up, she would not be able to relinquish control.

Haeith placed his left hand alongside Namid's face. "You have my pledge," he said.

Namid nodded and opened her defenses to him. It surprised her how easily he meshed his Power with hers. He swiftly built up the two semblances, while showing her all that he did.

One semblance would be of the group continuing to travel along the road, and the other of a nothingness that would cling to them and hide them as they left the road and cut through the open land. He showed her how to tie a line of Power to the semblance so that it almost maintained itself. She would just act as a conduit for the Power she pulled from outside herself.

He also showed her how to hook just a small amount of Power to the semblances that she would hold, to make them 'feel' more like the real people. Then he showed her how to place both semblances on everyone at the same time, but as yet inactive, and set them up to take effect the next time they all left the road.

Then he was gone. He left only the thinnest link between them to allow them to bolster each other's semblances, if needed.

Namid hadn't realized that she had closed her eyes until she opened them after he finished showing her everything. "That's remarkable work," she said as he helped her to her feet.

He shrugged. "I was well trained."

At that point, Namid realized that his training had been focused into this area of concealment and misdirection. And, although he did not have nearly the raw Power that she and Aahmes did, in this area they would not be able to best him.

Cameni jumped to her feet as they rejoined them. "That

was fast. Are you ready?"

"Yes," Haeith said.

Everyone gathered up the gear—again they would not allow Namid to help—and they returned to the road. They followed it for less than a candle-mark before Haeith indicated that they could leave it anytime.

"We've traveled the road long enough for any watchers to expect that we'll continue as we've begun," he said.

Namid studied the land around them but did not yet see any of the landmarks that she needed. Still, this was as good a place as any. The grass grew in clumps here and so they could at least get a short distance off the road without disturbing it and giving themselves away.

Namid moved first to the west side of the road, acting as if she needed to remove a rock from her boot. The instant she left the road, she felt a slight tug at her Power and the semblances came to life. If she squinted, she saw the semblance she held overlaid on each of them, mimicking their actions. Haeith nodded.

"Everyone can leave the road now," he said in a quiet voice.

Namid walked further away from the road, continuing west, and the others followed her. In a corner of her mind, she saw the semblance of nothing wrapped around them and the semblance of the group now moving further down the road.

"Is it working?" Cameni said. "I can still see us."

"We are visible to each other because we are inside the semblance," Haeith said. "From outside, we are continuing down the road. Look."

The others looked where he pointed, toward the semblance Namid held.

"We look like ghosts," Odasoro said.

"Only to us," Haeith said. "To anyone else, those look as real now as we look to each other."

"That's wonderful," Cameni said. "I didn't know you could do that."

Haeith shrugged.

"Now which way is going to be best?" Aahmes said to Namid.

"For now, we should angle over this way," Namid said and pointed roughly southwest. "We're still too far north for any of my landmarks, so you could use your swift travel for a while, if you wanted."

"Probably should," Aahmes said. "We've been losing time."

They started walking the direction Namid had indicated, and a few breaths-of-time later Aahmes started the swift travel. Namid noticed that this time the blur around them was much brighter, maybe because it was daytime.

And they walked.

Sometime later, Namid found Haeith walking at her side. "Any strain?" he said.

"No. But it does feel strange to have the Power just flowing through me like this."

He nodded, and they walked for a while in silence, while the others chatted behind them.

"What can we expect to find once we reach this Corentris?" Haeith broke their silence. "How many might we face there?"

Aahmes joined them at that point.

"Hard to say. When I was there, I think there were several score or more Dark Priests there pretty much all the time. Add to that a couple score followers and slaves who do their bidding. And the Dark Prince, of course."

"By now, I'd think, wandering Dark Priests would have been called back too," Aahmes added. He gave Namid a tight smile. "I've been saying all along that this is a fool's errand."

"I know you have," she said, while marveling that he could converse normally now while still holding the swift travel. He must be getting better at it with the practice. Or maybe it was just easier without the horses involved.

"So that explains why we're here," Aahmes said.

Namid gave him a sharp look. "We? You, yes. Don't include me in that description."

Aahmes grinned. "At least I had the promise of payment when I first got involved. What's your excuse?"

"Who else do you have to do all the dangerous stunts?" Namid said and grinned back at him.

"Ah. Now I see. I'm here because I'm a fool, and you because you're crazy...."

"Now, wait a—"

"What does that say about the rest of us?" Haeith said.

Aahmes and Namid looked at him. He just gave them an expressionless look, although Namid noticed the corners of his mouth twitch as he contained a smile. They all then glanced back at the others a short distance behind and, when their companions gave them quizzical looks, started laughing.

~ ~ ~

After a few candle-marks of walking, sometime around midafternoon—although the swift travel made it difficult to determine the sun's height in the sky—Namid suddenly felt dizzy and nearly fell. She checked the semblance, but it still held and the Power drain from her was minimal.

"Letting the swift travel go," Aahmes announced and dropped it.

They all staggered back into the normal world and Namid turned just in time to see Aahmes collapse. The others also dropped to the ground, but not as completely as he had. She tried to walk over to him, but her legs gave out under her, too. So, she settled for crawling across the dirt to get to him.

"What's happened?" Odasoro said.

"I feel so strange," Cameni said at the same time and also crawled toward Aahmes.

"Don't know," Namid said. "Something with the spell. Aahmes?"

263

He didn't answer, and she saw that he was barely conscious. Many long breaths-of-time more and she sat next to him. Cameni arrived at the same time and began what Healing she could. Aahmes looked at them both but did not seem to recognize them. The others crawled over to join them.

"Could it be another attack?" Odasoro said.

"I suppose," Namid said. "But I haven't felt anything like an attack. And my semblance is holding just fine."

"As is mine," Haeith added.

"Swift travel unraveled," Aahmes whispered, startling them. He gave them a weak, rueful grin. "Not so good for those inside." His voice sounded weak.

Cameni looked up. "Well, he's pretty much drained," she told them. "He needs rest."

Namid glanced at the sky to judge how much daylight they had left.

"Later," Aahmes said and struggled into a seated position. "We don't have time to coddle me."

"It's not coddling!" Cameni said.

He glared and clambered to his feet, wobbling a little. Namid noticed that her own legs felt stronger and she also managed to stand. The others gradually did the same.

"You're just asking to collapse again," Cameni warned.

He shrugged. "I'll make it 'til we all need to rest."

Namid looked at him doubtfully and he gave her an expressionless look in return. But his voice in her thoughts said otherwise. *~She's right, unfortunately. But I feel we don't have the time. Can you spare a bit of Power for me, so I can at least keep myself upright?~*

In response, Namid sent a tendril of Power in his direction. When he caught it, she started to siphon Power to him, much as she was doing for her semblance.

He looked surprised but accepted it. *~Thank you.~*

While Namid set this up, the others had moved around slowly, working kinks out of abused legs. Namid took the opportunity to do the same, and also looked around for any of her landmarks.

And she found one.

"Well, at least we're far enough south," Namid told the others. "See that rock formation over there." She pointed to where it sat a little south but mostly west of them. They nodded when they spotted it. "There's one of the landmarks. We need to get to those rocks."

"About how far away are we from Corentris?" Odasoro said.

"It's possible we could be at the cave entrance soon after sundown."

"Cave?" Cameni said.

"Oh. Yes. The city's underground."

CHAPTER 24

The journey to the rock outcrop took them about a candle-mark, which left plenty of time to travel from there to the next three. Each was positioned so that a person needed to stand atop one of them to spot the next one. Namid did not know if this was deliberate, but it worked out well.

When they reached the fourth jumble of rocks, Namid was stumbling with weariness, and she heard the others doing so too, along with some halfhearted cursing. They decided to rest and eat something. Haeith found a nearby depression that held some stagnant water and Odasoro set about starting a small fire and boiling some of the water from the pond to drink later.

Namid's hands no longer hurt, just felt stiff, so she helped where she could. But when her vision blurred, she decided she needed to sit for a while, and dropped down where she was. Aahmes hauled out some blankets and dropped a couple in her lap as he gracelessly dropped to the ground next to her. Namid noticed his face seemed even thinner than usual, with lines that she did not remember. He moved like he was in pain.

"You all right?"

He gave her a halfhearted smile. "Not really. But you can't be much better. You can't keep feeding me Power and still hold the semblance, too."

"I know. But I can hold things together for a little longer. And when you sleep some...."

He did grin then. "I won't have to be a drain on you," he finished. "Well, that's my plan. After some food." He looked at their companions a few moments in silence.

"Just keep Cameni away from me," he said. "She doesn't need to know how drained I really am, and I don't want her wasting Power on me just for this. I'll recover well enough on my own and we'll likely need her abilities more desperately later."

Namid studied his profile when he would not look at her. "Foreknowledge?" she said.

He shrugged. "Possibly. Sometimes I get a sense of future events. Sometimes it's even accurate, although I don't know until afterwards. But I'd still rather save our Healing ability. She's good, and that's something I can't help with. Nor can you, I suspect." At that last statement, he did look at her.

"You're right. My abilities don't lie in that area."

"So, she's all we've got."

Namid had no answer for that.

So, they sat, wrapped in the blankets as the air chilled. After a while, Odasoro brought them some of the food that Haeith had heated over the fire, some kind of stew. As he handed them the bowls, Odasoro gave them each a searching look, but said nothing.

From this group of rocks, Namid had already spotted the next, which marked the entrance to one of the passages into Corentris. But the entrance was farther away from this last landmark than she had remembered. They would not reach it until well after dark. She told the others this after they had finished eating.

"Perhaps we should wait until morning then," Odasoro suggested. "I think I'd rather be rested before venturing into this city of Dark Priests."

"But can we afford to wait?" Cameni said. "Who knows what they're doing to Enric."

"And we do have very few days left of the time Myung gave us," Namid said. "We still have to find this jewel that is part of the sword."

"How *are* we going to find this thing?" Cameni said. "We seem to have no information to help us other than it's in Corentris."

"How large is Corentris?" Odasoro said.

"I never traveled all through it," Namid said. "But I'd guess it's roughly the size of Rhadanthus."

Odasoro whistled softly.

"Indeed," Haeith said. "Perhaps something will lead us to this jewel, like the hilt led to the scroll back in Kilaadi."

"Perhaps," Namid said. "We can try pulling out the blade once we're in the city and see if it guides us anywhere."

"What about the shepherd's pipe?" Cameni said. "How does it fit in?"

Namid shrugged. The others all shook their heads.

"Perhaps while we rest, we should see if any of us can actually play the thing," Aahmes said. "That way we'll know if we also have to find someone who can, as well as whoever is supposed to wield the sword."

"Sounds good," Namid said.

So Aahmes pulled out the pipe, polished it on his tunic and tried to play it. Nothing happened, not a sound. He shrugged and passed it to Namid. She met with the same results and handed it to Cameni.

"I already tried to play it back in that ghost city. It didn't work for me, either," Cameni said as she started to pass it on to Haeith.

"Better try again, just to be certain that it's not a matter of *when* you tried to play it," Odasoro said.

So Cameni tried, with no more success than Aahmes and Namid had. She handed it to Haeith.

When he tried to play it, pleasant, soothing tones came

out of it. He stopped and looked at it in astonishment. "But I don't play any musical instruments," he said.

"Apparently, that doesn't matter," Odasoro said. "I'd say that you are the one."

Haeith stared at the pipe a moment longer, then raised it to his lips again. This time a wonderful rippling melody came from the pipe, lively and joyful, and Namid noticed her fatigue abating, and even her hands felt better. The others seemed more alert, too.

Interesting, Aahmes commented by hand-talk to Namid.

He leaned close and whispered, "I think you need feed me Power no longer."

Namid checked and saw that, while he still had not completely recovered, he did have some of his own reserve of Power back. He even looked much better.

She dropped the link of Power with relief. It had been more difficult than she had first thought to maintain the link to him and to the semblance, and still guide them to the correct landmarks. Haeith stopped playing long breaths-of-time later and put the pipe away.

"Well, that effect's very welcome," Odasoro said as he climbed to his feet. "I now feel ready to go on for a while yet."

"Once we enter the caverns, we'll have to be extra vigilant to avoid detection," Namid said. "Do we want to enter them tonight?"

"How long will we travel through these caves until we come to the city?" Cameni said.

"Several candle-marks, at least," Namid said. "Possibly as long as half a day. And that's assuming we can travel straight through. If we have to dodge Dark Priests, it could take longer."

"Will there be someplace not too far inside where we can hole up for some real rest after we get there?" Haeith said.

Namid pictured the passageways that she remembered. A memory flashed across her thoughts... plodding from the underground city to the surface and back—with other slaves of the Dark Priests—to carry supplies that had been left at the cave opening, counting passages along the way to avoid getting lost in the caves. She shook off the memory.

"Yes, there are some side passageways not too far from the entrance. We can go down one of those and find a place to rest that's not on the main path."

"Then I say we should go this night and enter under the cover of darkness," Haeith said.

One by one, everyone else agreed with Haeith, so they set off again.

A couple of candle-marks after full dark, they came to the cave's entrance. Namid almost missed it in the light of the single moon that had already risen, the waning Nidvi, although she knew what to look for. Aahmes was the one who spotted the opening half-covered with overgrown brush. They crept inside, while trying to disturb the plants as little as possible.

Just past the low entrance, the ceiling rose enough to allow them all to stand upright. They gathered to one side of the entrance.

"We're going to have to be as quiet as possible from here on," Namid whispered. "Several parts of these passageways echo horribly."

"What about light?" Cameni said in a quiet voice. "How'll we make our way through here without attracting someone to our light?"

"Don't use one for as long as we can," Aahmes said. "Remember, Namid can see very well in the dark. While I can't see as well, I can still make things out better than the rest of you. We can use a rope to stay together and Namid will lead, while I bring up the rear."

"That'll be awfully slow," Cameni said.

"Better than the quick way of getting ourselves captured," Aahmes said.

So Haeith hauled out a length of rope and everyone grabbed on to it. Then Namid took them deeper into the cave, brushing her fingertips along the rock wall as an extra precaution against getting lost. While she *could* see in the cave, it was murky, even for her. At least the floor in this area was packed dirt, so she had no worry of uneven spots or rock outcrops that would trip them.

The first twenty or so paces the floor sloped steeply downward, which forced them to tread carefully to avoid falling. But after that, the slope eased off, although they still traveled downward. Namid turned into the first side passage she came to. After several twists and turns, they came to a dead end.

"We can rest here," she said.

Namid called up a dim orb of light, just enough for the others to see to move around. Everyone pulled out blankets for warmth and left everything else packed. Namid took first watch and so had a few quiet candle-marks to herself.

Mostly she let her thoughts wander, although she did wonder if Staehw followed their semblance now. Down the thread of Power that connected her to the semblance, she checked on it. It still held strong and showed the little group in a cold camp near the road. Namid was tempted to try to locate Staehw but feared that the increased amount of Power she would need to use would attract unwelcome attention. So, she just watched down the passageway, thoughts drifting, and woke Odasoro when it was time for his watch.

Namid settled down to sleep in a spot further back in the cave. She felt bone-weary. The days ahead would not be easy, a nightmare trip into her past, she suspected, and the thought chilled her. But somehow, despite her fears, she fell asleep.

Much later, in her sleep Namid heard a sound down the passageway. Unnerved, she propped herself up partway to listen better. The cave was still. She could not even hear her companions' breathing. And her small orb no longer gave off any light. That should not have happened, and only added to her anxiety.

"Aahmes," she said softly. "Are you awake?"

Namid heard no answer, so she repeated the question. This time he gave a grunt that seemed to indicate that he had at least heard her. She said nothing further and strained her ears and other senses to find out what had disturbed her. She found nothing.

She started to lay down again and suddenly sat bolt upright.

A terror loomed there in the dark, pressing on her, smothering thought and action, nearly tangible in the blackness. She curled into a ball and tried to block it out. She told herself such fear was unfounded, tried to believe it. But still it engulfed her.

After an eternity, it began to ease, and again Namid thought she heard something in the passageway. It seemed closer, but the fear held her, and she could not move to save herself. But at least now she could talk.

"Aahmes! Are you awake?" She noticed that her voice sounded panicky.

She felt panicky!

"Yes," Aahmes said.

The effect of that one word amazed her. While the fear remained, it retreated and only crouched on the edge of her awareness like some wild animal, waiting for the next moment of weakness.

When she said nothing else, Namid heard Aahmes move. Sitting up, she thought.

"What's wrong?" he said in a quiet voice.

"I heard something… I don't know!" This time she sounded almost hysterical. But she could not seem to do anything about it.

"Namid?"

She heard him get up and move closer. But still, when he touched her shoulder, she jumped. He sat down nearby.

"What is it?"

With difficulty, Namid described for him what had happened. She had to force the words out past the returning terror. She started to tremble, but she finally got it all out.

He started to stand. "I'll take a look...."

"No!" Namid grabbed for his hand and missed. She still could not see.

He touched her cheek. "You're ice cold. I know—"

"Don't leave me!"

"I'm not. I'm just going over here for my blankets.... Now, I'm back."

He piled his blankets around her. "How's that?"

"Good. What about you?"

"Ah. I grew up with weather colder than it is in here. Now, I'll just take a look—"

"No! Don't leave me!"

"The others are here."

"They're asleep. Stay! Please."

He fell silent for a moment, then he agreed. "But let me rearrange things a bit." He moved the blankets and did something at the wall near her.

"Can you move over here?"

"Where's here? I can't see anything."

"You can't?" He sounded surprised. "Hmm."

Something touched her foot. Namid jumped again and just barely restrained a scream.

"That's me. Move over here. You can lean against the wall."

Namid crawled in the direction of his voice.

Aahmes had spread his blankets out on the floor and up the wall of the cave. He took her hand to help her over to him, then helped her get untwisted and settled again in her own blankets. She leaned back against the wall and tried to control her shivering.

After a long silence, Aahmes spoke softly. "You can let go, if you want."

Namid realized then that she had never released his hand, and had, in fact, been clutching it as if her life depended on it. She pulled her hand back.

"Sorry."

A voice came out of the darkness, startling her. Namid

curled up again.

"What's wrong?" It was Odasoro.

"I've got this," Aahmes said. "No need to interrupt your watch."

After several breaths-of-time, Aahmes said her name. Namid tried to answer, but the terror washed over her again, until she was drowning in it.

She could not utter a sound.

Aahmes pulled her close and wrapped his arms around her. Namid clung to him, shaking uncontrollably. She felt her heart pounding, could even hear it, and she wondered that he seemed oblivious to the noise it made. His voice came from a great distance, but she could not figure out what he was saying.

For long breaths-of-time, she sat paralyzed by the terror, certain that something lurked out there, that it stalked her, and when it found her, all the horrors she had experienced at the hands of the Dark Priests would be nothing to what it would do. She felt a touch of Power and cried out, or thought she did, but she could not hear her own voice. A few breaths-of-time more and she knew the something was just down the passageway and coming closer.

Then the terror vanished, leaving her limp and gasping for breath. And still in darkness.

But now she heard Aahmes' voice again.

"Namid? Can you hear me? Come back. Namid?"

Namid tried to speak, but her throat felt raw. "I'm back," she managed to croak.

"Thank the gods! What happened?"

"I don't know. Did you see my light go out?"

"Yeah, just a short time ago. Can you bring it back?"

"Oh. So that's why you sounded like you did earlier, when I said I couldn't see. Uh, I'll try."

Calling the orb was harder than it should have been. But as soon as she did, she could see normally again. The first thing she noticed was Odasoro standing a couple of paces away, looking concerned. He held an unsheathed short sword. He had purchased it back in the town where Enric was captured. The others still slept.

"Was it an attack?" Odasoro said.

"Not sure," Namid whispered. "Maybe."

"I didn't feel any Power to fight or block." Aahmes said.

Odasoro glanced at the others.

"Only against you. They want to get you in particular, don't they?" he said.

Namid shrugged and nodded at the same time.

"We overheard something to that effect when we went into town to try to rescue Enric," Aahmes said.

"Because of your fa—" Odasoro cut himself off and looked pointedly at Aahmes.

"He knows," Namid said. "And yes, probably it has something to do with who my father is. And who I am. I just don't know what or why."

"Should you even be here?" Odasoro said.

Namid gave him a long look, then looked at Aahmes. Neither of their expressions revealed their thoughts. She shrugged. "If we believe this prophecy, I'm supposed to be. Either way, I'm the only one here who can act as guide in this place."

Odasoro nodded. "I suppose so." He gave her a slight bow and returned to his watch.

"Think you can get back to sleep?" Aahmes said.

"Maybe." She suddenly realized something. "Oh, no!"

"What?"

"I've lost the semblances. Just like I lost the light."

"Well.... Nothing to be done about that now. Hopefully, they served their purpose."

"I hope...."

"Try to sleep," Aahmes said, and started to stand.

"Wait!" Namid grabbed the edge of his sleeve. "Aahmes... would you... I mean—" she faltered, afraid to say what she wanted to.

"What?"

"Don't go. If you don't mind...." Her face grew warm.

"I'd feel better—" She glanced up at him, afraid of what his expression might tell her, and afraid not to see it.

He looked startled, at first, then guardedly pleased. He sat again next to her. "Of course, I'll stay."

They rearranged the blankets then, so they cushioned them better against the wall. He pulled her close beside him and wrapped one arm around her, letting her use his shoulder as a pillow. Namid leaned there, conscious of his warmth, and his steady breathing and heartbeat, which eventually soothed her enough that she drifted off.

CHAPTER 25

The sound of someone clearing his throat woke Namid. She looked up to see Haeith standing a couple of steps away. He gave her an odd look, with a hint of a smile.

"Thought you might want to be up before the others," he said.

Then Aahmes shifted and Namid remembered the past night. She sat up and felt her face grow warm, again. Haeith just nodded and turned away to pack some blankets. Namid saw that Cameni still slept and Odasoro was just stirring. She looked at Aahmes to find him looking back at her.

"Tactful" he said with a slight smile. She just nodded.

Aahmes rolled off the blankets and started to gather them up. "Better?" he said in a quiet voice.

Namid helped roll a blanket and avoided looking at him. "Yes. And thank you."

"Any time." When she did not respond, he caught her chin and gently tilted her head up so that she would look at him. "I mean that, Namid."

Namid nodded and looked away, suddenly shy. She grabbed a pack and dug some food out of it. The others were awake by then and so she handed out food as they cleaned up the area. She managed to catch Haeith away from the others and told him about losing the semblance. He looked thoughtful, rather than worried.

"Probably you would've had to let it go today, anyway," he said. "A few candle-marks early should not have changed anything, and might even cause confusion to our adversaries."

"We can hope," Namid said.

After they had everything packed, and everyone had eaten at least a little, they again lined up with the rope and started back toward the main passage. After the first turn, Namid killed the light orb.

"Are we going to have to go the entire way in darkness?" Cameni said.

"No," Namid said. "Once we get to better-traveled areas, they'll have lights placed along the walls. Of course, we'll have other worries there."

"Yes, but at least we'll be able to see!"

Namid did not bother to answer that and just concentrated on leading everyone through the dark. She felt unsettled from the terror of the night before and so moved slower than before. That was probably all to the good, since, at best, the cave was dim to her, and the others just followed her blindly.

The journey through the passageways was anything but enjoyable. At least the floor remained smooth enough that Namid did not have to warn of things they might trip over. But there seemed to be many more side passages than she remembered. She knew she had not been alert the last time she had passed this way, but she felt certain there were more than before. After she had counted two more on her left than should have been there, she called a halt.

"What is it?" Odasoro said, keeping his voice quiet.

"We might have a problem," she said. "It looks like things have changed far more than they should have since I last came through here."

"Are you certain this is the entrance that you thought it

was?" Cameni said.

"Yes, that I'm sure of. The landmarks above were right."

"What's different?" Haeith said.

"Too many side passages," Namid said.

"Is it possible that some aren't really there?" Odasoro said.

Namid considered that. "Possibly. Wait here a bit. I'll be right back."

~*Should you go off alone?*~ Aahmes said in Namid's thoughts.

"I'm just going back a couple of passageways," Namid said aloud, for all of them. As she turned away, she heard someone draw a sword.

"We'll await your return," Haeith said.

While Namid returned the way they had come, she called up a tiny amount of Power, just enough to help examine the openings. The first two looked ordinary, both to her usual sight and when she scrutinized them with Power. But the third opening differed. When she first looked at it, she just saw the opening. But as she concentrated on it through the Power, she saw an insubstantial-looking cave wall instead of an opening. But she could feel the opening and even walked a couple of paces down it before she returned to the main passage. She made her way back to the others.

"Well?" Cameni said as Namid joined them.

"Something definitely odd. Haeith, would you come take a look at this. I think you know more about illusions than the rest of us."

"Of course."

So Namid guided him back to the third opening and quietly explained what she had seen. When they got there, he seemed to look it over for several long breaths-of-time. Namid assumed that he used some Power, but she never sensed it. Then he chuckled.

"What?"

"I might have an explanation. When you last came this way, how knowledgeable were you about your Power?"

Namid thought back to that time. "I knew that I had some, or at least suspected it. I don't remember which. But I had no idea how to use it."

He nodded. "The illusion here is the blank wall. The passage does exist and probably existed when you last passed through here. But then you did not use Power and so saw the illusion as reality. And now, I suspect you unconsciously use your Power to help you see in the dark, and so you saw right through the illusion without realizing it."

"Makes sense." Namid looked back at the opening and cursed under her breath. "Now I'll have to backtrack and check out every opening again to get my count right."

They returned to the others and Namid told them what Haeith had discovered. After some discussion, they agreed that Haeith and Namid would backtrack to correct her count of the side passages, while the rest would stay and wait where they were. Namid disliked splitting up, but it seemed the fastest way to get the thing done.

So, she and Haeith returned to the cave entrance, then made their way back down to the others. This time, she checked each opening carefully to determine which ones, if any, had been hidden the last time she had walked this way. By the time they joined the others, she knew what to look for to tell the passages apart and knew exactly how far they had come.

"Another three of the passageways I know from before and we'll take a side passage to the busier areas. Or at least the areas that used to be," Namid said.

"And then we'll have some light!" Cameni said.

Less than a candle-mark later, Namid called another halt. "We're almost there. I can see a hint of light ahead."

"I don't see anything," Cameni said.

"Probably too faint yet for you," Aahmes said. "I see it too."

They continued on.

When everyone could see well enough to follow Namid

without the rope, Haeith repacked it.

Just before the last bend in the passage, beyond which the lights began, they stopped again for a quick conference.

"From here, we can follow the lighted passages, which will be the quickest way to the city," Namid told them. "However, we're also far more likely to meet people than if we take another way."

"Although the danger is greater," Cameni spoke up first, "I think we must take the quicker way. We have far too much to accomplish to have the luxury of taking the safer, slower, route."

"I agree," Odasoro said. "I fear we must take the risk at this point."

Namid looked at Aahmes, who shrugged and fingered the hilt of one of his daggers. Haeith nodded.

"The quick way it is, then," Namid said. "Haeith, do you still hold the semblance over us?"

He nodded. "But it is becoming difficult to maintain intact. The Power is… stranger."

Namid checked for herself. The Power did feel different, even more untamed and unpredictable than just a few days earlier. Stronger, too. And something more, something she could not identify. But it made her skin crawl.

Aahmes had apparently also tested it. "Wild Power, mostly. The time is close, so I imagine it'll just continue to increase now. But that could work in our favor. If we can use this Power, the Dark Priests might not recognize what we are doing, since the Power feels so different to begin with."

"It could mask our use of Power," Namid said. "That would certainly help."

"But what if it doesn't?" Cameni said. "Won't we just be pointing out to them where we are?"

"There's that possibility," Namid said. "We should still be cautious in our use of Power, but I think we need not be too stingy."

"A moment, then," Haeith said. "Let me see if I can

adjust the semblance to use this Wild Power."

His moment stretched into nearly a quarter of a candle-mark, and by the time he finished, he looked strained.

"I couldn't work with it. But I *was* able to wrap my own Power tighter so no one further than a couple handspans from us should sense it. And I bolstered the semblance enough that it'll hold at least long enough for us to find a place to hide in the city," he said, sounding fatigued.

So, they headed out, Namid in the lead. This time Haeith took up the rear. The lights turned out to be torches, placed along the walls of the passage at wide intervals that left shadowy areas between. Namid wondered at the change. She remembered the Dark Priests using light orbs similar to hers.

They stayed close to one wall and started down the lighted passage. Several breaths-of-time after they moved into the dim area between the first two torches, they heard voices from ahead.

"Now to test the semblance," Namid whispered over her shoulder. "Be ready if they see through it."

She heard a couple of the others draw weapons as they crept after her. Namid let her poisoned stiletto drop into her hand as she approached the next bend. She peeked around it.

No more than a couple of paces away, close to one of the torches, stood two Dark Priests, deep in conversation. Namid eased around the corner, careful to make no noise, and started to edge past them. The others followed behind her just as carefully. In the moment Namid passed directly across from them, one Dark Priest looked up and seemed to look right at her. Namid froze and held her breath, ready to attack, if it became necessary. The others stopped behind her. For several long breaths-of-time, the Dark Priest looked in Namid's direction, then she frowned and returned her attention to her fellow. Namid took a deep, silent breath and hurried down the passage and around a curve, back into the dimness between lights. The others joined her.

"That was too close," Aahmes said.

"Did she see us?" Cameni said.

"Couldn't have," Namid said. "Or they'd have stopped us."

"Let's keep moving and get out of this tunnel as quickly as we can," Odasoro said.

No one argued and so they continued on as before. Several harrowing candle-marks followed. Every time they passed any Dark Priests, invariably at least one of them stared in their direction a time, before losing interest. Several of the groups of Dark Priests that they passed seemed to be arguing, but Namid did not want to linger to try to find out what was going on. Sometime after they passed the eighth or ninth group, they came to another side passage. Namid led the way into it and around several bends.

"Where are we going?" Cameni said.

"Just out of the way for a little rest," Namid said. "This is worse than I thought it would be."

When they reached a point where the light from the main corridor faded to a dim glow, Namid plopped down on the ground and took a few deep breaths to steady herself. The others joined her on the cave floor.

"How much further is it?" Cameni said.

"About another candle-mark, I think," Namid said. "Then we'll be at the city. I suggest we find someplace there to hide and use as a base while we find the jewel and Enric."

"I wonder what they're arguing about," Aahmes said after a few moments of silence.

Namid shrugged. "It's unusual. But I didn't really want to stop to listen."

"I just hope it's not something we should know," Aahmes said.

Namid considered that for a moment. "Well, if it is, let's wait until we've got that hiding place and then we can try to find out."

No one argued with that. After a few more breaths-of-time to steady herself, Namid led them back to the main passage.

This time luck seemed to be with them. They passed only one additional group of Dark Priests before the passage ended. It opened out onto a ledge partway up one wall of a huge cavern, a cavern large enough to hold an entire city. Which it did.

From their vantage point, Namid could see all the way across the cavern. She had never before been able to spot the source of light and still could not. It looked like the glow from a torch in the fog, but now much brighter than she remembered. The city itself was circular, a little smaller than the cavern, and surrounded by a paces-high wall. Four gates were evenly spaced in the wall. A wide street led from each gate to the city's center, which held a cluster of temples and other larger buildings. The rest of the buildings and streets in the city roughly formed concentric circles that extended out from the temple district to the walls.

On the buildings closest to the temples, a golden glint reflected the dim light. Many of them looked to be made of marble. Further away from the temples, the buildings looked poorer and less well kept. No streets extended beyond the city walls. There the cavern floor was visible, rough and rock-strewn.

This was Corentris, city of the Dark Prince and his Dark Priests, the city they had come to find. Namid caught her breath as she realized what she was seeing....

The layout of Corentris mirrored Rhadanthus in every detail.

Out of the corner of her eye, Namid saw Aahmes glance at her. She wondered what he thought but did not ask. He said nothing. She watched him as he looked back at the city so familiar to them both. He seemed to be picking out the well-known places, just as she found herself doing.

Almost straight in front of them stood Shadow Keep, the building Namid had called home for the past several years, or at least its subterranean twin. Off to the left and closer to the city walls stood the inn where she had spent so many evenings, baiting and being taunted by Aahmes. Everything looked like Rhadanthus, except no bodies lay in the streets from the passage of Sy'shythys, and most of the stones and wood looked darker. And, other than the structures and roads, Namid saw no sign that anything or anyone lived there. A faint breeze that carried the odor of dust blew in her face.

After several breaths-of-time of fruitlessly looking for signs of life, Namid looked instead for the way off their perch. She thought she remembered it was off to one side…. She spotted it to the right, a narrow continuation of the ledge that became a path leading down to the cavern floor. From where she stood, she could not see its entire length, because it doubled back on itself to pass beneath them.

Namid pointed it out to the others and they started down. At this point, she no longer needed to lead the way, so she let the others go on ahead and fell into step with Aahmes.

"I assume you'd have mentioned the likeness if you'd realized it existed," Aahmes said after they had walked several paces in silence.

"I don't know why I never noticed that the two cities are identical," Namid said.

"Hmm. Maybe you were kept from it. Have you thought of that?"

"No… but what would be the purpose? And why the duplication?"

He shrugged, and they helped each other over a broken section of the path.

"I have no idea," he said. "But I like this even less than before. We should choose our hideout with care and get there fast."

Namid nodded and considered potential places that she remembered from Rhadanthus.

"Perhaps we should avoid Shadow Keep," Namid said.

Aahmes gave her a sidelong look. "We could still go there if no one suspected that's where we were...."

She gave him a quick look. "Could it be, O Sneakier-Than-Me, that you are about to show me the secret way you have into Shadow Keep?"

He chuckled. "One, anyway." His grin widened at the look she gave him.

"Assuming the way is also duplicated here," he said in a more serious tone.

She nodded.

They continued down the rough path in silence and reached the bottom several breaths-of-time after the others.

"Let's get out of sight," Odasoro said. "I feel too exposed here." He started toward the nearest opening in the wall.

"But the semblance should still be around us," Cameni said as she followed with the rest of them.

"For now," Haeith said. "But we made some noise getting down here. Someone might have heard."

"Oh."

They reached the nearest gate without seeing any other living thing. The gate stood open and Namid saw rust on it. After they passed through, Aahmes took the lead and guided them through a series of narrow alleys. While the buildings and streets all looked as they did in Rhadanthus, the alleys held none of the refuse that Namid had grown accustomed to seeing. But a thin layer of dark greenish grit coated everything. Namid noticed no smell other than the ever-present dust odor.

They kept close to walls as they followed Aahmes and scurried across any openings that they had to pass. After many long breaths-of-time of this, Aahmes ducked into a narrow doorway and as quickly returned.

"In here," he said, his voice barely above a whisper.

They all filed in after him, tracking some of the greenish grit inside as they did, and followed him to steps leading down into what seemed to be an empty cellar.

"Down here," Aahmes said.

Namid turned back and peeked out the door they had entered, then waved to get Aahmes' attention. She pointed to the clear trail they had left outside in the greenish grit.

Haeith joined them at the door and nodded when he saw the problem. He sent out a thin tendril of Power that Namid sensed only because she stood right next to him. The grit shifted and flowed along the ground, until it lay as smooth as before, as far as Namid could see, erasing the signs of their passage.

"What *is* this stuff?" Cameni complained as she brushed at the grit on her shoes.

Aahmes closed the door and leaned against it while Haeith walked over to Cameni. He knelt next to her and studied the grit without touching it.

"It has an evil sense of Power to it," Haeith said after a moment.

The others gathered around and both Aahmes and Namid also reached out with tiny bits of Power.

Cameni stared at the grit that coated her fingertips. "I can feel death from it," she whispered.

Aahmes looked up. "It's Sy'shythys, somehow," he said.

Cameni's eyes grew wide.

"But not in the killing form that we saw," Aahmes said. "I can feel that it's the same, but this stuff is more like a residue. Annoying, but no Power to kill."

Cameni looked relieved. She pulled out a cloth and wiped her hands clean.

"Sy'shythys. Here," Namid muttered. "In a duplicate of Rhadanthus—"

Haeith whipped around. "I'd heard of such things...."

"What?" Odasoro said.

"Omoiosurgy. Using a duplicate of something to send the effects of the Power to the other. But such a scale... shouldn't be possible...."

"They made the killing-mist here, then," Odasoro said. "And then sent it to Rhadanthus?"

"Looks that way," Namid said.

Cameni handed cloths to everyone. "To get rid of the stuff," she told them. They wiped down their shoes, brushed the grit into a corner, and left the cloths there, too.

They descended into the cellar, then. Namid looked around the empty room.

"So, what is this place?" she asked Aahmes. "Is your secret entrance here?"

He nodded. "It was an abandoned shop back in Rhadanthus. In worse shape than here. Over here."

He indicated a portion of the wall that looked like all the others.

"Do you see it?" he asked Namid.

She studied the wall a moment and nodded.

"It takes Power," she said. "Of course."

She reached out with the smallest tendril of Power and tapped a brick at about knee height. A section of the wall slid away from them, then to the side behind the rest of the wall, to reveal the beginning of a narrow tunnel.

"This way," Aahmes said and led them inside. After they all stood in the tunnel, he waved a hand at the wall and it slid closed.

"I can't see a thing," Cameni said in a quiet voice.

"Just wait a breath-of-time," Aahmes said.

And in just that amount of time, a faint glow from the floor became visible, just enough to see to follow the tunnel. Many breaths-of-time later, Aahmes called a halt at a trap door in the ceiling. The door was secured on their side, and hand- and foot-holds stuck out from the brick wall beside them.

Aahmes reached up and released the latch, then led the way through the hatch. Namid was the last one up and she laughed lightly as she looked around.

"The Keep's old apprentices' room," she said.

Aahmes nodded and closed the trap door. Its outline faded away, blending into the floor. And Namid sensed no Power from it, at least not until she sent out a tendril of her own Power.

"This should do," Haeith said as he looked around the windowless room. He opened the one door and looked out — to a staircase leading up, Namid knew, if this place mirrored the Keep in Rhadanthus. Haeith closed the door with a nod.

They dumped their packs in the corners and plopped down on the floor to get some rest and decide on their next move. Namid pulled the blade of Akavos out and sat down with it.

While the others talked about possibilities such as where the Dark Priests were and how to find Enric, Namid focused her attention and Power on the blade. After she had stared many long breaths-of-time at its shiny surface without any hint that it would point out the jewel's location, she looked up to find Odasoro watching.

"Anything?" he said.

Namid set the blade aside. "Nothing. Not a glimmer. I wish Myung had said something about this black jewel, about how to find it."

"Perhaps we need Enric. He *was* the one the sword guided to the scroll."

"You're probably right."

"Can you find him here?"

"I think so. I do know where the Dark Priests keep prisoners. Or at least where they used to." Namid sighed. "This desertion of the city worries me. While they did not use it extensively, there used to be at least some activity. And they often kept their followers and slaves here, when they didn't have them working for them." Namid only then realized that she held her hands clenched. Odasoro placed one hand over them.

"Are you going to be able to do this?" he said, dropping his voice to a whisper. "Guide us to where we have to go, I mean. It'll mean going through where they held you and your sister, won't it?"

"You wouldn't be able to find the way on your own,"

Namid said. "I'm the only one here who can take us through that maze."

He nodded. "But I fear what returning here will do to you," he said and returned to the others.

Namid watched him cross the small room, but her thoughts were elsewhere. She also feared what returning here would do to her. After her sister had died, after she had returned home to find it run by the Dark Priests, she had not been herself for a time. And she already felt shaky again. She took a deep breath and held it, tried to find some calm. The last thing they needed was for her distress to project and a Dark Priest notice it. As she let out her breath, Aahmes called to her.

"Namid, would you check on this? I think I've located Enric."

Namid grabbed the sword blade and joined the others.

"Just like back in that town," Aahmes said. "But I'm not sure… the Power is so shifty. Not to mention the wildness seeping in. See if you feel it, too."

Namid handed the blade to him and closed her eyes to better concentrate. She just barely touched the Power in the vicinity and immediately noticed what Aahmes had said. It felt as strange as it had up in the passageway to the cavern, and now it seemed to slide away from her. As before, she stayed passive and cautiously reached out to see if she could feel Akavos' Power and the echo of it that was Enric.

After a few breaths-of-time, she sensed them both. Enric was where she expected, in the cells beneath the city that the Dark Priests used to hold troublesome prisoners. She was too familiar with those cells.

Akavos seemed to be close to him but having to fight the slippery Power left her uncertain of that. She also felt that particular taint on the Power that she associated with the Dark Priests but could not tell how many there were, nor how close to Enric they might be. She did not sense anything that might be the black jewel. She let the Power flow away and opened her eyes.

"Yes, he's here. And I know where."

"Is he all right?" Cameni said.

"He's alive, but I didn't check closer. That would probably have revealed me to any guards," Namid said. "Now I think we have a decision to make."

That caught everyone's attention.

"Of course, we need to get Enric away from the Dark Priests," Namid continued. Everyone nodded. "I've tried to locate this black jewel that we need, without success. Odasoro suggested that maybe only Enric can locate it, like he located the old scroll. So, we need to get the hilt and blade into his hands. I'm leery of carrying the blade in with us when we rescue him, but I don't like the idea of trying to hide it somewhere and trusting that it won't be found. I'm also concerned about all of us going in to get Enric.

"On the one hand, it might take all of us. Or fewer people might have a much better chance of slipping by. But I also don't like the idea of splitting up. Things are not normal here... well, normal for this place. There should be more people in the city and we have yet to see even one of the Dark Priests' followers or slaves. So far, everyone we've encountered is a Dark Priest. They used to keep a large number of hangers-on and slaves. I wouldn't think that would have changed."

While Namid spoke, Odasoro pulled out some food and passed it around to everyone. When he handed some to her, he whispered, "Better eat while we can. I've a feeling that things are going to get rough, now."

"And we also need to find the person to wield this sword against the evil?" Cameni said.

"So we've been told," Namid said. "But, so far, a number of things have just happened, without any real action on our part. I'm thinking one of us is the intended wielder of Akavos and that we'll learn who it is in time."

"Like with the shepherd's pipe," Aahmes said.

Everyone exchanged looks and shrugs.

"I dislike the idea of splitting up, and also of hiding the

blade somewhere," Cameni said. "I… I know that I'm basically useless in a fight, but I *can* Heal. So, I need to be where we're most likely to need that."

"Which is likely to be where Enric is," Namid said with a nod. Cameni turned pale but said nothing further.

"Are we going to continue to have the benefit of our semblance?" Odasoro asked Haeith.

Haeith frowned. "Right now, it's still there. But I feel it beginning to shred with this unstable Power all around. And under any kind of assault, it will drop entirely."

"Perhaps you should just let it go and save your strength and Power," Aahmes suggested. When the others agreed, Haeith let it go with a small sigh of relief.

"Sounds like we're all going then? And we keep the blade with us, right?" Namid said.

No one objected, so she continued. "What about the shepherd's pipe? Bring it, too? Keep in mind that anything with Power that we carry could possibly be detected by the Dark Priests."

"Granted," Odasoro said. "But I think the same argument applies to the pipe as to the blade. We don't want to hide it somewhere and hope it'll stay hidden."

"At least if we carry these things with us, we have the chance to oppose their removal from our possession," Haeith added.

Aahmes smiled. "Fiercely, I imagine."

Haeith nodded.

"So… we all go, keep the blade and pipe with us, and get Enric out of there," Namid said. "Let's get ready, then."

"A couple more points," Aahmes said, stopping them all in the process of rising. "First, we won't have the luxury to discuss or argue decisions while we are in there…." He looked at Namid. "I assume that he's in some sort of dungeon?"

When she nodded, he continued. "So, we all need to follow Namid's directives, and immediately, even if we don't understand the why behind them." Here he gazed at Cameni until she nodded. The others also agreed.

"Since when am I in charge?" Namid said.

"You've been taking on that role more than any of the rest of us," Odasoro said.

"And leading well," Haeith added.

"And you know where we're going and what we're getting ourselves into," Aahmes said.

Namid laughed at that. "Well, to a point," she agreed. "All right, I'm giving the orders, at least for now. What's the other point?"

"I suggest we hide as much of our gear as we can, and travel lightly," Aahmes said.

"Well-advised," Haeith said. "But I suggest we find someplace that'll be along our most likely escape route. I imagine we might have to leave in a hurry."

Namid nodded. "Unfortunately, you're probably right. All right, quick plan. The cells where they have Enric are beneath this city. In fact, I think there are several levels of caves under us, but I never saw all of them. The easiest access is through one of the temples in the city's center, so let's find a place there to stash our packs. Then they'll be nearby when we come racing back out of there. As I imagine we will. We'll go in, get Enric out of there, and, if possible, hide out in the city until we find the jewel."

"And then all we'll have to worry about is killing a god," Aahmes added. "Not a problem."

He turned away and started preparing. Nobody laughed at his comment, although Namid did smile to herself. If only that was all to worry about.

CHAPTER 26

They all prepared much as Aahmes and Namid had days earlier when they had gone searching for Enric. They planned to bring every weapon they had with them, and to hide everything else. Namid took the time to rebraid her hair and this time added a little surprise that she used sometimes.

She pulled over a dozen thin needles from their hidden pocket in one of her armguards and carefully inserted them into her braid. The sharp points on both ends of the needles would give anyone grabbing her hair a nasty surprise. Aahmes watched her make these preparations and grinned.

"I'm glad you weren't using those when we had our little bout," he said. "If I'd caught your hair, I would've been very unhappy. Do those also have poison on them?"

"No. I tried that once, but the poison tends to eat through my hair."

He looked startled, then laughed. "So that explains what happened a few winters back. And I just thought you'd had one of the tyros cut your hair."

Namid smiled. "In truth, I did… after the poison had eaten through it in chunks."

Aahmes shook his head, still laughing softly, and

continued his preparations.

Finally, they were as ready as they would be. No one wore any kind of cloak, and all but Haeith dressed similarly to Namid and Aahmes.

Haeith wore his habergeon under a black tunic. He had secured the blade of Akavos somehow within the sheath of his great-sword. He also carried the shepherd's pipe, tucked into a small pouch at his belt. Namid left off her overtunic and wore just her lighter undertunic over her shirt. She carried her knives and sword, and a couple of extra knives they had taken from Lann's clansmates days ago. Cameni wore a tunic and trousers taken from the clansmates and carried a knife. Namid tied up Cameni's hair in braids with laces taken from one of her gowns. Aahmes tied his hair at the nape of his neck. Odasoro carried his short sword and also wore some of the clothes they had taken from the clansmates.

They left their hideout the way they had entered and moved warily through the city. Haeith had put up a veneer around them that he said was easier to maintain than the semblance and would make anyone seeing them think they belonged there. Namid hoped it would work. Haeith also periodically sent a small puff of Power behind them to smooth out their tracks in the greenish grit.

Namid led this time and took them through small streets and back ways to the temple district. Ironically, the entrance she knew lay beneath a temple that in Rhadanthus had been dedicated to Ilenii. Namid hoped this was a good sign.

On their journey, they met no one and Namid saw no signs that anyone had passed that way recently. When they reached the temple district, she and Aahmes scouted ahead, while the others hid in a small courtyard.

As they approached the building they wanted, Namid heard voices. She and Aahmes found a good vantage point to see who was talking.

Not far from their hiding spot stood three Dark Priests. While they stood close to one of the other small temples, they had an unobstructed view of the open courtyard that led into Ilenii's temple. Namid looked around and considered options, only half-listening to their conversation.

Then something they said caught her attention. It sounded like there was some split within the Dark Priests, and that the First High Priest no longer had the unquestioned loyalty of every Dark Priest because of something he was doing or was planning to do. That was all she picked up before Aahmes diverted her attention.

Can't go this way, he said by hand-talk. *Is there a back way?*

Namid shook her head, then replied the same way. *There are windows….*

Good enough.

They returned to the others and soon they all clambered through some large windows at the back of Ilenii's temple. Inside was a mess. Everything portable had been broken up and tossed haphazardly around the room, forming several clumps of debris.

They placed their packs next to one clump and Haeith put a semblance over them to make them blend in with the debris. Then Namid led everyone further into the building, down a short hall and into what looked like a kitchen. A narrow door on the back wall opened on stairs that led down.

"Why isn't it guarded?" Cameni whispered.

"Who do they have to guard against?" Namid said. "Everyone's either a Dark Priest, a prisoner, or under their control. Come on."

The narrow steps, not too steep, took them down what would have been about a story and a half if they had been in a building. The small room at the bottom was deserted and had three openings off it. Namid took the middle opening and warned the others to be ready for an attack at any time.

At first, the passage was too narrow for two people to walk next to each other, but it soon widened. It was cold, but Namid feared they would soon enough have plenty to keep them warm. The floor sloped downward, and widely spaced torches provided dim light. They passed several side openings before they came to the one she wanted. A quick check with the Power showed her that both the hilt and Enric lay that direction and she told the others.

They started down the passage and, after a short distance, came to one group of cells that the Dark Priests maintained. Namid saw no guards and her anxiety doubled. At that moment Aahmes tapped her arm to get her attention and leaned close.

"This seems too much like a trap. No one fails to put at least one guard on an important prisoner," he whispered. "But I don't feel anything through the Power. You?"

"No, just Enric and Akavos' hilt," Namid whispered back. "I felt Dark Priests earlier, but don't now. Not nearby, anyway."

"Are you sure you're sensing the real things?" Aahmes asked.

She double-checked. "Enric is down five cells on the right. The hilt is in the one beyond him. This is too easy."

She noticed the others watching them intently while they whispered. Cameni looked like she wanted to say something, but she kept quiet.

"Yes. I think perhaps they already know we're in the city and don't care if we retrieve Enric and the hilt," Aahmes said. "But I think they'll know when we *do* retrieve them."

Namid nodded. "But we're rather committed now. Be ready."

Aahmes nodded and whispered to Haeith. Namid pulled Cameni close and told her about Enric's location, and the hilt's, and the possibility of a trap because of the lack of guards. Cameni passed the word to Odasoro.

Haeith and Odasoro drew their swords, and Haeith moved to a position behind Aahmes and Namid. Odasoro and Cameni put their backs to the wall, prepared to stay where they stood as the rest moved toward Enric's cell.

Aahmes and Namid kept to the walls on either side of the passage and gave each cell they passed a quick look. Namid saw nothing in any of the cells and Aahmes indicated the same. Haeith stayed roughly a pace back from them and kept watch back toward the others as well.

Namid and Aahmes came to the door to Enric's cell, a solid, iron-bound thing. It was locked. Namid motioned to Aahmes to join her.

"No traps so far?" she whispered.

"Not a thing, Powerful or not."

"Me neither. See if the door is locked where the hilt is."

He moved to the next door and tried it. He shook his head.

"Get the hilt while I work on this," Namid said.

She turned her attention to the lock. She sensed no hint of Power about it and it looked simple enough to pick, but she decided not to take the time. Instead, she sent a sliver of her Power into the lock and popped it open. Namid opened the door.

Little light penetrated the room from the torch outside but Namid spotted a figure tucked into one corner. She assumed it was Enric. One step into the cell and Namid had to fight memories that threatened to overwhelm her.

It had been a cell like this....

No, she refused to remember!

Namid pulled out a dagger, just in case, and crept up to the figure. Haeith guarded her back. She still saw no sign of Power or traps and so reached out a hand to touch the figure.

It started up with a gasp and startled her. She jumped back, suppressed a curse, and just barely kept from throwing the dagger. Haeith steadied her with a hand on her back.

"Namid?" the figure in the corner croaked. The voice was rough and sounded abused but was unmistakably Enric's.

"Yes. Hush." Namid hurried back to him, sheathing her dagger, and set about trying to get him on his feet. She was surprised to discover that they had not chained him to the wall, unlike their usual practice.

Enric insisted on talking, although softly, but she paid no attention and concentrated on hurrying them out of there. Then she heard the clash of metal from the passage outside.

"—a trap!" Enric's words finally penetrated. "They want you."

For just a moment, Namid froze in horror. The worst had happened.

The next moment she hauled him to his feet, ignoring his exclamations of pain, and half-dragged him to the door. Haeith was there before them and already out in the passage. He and Aahmes held off a group of Dark Priests who had apparently come from the cells beyond Enric's. Clearly, the time for silence was past.

Namid started toward Cameni, shouting for her and supporting Enric. Cameni and Odasoro ran to Namid and took Enric off her hands.

Just in time.

A blast of Power streaked toward the others from beyond those they fought. Namid deflected it and sent back one of her own, un-aimed, hoping it would at least alarm the other mage. She reached back and pushed Cameni back the way they had come in.

"Run!" she ordered and just barely blocked the Power that flew toward her.

Haeith and the others were being pushed back toward Namid and so she backed up as well, hoping that Cameni, Odasoro, and Enric had taken the way out. The men in front of her were holding their own, so she concentrated on preventing any Powerful attacks from reaching them.

At least three Dark Priests now flung Powered attacks at them. She would not be able to keep up for long. She started to pull Wild Power to help but had to fight to use it as the slipperiness they had noticed earlier interfered with her control.

They were forced further back toward the entrance, the Dark Priests walking over their own injured and dead to come at them. Something touched Namid's arm and she almost threw a blast of Power before she realized it was Cameni.

"We're blocked that way," Cameni shouted. "Is there another way?"

"Second passage on the left," Namid shouted back over the din of battle and screams of the injured. But a moment later, Cameni returned, Odasoro and Enric with her.

Enric grabbed Namid's sword out of its sheath and she heard him fighting behind her. At least Cameni had Healed him, Namid thought as she blocked another bolt. Enough of the Power got through that time, however, to make her skin tingle. And she was having trouble hanging on to the Wild Power. The next blast of Power might just blow her defenses away.

She tried to remember any other escape routes and realized that the Dark Priests had them well and truly trapped. Unless they could manage to cut their way out.

Namid yelled to Aahmes through thought-speech, hoping she was doing it right and he would hear. *~Take over for me! I've got to focus on the way out!~*

She turned her attention to blasting the Dark Priests who stood between them and the way back up to the city. She felt no further Powerful attacks from behind, so Aahmes must have heard her. Namid stayed right behind Enric as he cut at any who faced him. Odasoro now held Cameni's knife as well as his short sword and attacked around Enric as well as he could. Cameni kept a hand on Enric's back, apparently constantly Healing him. And Namid sent bolts of Power past him into the crowd beyond, trying to cut down as many as possible with each attack.

At first it worked, and they edged toward their goal. Then something got past Aahmes and blinded Namid. When she could see again, Cameni lay on the floor, stunned. Enric and Odasoro still fought, but with no shelter from the bolts of Power that tore into them. Behind Namid, Aahmes had dropped to his knees. Haeith still fought fiercely but was vastly outnumbered. Then Namid realized that she could not draw on any Power. They had blocked her somehow!

Namid drew two daggers and started to help Haeith, but at that moment a final Powerful attack dropped on them.

She blacked out.

~ ~ ~

When Namid came to, the Dark Priests had already stripped them of all their weapons. They drug them all to an open area on the floor and searched them all roughly and thoroughly.

Namid tried to fight back and took several blows for her efforts, nearly blacking out again. When they had finished, they had even taken both her armguards and the daggers hidden in her boots.

Then they brought out the chains and manacles. And the memories washed over her.

No, not again!

The Dark Priests soon had the others all secured to their satisfaction, manacles on wrists connected by short chains, with a longer chain to attach to something else, and fetters on ankles, again with short chains between. It was certain they would not walk with any speed while they wore those.

But when they came to Namid, she fought madly. She fought the memories, the chains of the past, the chains they wanted to put on her now. But finally, beaten and exhausted, and shaking so much she could hardly stand, she could oppose them no longer and they chained her as they had her companions.

Then a couple of Dark Priests moved from one to the next pouring something down each prisoner's throat. Namid had a sinking feeling she knew what it was, and when it came her turn, her suspicion was confirmed.

Although she tried to fight again, they got the stuff down her throat, more of that drug of Lann's, and she picked up a few more bruises for the trouble. At least the dose of the drug seemed to be correct this time. Namid did not black out from it, although she felt woozy. So, she knew she could not count on using any Power for some time.

The Dark Priests left them alone then to tend to their fellows. And Namid saw that the Dark Priests now had both the hilt and blade of Akavos.

Namid peered at her companions to gauge their condition. Everyone looked as dazed as she felt. Enric did look better than he had, not counting the effects of the battle. Odasoro was still alive, which was a relief, but looked rather battered. Both Haeith and Aahmes were bloodied, but neither looked too injured, so Namid assumed most of the blood was not theirs. Cameni did not seem to have taken any wounds, and other than bruises, neither had Namid somehow. But her head hurt badly enough from that last attack of Power and fighting off her memories that she tried to avoid moving too much.

After tending to their injured fellows, the Dark Priests hauled Namid and her companions to their feet by the chains. Namid was relieved that she could at least stand. One Dark Priest came along with a longer chain and attached their lead chains to it. With a tug, the Dark Priests led them back toward the entrance they had come in.

They had no chance to communicate with each other. At least one Dark Priest walked between each of them. Also, the Dark Priest who led them set a fast-enough pace that Namid had to concentrate on not tripping with the short chain keeping her stride to tiny steps.

Before they reached the stairs, the Dark Priest in front turned down a passage on the left and took them into an area Namid did not recognize. The floor here was rougher than elsewhere, which made walking that much more difficult.

Then the inevitable happened. Namid caught a foot on

a small protrusion of rock and could not recover in time. She fell to the ground, hard, halting their progress. Before she could even attempt to regain her feet, one of the Dark Priests pulled out a short whip.

Namid just had time to protect her face when he lashed out at her, catching her shoulder and cutting right through the fabric of her sleeve. Blood ran down her arm.

She heard an inhuman-sounding roar from near the back of the line. Most of the Dark Priests hurried back there and Namid caught a glimpse of Aahmes as he insanely tried to fight free of them, shouting at them incoherently. He went down behind the press of bodies and Namid no longer saw him. The Dark Priest with the whip came back toward her and raised the whip again.

"Hold!"

A new, authoritative voice brought all motion in the corridor to a halt, even the scuffle where Aahmes was.

Namid looked toward the new voice and saw a different Dark Priest near the end of their line. He stood no taller than the others, but radiated authority and Power, although she could not sense Power right then. He was handsome, cleanshaven, with pale skin and pale blond hair, almost white, and striking features. But his blue eyes were cold and his expression cruel.

He wore dark green-gray robes of a much finer material than the other Dark Priests there and the amount of decoration on them declared his higher rank. He carried an ornate dagger sheathed on his belt. The Dark Priests who guarded the small group gave him respectful attention.

After a moment, Namid recognized the decorations on his robe and knew him to be one of the High Priests, which made him one of the immediate underlings of the First High Priest. He also seemed familiar somehow, although the memory would not come clearly. But Namid felt cold with dread.

He paced along the line and studied each of Namid's companions. Namid watched him and thought she saw him give a start of surprise when he saw Aahmes. She was certain he gave the former Shadower a longer look than he gave the others. He stopped when he came to her. His gaze traveled from her wounded arm and bloodstained sleeve to the whip the Dark Priest nearest her still held. Without warning, and faster than she would have expected, he grabbed the Dark Priest by his collar and pulled him close.

"Do you forget your instructions?" he hissed into the man's face.

The man he held babbled out something to the effect that he did not. He shook so hard that he was almost unintelligible. The High Priest threw him back against a wall, hard, and he immediately dropped to the floor to grovel at the High Priest's feet.

"Report to your superior for chastisement," the High Priest ordered him. "Now."

The man dropped the whip right there and ran back the way they had come. The High Priest retrieved the whip, coiled it, and absently tapped it against his leg as he turned back to Namid. As he looked down at her with an expectant smile, a flash of memory came to her, and she knew. His name was Randoq. She had been a child when she had last seen him. The fear she had known back then engulfed her. He nodded, and his next words confirmed that all this had shown in her expression.

"Yes, you remember. It was inexcusable that your bitch of a sister had the effrontery to die and take my child with her.... And I haven't forgotten your part in it."

Namid heard expressions of surprise from her companions but kept her attention on High Priest Randoq. At his words, her fear flashed into fury. He laughed at her, a harsh sound with no humor in it.

She narrowed her eyes. "You mean the part where I tried to save them? The baby came early, you misborn ass, and I knew nothing of childbirth! You and all your cronies had Power. You could've done something. But you were too engrossed in your puerile dominance games!"

Randoq's face twisted in anger. He drew back a hand, prepared to strike her. She straightened, lifted her chin and stared into his eyes, daring him.

Slowly, glaring, he mastered his anger and lowered his hand. He leaned toward her until his face was a mere finger-width from hers.

"Breaking you will be my immense pleasure," he hissed.

She returned his glare but said nothing.

"This one comes with me," Randoq told the other Dark Priests, who scrambled to unhook Namid's chain from the others and place it into his hands. He hauled her to her feet by the chain, then studied each of her companions in turn. His gaze lingered on Cameni, and Namid saw Enric clench his jaw in anger.

"Make sure these others are well secured," Randoq ordered the other Dark Priests. "And be certain *that* one is not damaged too much." He pointed at Aahmes. "His Eminence might want him, too."

Randoq pulled Namid to the side for the others to pass them. No one said anything, but she saw fear and anger in her companions' expressions. When Aahmes came even with them, Randoq stroked her hair at her temple. He laughed when she pulled away, and at Aahmes' impotent fury. Then her companions were gone.

Randoq headed back the way they had come and hauled Namid along with him. She was surprised enough that he had not taunted and tormented her further, as she remembered he used to, that she actually asked where they were going.

He surprised her even further by answering.

"His Eminence wishes to see how the scrawny princess of years ago has turned out," he told her.

"Why?"

He laughed. "You'll learn that in time."

They spoke no further.

Randoq took Namid through a confusing number of passages, ones unfamiliar to her. He finally stopped before a set of carved double doors. Although she had not recognized the route to get to this place, she knew where they were now and suspected what they planned for her. She tried to steel herself for the torment to come by reminding herself that she had been through this before. And she *was* still alive. Despite this, Namid could not keep from shaking as the doors swung open.

The room beyond was large, its walls shrouded in shadows. Namid heard the murmur of many voices from the Dark Priests gathered there but barely saw them in the shadows. By their robes, most of them belonged to the lowest ranks, the recently initiated.

In contrast to the shadows that hung around them, the center of the room was well lit by an orb about the size of her hand. The orb hovered between two pillars. Its stark light fell on the waiting chains and manacles that hung from the pillars and on the strong metal rings that had been fused by Power into the floor. At the edge of the light cast by the orb, an ornately decorated chair sat facing the pillars.

A long whip lay coiled loosely around one of the metal rings on the floor. A faint greenish glow clung to the edges of the whip. They had imbued it with some Power, although she could not sense it. The part of her that was not gibbering in panic wondered for what purpose. This room existed to chastise erring slaves, Dark Priests too, to lash them mercilessly, and demonstrate that chastisement to all.

Namid had been here before.

As she and Randoq stood in the doorway, the room grew quiet. At first, Namid thought the assembly had noticed them, but then she saw a single hooded figure cross the room, coming from their right. It was clearly a man, tall, and judging by the amount of gold on his robes and hood, she guessed that this was the First High Priest. Strangely, even when he moved through the light in the center of the room, she was unable to catch a glimpse of his face. She wondered at this concealment. He took his place in the ornate seat and beckoned toward Randoq.

Namid fought Randoq all the way across the floor, with the result that she picked up even more bruises. While he switched her to the bindings on the pillars, Randoq slit her tunic down the front and took it from her, leaving her only her shirt. He secured her between the pillars, facing away from the assembled Dark Priests, with her arms stretched to the sides and above her head, and her ankles locked to the rings in the floor at the width of her shoulders. Then Randoq tore the back of her shirt, baring her back.

Namid shivered from the chill in the room and fear of what was coming, too exhausted to continue fighting for the moment. She gripped the chains that held her arms. Too soon they would be her only support, she knew. She tried to remember the calming exercises that she had learned at Ilenii's temple, but being in this place again, like this, she teetered at the edge of the terror that she had known here before.

Randoq moved out of Namid's sight and then spoke from somewhere behind her.

"As you all know by now, this errant slave has returned to us at this critical time. Although His Eminence has decreed we cannot currently exact the full penalty her desertion warrants, still an example must be made. You are all here to witness. In addition, you will also bear witness to the trial of a spell originally set into her very flesh many years ago. We can now, at last, assess its efficacy."

Namid's head came up at that last. What was he talking about? What spell had they cursed her with?

There was silence then, except for some scuffing sounds. Namid nervously wondered what they could be doing. She heard footsteps approaching. They stopped somewhere behind her. Randoq, she assumed.

Namid tried to escape within herself, while at the same time strained her ears for the distinctive whoosh of the whip, hunched up in dread of the exact moment.

Nothing.

Randoq had not even retrieved the whip at her left foot.

But something had changed. Was the green glow brighter?

"Now!" Randoq said, and she jumped.

Namid screamed, then, as her back exploded with the stinging burn of multiple lashes, all tearing into her skin at once. The coiled whip's green glow flashed momentarily into blinding brilliance at the same time. But nothing had touched her. She heard murmuring from the Dark Priests behind her.

"Excellent. Again." One man's voice rose above the others.

The ordeal continued. Namid did not even try to count the number of times the voice said "again", and the lashes somehow sliced into her back without any contact from any whip. Soon she could not have counted even if she had wanted to. The pain threatened to drag her into darkness, a battle she was losing, when the nightmare finally stopped.

Namid hung from the chains, barely aware of her surroundings. When they released her from the shackles, she dropped to the floor, mostly unaware of the relatively minor pain of hitting the floor over the agony from the lashes. She felt the blood run down her back. She heard several voices speak. One said something about a partial success. Then she could no longer make out the words and lost track of what was happening.

~ ~ ~

The next Namid knew, she was being half-dragged half-carried along one of the passages. Her shirt felt stuck to her back in places, which kept it from sliding off her shoulders. Elsewhere, she felt blood still running down her back, so she decided only a little time must have passed.

"She's back with us, Notable," said the Dark Priest who helped support her on her right. She must have done something to betray her return to awareness.

"Excellent," came an unfamiliar voice from behind her. "Turn aside at the next intersection. There is something His

Eminence wishes her to see."

The Dark Priests continued to support her as they turned down the new passage. A few paces further, they stopped in front of a curtained opening and left her standing on her own. Barely. Namid still felt she could collapse at any moment and so steadied herself against the wall. They had not put her back in chains. Considering her current condition, they probably had no need to.

With a savage smile for her, one of the Dark Priests pulled aside the curtain to reveal a small room with two people chained to the blood-encrusted wall across from the entrance.

"Kalon and Jiro await you," the Dark Priest said.

Her older brothers! She did not see their other brother, Tal, who had last been traveling with them. Namid feared what the Dark Priests might have done to him. Two more Dark Priests stood by her brothers' tortured and mutilated bodies.

Cold pain erupted in Namid's chest and flooded her body. Her vision narrowed to the two figures on the wall. She realized she had stepped toward them only when the Dark Priest at her side prevented her from going any closer.

Someone kept repeating "no" in her voice.

She forced herself to study the bodies... something looked odd about them. Then she realized they both were shrunken and dried. No telling how long they had been dead. She saw the Dark Priests had done nothing to their faces. She could still somehow recognize them.

She felt that her brothers' spirits touched her, tried to tell her something important. But she could not understand the message through the growing noise in her head. Namid struggled to go to them. She fought the Dark Priest holding her back, but he was stronger.

Namid realized not only did she feel her brothers in the room, she detected a faint hint of their forms hovering near their bodies. And something tied them to those bodies. She shuddered.

The Dark Priest who restrained her laughed as he pulled her closer and said that she could be next. One of the others denied that but said that her friends would be.

The other Dark Priests in the room caught Namid's attention. They were performing a ritual Namid had heard of only in whispered tales, a ritual to harvest Power from the continued pain and suffering of a spirit bound to its dead body.

Namid went still, unable to move if she wanted to. A knot of hatred, anger, and grief tightened at the back of her head and grew, accompanied by a terrible heat. The throbbing increased, and the heat suddenly burned through the disorientation from the drug they had given her earlier. With an inarticulate cry, she called all the nearby Wild Power to her. A red haze clouded the edges of her vision and began to cover her sight. She trembled as the first tears slid down her face. They vanished in the growing heat.

The Dark Priests performing the ritual turned toward her and terror twisted their faces. Their mouths moved, but she heard no sound over the roaring of flames. Kalon and Jiro would have a proper funeral pyre, a cleansing fire to send their spirits forever out of reach of this evil!

A spinning inferno exploded in the room, tore the Dark Priests near Namid away from her and consumed the mangled bodies on the wall. With Power-enhanced senses, Namid felt her siblings' spirits escape the fetters that had been placed on them, escape the tortured bodies, and fade away. It seemed they smiled.

And her tears fell.

She noticed the intense heat in the small room then, and the roar became nearly unbearable. Her hair lifted on a ghostly wind, unbraided. Faintly, she heard the small tinks of the needles that had been in her braid hitting the floor. She finally heard the shrieks of the Dark Priests as the flames devoured them all.

Namid's sight cleared then. Through the whirling flames, she saw that the far wall stood blackened and bare, the bodies gone, and even the manacles and chains melted. The flames began to die. She felt spent, drained of Power and empty of emotion, except for the bitter ache in her heart.

"Finally, the proof," said a familiar voice from behind her. "She is indeed the one."

Namid started to turn, but something Powerful struck viciously at her mind. Pain exploded behind her eyes as she desperately tried to grab shreds of Power to protect herself. She screamed, vulnerable, as all her defenses buckled. Darkness swept over her.

But her brothers' voices followed her into the darkness, soothing her, repeating two words.

"Tal escaped."

Tal escaped....

CHAPTER 27

Namid lay on a frigid, rough stone floor. After a time, she recognized that she lay there in fact and not in the midst of some dream. She seemed to remember horrible nightmares, but the details escaped her. She opened her eyes to darkness, not even a glimmer of light. She hurt, more than she remembered ever hurting before.

She tried to move and discovered that she could, if she was willing to endure the increased pain. It seemed that even her hair hurt.

Where was she? And why?

Namid heard a noise then and froze, and directed her attention outward rather than inward. Was that metal hitting something? Stone perhaps? It was not repeated so, after several breaths-of-time, she returned her attention to her plight.

One thing at a time, she told herself, as you learned.

All right, hands. Palms ached. Something about fire there? She could not yet remember, so did not dwell on it. They did not hurt all that much. A good thing. Rough stone under hands, not stones fitted together like in a building. Continuous, like a cave, maybe. Something there too, that would not come to her. So… feet. Cold toes in boots, but no pain there. Ah! She still had her boots. And fetters on her ankles, with a short chain between.

Chained again.

No, not again!

She started to shake, and not from cold.

She forced herself to concentrate, to continue her assessment. Arms and legs. Knees felt banged up. She seemed to remember falling. Arms did not feel too bad, but shoulders and neck felt strained. She remembered holding herself up…. Nothing further. Oh well, moving on. Torso. Chest and belly cold, lying pressed against the rock floor, the chill seeping through her shirt…. Where was her tunic? Ah, fabric next to her left hand. Felt about right to be her tunic. Back… also cold and…. Oh! There was the worst of the pain….

And the memories rushed back, accompanied by a terrible pounding in her head… the whip… the Dark Priests… fire… her defenses crumbling….

Kalon and Jiro!

Namid choked back a sob as she remembered it all.

"Namid?" came a voice out of the darkness, not much above a whisper.

She went still and shoved a fist against her mouth to suppress the sobs, although the motion sent waves of agony across her back.

"Namid?"

Then she knew the voice. "I'm here."

"Thank the gods," Odasoro said, from somewhere ahead and to her left. "We'd feared the worst."

"I'm here," Namid repeated. And everyone started talking. Listening to the voices, it sounded like most, if not all her companions were there with her.

After several breaths-of-time, Haeith raised his voice over the others and hushed them. "Quietly! There might be unwelcome ears."

"Where are you all?" Namid said in a quiet voice into the

ensuing silence.

"We're along the walls," Odasoro said. "They have us chained here."

Namid took that in as she tried to sit up. She could not suppress a groan as she moved her tortured body, but she made it to a kneeling position. She pulled on her tunic and felt a little warmer. Unfortunately, her motion split open one of her wounds. She felt blood running down her back under the tunic. She tried to ignore it.

She dug into a hidden pocket in her boot and pulled out a couple of the tools for picking locks and started on the locks on her fetters. The simple locks caused her no problems and she had them open in no time. Free from chains again, she at once felt better. Not much, but enough for the moment. She tucked the lockpicks back in her boot.

"Are you all right?" Cameni said. She seemed to be almost straight ahead of Namid.

"I've been better," Namid said, unwilling to give details. "Any idea how long it's been?"

"They brought us here almost directly after we left you," Haeith said. His voice came from her right. "They brought you here a couple of candle-marks later. But you were out for a long time. It could be dusk, or later, in the world above."

"I was out that long?" No one needed to answer that.

Namid tried to get up and realized she was not ready for that yet. "Ah, did any of you see where they dumped me when they brought me here? How close am I to the door?"

"The door should be less than half a pace from you," Haeith said. "Toward your feet, if you are still lying on the floor."

"Ah, no, I'm sitting. But I have my bearings now. For the moment, anyway. Just to ease my mind… it *is* totally dark in here, right?"

"Yes. Why?" Enric sounded puzzled.

"Good. I just wanted to make sure that I hadn't gone blind."

"They tried to blind you?" Cameni sounded horrified.

"No!" Namid said, then changed the subject before anyone asked what the Dark Priests *had* done. "I'm going to make my way over to you. Are there any hazards I should be aware of on the floor between me and you?"

"No," Haeith said.

"Good. Now, don't hold your breath. This is going to take a while." Namid decided to go toward Haeith's voice and so started to crawl to her right.

"Why?" Cameni said. "Are you injured?"

"What do you think?" Aahmes spoke for the first time, and a concern that Namid had not acknowledged vanished at the welcome sound of his voice. But another worry replaced it. He sounded awful and Namid wondered how badly *he* had been hurt.

The others stayed silent after that, for which Namid felt grateful as the crawl took every bit of her concentration, particularly since she was determined not to cry out at the pain. Finally, she reached a wall, and told everyone so.

"You sound close," Haeith said, from her left, now. "I believe I'm the first one on this end."

"All right, I'm coming."

Namid found nothing on the wall to grab to pull herself to her feet, so she continued her crawl, keeping her right shoulder brushing the wall. Not too far along, beneath her hands she felt a circular rock set into a slight depression on the floor, the lid on the crude privy arrangement these cells had. If this cell matched others she had been in years ago, there would be one for every set of rings in the wall, one per prisoner. She would need to be careful if she continued to follow the wall to reach everyone. She started forward again and bumped into someone's feet.

"That's you, I hope," Namid said.

Haeith chuckled. "Yes. I'm seated here."

"Fetters on your ankles, too?" she said.

"No, just manacled wrists. Here." Haeith's feet moved, then Namid heard rattling chains against stones and a hand touched hers. She clasped his hand for a moment, then found the manacle on his wrist and followed the short, attached chain to the thick metal ring set in the wall.

"Both wrists?" Namid said.

"Yes."

"All right," she said, "let's see what I can do."

She dug out her lockpicks again and tried to find a somewhat comfortable position to work from. The movement sent waves of pain through her. She hissed softly. The pain in her head now rivaled the pain in her back. Haeith leaned toward her, his breath warm on the side of her face.

"Namid, how badly *are* you injured?" he said, barely vocalizing his words. "I can smell blood."

"It's mine," she whispered back and hoped that only Haeith heard her. "And it's not good, but I don't want to alarm anyone. We don't dare have Cameni Heal me, even if the drug's worn off so she can. That'll alert every Dark Priest in this place. I'll recover in time."

Namid found the lock on one of Haeith's manacles and began to work on it. Finally, she got the feel for it and it opened. But then and there, she decided that trying to do something like this in total darkness and this severely injured was one of the dumbest things she could remember doing. The second lock was easier because she had a better feel for the type of lock they used.

"Hold a moment," Haeith said after she had freed him, before she even tried to move on to the next person. She heard cloth rustling and he pressed something into her hands.

"Put it on," he whispered. "It's my outer tunic and it's black. Likely no one will notice any blood seeping through."

Namid thanked him and slipped it on. He helped her as they moved around to each of the others and she picked the locks on their manacles, too. By the time they reached Aahmes, who was the last one, Namid felt she might be ready to try standing. When he was free, Aahmes caught her in a sudden embrace that made her gasp with pain. He stood and helped her to her feet, and they all eased over to the door.

"Good thing you got me those lockpicks," Namid murmured to Aahmes.

"Especially since they got mine."

"Next time don't stash them where they'll find them so easily."

"I'll keep that in mind...." From his tone of voice, Namid readily pictured his look of exasperation. She smiled to herself.

"Loan me yours," he said. "I'll get the door."

Namid handed them over and leaned against the wall to muster her strength. She knew that once they moved into any light, she would need to look much better than she felt so the others would not fuss or hold up for her.

A moment later, Aahmes laughed.

"What?"

"Almost too easy. Someone ought to tell them their locks are nearly worthless. Here." He handed her tools back and she slid them down into her boot.

"Are there likely to be guards out there?" Cameni whispered.

"Who knows," Aahmes said. "Everyone be ready. I'm opening it."

A sliver of light crossed the room when Aahmes pushed the door open just a crack. Namid thanked Ilenii that the Dark Priests kept the hinges well-oiled, so they did not squeak. She still stood in darkness, but she could now see her companions well enough to assess their conditions. All of them had been ill-treated, but Aahmes looked the worst. His face was swollen and badly bruised and he moved with less grace than usual. He opened the door further. Namid wondered how bad she would look to them, then dismissed the thought as unimportant. She concentrated on keeping her expression bland to avoid showing any of the pain she felt and stepped up behind Aahmes to peer around him.

The door from their cell opened out into a room that was poorly lit by a single torch. The room held a couple of chairs, with a thin rug on the stone floor. It was unoccupied.

With sighs of relief, they all ventured out into the room and Aahmes shut their cell door again. No other doors led from the room, only an opening in the wall to the left of their cell door. The light from the torch showed a passage leading from the opening. The passage made a sharp turn just at the edge of the light.

Aahmes glanced down at his hands and turned sharply to Namid, deep concern in his expression. She saw the red stain of blood on his hands—hers, from when he had touched her back—and she looked up to meet his gaze. He started to say something, but she stopped him with a shake of her head. He looked ready to argue but just closed his fists around the telltale stains.

"Let's get away from here!" Enric said. He grabbed the torch and headed for the opening. The rest of them followed.

"Do you know where we are?" Cameni asked Namid.

"In a general sense."

"Well, can't you... you know... look using Power?"

Without thinking, Namid reached out for the Power. And nothing happened. She barely kept walking while she suppressed sudden panic. She remembered the drug burning away in the Power she had called for the fire, and she did not feel like she had been given more, but she still sensed no Power. Nothing. What had that attack been that had knocked her out? She had heard tales that a person could burn themselves out with too much Power. Had she done that? Had it been done to her? She tried to pull her thoughts together as Cameni gave her a worried look.

"I can't right now," Namid told her. She sounded shaky to herself and hoped Cameni did not notice. Namid raised her voice a little for the others to hear, too. "In fact, we probably shouldn't use any Power, once the drug has worn off. As soon as they realize we're gone, they'll be watching for it."

"How will we find everything, then?" Odasoro said.

"I know where the black jewel is," Enric said. "I've seen it."

"Do you know how to get there?" Haeith said.

"No, but I can somehow feel it pulling me. And I can feel where they have the hilt.... And the blade too, I think."

"What about the pipe?" Namid turned to Haeith, as she remembered that he had carried it.

He nodded. "They took it, too."

"There's something else with the hilt and blade," Enric said. "Perhaps it's that."

"What about weapons?" Odasoro said. "I don't think we want to travel too far here without them."

"I would feel most comfortable with my own blade," Haeith said.

"Once we get to someplace more familiar," Namid said. "I should be able to get us to the place where they probably put our things. If nothing else, we'll be able to arm ourselves adequately there, I think."

So, they continued along the passage. It curved and twisted, but they found no side passages off it. Namid had horrible images of meeting Dark Priests coming at them while they were trapped there, but nothing of the sort happened. Not that this reassured her... more Dark Priests should have been around.

Finally, they came to an intersection. Enric paused and faced each new opening in turn, then led them down the right-hand one. This passage widened after a short distance and they came to an area where the wall sconces again held lit torches. Enric put out his torch but kept it. Maybe to use as a weapon, Namid thought.

They continued, and passed numerous side passages, but stayed with the main one, hoping to reach their destination fast enough to avoid discovery. Their luck held, and they came to a closed door without encountering anyone.

"Beyond here," Enric said in a quiet voice. He handed

the torch to Haeith and tried the door. It opened smoothly away from them. Enric slipped inside and the rest of them followed. Namid happened to be watching Enric as she stepped into the room. His gaze traveled around the room and stopped at a point somewhat to his left and ahead. She saw him flinch and he looked away. Namid turned her attention to the room and froze, incapable of taking another step.

The orb of light shone brighter than it had earlier, which only made matters worse, for there stood the pillars with their chains, and the ornate chair facing them. And there on the seat of the chair lay the whip. A faint green glow still clung to it. Namid started to shake and none of the calming disciplines that she had learned made any difference. Enric walked toward the ornate chair and the others followed, but Namid found herself backing away until she backed into the wall and could go no further. She could not even make herself go back out the door because that meant taking just a step or two closer to those pillars, to the chains, and the whip. She fought to regain control of herself before someone noticed, but a moment later it made no difference.

Aahmes glanced back and spotted Namid. He turned to follow her gaze, then looked back at her. The stricken look of sudden understanding on his face warred with fury. He returned to her but stopped about half a pace away and stepped in front of her, deliberately blocking her view of the area by the pillars. She slowly looked up at him. Whatever he saw in her face tore a strangled cry out of him. He eased her into his embrace and vowed all sorts of inventive and painful retributions on those who had done this. Bit by bit, she relaxed in his arms and finally stopped shivering. Then she pushed at his chest until he released her. He gave her a confused look.

"The others," Namid said.

He glanced back over his shoulder and nodded. "They won't know from me," he said. Then he showed her his freshly bloodied hands. "No one has noticed yet, but we're going to have to do something about getting you bandaged." He glanced back at the others again. "They're busy at that chair. I think Enric is prying out one of the jewels."

"So that's where it's been," Namid said. "Right under their noses."

Namid looked up at him again. She lightly touched his face in one of the few spots not swollen or bruised.

"We're quite a pair, aren't we?"

He gave her a pained smile. "Used to get worse when I wrestled with my brothers," he said. "They turned out a lot like Haeith. I was the small one in the family." Then he changed the subject. "From here, can you get us to a place where we can rest and maybe get a chance to recover at least a little before we go to oppose this 'great evil'? I can't yet touch the Power because of that cursed drug, but I feel it beginning to wear off."

Namid thought a moment and nodded. "I have a place in mind. And the place I think they put our weapons is on the way. Best of all, we can travel almost the entire way using passages that the Dark Priests seldom walk — or at least that was true when I was here before. They'd send their slaves running to the storerooms for anything they wanted. Except the room where they'd dump people's weapons."

"Good." He stepped back from her, but still blocked her view. "They're returning."

The others joined them soon after. Enric carried a black jewel about the size of his thumb. And Odasoro carried a folded piece of parchment.

"Found it behind the jewel," he explained at Namid's questioning look. "Seems to be an ancient form of musical notation."

"For the shepherd's pipe?" Namid said.

"I think so."

"Now for weapons," Haeith said. "And then the hilt, blade, and pipe, yes?"

"Do you know where we are now?" Cameni said.

Namid nodded. "We'll need to go out those doors, though." She pointed at the double doors and started toward them. Aahmes kept himself between her and the pillars. She gave him a grateful look when she thought no one else would notice.

They slipped through the doors and closed them behind them. Namid took the lead again and hurried everyone into the least-used passageways. Of course, this meant they were also poorly lit. Close to a candle-mark passed before they came to the room she thought might hold their weapons. Enric stopped her hand just as she reached for the door.

"I feel the hilt and blade are close," he said. "Shouldn't we get them sooner, rather than later?"

"They're more likely to be guarded than the rest of our stuff," Namid said. "I'd rather be armed when we go for them."

He considered that, then nodded and reached to open the door himself. It was locked.

Aahmes slipped Namid's lockpicks out of her boot as he passed her and stepped up to the door

"I've got this," he said.

"Show-off," Namid muttered.

Aahmes flashed her a grin over his shoulder and after a few breaths-of-time, swung open the door. He returned her lockpicks with a jaunty bow.

She glared at him.

They filed into the room and closed the door behind them. Aahmes whistled as he looked around. The room was not large, but everywhere they turned they saw weapons and shields, even some pieces of armor, all things the Dark Priests had taken from their prisoners over the years. Here and there the glint of gold or sparkle from a gem was also visible. The loot was somewhat grouped by type, but otherwise just stacked on crude shelves.

"Quite a treasure trove," Aahmes said with a familiar gleam in his eyes.

Namid swatted him on one arm. "Not now."

He gave her one of his old roguish grins and glided over to a shelf of daggers. Namid joined him. After several breaths-of-time of poking through the stack, it was clear that their own weapons were not among them. So, they started picking out the best of what was there. Then Cameni called them all from across the room.

"I think this is ours," she said.

She was right, as they all saw when they joined her. With a pleased smile, Namid pulled out her armguards with their stilettos, and the rest of her knives. But her sword was not there. While the others sorted out their items, she looked around for it. But she came up empty. Namid noticed that Haeith had found his armor, and Aahmes and Enric had each found some leather armor that looked like it would fit them. She looked for some armor as well, but none of what she found would fit her well enough, or any of the rest of them either. So, she joined the others back at the door.

"What's wrong?" Odasoro said.

"My sword's not here."

He gave her a long look. "They could have good reason to want to keep that."

Namid nodded, with a frown. "I know. I'd just hoped they wouldn't realize what it was."

"What's this about?" Cameni said. "And don't evade the question like you've evaded others. You've kept secrets all along and I think we need, and have a right, to know more than you've been telling us."

Namid looked into her eyes for a long moment and debated what to say. Cameni did not flinch from her appraisal.

Namid nodded. "All right. But not here. We need to get someplace safer first. Agreed?"

"Agreed."

"Do we go after the hilt, blade, and pipe now?" Odasoro said.

"We're probably going to have to fight for them," Namid said.

"We should find someplace where we can hide for a while," Cameni said, "and tend to our injuries first. Going into a fight in our condition is just asking for failure."

"I agree," Aahmes said. That drew a startled look from Cameni and a slight nod of agreement from Haeith.

"Akavos and the shepherd's pipe are close," Enric said, "but it feels like they're below us." He gave Namid a questioning look.

She nodded. "There's at least one other level below this one. But I don't know that level, don't know if it's got any hiding places."

"Then let's stop on this level for a while," Cameni said. "Do you know a place?" She turned to Namid.

"Yes."

"Good. How about some food, too?"

Namid gestured back the way they had come. "If we wanted to backtrack, there are storerooms back there. But I wouldn't recommend it."

"Draw the path for me," Aahmes said. "I'll go. I can find my way and they won't even know I've been through there." He gave Namid a grin. "Just leave me marks to find you after."

Namid nodded. She scratched a rough map on the floor and described the route to Aahmes. When Namid finished, Aahmes headed out.

"You certainly know your way around here well," Enric said, a hint of challenge in his voice.

"Remember I said I'd been brought here from Kilaadi…. The Dark Priests kept us all as slaves, doing any work they thought of… carrying food to the cells, keeping the storerooms… that sort of thing…." She met his gaze and he looked away after a moment.

Namid scratched over her makeshift map so no one else could read it for what it was and led the others in the opposite direction, pausing from time to time to leave a cryptic mark for Aahmes to follow. To anyone else, the marks would just look like random scratches high on the wall, if they even noticed them at all. But to Aahmes, they would be the trail to find them again.

They had not thought to grab a lit torch again when they had the chance and so were eventually reduced to feeling their way along in the dark again. The passageways were so seldom used that they were not kept lit, and flint and steel had not been in the room with their weapons. Namid counted passages to guide them and finally found the secluded spot she wanted, a small side passage that curved then widened out into a small room. They settled along the walls of the room to await Aahmes' return.

CHAPTER 28

A soft tap of stone on stone pulled Namid from the daze she had allowed herself to help endure the pain. The barely heard sound continued, coming from back the way they had come. Namid realized it formed a beat that she recognized from one of the Shadowers' favorite drinking songs.

"Aahmes."

Namid heard Aahmes come into the room. "Where's the torch?" he said. "I've got a tinder box."

"Here," Enric said, and within moments they again had light. Aahmes dropped a good-sized bundle on the floor and regarded them with a triumphant grin. "You may all thank me at your leisure," he said, with a jaunty glint in his eyes.

"Maybe after we eat," Namid said. "I'm starved."

Aahmes just laughed and started separating out what he had brought. The bundle included a number of clean cloths, which he gave to Cameni. For bandages, Namid assumed.

They devoured the provisions Aahmes had found. Namid was far more interested in stopping her stomach's complaints than savoring the food. She suspected the others felt the same. Then Cameni gathered up her cloths and a full waterskin.

"So, who's first?" she said.

No one answered right away and Namid noticed both Aahmes and Haeith pointedly avoided looking at her.

Namid sighed. "Considering your speech about secrets, I guess that would be me," she said.

Cameni raised her eyebrows at Namid and started toward her. She, and the others, too, looked surprised when both Aahmes and Haeith joined her.

"Extra hands will make this easier, I think," Haeith said.

Namid grimaced but nodded her agreement.

"What?" Cameni looked back and forth between the two men. "What do you know that I don't?" she demanded.

"My injuries are rather more severe than I have let you know," Namid said and got to her feet with Aahmes' help. "This is likely something you have not seen before. And without a doubt will cause me further pain before you are done." Namid took a deep breath to steady herself. "Just remember that I have been through this before. Do what you have to."

"That's Haeith's tunic," Cameni said.

"I gave it to her." He gave Namid a sympathetic look. "And I think it best if we just cut it off, rather than trying to save it."

Namid nodded and pulled her long hair over one shoulder, tugging free some strands that stuck to the dried blood. She turned around to brace herself by leaning her forearms against the wall.

Aahmes sidled around to be able to see her face. "Wouldn't you rather sit?"

"Not yet. I'll be on my knees soon enough, I expect. But I can better brace myself for this standing."

Namid stifled a cry as Haeith inadvertently pulled open one of the wounds when he started to free the cloth from where the blood had dried and plastered it to her back. She felt some cool water soak through the cloth and heard that cloth tearing. She concentrated on the rock wall in front of her and tried to distance herself from the renewed pain as

Haeith and Cameni worked at removing the black tunic, then her own. After that, she was left with her torn shirt, soaked through with blood at the back. And, as Namid had predicted to Aahmes, the pain had driven her to her knees.

Aahmes stayed with her, a steadying presence as he gripped her arms. She felt the chill air touch her back as Haeith peeled away the last of the bloody cloth. Cameni gave a small cry of dismay. Then total silence gripped the room.

Namid clutched the remnants of the shirt to her chest and managed to turn around, confused at the silence. She found everyone staring at her with looks that ranged from horror to pity to anger. When she turned, Aahmes made a strangled sound.

Odasoro broke the silence first. "My dear, if I had known, I would never have countenanced your return…."

"What? Oh." Namid realized the cause of their shock and dismay. Beneath her current wounds lay the many crisscrossed scars from the previous times the Dark Priests had deemed it necessary to punish her transgressions—real or imagined—against their various rules for their slaves. Namid had worked hard to forget the physical scars they had given her.

"I did say that I've been through this before."

"As usual, you failed to provide details," Cameni snapped at Namid, her angry tone belied by the concern on her face.

Namid shrugged and winced at the pain even that small movement caused. "There are details of a number of things that I don't wish to talk about," she said.

"I must Heal this," Cameni said. "As soon as that horrible drug wears off. Or you'll be even more badly scarred."

"No!" Namid snapped at her. "No Healing. That'll bring them down on us as fast as if we just sent them a message saying, 'here we are'. Do you really think scarring matters at this point?" To her chagrin, Namid's eyes filled with tears.

"I am *years* beyond the time that could make any difference!" she said and turned her face away.

The silence stretched, then Namid felt a gentle hand on her arm.

"I'm sorry," Cameni said. "Let me just clean and bandage your injuries."

Namid nodded. She turned back to the wall and avoided Aahmes' gaze, unwilling to face what she might see there. Cameni had a gentle touch but still could not avoid causing her more pain. Namid squeezed her eyes shut against the burning tears at the pain, the recent terror, and her new fear at her apparent loss of Power. And Kalon and Jiro.

After a few moments, Aahmes clasped her hands and she returned the grip while hanging her head to hide her face. When Cameni finished cleaning Namid's wounds, she shooed Aahmes away, so she could wrap Namid in bandages. When she finished, Namid was covered by bandages from her waist to her armpits, well enough that she could have gone without a tunic, but Cameni handed her one anyway—Aahmes' overtunic, Namid noticed—and helped her slip it on. Then Cameni moved off to tend to one of the others.

Namid stayed where she was for a time and worked to regain her composure. She braided her hair again—hissing softly at the pain the movement caused—and tied it with a strip of torn cloth. She had to smile to herself when she heard Aahmes softly cursing Cameni, no doubt as she tended to his injuries. And Namid felt able to again face the others. She turned around to find almost everyone studiously avoiding her gaze. She looked at Aahmes.

He gazed at her intently, but Namid could not read his expression.

Maybe tell everything else, too, he said by hand-talk. *They're worried. Confused. A bad way to go into what I think we're headed for.*

After a moment, Namid nodded. He probably had the right of it. Tentatively, she cleared her throat, and found herself the center of attention. A wan smile touched her lips.

"As pointed out earlier," Namid said, "you all deserve some information. Just try to understand that much of this I have needed to keep to myself for a long time. For my own protection." No one moved or spoke, although Cameni continued to tend to Aahmes.

So Namid told them what she had told Aahmes so many nights before, the tale of who she was and the imprisonment she had endured at the hands of the Dark Priests, what they had done to her parents, and about her eventual expulsion from her father's house and city. She told them about seeing her brothers and what she had done to their killers before being dumped in the cell. She kept her gaze on the floor, not wanting to see anyone's expression. After that, Namid had to stop, unable to speak around the lump in her throat.

"And your sword?" Cameni said.

"A family heirloom," Namid said. "And it's possible that in the Dark Priests' hands it could be used somehow to legitimize their control of Kilaadi, and by extension, Paronia and the rest of the Six Realms."

"That seems probable," Odasoro spoke up. "They likely see you as heir to your father's throne."

Namid looked up at that. "Not me! My brother Tal escaped. He's the elder. He's next in line."

"But you are here," Odasoro pointed out. "Almost within their grasp. I suspect they plan to use that to their benefit."

Namid shrugged, but secretly agreed. "I think that's everything," she finished.

"Not quite," Enric said. "Just how much magic do you command? What can we expect from you?"

Namid looked away again. "I'm not sure—"

"Oh, come on! No more secrets, right?" Enric practically shouted at her.

Namid glared at him and her disquiet flashed into anger. "Fine! Nothing! That's what you can expect from me for Power. Absolutely nothing!"

"What? But we've seen—"

"Since my brothers... since whatever hit me... I can't feel any Power. Can't touch it. So, nothing!"

Namid realized then that she had risen to her feet and stood shouting at him. She felt guilty when he flinched back from her. She turned away.

"I might've burned myself out," she said in a lower voice. "Or maybe they did it to me."

Again, Namid heard the voice saying that she was the one. She wished she could identify the voice, but that still eluded her.

"Perhaps you should back off," Aahmes said into the silence. "She's been through a—"

"So have I," Enric interrupted him. "So have we all. And naturally you'd try to shield her. But we have something that we have to do."

"*You* have something that you have to do!" Aahmes shot back. "Remember, it's *your* quest! And what's this 'naturally'?"

"It's plain to see—"

"Please," Namid interrupted him. "We all have our secrets, things we don't want to talk about." She glared at them until they nodded. "Mine just happen to be tied up in all this. Accept my apologies for keeping you in the dark. Much of what I've told you is... distressing. I don't enjoy speaking of it... remembering...."

The others nodded and Enric looked rather sheepish. "Please accept my apologies, as well."

"Certainly."

"And mine," Cameni chimed in. "All the things I've said to you...."

Namid laughed. "If that sort of thing bothered me, do you think I could have lived in Rhadanthus these past several years?"

Cameni shook her head. "I suppose not. But still, I shouldn't have spoken to you that way, Your Highness."

Namid groaned. "I'll forgive you as long as you *never* call me that again."

"But you are—"

"Never."

Cameni looked perplexed but agreed.

Namid sat back down, exhausted, more from the shifting emotional exchange, she suspected, than from her wounds. After almost a quarter candle-mark more of Cameni's ministrations, Aahmes joined her.

"Is the drug wearing off yet?" Namid asked him.

"Slowly. I might need another candle-mark, though, before I'm up to anything substantial."

Namid nodded.

"You really have no Power left to you?"

"Not that I can tell. It's possible I'm being blocked, I suppose. But I can't tell that either."

"I could see if I can sense anything…."

"Maybe later, after we've already revealed our presence again. I'd rather not have them breathing down our necks any sooner than we have to."

He nodded and fell silent. But he took her hand again and smiled at her when she looked up at him. Namid leaned her shoulder against his and closed her eyes against all that had happened. She tried to clear her mind and hoped that some brilliant thought or plan of action would come, but she could not concentrate. She felt that someone was watching her, and the regard felt unfriendly.

She opened her eyes and looked around the room, and caught Enric quickly turning his gaze elsewhere. None of the others paid her and Aahmes any attention. She waited to see if she had seen correctly, and again caught Enric staring at her with an unfriendly expression. And he looked away when he saw her looking back at him. Namid slipped her hand from Aahmes' grasp and levered herself to her feet.

Aahmes looked up at her. "Want me along?"

"So, you saw it, too?"

He nodded.

"No. If I need to strangle him, I can handle that myself."

Aahmes smiled at that.

Namid walked up to Enric and sat down right in front of him.

"What is it?" she said.

He would not look at her. "What?"

"Something is plaguing you. Something about me, I think. What is it?"

He looked down at the floor and was silent so long that Namid thought he would not answer. Then he spoke, so quietly that she had to lean closer to hear him. "On the way here, the Dark Priests talked. About a lot of things, but one thing that pleased them greatly was someone who was passing information to them. About us. Often, and accurate. And they talked a lot about you, that you're something important to them."

"I see." Namid saw only too well. "And what do you think?"

"I don't know what to think! A lot of what they said makes sense and fits what has happened, but…."

"But… we've traveled together and been through some difficult spots…."

"Yes. But you're also expert at evading questions and hiding things." Now he did meet her gaze, a challenge clear in his expression.

"Can you see why that might be?"

He looked thoughtful. "If all you've said is true, then I can agree you would've learned to do so to survive. Still…."

Namid nodded. "Still. There's really no way to verify what I've told you, while we are here. And so, you don't feel you can trust me because the Dark Priests might've spoken truly."

He nodded and looked miserable.

"Understandable, given everything that's happened." Enric looked at her in surprise, like he had expected a different response. "But also, please, consider that they might've said all those things in your hearing just to sow distrust among us."

"I suppose." He did not sound convinced, but Namid thought he would at least consider the possibility.

Namid stood and looked down at him, and kept her misgivings to herself. "I just ask that if you decide I'm what they say, please don't just up and stab me in the back. You might need me."

He gave her a shocked look, then flushed and looked away. Namid stayed a moment longer, studying him, then returned to her place next to Aahmes.

"Did you find out what that was all about?" he said as he reclaimed her hand.

"On his journey to Corentris, the Dark Priests told him some tales."

"Hmm. About little ol' innocent you?"

Namid smiled, which was probably what he intended. "Well, innocent of these things anyway. But now he doubts...."

"Ah." He fell silent for several breaths-of-time, then said, "I'll watch your back."

Namid nodded and leaned against him. "Thank you." She closed her eyes, and again sought that elusive spark of inspiration.

CHAPTER 29

Someone shook Namid's shoulder. She batted half-heartedly at the insistent hand and mumbled something about being left alone. Her motion or voice must have startled Aahmes, however. He started up, with a dagger in one hand, jostling her. Of course, at that point, she was wide awake as well.

"How long?" Namid said and tried to focus on Haeith, who stood over them. She seemed to be asking that question too often.

"Longer than we'd intended," he said. "I also fell asleep and I'd planned to watch."

Namid sat up and looked around. The others stirred, but no one was up yet. "A spell?" she said.

Haeith shook his head. "No, just reaction to recent events, I'd say. Come on, we need to be going. I believe it must be near dawn above."

Aahmes and Namid struggled to their feet, both stiff from their injuries. Namid still hurt, too, but at least the pain in her head had subsided some. She still could not feel any Power, but she could move now without having to fight to keep from blacking out.

Namid found that moving around helped ease the stiffness, which came as a relief. Everyone gathered up their things and they set out, with Enric again in the lead.

However Akavos pulled him, it seemed to work well. After about half a candle-mark, they came to stairs that led down. Some light came from below, so they snuffed out their torch and eased down the staircase, weapons held ready.

At the bottom, they found themselves in a carpeted hallway. Colorful tapestries covered most of the rock walls and sconces held small orbs of Power that gave off enough light to imitate daylight. No one was in sight.

"Can you tell how far?" Namid whispered to Enric.

He pointed down the hall to a door about fifty paces away. "Beyond that."

They hurried to the door. Aahmes put his ear to it and, after a breath-of-time, told them he heard voices, four or five he estimated.

He looked at each of them in turn. His expression asked if they were ready. After everyone nodded, he flung the door open and they all rushed in.

The battle was swift and bloody. They caught the Dark Priests by surprise, but they were armed and experienced with their weapons. Namid and her companions just happened to be better. Enric picked up a shallow cut on one arm, but otherwise they all escaped injury.

While Haeith and Aahmes dragged the bodies to one side, Namid looked around the room. It was decorated as lavishly as the hall outside, in blues and golds, with plush chairs spaced randomly around the room. She saw no sign of the pieces of Akavos or the pipe. She gave Enric a questioning look.

He shrugged. "It felt like they were in here."

"Another trap?" Namid said, worried.

"I think I hear someone at the stairs," Cameni said from the door. Aahmes joined her, glanced down the hall and shut the door.

"This doesn't have the feel of a trap," Haeith said.

"Could the pieces of the sword be somehow disguised?" Odasoro said. "Maybe under an illusion?"

"I suppose," Enric said. "I do still feel that they're here, but I don't get any particular direction."

Haeith looked at Namid. "Shall I?"

"I don't see that we have much choice," she said. "Just try to disturb the ambient Power as little as possible."

"I will."

He closed his eyes but seemed to do nothing else. After many breaths-of-time, Namid gave Aahmes a questioning look. He shook his head.

"I don't feel what he's doing. We should be all right."

About a quarter candle-mark passed, then Haeith opened his eyes again and scanned the room.

"There are no illusions here," he said. "But I think you're standing on a door," he told Enric, who jumped away from where he stood and gave the rug a suspicious look.

Aahmes began to roll back the rug and soon exposed a heavy wood door beneath it. Haeith was the only one strong enough to open it alone. Beneath, they found another set of steps that led down.

"That's odd," Enric said. "Now it feels like they're down there."

"I wonder if someone could be interfering with that," Namid said. "Drawing us in by using the Power."

"I think it's been someone else's game from the start," Aahmes said. "But we're here. I think we can agree these Dark Priests need to be opposed, whatever else this 'great evil' is. So, we just see this through, fighting to come out intact at the end."

He grabbed a light orb from one of the ubiquitous sconces and started down the stairs. After a moment, the rest of them followed. Haeith took the rear and closed the door behind them. Namid wondered what good that would do with the carpet turned back and the dead bodies along one wall, then dismissed such thoughts. It probably did not matter one way or another at that point.

At the bottom of the stairs, they came to a room about the size of the one above, and decorated as much, although this time in gold and red. Three doors led from this room, all closed. Enric walked to the door directly across from the bottom of the stairs.

"This way," he said.

"Careful," Namid said. "I think we're close to the place where the Dark Prince sleeps. Or slept."

"You think?" Enric said.

"When they held me, slaves and prisoners were rarely taken below the level of the cells," Namid said. "Tales were passed among us. This seems something like some of the tales I heard."

Enric gave her a curt nod and turned back to the door. He listened for several breaths-of-time with an ear pressed to the door, then shrugged and opened it. Darkness filled the room beyond. The stink that rolled out the doorway drove them all back, retching helplessly at the stench of terror and blood and death.

Haeith, Aahmes, and Namid gained control of their stomachs first and approached the door together to peer into the room. Namid held the end of her tunic over her nose and mouth to try to keep out the stink. The two men struggled to breathe shallowly. The light from the orb Aahmes carried revealed an evil sight. They saw a rectangular room, and along the walls on both sides, scores of mutilated bodies lay in piles that reached higher than Namid's waist. Many looked much too fresh. Dried blood covered the parts of the floor that the bodies did not.

Aahmes and Namid shared a look.

"The slaves?" he said.

"Looks like."

"Explains why we didn't see them above."

The three backed away from the door to take in the clearer air in the first room. Enric looked up at them, his complexion somewhat green. Cameni knelt in one corner, facing away from the open door. Odasoro crouched next to her and talked softly to her.

Namid took a second look at the pattern in the carpet. Much of what she had thought a design was, in reality, blood that had soaked in. She suppressed a shiver and did not mention this to the others.

"Perhaps we can take a different route to our destination," Odasoro said, with a look at Enric.

"Maybe one of the other doors?" Enric said, as he worked to control his nausea and revulsion.

Namid closed the open door as Aahmes stepped toward the door to the left of the stairs. He opened it a crack, leaned close to peer through, and lurched back, coughing. He closed the door and shook his head, trying to regain his breath.

"No good. Same thing. But worse," he croaked.

Namid looked at the final door but made no move toward it.

"I'll wager we find the same there, too," she said.

"I won't take you up on that wager," Haeith said. "But we'd better make certain, anyway."

He borrowed the orb from Aahmes, and repeated Aahmes' actions at the last door, right down to the choking retreat.

"We'll just take the most direct route," Enric said, and returned to the first door.

"Wait," Cameni said and pulled out a few bandages that she had not used. "If we tie these over our mouths and noses, it might help."

Enric gave her an uncertain look, shrugged and took one of the bandages from her. He waited until they had all tied on the strips of cloth, then opened the door again and stepped inside.

The trip through the room took few breaths-of-time but felt like candle-marks as they picked their way around parts of bodies and tried not to step on anyone. Namid noticed that not one of the bodies was still in one piece. She suspected much of that had happened before they died. After that pleasant thought, she tried to concentrate solely on placing her feet safely.

"Why did they do such a thing?" Cameni said as they neared the end of the room.

"One way the unscrupulous can grab more Power is through the deaths of others. Supposedly the more lingering the death, the more Power they can strip from their victims' waning lives," Namid said.

Cameni shuddered and looked even more ill.

"You sound familiar with this sort of thing," Enric said, with a suspicious look over his shoulder for Namid.

"I was held here for a time, remember?" she said. "Everyone shared tales about the Dark Priests' doings as we all tried to figure out how to survive. Naturally I heard tales of what the Dark Priests were supposed to be capable of."

"Most of these bodies seem relatively fresh," Odasoro said. "Why would they need to raise such magic so quickly? And why now? Shouldn't this 'Wild Power' provide enough magic for anything they might want?"

No one had an answer. After a short silence, Aahmes spoke. "The Power here does have an evil feel," he said. "Parts of it anyway. Tainted whorls. And slimy. This is probably what we felt a hint of earlier, that we couldn't identify."

"Can you still use it if you must?" Namid said.

He looked thoughtful, head cocked slightly. Testing it, Namid imagined. Then he nodded. "As long as I'm careful not to grab the tainted parts." Namid gave Haeith a questioning look.

He nodded as well, and added, "The Wild Power is also problematic for me. But I'll do what I can."

Enric picked his way over the last of the bodies and paused at a door at the far end of the room.

"Everyone ready?"

"As ready as we can be," Aahmes muttered, while everyone else nodded. "There's a nexus of Power beyond that door," he said a little louder. "I can feel Akavos now, but also the taint, the Wild Power, and something else."

"The Dark Prince?" Cameni said.

"It seems likely."

For a moment, they all just looked at each other. Then Namid broke the silence. "This is it, then." She reached to open the door, but Enric beat her to it and swung it wide.

The altar-like table that stood in the center of the circular room caught Namid's attention first. A gaunt, dark-haired man lay atop it, unmoving. Dim light in the room came from an unseen source, much like the light in the huge cavern above them. A brighter light, also from an unidentifiable source, illuminated the man on the table. Through the doorway, Namid saw three openings in the wall across the room. The openings led into darkness.

Enric eased into the room first, his sword held ready. He at once turned to the right and focused on something Namid could not see. He pulled the strip of cloth from his face and walked that direction as the rest of them entered the room, all with weapons ready. Namid entered last and closed the door behind her. She removed the cloth she had tied across her nose and mouth. The others did likewise. Namid studied the room but avoided looking too closely at the emaciated man on the table.

Enric returned from the right, holding the black jewel, along with the hilt and blade of Akavos raised high, his expression triumphant. He had sheathed the sword he had carried. Haeith was a step behind him and held the golden pipe. As he walked, Haeith seemed to be studying the man on the table, from a distance.

"So how do we piece the sword together?" Cameni whispered. Keeping their voices quiet seemed appropriate.

"I have no idea," Enric said, also in a quiet voice.

"The sword gives you no clues?" Haeith said.

Enric shook his head.

"I believe this music is the key." Odasoro held up the ancient musical notation.

"But I know nothing of reading music," Haeith said.

"I believe I can guide you," Odasoro said.

Namid explored as the others continued to discuss the matter. The room held no other furnishings, neither was it decorated like some of the others. She counted two more openings that had not been visible from outside the door. She saw old blood under the table, but nowhere else. Namid tried to ignore the figure in the center of the room, but her gaze kept returning to him. So finally, she edged closer.

And stopped, held motionless by the clear, sweet, incongruous sound of the pipe. A deep bell-like tone rang in the room and the man in front of Namid sat up and turned toward her.

CHAPTER 30

Namid scrambled back and stared at him. While wasted, his face was otherwise almost indistinguishable from the face that she saw whenever she looked at Aahmes, or looked in a mirror. Somehow, she knew that she stood before Sesaisyd. She tried to say something to warn the others but could not make a sound.

Sesaisyd's haggard eyes held hers and drew her into their gray depths. Images came to Namid, and knowledge. She saw Sesaisyd and several others grouped around a table, laughing and drinking and spinning illusions and dreams out of whorls of Power. They spoke of the gods and plans to overthrow them. She recognized Ilenii in the group, as eager and vocal as the rest.

Namid saw them again, now dwindled to half their number, uncounted years later she knew somehow. They stood in the bitter wind of a northern winter, sharing with each other the fantastic knowledge that the gods could not be found, that they seemed to have vanished from the world many millennia earlier, before this group came to Power. They decided to take the places of the gods.

Images of conflict swirled past Namid, too swiftly to

grasp the details, many hundreds of years of gathering and taming ever greater amounts of Power to their own desires and stretching their abilities to the limit and beyond. And their numbers dwindled further, mostly through their own actions. She saw what they did to each other and to any who seemed to stand in their way, none of them innocent of cruelties and atrocities. She saw an intense argument between Ilenii and Sesaisyd. Others joined, and the argument became a battle of Power.

She saw Sesaisyd lying on the table, but she knew the moment she saw lay many hundreds of years in the past. Dark-robed people filed into the room and one, their leader, held his hands above Sesaisyd's head and tore Power from the insensible man. This image repeated itself many times and the Dark Priests grew in Power and control of their god.

Then darkness blanketed Namid's vision, punctuated by stars. She drifted downward. In front of the stars, she counted five dark, rounded shapes. The moons, all dark. She saw the sun rise and, with it, the Wild Power rose to lap about her ankles.

Namid returned and found herself still staring into a pair of gray eyes that nearly matched Aahmes', aware that mere breaths-of-time had passed. And she realized that she had learned more than the god might have intended. While he looked only a little older than Aahmes, Sesaisyd felt timeworn and spent by the passage of the millennia, broken from the Power theft. He did not expect to live much longer.

His eyes widened, as they held hers, and he just then seemed to focus on her. "You look like her... my twin..." he said in a rich, deep voice that nevertheless sounded rough with disuse.

His voice caught the others' attention. Namid heard them come up next to her as the music from the pipe faded away.

Sesaisyd's eyes shifted to the person at Namid's left. Aahmes.

"Another?" Sesaisyd said. "What trick is this?"

Namid sensed motion from Enric and reacted just in time to catch his arms, to block the downward swing of Akavos.

"Wait! Things don't seem to be as we were told."

"No. But they sufficed to bring you here at the right time," came a new voice, the voice Namid had last heard behind her as she was attacked and fell into darkness.

Namid and her companions turned toward the dark opening from which the new voice came. From the corner of her eye, Namid saw Sesaisyd shudder at the sound of the voice and slump as if under a great weight.

"Myung?" Enric said hesitantly.

He was right... the voice sounded like Myung's. And yet unlike. But still familiar.

The man the voice belonged to stepped into the room. His face was Chendrukhar's, mostly, and he wore the gilded robes of the First High Priest. Several lesser Dark Priests filed into the room in his wake, like so many shadows. They took positions around him. One carried Namid's sword.

"What? How?" Enric stammered.

The First High Priest smiled. "Yes, I am Myung. And Chendrukhar. Others, even." He looked at Namid. "Karile...."

Namid fought down a surge of anger at this revelation. And a wave of grief.

He turned to Enric. "And Lyvoa...."

"She was my sponsor to Vlatas' temple," Enric said, sounding stunned.

The First High Priest favored him with a fierce grin, then continued. "Some years ago, I took the Power of the priest Myung, and with it came his knowledge and other aspects, his essence if you will. He didn't last long after that. The same with all the others. You can just think of me as Wesh, to help keep things straight." He gave them all the feral grin, then.

"You sent me to Rhadanthus!" Enric said. "How much

else of this have you dictated?"

Wesh shrugged. "I steered events in the direction I needed from time to time. What did you think of my ancient scroll in the library in Kilaadi? I thought that was particularly well done. It even contained many truths."

A burst of Power crashed into Wesh, coming from another of the dark openings, this time to their right. High Priest Randoq stood in the opening, with his own following of lesser Dark Priests, and several other High Priests, arrayed in front of him.

Wesh shrugged off the attack but took a step back. "What? You dare?"

Randoq gave him a nasty smile. "While you've been busy *steering* events, I've been busy preserving the priesthood, bolstering it, gaining greater Power for us. As a true leader should." He cocked his head toward Namid and her companions. "They know. They've seen the refuse." He threw another bolt of Power at Wesh, which the latter blocked and sent back at him.

"This will get nasty quickly," Aahmes murmured. "He's the one with the blood Power. Some of it's even from those who fell to Sy'shythys."

"And the first one has forged a link to the Wild Power," Haeith muttered.

Namid heard them but could not respond. She knew about the link Wesh had forged to the Wild Power... it went through her. The moment Randoq had appeared, an overwhelming binding of Power had engulfed her mind and body, holding her motionless. And through the binding came some unanticipated knowledge: Wesh had set the binding in her right after she had exhausted herself with the fire for her brothers.

This binding locked her away from the Power and he twisted it now to control her. But beyond the binding's obstruction, Namid again felt Power. Wesh's presence tried to overwhelm her thoughts, but there she fought, and for the moment held him at bay. She began working on forcing her way out of the bonds, but she remained trapped inside her body, for the moment anyway, which he controlled. Namid lost track of what happened in the room as she struggled to break the binding.

Oddly, chunks of Wesh's thoughts and plans seeped through to her. Sesaisyd was doomed... the Power of gods who died passed to any descendant who was closest at the time.... He knew Sesaisyd and the others had made themselves 'gods'.... Aahmes' existence had been a surprise.... She and Aahmes must be descended from Sesaisyd — gods' descendants sometimes had their ancestor's features.... With his death, Sesaisyd's Power should split between them.... And Wesh would take that Power from them, along with their own substantial Power — as he had taken Myung's and Chendrukhar's but been unable to take Sesaisyd's completely these many years. Then he would repeat what Sesaisyd and the others had done... he would become a god. He thought that Randoq must have similar plans.

Namid felt Power growing in the room and strained to reach it, while Wesh pulled Wild Power through her to battle Randoq. She was vaguely aware that she walked toward Wesh and wondered what he was having her do. Then she lost interest as a second binding slammed into her. From Randoq, this time. She staggered from the two opposed bindings.

As with Wesh's binding, Randoq's thoughts and plans seeped through to her. His binding came through blood Power, through her torment under the whip. He would oust the First High Priest... gain power over the Six Realms.... He had thought to do *that* through Namid's sister....

Namid would have laughed, if she could: the tired old ploy of marrying the princess to gain the kingdom. Really?! This felt like one of Odasoro's tales.

More of Randoq's thoughts came to her. He would finally get the blood Power of the god—something he had so far been unable to manage—from Aahmes, after his heritance from Sesaisyd came to him…. The existence of another descendant was a welcome surprise…. These others might be a rich source of blood Power as well…. He would break her… control her through the binding…. When she was no longer useful, he would get the rest of the blood Power of the god then.

Namid became aware again of the room when Wesh turned her to face the others. A three-way battle raged, with both Power and more mundane weapons, and she found it difficult to see details through the bright flashes of hurled Power.

Namid glimpsed Haeith, Aahmes and Enric battling with some of the armed Dark Priests. Randoq and Wesh threw bolts of Power at each other, and also at Namid's companions. Aahmes blocked anything they threw his way and protected the others, but he looked strained. Amid all this, Sesaisyd sat on the edge of his table, apparently watching, but doing nothing, his lips twisted in a self-satisfied smile. Through the binding to Wesh, Namid sensed that he pulled heavily on Sesaisyd's Power. And he thought that Randoq did also. Namid fought both Dark Priests' bindings and picked away at them as if picking at mortar with her fingernails. She concentrated on her left hand and willed it to move. And, oh so slowly, it responded. She formed the hand-talk gesture for 'Help!' and hoped Aahmes would notice soon.

Something new came from Randoq. Through the Power, he paraded in her thoughts all she had endured at the hands of the Dark Priests, drug out all her pain and torment, battered her with horrid memories. She felt his intent, remembered his promise to break her. She snarled and pushed back. True, she had been hurt, she carried the scars, but she had learned to live with them. He could not use them, or her memories, against her. They were hers! Fury washed over her. The bindings cracked and began to fall away.

At a brief lull in the battle, when Namid's companions

dispatched the Dark Priests facing them all at once, Enric's gaze fell on Namid where she stood at Wesh's side. A moment later, Aahmes' gaze followed Enric's and found her. At first, he did not seem to notice Namid's hand-talk gesture, then his eyes widened, and he stared into hers.

"I knew it!" Enric shouted. "She's betrayed us!"

Aahmes shook his head, refuting Enric's assertion, but Enric seemed beyond paying any attention to him. Namid clawed at the restraints of Power that held her in place and held her mute. And the Wild Power came to her, through the holes in the bindings. It further splintered the hold the Dark Priests had on her.

Too late.

Time slowed to a crawl. Enric lunged toward her, Akavos raised to strike. Aahmes raised a hand and sent Power to block Enric's attack.

Too late.

Still held immobile, Namid watched the Powerful sword descend toward her. Then Sesaisyd was there, so fast she had not seen him move. He placed himself between her and Enric at the precise spot the killing blow would fall.

Akavos caught the god in the neck.

An ear-splitting screech came from the sword. Enric dropped it with a cry of pain and cradled the hand that had held it. Sesaisyd's body and severed head began to fall. At that moment Namid felt a sudden surge of Power, and Sesaisyd's motion stopped. His head hung suspended in midair, blank eyes staring, and his body remained tilted away. All sound in the room ceased, and all motion, almost as if everyone was bound as Namid was.

Then Cameni gave voice to a small shriek and hid her face. Haeith and Aahmes exchanged looks.

Aahmes shrugged. "I've never seen a god killed before either."

A moment longer, Sesaisyd's body and head hung there. Then, in a brilliant flash of light, they crumbled into ash that fell to the floor. A wisp floated up from the ash, drifting to an unfelt wind.

Sesaisyd's voice came to Namid, in her thoughts. ~*Such strength... my many-times-removed daughter.... Should not fall to such as these....*~

And knowledge came to her, too from Sesaisyd. He had long known that he would not survive this. While they stole his Power, he had reached through the link they forged to whisper in the darkness of the Dark Priests' minds... to embolden them in their intrigues against each other... twisting their plots... to ensure Namid would return—heir to his Power—to foil the outcome of their scheming.

While the god's death held Wesh's and Randoq's attention, Namid grabbed for more of the Wild Power, called it to her, much as she had called it for her brothers' pyre. It roared into the room as a raging wind and into her mind and body, transfixing her in her own personal maelstrom of light and sound. Both bindings disintegrated, their remnants flung away from her.

As both Dark Priests reeled from the sudden backlash of the broken bindings, one last bit of knowledge slipped through from Wesh. He had delayed Dar in Rhadanthus, made certain Sy'shythys caught the Shadowers' leader, because Dar had realized that he had usurped Chendrukhar. As part of his 'steering of events', Wesh had killed the man he had claimed was a friend.

With a cry of rage, Namid spun, twisted her right wrist to release her stiletto, and drove the knife toward Wesh's chest. He saw and turned just enough so that it plunged into his shoulder instead.

Then he shrieked, high and loud. Namid stared in horror as the Wild Power she held cascaded down her arm into her blade, into the poison on its edges, and through that into the wound, forming a sickly yellow-black blotch that flowed up Wesh's neck. The stiletto's blade melted into the wound, in the wake of the Wild Power, leaving her holding the hilt. She flung it away from her.

Wesh's scream pierced her ears. The others in the room

covered their ears to try to block out the horrible sound. All except the Dark Priests who had followed the First High Priest. They stood rigidly upright, their faces masks of horror, like they shared what happened to him.

Then, one by one, they crumpled, lifeless. Namid's sword hit the floor with a clang. Wesh fell last, mere breaths-of-time after she had stabbed him. His body dissolved into a glob of noxious yellow-black goo.

An ominous silence cloaked the room. The winds died and Namid's companions put their backs to the nearest wall. All of them sported various injuries, but no one seemed seriously wounded. The door they had come through no longer existed and the bodies in the room beyond had been incinerated, just like Namid's brothers' bodies. Akavos lay on the floor where it had fallen.

"I must thank you for dealing with that minor problem for me," Randoq said and stepped all the way into the room. His supporters numbered half what they had earlier, but they still outnumbered Namid and her companions. Randoq looked from Namid to Aahmes with an eager expression.

"I would expect your heritance to come to you, likely both of you, at any moment now," he said.

Aahmes looked confused and glanced at Namid. Through thought-speech she told him to open his thoughts to her and she shared what she had learned through the bindings, taking a fraction of the time she would have needed to explain it all aloud. Another bit of knowledge that she had not known she had received came to her. The blade Akavos had been forged with Wild Power for just one purpose, to bind Sesaisyd. But sometime later, someone had distorted that into an imperative to kill him but bind his Power.

Namid glanced down at the sword to see it rimmed with a faint glow. She felt Sesaisyd's Power within it. She looked up to find Randoq's attention on the sword. He raised his gaze to hers for an instant. Then he glanced over at Enric, no more than a flick of his eyes. Namid noticed a satisfied smile on Randoq's lips, then saw the link of Power between him and Enric. And Enric lunged for the sword, a strange light in his eyes. Namid shouted at Aahmes with thought-speech and voice to keep the sword away from Enric and dove for it herself.

Aahmes and Haeith also darted for it and the four of them clashed at the blade. In the confusion that resulted, Namid tumbled under the table to avoid being trampled, Enric struggled in Haeith's grip, and Aahmes' momentum carried him across the room, almost to Wesh's remains. But Aahmes held the sword. Incredibly, a streak of Power flew from Cameni's hands to attack the link that bound Enric to Randoq.

Namid rolled to a stop at Randoq's feet. She tried to scramble away, but he caught her with a painful grip on her arm and hauled her upright. She barely noticed… Aahmes held her attention instead. He stood poised by the stone table with Akavos raised high over his head, prepared to bring it crashing down on the table's edge. Randoq noticed his intent and sent his followers running from the room. He tried to drag Namid after them, but she fought enough that he made no progress.

The sword struck the table and, with a shriek worse than Wesh's, shattered into myriad luminous shards within a blinding column of light that rose to reach through the ceiling. Out of the light, half the shards flew to Namid and pierced her skin, sending waves of agony flooding through her, pangs unlike any she had experienced before. She could not breathe or make a sound for the agony of the shards working their way into her body. The rest flew to Aahmes.

With a roar, the table split where the sword had hit and crashed to the ground. Pieces of the ceiling began to fall and created a choking dust in the air.

Randoq dropped Namid's arm and fled. Namid remained frozen in place as the shards melted into a Power that poured into her, untamed and unsafe, a light that deafened her, a blinding sound, a wind that flooded through her, shredded her and reformed her around this deluge of Power that was more than she had ever dreamed she could hold and survive. And the Wild Power rushed to her as well, swirling into the chaos that engulfed her. She spotted Aahmes frozen in place as she was, a vague shape almost invisible through the expanding glow.

After a time, the agony began to ease, although the intensity of the light increased. More of the ceiling fell and the air grew even thicker with dust, making breathing a trial. Someone grabbed Namid's arm and she nearly struck before she recognized Haeith. Dimly she saw the others grouped behind him along the wall, except for Aahmes.

"We have to get out of here!" Haeith shouted in Namid's ear.

"Where's Aahmes?" Namid shouted back.

"This way." He started to guide her, and she glimpsed Aahmes coming toward them. Then most of the ceiling crashed down in the middle of the room between them.

"Aahmes!" Namid shouted over the din. No answer.

"It's no good!" Cameni yelled. "The whole thing's coming down!"

"Which way is out?" Odasoro shouted and grabbed Namid's other arm.

"We have to get Aahmes!" Namid shouted.

All at once, Haeith's presence rolled over her thoughts and forced her to focus.

"We can't get to him from here," Haeith yelled to be heard. "You have to get us out of here. The Power in here is too wild for me, too much. I can't do what's needed! Use the Power, reach out to another place and step us out of here!"

In her thoughts, he showed her how it worked. It needed a lot of Power, not a concern for her at that time. Namid wavered, needing instead to blast the rock that had fallen and cut Aahmes off from the rest of them. Then the choice was torn from her control as the rest of the ceiling fell. She yanked at the Power, not caring what it did to her, and wrapped it in her desire to bring them all, Aahmes included, from that place. Namid cast her thoughts out to the entrance they had used to get into the caverns.

She stepped.

~ ~ ~

Namid stumbled as the ground solidified beneath her feet. She had taken them in an instant from far beneath the ground to just outside the cave entrance. She coughed the dirt out of her mouth and looked around. It worked! But her elation at her success vanished when she saw that Aahmes had not made the journey with them.

She again drew Power to herself and reached out into the crumbling chaos that was Corentris. She touched their packs in passing, where they still lay, left behind in the temple. A brief diversion of Power, a slender tendril thrown out, and she flipped the packs to her companions' feet. She stretched further…. There! She pulled, but her sense of him vanished, with the feel of something, or someone, blocking her. Again! Nothing.

She felt raw from the Power that had come to her, but she recklessly gathered more and felt Aahmes' faint presence, still back in the caverns. She tried to pull even more Power to step back to his side, but the agony was too great, and her control began to slip.

Namid darted toward the cave entrance with a half-formed plan of building a bubble of Power around herself to protect her on the way back in. Haeith caught her just inside.

"Let me go!" Namid screamed at him. "He's still alive! I can feel it!" She fought him with every dirty trick she had learned in Rhadanthus. But he countered every one.

"You can't return. You'll never make it back to him. Listen!"

As he pulled her back from the cave, she became aware of a rumbling sound coming from deep in the ground. It grew to a roar, louder than thunder. The cave and ground in front of her collapsed and fell into a pit leagues wide and many paces deep, burying the cavern system. Through the Power, Namid touched Aahmes, thought he tried to respond. Then nothing.

Haeith stayed with her while she howled her sorrow and anger, cursing the gods who were not gods, and the Dark Priests alike. The Power had slipped away from her. She was in no condition to control it. When she exhausted herself enough that she stopped fighting him, Haeith half-carried her the short distance away to the makeshift camp the others had set up.

There he sat her down on some blankets and made certain that she was wrapped up against the cold. Namid felt numb and drained, colder inside than out, and all but oblivious to anything the others did. They spoke to her, but her despair and grief swallowed up their words and kept them from reaching her. After a time, they let her be. Namid wrapped herself in the Power, the little she still commanded, and sought for Aahmes.

Time passed. When she had spent the last of her Power and could no longer control any she pulled from around her, Namid was forced to return to herself, and she became aware of her surroundings.

Night had fallen. Clouds covered the sky, which made it impossible for her to determine how far into the night it was. The fire was little more than glowing coals, but she felt some heat from it that helped offset the piercing breeze. Bundles scattered around the fire showed her where her companions slept. She wondered, in a vague sort of way, who was on watch, or even if anyone had set one. A movement to her left caught her eye.

Namid discovered Haeith watching her. He sat with his bared sword across his knees, although she sensed no danger nearby. His eyes reflected the faint glow from the remains of the fire. He nodded toward a bowl that sat by the coals.

"We saved some food for you."

Namid glanced at the bowl that she had not noticed earlier, then looked back at him.

He sighed and retrieved the bowl, placing it in her hands. "Eat."

She considered defying him. She had no interest in any food. But she also had no real interest in defiance, so she ate. She tasted nothing, but at least it helped warm her. When she finished, he took the bowl and set it aside. Then he sat next to her.

"I just can't believe it," Namid said an eternity later.

"He was a good man."

"I had just…. We…." She choked up, unable to continue.

Haeith gifted her with his companionship and with his silence as she cried out her anguish. Then he wrapped her again in blankets as she drifted into an exhausted sleep.

Chapter 31

The next morning, Namid scrambled and slid down into the crater of Corentris. She picked her way over the broken ground, headed toward the center, and extended tendrils of Power down through the rubble, searching. Using her Power was still agony, even in such a small amount, but she did not care. At some point, someone handed her some food, which she ate, her attention elsewhere.

Time passed and still she searched, heedlessly using her almost-drained reserve of Power to reach far beneath the ground, looking for Aahmes, looking for anything. Sometimes she was aware of her companions nearby, keeping pace with her. Sometimes she did not notice.

Around midday, her reserve again depleted, she began pulling on the Power around her. The Wild Power came to her, more sluggish than before, but still hers to control. She diverted some from her search to keep herself going.

Late afternoon, she felt a strange Power twinge from far below and a little ahead. She stumbled over to stand above it. She strengthened the tendril of Power that touched it and tried to decipher what it was.

"What is it?" Cameni said from somewhere behind her.

"Did you find—"

"I can't tell," Namid said, her voice hoarse. "Power...."

The others approached but backed away again at Namid's signal. She too backed up, then extended one arm toward that spot, fingers held stiff, to help her direct the Power. A moment to focus, and she sent a spear of Power blasting into the ground. Debris flew up and out, and somehow missed everyone, although the dust that floated down coated them all. Namid backed up again and directed the Power out and around to begin creating a hole.

"Haeith? Can you help with the sides?"

The big warrior stepped up to her side and studied the hole several long breaths-of-time. Then he used his Power to hold the sides, fusing the dirt together, to keep the hole from falling back in on itself.

"This will only hold a few days," he warned her. She nodded.

The others scrambled to help clear debris with bare hands and stayed out of the way of the Power.

When it got too dark for most of them to see, Namid called up some Power orbs for light, and they kept digging.

They continued in this fashion until exhaustion forced them to stop. Someone—Namid had not seen who—had brought all their gear to a spot near the new hole. So, they rested, slept and ate a little, and started up again.

Namid lost track of the time, just kept pushing herself. When Haeith could no longer control his Power—while he recovered—she spent the time crafting a ramp that spiraled down into the hole. She fused the dirt as she had seen Haeith doing to hold it firm and returned to digging as long as she could direct the Power. She begrudged the times she needed to rest and returned after the shortest time possible to continue, despite the near constant agony she felt using Power.

In the evening of the second or third day—Namid did not know which—she caught a glimpse of a sparkle at the bottom of the hole.

"Stop!" she yelled and suited action to word. She called up a light orb and hurried down the ramp. She heard the others behind her. The last several paces of the ramp were incomplete, so she just slid the rest of the way into the hole, then picked up the lump of metal that had sparkled at her.

"What is it?" Odasoro said.

"It used to be the hilt of my stiletto," Namid said and turned the blackened metal lump over and over in her hands. She looked around and noticed that this whole level of rubble looked charred.

She yanked in the Wild Power, stifling a cry at the pain, and sent it back out in waves around her to search through the debris. The aftertaste of Power here told her this had been Sesaisyd's prison room. She touched on small chunks of rock from the table. And nothing else. No bodies, no hidden escape tunnels. No Aahmes. Just scorched wreckage.

The last of her Power flew out into the twilight and the lump of metal slipped from her fingers. She dropped to her knees and wept.

~ ~ ~

Days flowed past Namid in a gray, joyless fog. She walked with the others as they traveled away from the ruin of Corentris. She ate what they handed her and slept when they did. She noticed when Cameni Healed her physical injuries and removed her bandages but cared little. She noticed that it snowed... maybe more than once. How many days passed this way Namid neither knew nor cared.

All her Power-related injuries healed. But not the gaping hole left by Aahmes' absence. She again controlled the Power, in a far greater amount than before, and when she cared to notice how much she carried, she felt surprised that she did not glow. But most of the time she cared little one way or another. She did nothing with this great reserve of Power. There seemed no point.

As the days wore on, Namid woke in the mornings hoping it had been a bad dream. As they walked, she expected to hear Aahmes' voice raised in an argument or tossing out some sardonic remark. She looked to see his grin, the way he pushed his hair back from his face. But always, he was not there. After a time, she thought she heard his voice or felt his touch on her arm, but when she turned to look, she was always disappointed. Even asleep, she could not escape the loss. This continual eager hope followed by crushing despair wore at her until she retreated into her gray fog and wrapped it around her, trying to feel nothing at all.

Then one evening, as they all sat by a cheerful fire, Namid realized she was hearing some of her favorite tunes played on a lute. Odasoro played as a background to the conversation. Somehow his lute had come away intact.

Why not Aahmes? And why not her brothers, too?

Namid squelched those thoughts before she started to cry again. She was sick of crying, and it was not helping her feel any better, anyway.

As Namid listened to the familiar tunes, the fog that had dogged her began to recede, leaving her drained but clearheaded. Her grief still lurked nearby but seemed less inclined to leap up and drown her again. Namid looked up to Odasoro's smile. He nodded at her and launched into one of the wilder tunes that she had liked as a child. She gave him a small smile. The expression felt strained, but he did not seem to notice.

Namid looked around at the others, who all gave her smiles and kind words of greeting but did not make a big fuss. For which she felt grateful.

"We've been discussing the town we'll arrive at tomorrow," Haeith said.

Namid nodded. "I think I caught some of that. Which town?"

"Cortohn," Cameni said.

Namid recognized the name… it was a good-sized town in the realm of Izrediuz. She pictured a map she had studied as a child. The town sat close to the border with Yiruny and Paronia, far northwest of Corentris. "We've come so far already? How long—" She broke off as she noticed their expressions had changed to worry. "Never mind. I don't think I really want to know."

No one said anything to that and a couple of them looked away from her.

"I have to say this," Enric said to Namid. "I owe you my most profound apologies for the way I acted toward you and for what I was thinking back there." He walked over and knelt in front of her. "I will be satisfied if you can someday forgive me."

"Oh, get up! Of course, I can forgive you. I saw the Power Randoq was using on you. You had no choice in the matter."

He stood. "But I was certain it was you working with them. Certain you'd betrayed us. I could've killed you!"

"But you didn't." Namid looked away from him. "And it easily *could* have been me. Both Wesh and Randoq tried to make it so."

"But you didn't give in to them."

"It didn't come to that, no. But I was lucky. Also, I wasn't facing them alone." Namid choked back the tears that threatened to come. "I'm just sorry we couldn't reach you sooner."

Enric shook his head at that. "Everyone's filled me in on what went on. I don't see how you could've come any faster. Your speed was amazing as it was."

"Be that as it may," Namid said and changed the subject. "Tell me about the town. What's the plan?"

Cameni grinned. "A long rest in a nice inn. A hot bath. And no more hiding and sneaking!"

"There's no question that we can afford it," Enric said. "And I think we've earned it."

"There could still be some Dark Priests who escaped the destruction of Corentris," Odasoro cautioned.

"They should be Powerless, or almost," Haeith said.

"And rather confused, I would think."

"I believe if any offer us any harm, I can deal with them," Namid said. Their reaction to her statement surprised her. Not one of them would meet her eyes. "What?"

No one spoke for several breaths-of-time, then Cameni glanced at her, looked away again, and said, "May I ask you something?"

Namid realized then that they were treating her as if she were fragile and might break with a wrong look. This both gratified her—it showed their concern—and somewhat irritated her. She did not feel that delicate. She just felt worn and tired with grief and being pounded by Power.

Namid nodded. "I just can't guarantee I'll have an answer for you."

Cameni hesitated, took a deep breath, clasped her hands together, and plunged ahead. "Are you going to be all right? I mean… all that Power…. Are you… safe?" She seemed to hold her breath as she waited for Namid's reaction.

Namid considered her words, uncomfortable with everyone's attention focused on her. Her first impulse had been to give Cameni a flip answer, but she decided it was not the time for such things. Namid took a quick survey of her condition. She still felt somewhat raw from the Power that had flooded into her but did not feel overwhelmed by it. And the hurt was less than it had been. She sensed the great reserve of Power she now had. The Wild Power had subsided, she no longer felt any lurking about. She felt like herself, just with more Power. She wondered what had prompted this particular concern, then thought she knew.

"All right, how long *has* it been?"

"Over two weeks," Odasoro said in a quiet voice.

Namid whistled at that. She had not thought that she had been out of it for so long. "I suppose I haven't been acting particularly lucid," she speculated and grimaced at their nods. "But I'm all right. I still ache from absorbing all that Power, but it's under control. I'm not a danger, unless I need to be to protect us."

They nodded and looked somewhat reassured.

Then Haeith handed her a bundle. "Here are these back."

Namid opened it. Inside were all her blades, minus the poisoned one destroyed back in Corentris. Even her sword was there. She must have pulled it out of the caverns with everything else. She gave Haeith a questioning look, but it was Odasoro who answered her silent query.

"Haeith spoke to us of fellows of his who, in their sudden grief, sought to join their lost comrades. We... we did not want you to take that path."

Namid looked at each of them, astonished. "That bad?"

"You have not been yourself," Haeith said.

Namid sighed. "I understand your concern. And thank you for it." She yawned then, without warning, and gave them a rueful grin. "It seems I still have some recovering to do."

"You *should* sleep," Cameni said.

Namid nodded. Cameni helped her get settled, then returned to the others. Namid fell asleep to the sounds of soft conversation and music.

~ ~ ~

They entered Cortohn about midmorning. During the journey Namid had almost wished to return to her unfeeling, detached fog. Almost.

The town was noisy, and everyone seemed dressed in their finest. Unusual for a late autumn day.

"Some harvest festival?" Enric wondered.

"Should be too late in the season for that," Namid said.

"We might have trouble getting rooms," Haeith said.

Enric grinned. "I believe our funds will allow us to get a place."

Haeith stopped a pretty woman to ask directions. She looked him over as they spoke and smiled a lot. They talked for many breaths-of-time while the others waited. He returned to them with a strange expression on his face.

"They are celebrating the demise of the Dark Priests' hold on the town," he said. "A bit over two weeks ago, the Dark Priests all just dropped to the ground at the same instant, in the middle of whatever they were doing. The townsfolk talk of a pillar of light that shot up to the sky. They say that it signaled their deliverance. And as soon as the Dark Priests fell unconscious, their hold on everyone was broken. So, the town rose up and eradicated them."

They all exchanged looks as they absorbed this.

"Did you find out where an inn is?" Cameni said.

"Yes, this way." Haeith started down a side street. "I learned also that there are tales of a band of bold heroes who caused the downfall of the Dark Prince and his Dark Priests."

"What?" Namid turned to Odasoro. "How?"

He shrugged and looked far from repentant. "We met a few travelers on our way here and I might have told a tale or two." Namid glared and he laughed. "That *is* part of why I came along, remember."

"I don't want to be mobbed if they find out it was us," Namid said.

Haeith chuckled. "I doubt they'd recognize us as the heroes of the tale."

"The heroes are all noble warrior ladies and lords from many lands," Cameni added. "And I'm certain they would never be seen in our condition!"

Namid sighed while they laughed. "I suppose. And speaking of 'our condition', is the inn much further? I think I've worn holes in my boots and I'm certain I can hear that bath calling to me."

"Just up ahead," Haeith said.

At first the innkeeper looked down her nose at them, dirty and road-weary as they were. But when Enric held out several navns, her manner changed in an instant at the sight of the gold coins. She could give them just two rooms, because of the crowding, but they were two of her finest.

They shared a common sitting room, and each had its own private bathing room.

While Namid and her companions took turns washing up, the innkeeper's son gathered up their clothes to clean them and left them each a comfortable, warm robe to wear. Namid did not let the boy take the tunic she wore that had been Aahmes'. She just rolled it up and tucked it into the bottom of the pack that had been his. She might clean it herself, carefully, later.

After her bath, Namid joined the others in their sitting room and enjoyed some of the inn's excellent food. Then she leaned back in a padded chair, with her glass of Karinthe at hand, and relished the warmth and the comforts of being indoors again, while she watched the others.

Cameni and Enric engaged in an animated conversation that had something to do with their families. They smiled at each other and touched hands often. Namid envied them their companionship. Namid gave a brief thought to Enric's quest—incomplete, since he had no Powerful sword to show for his efforts—and decided he had returned with something better.

Haeith sat in one corner and examined his armor and weapons for any damage needing repair. Namid considered emulating him. She doubted her own blades had escaped undamaged. But she felt too comfortable to make the effort.

Odasoro perched on the edge of a chair and tuned his lute. Then he played snatches of songs, a jumble that still made a pleasant sound.

Overall, a perfect picture of the calm after the storm, Namid thought, except for that gaping hole where the last member of their group should have been. She let her tears fall, unnoticed by the others.

Namid finished her Karinthe and settled into an even more comfortable position in her chair. As she continued to watch the others at their pursuits, Aahmes took shape in front of her. Her heart ached looking at him. At the same time, it amused her to think that she had fallen asleep and still included the sitting room in her dreams.

Her dreams became a mix of memories of her time as a Shadower. After a time, Aahmes returned and he seemed to be speaking to her, but she could not hear him. Then he retreated from her, floating rather than walking, and his face faded into Odasoro's, who leaned over her.

"Namid? Everyone's going down to the main room. Would you like to come?"

"Hmm? Oh. Maybe for a while. Are our clothes back?"

"Most of them are in bad condition. But Enric and Cameni stepped out earlier and brought back some things for us."

Namid noticed then that Odasoro wore a nice burgundy doublet, with matching trousers and low, indoor boots. He pointed toward the chair to her left, almost hidden beneath the various pieces of clothing piled on it. He smiled at the expression on her face.

"You've slept the afternoon away. If you need help with any laces, the innkeeper's daughter is right outside the door for you. Meet us downstairs?"

Namid nodded and started looking through the clothes as he left the room. Fewer were piled there than she had thought, just two sets… one a beautiful sapphire-blue velvet gown with a fine white chemise to go under it, the other a soft gray velvet tunic with trousers of the same color. Namid decided on the gown and asked the girl to help with the laces.

When the girl had finished, she stepped back from Namid, her eyes wide.

"Lady, you're beautiful," she whispered.

"I am?" Namid smiled, bemused. She'd never thought of herself as such.

"Yes, come see." The girl grabbed Namid's hand and pulled her over to the mirror on the bedroom wall. Namid studied her reflection and granted that the girl might have something there. The color of the gown suited her. Namid had left her hair loose after her bath and now it streamed over her shoulders and down past her waist in black waves. Her eyes looked haunted to her. No surprise there.

"See," the girl said with a smile. "You could be the lady out of a story!"

Namid smiled. "Perhaps you're right. But this lady is hungry and should go join her friends."

The girl blushed and bobbed a curtsey. "I'm sorry. I'll take you right there."

"No harm done," Namid assured her as she followed her downstairs.

The common room was noisy but did not smell of stale drink and unwashed bodies like other such rooms Namid had frequented not that long ago. The girl led her to the table where the others sat—all in clothes as fine as Namid's—and left her with a promise to bring food.

They all greeted her, then returned their attention to the food before them. It smelled wonderful and Namid started on hers when the girl brought it. Namid let her companions' conversation flow around her, there if she chose to join in, a pleasant backdrop if not. After she finished eating, she looked around at the others who shared the room with them—a festive bunch—locals, she guessed. The wealthiest of the locals. The group's velvets and silks fit right in.

But Namid felt she did not. And she knew then what she would do.

~ ~ ~

The next morning, Namid saddled a horse that Enric had insisted on buying for her and, over her companions' protests, headed out of town, following the road that would take her north to Rhadanthus. The city had been her home most recently, the home she had made for herself. She felt drawn to return there, to see its true state.

While cold, her journey was not difficult. She was well provisioned and felt unconcerned with any of the typical dangers of the road.

She lost track of the days and topped a hill to see Rhadanthus' South Gate below her sooner than she had expected. She rode toward it, studying the gate. It looked intact, new, and stood open. So, some people were there, were repairing the damage.

No guards or Warders stood at the gate, so she rode in without stopping. Within, the city looked about as she had expected it might. Ruined buildings all around, looking melted. But no bodies. And here and there she saw signs of repairs, saw more people than she had expected going about their pursuits. Most of them paused to watch her pass. She did not recognize anyone.

As she approached the part of town she had frequented most, the part near Shadow Keep, her stomach clenched, and she shuddered. She feared what she would find, but decided she needed to see.

She dismounted and led her horse through the narrow streets. She saw fewer people here, and fewer repairs. At the last corner, she paused to take in what lay before her.

The area around Shadow Keep had been partly cleared and now stood emptier than she had ever seen it. And the Keep itself looked in the process of being rebuilt. The two walls she could see from her vantage looked—from the outside anyway—much as they had before Sy'shythys, although the stones differed, and the single wood door looked new. The walls stood not quite high enough to be ready for the ceiling that would be the second-level's floor and Namid wondered whether the other two walls even stood that high yet.

Namid's gaze was drawn to the door a little down the street to her right. It opened, and a man stepped out, looking around. He caught sight of her and grinned.

"Namid! You came back t' us!"

"Thes? What're you doing back in Rhadanthus? I figured you'd stay with the roadside banditry after this." Namid waved a hand at the general destruction that surrounded them.

"Funny thing," Thes said. "After you raced off with the Prazny chasin' after you, and your Prazny friend headed back the way you lot had come, Wesh just left. No warnin', no directions for anyone, just gone. A few o' the others wandered off after a day or so. The rest o' us waited a bit. But when we saw that great light off the way you'd gone, we decided we'd best be leavin'. So, we came back t' the Keep, t' our home."

Namid nodded.

When Thes motioned her forward, she led her horse toward the door. "Come on in. Your horse, too."

Thes looked around again. "No Aahmes taggin' along? Did you finally put a dagger in him—" He broke off at something he saw in her expression.

"Oh." He looked away for a breath-of-time, then back.

"Not the best liked o' us," Thes said, his voice sounding rough. "But he was one o' the most skilled. Hard t' think that somethin' took him out…."

Namid just nodded and blinked against the burning in her eyes.

With a gentle touch on her arm, Thes led her inside the Keep. She saw that she had guessed correctly… the other two walls stood shorter, less complete.

"Those o' us who came back are holed up in the underground rooms for now," Thes said, closing the door behind them. "Just let the horse stay here for a breath-o'-time, so you can unpack. Then we can put him with the others."

"The others?"

Thes grinned. "Aye, when Wesh left, he left everythin' behind. O' course we packed it all up and brought it back with us. Horses, too."

Namid matched his grin. "Of course."

Thes watched her as she looked around, taking in the complete destruction that still marked what had been the Keep's interior.

He grinned at her expression and clapped her on the

shoulder. "Welcome home."

~ ~ ~

Namid settled in with the remnants of the Shadowers, falling easily into a leader's role, along with Thes, and worked with them to continue rebuilding the Keep. No longer hiding her Power, she used it to help, so the work progressed faster than it would have otherwise.

Nearly two weeks after her return, one of the younger Shadowers interrupted her attempts to fuse some rocks together the way Haeith had fused the dirt back at Corentris. The Shadower's arrival broke her concentration and the rocks rained down across her lap in a shower of pebbles. She brushed them away with a questioning look for the girl.

"I'm so sorry, Leader. But we've news there's some noble lady asking around after someone who sounds like you. She's odd, though. Not got so much of that better-than-all-of-us manner that nobles usually have. She's got another noble with her, and a minstrel and a guard—"

Namid jumped up, her task forgotten. "Where are they?"

"Inside the South Gate. Near the old tannery."

Sending the girl to pass the news to Thes, Namid hurried off.

She found Cameni and Enric, Odasoro and Haeith leading their horses through one of the worst parts of the destruction, an area that no one had yet started clearing.

"How do you come to be here?" Namid said after they exchanged greetings.

"We're heading to my home," Enric said.

"Hoping to get there before the winter storms start," Odasoro said.

"But I insisted we stop to see you," Cameni said. "See that you're doing well…."

Namid looked away for a breath-of-time. "Well enough," she said. "The Shadowers who were with Wesh returned here. We're rebuilding…."

"Good to have a task, and with comrades," Haeith said. Namid nodded.

Cameni impulsively hugged her, then with an arm around her shoulders, led her a pace away from the others. "I wanted to ask you... well, Enric and I plan to wed... and.... I have few friends, as you might have fathomed. Truly, no one other than us.... Would you be willing to stand with me? When Enric and I wed?" She gave Namid a half-fearful, half-hopeful look.

At hearing that Cameni and Enric planned to wed, the ache of loss that clung to Namid flared into anguish that tore through her before subsiding again. After a breath-of-time, she managed a slight smile for Cameni's sake. "Yes, certainly."

Then she gave Cameni a truer smile as she brushed her hand over her stained, dusty clothes. "Of course, we'll have to get me something better to wear."

Cameni looked pleased and hugged her again. "Assuredly. We won't wed until the summer anyway, at the earliest. Nobles... as you know." She shared a wry grin with Namid.

Cameni turned back toward the men, smiling. "She said yes!"

Enric grabbed Namid's hand and bowed over it. "You honor us. Thank you."

Namid extricated herself. "Just send me word—"

"Why not return to Kilaadi?" Odasoro said. "I'm heading there when these three travel to Cameni's family. It'll be easier to get word there...."

Namid shook her head. "I can help here right now."

"Then come in the spring," Odasoro said. "After you've got everything here settled."

Namid tilted her head and considered. "It's probably time I returned... for a time, even if I don't stay—"

"Then I'll see you there in the spring," Odasoro said.

"And now we must go," Haeith said.

Namid nodded. "The storms usually don't start this

early, but it's best to get your traveling done as quickly as possible this time of year."

Namid showed them an easier path through the city's destruction back to the gate. From there, she watched them until she could not distinguish them in the distance, then returned to Shadow Keep.

Thes met her at the door. "All's well?"

At her nod, he held out a folded piece of parchment to her. Her name was written on it in a familiar hand… Dar's.

"What's this?" she said without taking it.

"Somethin' Dar gave me a while back t' give t' you if somethin' happened t' him. I just t'day managed to dig it out o' m' hidin' hole where I'd put it for safekeepin'."

After Namid took the parchment from him, Thes disappeared back inside the Keep.

Namid turned her back to the door and slowly unfolded the parchment. She could feel that there was something inside. The parchment held no other writing, but within she found a small, thin box. The box was filled with clay that held the impression of a key… a key unremarkable except for the distinctive, rough star-shape of its bow.

~

Notes and Pronunciations

A week is eight days long.

A "candle-mark" is roughly equivalent to an hour.

A "breath-of-time" is an indeterminate short amount of time, roughly seconds to a few minutes.

The five moons, in order from largest to smallest: Itieka, Nidvi, Trisi and Tursa (the "twin moons"), and Gopan.

Aahmes -- AH mehz
Aahmestharq -- AH mehz thahrk
Akavos -- ah kah VOHSS
Aytivsardz shirav --
     AY tihv sahrdz SHEER uhff

Belaraketh -- bel AHR uh kehth
Boudra -- BOO druh

Cameni -- KAM uh nee
Chendrukhar -- CHEHN droo kahr
Cielila -- see EL ihl uh
Corentris -- kohr EHN trihss
Cortohn -- kohr TOHN

Dar -- DAHR
Das -- DAHSS
Dytel -- D-EYE tuhl

Elnathan -- EL nuh thuhn
Enric -- EN rihk

Fathir -- fah THEER
Fellin -- feh LIHN
Foroughi -- FOHR oh ee

Gopan -- GOH pan
Gwelasius -- gwel AZ yuhss

Haeith -- HAY ihth
Harunsson -- HAHR uhn suhn

Ilenii -- ihl EHN ee
Inezha -- ihn EH zhuh
Itieka -- iht ee EH kuh
Izrediuz -- ihz REHD ee uhz

Jiang -- jee ANG
Jiro -- JEER oh
Jelth -- JELTH

Kalon -- KAL uhn
Karile -- kahr EYE-L
Kazkalar -- KAZ kuh lahr
Kilaadi -- kih LAH dee
korz -- KOHRZ

Lann -- LAN
Lyvoa -- lih VOH uh

Macai -- MAH kay
Myung -- mee UHNG

na'ak eh zandh -- NAH ak eh ZAHND
Naalin -- NAH leen
Namid -- NAH meed
Narqir -- nahr KEER
Navele -- nuh VEEL
Nazextas -- naz EHKSS tuhss
navn -- NAH vuhn
Nidvi -- NIHD vee

Odasoro -- oh DAHSS oh roh
omoiosurgy -- oh moy OHSS ur jee

Ophele tez za seidalar --
 OH feh leh tehz zah SEYE duh lahr
Oyanzaynye -- oi yan ZAYN yeh

Paronia -- puh ROHN yuh
Prazny -- PRAHZ nee

Randoq -- RAN dok
Raphahan -- RAFF uh han
Rhadanthus -- ruh DAN thuhss
Roivah-neheb -- ROI vuh NEH hehb

Sainamid -- sah EE nah meed
Sesaisyd -- seh SAY sihd
Shartov -- SHAHR toff
Shiara -- shee AHR uh
Staehw -- STAY oo
Sy'shythys -- sih SHIH thihss

Tal -- TAL
Tamanend -- TAM an ehnd
Tanyala -- tahn YAH lah
Thes -- THEHSS
Trisi -- TRIH see
Tursa -- TUR suh

vikl -- VIH kuhl
Vlatas -- VLA tuhss
Vlenorx -- vlehn OHRKSS

Wesh -- WEHSH

Yiruny -- YIH ruh nee

Zelimir -- ZEL uh meer

~

Author's Note

Thank you for reading my book. I hope you enjoyed it!

Please consider leaving an honest review on the book's
product page at your favorite online bookstore
and on Goodreads. Reviews from readers like you are
powerful and greatly help other readers
discover books they might enjoy.

-Lynn

About the Author

S. Lynn Helton lives in the foothills of the Rocky
Mountains, U.S.A., with her family and a couple of crazy
cats. Lynn enjoys camping and hiking, playing games,
crafting, reading (a lot) and, of course, writing.

Read more about her books on her website:
www.slynnhelton.com